DO651275

"[A] RICHLY TEXTURED TALE OF CRIME AND PASSIONS."
—*The San Diego Union-Tribune*

"The plot will keep you guessing. . . . Mewshaw has a real gift for locale and dialogue, and TRUE CRIME is worth reading."
          —*The Cleveland Plain Dealer*

"Outstanding . . . Mewshaw has captured superbly one man's struggle to come to terms with both past and present; that he provides also an absorbing puzzle merely increases the readability of what must be one of the year's best mysteries. Highly recommended."
          —*Library Journal*

"An accomplished writer of both fiction and nonfiction, Mewshaw again displays his storytelling talent. . . . A splendidly written, expertly plotted suspense thriller—alternately deeply touching and riotously funny, always a delight."
          —*Publishers Weekly*

"Mewshaw is a shrewd and vivid writer with an eye for telling detail."
          —*Entertainment Weekly*

Also by Michael Mewshaw:

Fiction:
BLACKBALLED
YEAR OF THE GUN
LAND WITHOUT SHADOW
EARTHLY BREAD
THE TOLL
WAKING SLOW
MAN IN MOTION

Nonfiction:
PLAYING AWAY
MONEY TO BURN: The True Story of the Benson Family
  Murders
SHORT CIRCUIT: Six Months on the Men's Professional
  Tennis Tour
LIFE FOR DEATH: A True Story of Crime and Punishment

TRUE CRIME

Michael Mewshaw

FAWCETT CREST • NEW YORK

A Fawcett Crest Book
Published by Ballantine Books
Copyright © 1991 by Michael Mewshaw

All rights reserved under International and Pan-American Copyright Conventions. Published in the United States by Ballantine Books, a division of Random House, Inc., New York, and simultaneously in Canada by Random House of Canada Limited, Toronto.

Library of Congress Catalog Card Number: 90-25691

ISBN 0-449-22132-6

This edition published by arrangement with Poseidon Press, a division of Simon & Schuster, Inc.

Manufactured in the United States of America

First Ballantine Books Edition: September 1993

For Pat, Karen and Kris

BOOK ONE

1

That airless night in early August, a persistent buzzing noise ripped through the rumpled fabric of my sleep. At some level I must have been aware of the phone, even feared it at this hour. So I willed myself to go on sleeping and incorporated the sound into my dreams.

I dreamt I was a little kid and I was with my mother in the kitchen back home. She was young again, her hair in a pageboy style with bangs cut straight across her forehead. Standing at the stove, she fixed my breakfast and talked to me about school. I could smell bacon, could hear it hissing in the skillet. She had the radio on, and a loud voice urged us to try something new and different.

I didn't want to wake up. I clung to that dream the way I had clung to my mother as a kid. For as the noise gradually roused me closer to consciousness, a clear thought knifed through the final defense—my mother was dead and I would never see her again in the waking world. Dreams and memories were all I would have of her.

I came to with my head on my arms, my eyes a few inches from the luminescent dial of my watch. It was four-thirty A.M. Fully dressed, a ballpoint in my hand, I had fallen asleep at my desk, in a tower looking out over the darkened domes and cupolas of Rome. Marisa was beside me, her hand on my shoulder, shaking me.

My first reflex was to hide what I had been doing. When Marisa went to bed, I had told her I intended to stay up packing for our annual trip to Sardinia. But I wound up working. Or rather fretting that I had no new project to

work on. I was between books and was reduced to reading
and taking notes from the clippings my agent faxed to me
every few days.

Although my office was just above our bedroom, Marisa
rarely climbed the spiral staircase, and she warned the
boys to stay away from what she called my "porno den."
Tonight there were no autopsy reports on the desk, no
crime-scene photos, no mug shots or morgue shots of
corpses spraddle-legged on slabs. But there was the Xerox
copy of an article from a professional journal aimed at
medical examiners, and I covered it with my hands the
way some men might conceal a girlie magazine or a picture of a mistress.

"Your brother," Marisa said, "he's on the phone."

On those rare occasions when Buck called, he invariably
forgot the six-hour time difference. Hurrying downstairs,
I hoped for some unexpected good news, any diversion
from the predictability of this fallow period. Perhaps he
was finally bringing his family over for a visit.

"Bucko," I shouted through static.

"Tommy." He sounded subdued. "Something's happened to Big Tom."

I sank down on the edge of the bed, thinking. A fall. A
heart attack. An automobile accident. Now in his late sixties, my father was a heavy drinker, a bar eater at risk for
everything, anything. "What is it?" I asked.

"Somebody shot him," Buck said.

Seeing my reaction, Marisa tensed as if to rush to me
or run for help. With a wave of the hand, I signaled I was
all right.

"Tommy, you there?"

"How bad is it?"

"Not good. Hit him in the chest. A through and
through. Nicked the heart and collapsed a lung." The
scratchy connection seemed to flatten his sentences. Then
again, Buck was a public defender and had had plenty of
practice at dealing dispassionately with forensic evidence.

"The doctor's less worried about the heart than the lung. You know, keeping it clear, making sure he can breathe."

"Where'd it happen?"

"In the driveway next to the house. Bastard just stepped up and plugged him."

"Is he conscious? Did he see who did it?"

"Cops say he mumbled about a woman. But the guy next door, the one-legged dude—"

"Luke?"

"Yeah, Luke the spook, he's our only witness. Of course he was probably full of gin, but he claims it was a white male with long, blond hair."

"This is nuts. Who'd want to shoot Big Tom?"

"Anybody on the block. Take your pick."

"Luke said the guy was white."

"You believe that, you're the right fish to buy an Edsel. Had to be a homeboy on crack pulling a B and E."

My sons had blundered into the bedroom. Kevin was tall and gangly, just as I'd been at the age of eleven. He went to his mother while Matt climbed onto my lap. Six years old, Matt was short, compact, and dark like Marisa. His skin was warm with sleep and his hair was sweet smelling.

"This pipe-head picks the wrong house," Buck ran on, "doesn't realize King Kong lives there. Case you forgot, Big Tom has a real gift for rubbing dusky-skinned folk the wrong way."

"What do the cops make of it?"

"The cops make a report, that's what they make of it. You know how it is. I'm as upset as you and I been asking the same questions. There's just not much to tell yet."

"I'll catch the first flight tomorrow. Call you from Kennedy."

"You like, I'll meet you at the airport in Baltimore."

"Good. See you then. If, you know, if—"

"Anything happens, I'll call back."

"Thanks, Buck."

When I hung up, Matt asked, "Who shot Grand-daddy?"

"They don't know yet."

"You boys should be in bed." Marisa was alarmed and fighting not to show it.

"Is he going to die?" Matt asked what I was thinking and didn't dare mention.

"Of course not," Marisa said.

"He's in the hospital. The doctors are taking care of him." I stood up, holding Matt for ballast.

"I'd like to see him," Kevin said. "Can we go with you?"

I decided I'd better set Matt down. Suddenly unsure of my footing, I was afraid of dropping him. "No. In a few days you'll all go to the beach with your grandparents." Marisa's family had a villa on Sardinia, and we had planned to join them there as we did every August.

"We could help you catch the killer," Matt pleaded.

"There is no killer," Marisa snapped. "He will be fine, just like your father said."

But I hadn't said any such thing and I feared the oppo-site. "I have to pack. You guys get back to bed."

Marisa herded them toward their room, leaving me to sag down onto the bed again. Like every man in his for-ties, I had attempted to imagine my parents' deaths and how I'd feel. When my mother died, the grief I experi-enced was precisely what I had anticipated. It was as pow-erful and uncomplicated as the love I had felt for her. But Big Tom was a different and more difficult matter. I had had years to prepare myself for the terrible end I had al-ways feared would befall him—and this wasn't too far re-moved from what I had expected. Still, I wasn't ready.

Marisa came back and kissed my forehead. "Please, tell me the truth. Is he already dead?"

"No. It's bad, but he's got a chance." I slipped an arm around her waist. The curve of her hip, the tilt of her belly, the texture of her skin, were as familiar to me as braille to a blind man's fingertips.

"I'll go with you," she said. "The boys will be fine with my parents."

"No, I'd rather you didn't."

We had been married for fifteen years, and Marisa was still mystified by my family. She didn't understand why we didn't see more of my father and Buck and his wife and kids, and I found it impossible to explain. But especially now that Big Tom had been shot, I believed it was urgent to shield her from . . . what? The past. The pull of my ambivalent emotions. There were so many things I wanted to keep separate from my life in Rome.

"I'll call you from the States," I said. "If there's anything you can do besides hold my hand, I'll holler for you."

"I like holding your hand." She twined her fingers with mine. After weeks of sunbathing on the terrace, she looked almost Levantine—a supple, busty harem dancer. On Sardinia she and the boys would soon be dark as aborigines. "I wish there was some way you'd let me help you," she said.

"You're helping by being patient, not complaining about being left behind."

"Maybe you will be back in time to join us."

"I hope so." This wasn't the truth, as I'm sure Marisa suspected. At loose ends, debating what to do next, I had little appetite for an aimless month on a sun-scorched, windswept island.

Over the years, whenever I traveled, it had become our custom to make love the night before I left. But it was morning now, the sky pearl-gray, the Alban hills etched in gold as the sun rose behind them. "I have to put away some stuff upstairs."

I kissed her, then climbed to my office and tore the copy of the article into confetti. It wasn't the kind of reading I cared to do on this trip. "Forensics, Insects and the FBI" was the title; the text described how lab workers had developed a new technique for murder investigations. Now they not only autopsied the victim; they examined the insects feeding on the corpse. From these bugs they could determine the time of death and whether the body had been moved.

It's a hell of an education, my line of work. But I can't say what it teaches you to do except stay on the same track. In the past decade I've tried my hand at pieces on sports, politics, and travel, but I remain best known for my books about murder cases. "True Crime," that's how my writing is catalogued in libraries; that's how publishers have me pigeonholed. Some critics call me a muckraker, a carrion bird. Those more favorably disposed view me as an investigative journalist. Whatever the label, it doesn't change what I do.

With sworn affidavits and newly discovered evidence, one of my books proved that an innocent drifter was executed in Florida for a murder he couldn't have committed. In another, I persuaded a million readers—and a federal jury as I successfully defended myself against a libel suit— that a rich California businessman had gotten away with killing his wife and dismembering her body. In my most popular book, which became an even more popular TV miniseries, I showed that a fifteen-year-old girl had indeed slain her father, but she had been savagely abused and he deserved to die. She wound up—with my help, I like to believe—in a psychiatrist's care instead of a maximum security cell.

The trouble was, I often had cause to feel imprisoned by, and squeamish about, my success. Each day the mail arrived with a raft of hair-raising proposals and horrifying pictures. Editors offered contracts to cover a serial killer in Seattle, to spend a year living with an outlaw polygamist clan in Utah, to reopen an investigation of the twenty-eight black boys murdered in Atlanta. Prosecutors tantalized me with bootlegged transcripts of grand jury hearings and tidbits of sensational inadmissable evidence. Killers dispatched letters from death row, their style stunningly tendentious, as though they'd read too many dull law books or swallowed too much Thorazine. Even psychopaths on the loose pressured me to cut a deal for their life stories. Some professed to be innocent; most didn't bother; but everybody believed he had a spellbinding yarn to tell in exchange for a percentage of the profits.

Hysterical strangers left messages on my answering service or passed me notes on airplanes. They had, they claimed, been with Elvis at the end. They alone understood the intricate conspiracy of Irangate. They could lead me to Jimmy Hoffa. Some of these tales may have been true. Some of these deranged souls may have been motivated less by greed than by mania for revenge or, far more worrying, by misplaced faith that only I could discover the truth, right a wrong, guarantee justice. I no longer needed to search for stories; they pursued me. Sources sought me out and spilled their guts the way vultures spit up food for their young.

In lighter moments Marisa taunted me that I could set out to pen a valentine to Mother Teresa and wind up writing a withering indictment. In anguished moments and in recent years these had become more and more frequent—she accused me of having a fixation with violence and death, and she rapped my office file cabinet as if it were the seat of my obsessions.

"Just looking at these pictures, keeping such things in our house, how do you expect to be happy?"

I assured her that I was as happy as I had ever been, and I promised not to leave autopsy photos lying around again.

But now that this had happened to Big Tom I wondered whether Marisa hadn't been right. I couldn't shake the suspicion that something I had written in the past had caused my father to be shot. For years I had been surrounded by a royal flush of sick tickets. Was one of them twisted enough to strike out at me through Big Tom? Or since we had the same name, was it possible the gunman had stalked me and hit him by mistake? Some psychopath I had put in a book? One I edited out? Had an anonymous tipster decided to back up his unanswered letter or maniacal phone message with evidence that he merited a mini-series?

What I feared most was the free-floating dread my work wakened in Marisa. Although at this moment she wouldn't torment me with such an accusation, I was sure she believed that to spend my life mulling over crime and its bloody aftermath was in itself sufficient to cause catastrophe. I was a carrier and Big Tom had caught the disease.

2

I offered to take a taxi to the airport, but Marisa insisted on driving me. She said she welcomed the chance to be alone with me a little longer. This didn't mean we exchanged any last-minute declarations of love and fidelity. In fact, we scarcely spoke.

Marisa was at the wheel. She insisted on that too. She didn't care for my driving. It wasn't that I was reckless or lead footed. To the contrary, I was too cautious for her taste. She said I lacked an intuitive feel for Italian traffic, in which the best defense is an aggressive offense. One dainty, sandaled foot planted hard on the accelerator, the other poised above the brake pedal, she slalomed along the Raccordo Anulare with the headlong speed of a downhill skier, her windblown hair iridescent as a raven's wing.

There were many moments in our marriage when Marisa had nothing to say, and neither cultural differences nor language difficulties—she was perfectly bilingual—accounted for these quiet periods. Before I knew better, I used to kid her that she was more closedmouthed than a mafioso.

"That shows how little you understand," she replied. "You're the Sicilian in this family. I've never met anybody so secretive and scheming, so full of conspiratorial theories."

Although she wouldn't admit it, part of her reluctance to talk was probably rooted in a feeling that she didn't want to resemble the other people in my life. "Why do they tell you so much?" she asked in amazement. "You're the Don Juan of listening. You like to hear everything from everybody. What do they get in return?''

"Attention," I told her, and left it at that, satisfied to have her as a wife, not a source, not another voice in my chorus of informers and confessors. What I loved most about Marisa was her flesh-and-blood presence, her warmth and steadfastness. She had a careless, tumbled elegance and physical grace that struck me as crucial ingredients in loyalty. It was easy to believe in somebody who had such confidence in herself; it was easy to go off, as I did several times a year, knowing she'd be waiting when I came back.

When she dropped me at Fiumicino, I said, "I'll call." She said, "I'll be here." Then I kissed her, and she drove off.

I bought a full-fare business-class ticket and the Pan Am agent bumped me up to first class. In my frame of mind, the complimentary champagne and caviar, foie gras and London broil, mattered less than the extra leg room—I'm six feet three—and the privacy.

After takeoff I downed two glasses of Chianti *classico*, lowered my seatback, and closed my eyes. I hoped to sleep, hoped not to waste the next nine hours fretting about my father. In self-defense I tried to think about my mother, concentrate on her healing influence. She had been the fixed point in the family, the linchpin, the one who encouraged Buck and me to believe that with effort we could accomplish . . . no, not everything; she was a realist; but we could better ourselves. She was also the reason—one of them anyway—why people told me so much. She had taught me to listen, to stay quiet as a spider and study the signs, testing for danger. Married to an alcoholic, she had had to develop survival skills and pass them along to her children.

But thinking about Mom, I realized how many threads ran back to my father, how much of her character—and mine, for that matter—was formed in reaction to him.

As for Big Tom himself, his character couldn't be separated from his drinking. Amid the chaos of impressions and misapprehensions that converge in the man, it's his boozing that first comes to mind, dominating all my other recollections. Even as a kid I was aware that I resented him for being a drunk, yet I loved him too and desperately wanted to know why he did it. Over the years I put the question to him point-blank in bars, in holding tanks, in emergency rooms, and once in an insane asylum when his truculence tilted toward the pathological. "I drink," he usually said, "because I like the taste." At other times he told me, "I like what it does to me."

Along with making him punchy and pugnacious, what alcohol did more often as he aged was make him very sick. He got the shakes, his big body shuddered, and he roared in pain and couldn't hold anything in his stomach except a few sips of beer.

After he retired and Mom died, he began to go on benders, wandering in his car from Maryland to West Virginia and Pennsylvania, listening to country-and-western music on the radio, riding with a bottle of Jim Beam between his legs. Sometimes late at night in Rome the telephone would ring, and I'd grope for the receiver and hear an international operator: "Collect call for Tommy."

Then a slow, deep voice warbled across the Atlantic, as if he were shouting from the bottom of a well. "Tommy, this is Big Tom."

"Where are you?"

"That's why I'm calling. I can't figure it out. Seems to be a tavern, the Tick Tock. That's what the sign says. I'm lost."

"Ask the bartender where you are."

"He'll think I'm crazy and call the cops."

"Step out to the parking lot and check the license plates. They should tell you what state you're in."

"Yes." He waited for me to go on.

"Next thing you do, stop at a gas station and ask the

best route to Washington. Hey, are you in any shape to drive? You'd better call Buck to come get you.''

''The hell are you talking about? I'm a little tight. That's all. The day I can't drive's the day I'm dead.'' Then he'd add as if I were the one adrift and seeking direction, ''When are you going to quit pissing away your life and move back home? Italy's no place to raise those boys.''

''Let's talk about it next time I'm in the States. Look, promise me you'll at least have a cup of coffee.''

But he'd be gone and I'd be left with a dead receiver and a gnawing regret that I hadn't said the right thing. In my work, I've heard psychiatrists refer to people who depend on drink or drugs as ''self-medicators.'' Maybe that's what Big Tom had been doing for decades—swilling down a bitter home remedy. But I had never been able to get past the symptoms to the source of his pain.

A self-described hick from Santee, South Carolina, Big Tom indulged his appetite for eating and drinking, for hell-raising, outrageous humor, and I suspect, a string of dalliances. (''A wise fox fucks far from home,'' he told Buck and me as teenagers, and that, in his estimate, fully discharged his duties as a sex educator.) But one thing he never indulged in was self-analysis or excuses. He did what he did and afterward, sometimes said he was sorry. But he never copped to a less serious charge or blamed his problems on being poor and unlucky. Although he warned us that ''every man has to eat a mile of shit before he dies,'' this fell under the heading of practical guidance, not cynicism. What he got in life—the bad as well as the good—struck him as being just about right.

Sometimes what the other fellow got infuriated him, however, and he railed against those who grabbed what they hadn't earned, and he goaded Buck and me to be fighters, to beat the other guy to the first punch. When drunk, he dramatized this lesson by walloping us—driving home the point that anybody who dropped his guard deserved to be punished.

Big Tom professed to be contemptuous of education,

and when Buck and I went on to college, he taunted us that a degree and a dime wouldn't buy a cup of coffee. "Remember the old proverb," he said. "The higher the baboon climbs, the more the world sees of his naked purple ass." Yet once we completed the University of Maryland, he appeared to be proud of what we had accomplished—as proud, Buck wisecracked, as a man who's trained his dog to drink beer from a glass.

Mechanical competence was what he admired. He was the type who could break down and reassemble anything from a toaster to a truck. His two boys, he complained, never owned a car that ran right; we didn't know our dicks from a distributor cap.

Having learned to barber in the Navy, he cut our hair until we were teenagers, and I remember the feel of his thick fingers inclining my head toward the scissors. It was one of the few times he touched me—unless he was hitting me. He wasn't like Mom. "No cuddling and kissy-face for me," he said. Still, after dinner as he sat watching a ball game on TV, he would squeeze Buck and me into the chair beside him and let us have a drag on his cigarette and a sip of his drink.

Although Mom was the one I usually went to for advice, I recall a time in college when I turned to Big Tom. A girl I loved, the first one who truly mattered, had ditched me and disappeared. Positive that she loved me too and that it was her family that had pushed her into leaving, I traced her to Texas, then hesitated, baffled about what to do next.

I feared I'd be annihilated by Big Tom's scorn. Or maybe that's what I hoped would happen—that he'd scourge me of my feelings and convince me to forget her. But Big Tom surprised me with his patience in listening, then his sympathy in speaking. "You sure you love her?" he asked.

"Yes."

"You sure dumping you wasn't her idea? I mean, if she let her parents push her into leaving, what's to say she won't take off again?"

Since there was no way of answering that question, I simply repeated that I loved her.

"Say you get her back, it's a hundred to one she won't stay. What you tell me, Tommy, this lady's in a different league. You ready to lose?"

"Yes."

"Then go ahead. You ain't my son, you ain't worth shit, if you don't go after something you want that bad."

What happened next, I didn't care to dwell on any more than I cared to picture Big Tom in a hospital bed, lung-shot and heart-wounded. Waving to the stewardess, I called for a refill of wine.

At Baltimore-Washington International—for me it would forever be Friendship—I stumbled through the terminal. Jet-lagged, half-cockeyed from Chianti, I passed Maryland memorabilia boutiques and food stalls with whole aisles given over to potato chips and corn curls. As always when returning to the States, I was struck by the spendthrift abundance of space and light and refrigerated air.

Buck had instructed me to meet him at the crab. "The what?" I had asked long distance from Kennedy.

"The Chesapeake Blue Crab."

I assumed he was referring to a bar or restaurant. But a rent-a-car agent directed me to the main lobby where my brother was waiting beside a sculpture of an enormous crustacean. Constructed of stained-glass panels and stainless-steel struts, it must have been twelve feet from tip to tip.

As I've learned from reams of unreliable testimony, it's hard to see a person without inserting something of yourself into the picture. It's harder yet to gaze at yourself without fogging the mirror with your breath. But I believe it's safe to say that few people would guess at a glance that Buck and I are related. Two years older, he looks younger, his thickset body radiating kinetic energy even in repose, his reddish beard and hair framing an impish mug. I'm fair-haired and a few inches taller, and although

I've filled out to a hundred and eighty pounds, I appear frail compared to my brother.

He didn't notice me until I said, "I'd like to have the backfin meat from this sucker."

"Tommy!"

I dropped my bags and embraced him, doing as I would have done with an Italian friend. "Whoa, man," he said. "Welcome back. But don't go homo on me." He held me at arm's length. "How you feeling? Body-clock-wise, it must be midnight."

"I'm holding up. How's Big Tom?"

"Okay. At least he's out of the oxygen tent." He snatched up my suitcases as if afraid I might hug him again. "You don't mind, it's easier to walk to the car than drive it around."

He led me out of the terminal, into the heat. The air had the weight and feel of a kitchen sponge slimy with detergent; the asphalt was gummy under my feet. I shrugged off my suit coat, loosened my tie.

Trudging along beside me, broad as a dray horse, Buck wore a tweed jacket and purple knit tie, a pair of cavalry-twill trousers and desert boots.

"What are you doing," I said, "dressed like that?"

"Had a court hearing this morning."

"But tweed in the middle of summer?"

"You inherited the taste in clothes, Tommy. I inherited the family brains and beauty."

This was a touchy subject, a minefield of old misunderstandings. "I just mean you're a walking advertisement for heat prostration."

"We'll be back in the AC in a sec."

Buck owned a four-wheel-drive Isuzu truck with fat, cleated tires designed for snow or the Sahara. He shoved my bags into the backseat between cardboard boxes overflowing with status reports, evidence folders, depositions, and legal texts, including the Bible of his profession, Bailey and Rothblatt's *Crimes of Violence: Homicide and Assault*. I had a copy in my office.

Up front, the floor was carpeted with pop-tops, Slurpee cups, soft-drink cans, and an army of action figures and Masters of the Universe.

"How are Peggy and the kids?" I asked.

"Terrific till this thing with Big Tom." He let the truck idle a few seconds before he punched the MAXI-COOL button. Warm air rushed out of the vents, moist as spray from a shower nozzle. It got gradually cooler as we headed west, into a glinting sun. Traffic advanced with what seemed hypnotic slowness. Accustomed to the demonic speed of Italian driving, I had to bite my tongue to keep from telling Buck to step on it.

"Marisa wanted to park the boys with her parents and come with me," I said. "I thought it'd be better to wait until I saw what the situation is. Anything new from the police?"

"This ain't one of your books, Tommy. No clever detective is out there sweating blood to solve the crime. Nobody like you is panting to write about the case. Unless somebody rats out the shooter, we'll never know who did it."

I kept my mouth shut and my eyes on the treadmill of cars ahead. I knew there might be more to his irascibility than too little sleep and too much worry about Big Tom. For years we had had our differences, and it didn't take much to push these nettling grievances to the surface. Although it had to have pained him to do so, Buck once summed up our problems with comic incisiveness. "Show you what a crock of shit both heredity and environment are. Here we had the same parents, same schools, same boyhood experiences. We crawled out of the same gene pool. But you became Prince Valiant and I mutated into the Creature from the Black Lagoon."

Actually, I was the mutation. Buck had remained the same—irreverent, rambunctious, inclined to outbursts of enthusiasm indistinguishable from mayhem or misdemeanor. Nothing could curb his high spirits; nobody had managed to housebreak him. College, then law school, had led to a profession, but he had learned no grace notes and wasn't persuaded he needed a new set of party skills. With an LLB from Baltimore University, he introduced himself as a graduate of Agnew U. and boasted that Spiro had been his professor of Legal Ethics. A fierce defender of hopeless cases, he dubbed himself "the St. Jude of the judicial system" and startled prosecutors and juries with his audacious courtroom antics. If he had trimmed his beard and trimmed his belief that excess was best, he could have developed a private practice and earned a handsome living. But he preferred to be a legend in poolrooms, biker bars, and holding pens, depending on humor, the blacker and more coruscating the better, as his heat shield against life's disappointments.

Still, it rankled him that I had made a name for myself, as well as a great deal of money, by doing essentially the same thing he did interview defendants and witnesses, review legal documents and attend trials. Although he usually tried to be good-natured about his baby brother's success, he became prickly whenever I disagreed with his reading of the law.

There were also the awkward moments when his wife, Peggy, demanded of me, "Why don't you do a book about Buck? He's had hundreds of fascinating cases and he's a helluva lot better lawyer than Racehorse this or F. Lee that."

On such occasions I babbled about the vagaries of the publishing industry, the prejudices of editors, the fickleness of readers. But what it boiled down to was not all murder cases qualified as "true crime." With rare exceptions, best-selling books had to depict the gaudy vices of the rich or famous, not the infamies of Buck's roster of indigents. They had to open a door on the gamey secrets of privilege, offering readers entry to a world they could simultaneously envy and despise. People didn't want to have their noses rubbed into the gritty realities of lives not all that different from their own.

At the East Pines exit, Buck coasted down off the parkway and into Riverdale, past landmarks from our adolescence.

There were a few new housing tracts and apartment projects with billboards promising easy terms and no down payment, and there were older neighborhoods where the vegetation had run riot, and honeysuckle and wild-grape vines added a raffish tropical touch to the general decay. Otherwise the area looked as I remembered it.

This part of Prince Georges County, poor close relative to Washington, D.C., was, according to sociologists, America's first suburban slum. Streets glittered with broken glass; rusty cars were jacked up on cinder blocks, their doors hanging by broken hinges. Mom-and-pop stores had signs assuring customers that they accepted food stamps. On front porches, men with rolled-up shirtsleeves and women with rolled-down hose sat waiting for an evening breeze, swigging at bottles in brown paper bags. Boys congregated on the same corners as they had in my day, undoubtedly discussing the same subjects—fighting, fucking, football, cars, petty crime (more serious capers were planned in secret), cops, and prison.

It was a district where kids learned early how to calm mean drunks and listen sympathetically to sad ladies with bourbon on their breath, lipstick on their teeth, and cigarette smoke in their hair. Success fantasies were constant and in Technicolor; reality was sepia toned. Life here had the shape of a telescope extended, each segment narrower than the previous one. After a brief childish illusion of freedom came the long process of locking in. Every choice, every pleasure, led to a trap. Assuming you didn't go haywire at the start and do a stretch in reform school, you got a girl, you got her pregnant, you got married, you got a dead-end job, and eventually wound up in one kind of jail or another.

"What you wonder," Buck said, his thoughts thudding along in the same groove as mine, "is why Big Tom stayed. He had the money to move. He'd be better off down in Anne Arundel County near us."

"I always hoped he'd spend time with me in Italy."

" 'Scuse me, bro, but I don't feature him living la dolce fucking vita."

* * *

I didn't recognize the hospital and thought it must be new to the neighborhood. But then I noticed the original structure embedded in a broad red-brick facade like a cottage that had been swallowed by a factory.

The lobby, like the rest of the building, had been expanded, spruced up, and freshly painted. Posters of sunsets and autumn leaves were pasted to the walls amid signs in English, Spanish, and Mandarin Chinese advising patients, "Know your rights" and "Have your credit card ready." On the bulletproof Mylar shield barricading the admissions window, there were stickers for American Express, Visa, and MasterCard. You had to speak into a microphone and shove your card through a slot.

Buck greeted people by name—nurses, custodians, administrators—while I lagged behind him, wobbly in the knees. These days being in the emergency room of any urban hospital was a nerve-rattling experience. Patients with broken limbs and blood crusted wounds slumped in plastic chairs. Gurneys lined the walls, full of gunshot victims, car crash survivors, kids who had overdosed. Some were lashed down with leather straps and fought to bust free, braying at the security guards.

"This one's tweaking!" A nurse hollered for help with a man in crack psychosis.

Orderlies wheeled away a teenage boy who had antishock trousers inflated on his legs. A woman—his mother?—hurried along beside him, plucking off his gold chains, his rings, and the beeper from his belt before he was rolled into the operating room.

In the elevator to the intensive care unit, I said to Buck, "You seem to have lots of friends here."

"You're a lawyer, the kind I am, your clients naturally wind up in the hospital from time to time."

On the ICU floor, a nurse told us Big Tom was sleeping, but when Buck explained that I had flown in from Italy, she didn't insist we wait for visiting hours.

In the dimly lighted room he appeared to hang suspended like something snared in a spiderweb. Two tubes had been inserted between his ribs—one to drain blood and fluids from his pulmonary cavity, the other to siphon off air. There was a smaller tube in his nose, an IV dripping into his arm, a catheter snaking up under the sheet, and wires to register his vital signs.

"Believe me," Buck whispered, "he looks better than yesterday."

To accept that I had to forget how Big Tom looked the last time I saw him—brawny, his arms like slabs of burnished mahogany, his face florid from hard work and hard drinking, his hair a wiry brush with a few silver bristles. He had driven a truck until he was sixty-five, delivering soft drinks, carrying three and four cases at a time, wearing his starched, blue company uniform like a member of an elite military unit.

Now he inhaled and exhaled with a strangled gasp. His complexion was putty colored, his hair lank and matted. His hands lay palms up, pale as the sheet, and the flesh on his arms hung in loose folds so that he appeared to wear his own skin like a sweater three sizes too large.

The strangled sound deepened and his fingers flexed. His eyes opened, blinked, then opened again. Buck said, "Look who's here, Dad. Tommy's here."

His head rolled toward the sound, his pupils swimming without focus. I gripped the old man's hand and was heartened by how much strength he had. He stared at me, actually seemed to recognize me, and managed to move his lips. I thought he was mumbling, "Why? Why?"

"I don't know, Dad." I felt my eyes burn. "I don't know why."

His hand tightened and he moved his mouth again, making the same garbled sound. Buck and I leaned closer until I understood what he was muttering.

"No," I said, squeezing the hand that squeezed mine. "You're not going to die."

3

By the time we left the hospital, it was nightfall, but the air was still smothering, and my brother and I still didn't find it easy to talk about Big Tom. Buck drove down the dreary length of U.S. 1, past body shops and car dealerships, boarded-up buildings and fenced-in lots overgrown with weeds and guarded by growling dogs. "Tell you what let's do," he said. "Let's go to my place, pour a couple trash-can-size drinks, and put you to bed."

"Thanks, but I'd rather stay at the house." In fact, I would rather have checked into a hotel, the Four Seasons, where my publisher put me up whenever I was in D.C. to do talk shows. But I knew better than to mention this to Buck, who'd see it as further evidence that I had gotten too big for my britches.

"Hot as hell at home. Big Tom finally bought a window unit for his bedroom, but that's it."

"I'm so tired it won't matter." I needed to be alone, needed to think, and definitely didn't want to be at close quarters with Buck and Peggy and wind up arguing with both of them.

"Look, Tommy, thing of it is, what if that toad swings back to grab whatever he was after last night?"

"I'll make a citizen's arrest."

"I know you, you'll make a mess in your pants. But suit yourself."

Off the main drag, the Isuzu pounded through potholes and over an unpaved road where workmen had set out barricades and warning flares. Black kids darted in and out of flickering wells of light, listening to ghetto blasters and chanting rap songs. A few of them carried cellular phones and wore bulletproof flak jackets. "Yo, white folks, you buying? Got rock. Got shake. Twenty dollar. Twenty dollar."

Buck said, "Big Tom tells me he's not going to let a bunch of boogies chase him out of the neighborhood. But how I have it figured, he likes it here—the excitement, the adventure. He's Ramar of the Jungle."

We stopped at a tall, ungainly house that seemed it might once have been a larger home that had been sawed in two and separated from its Siamese twin next door. In front, it was finished with fake fieldstone. Aluminum siding covered the other walls. Big Tom's fifteen-year-old Oldsmobile Toronado was parked in the drive.

"I'll come in," Buck said, "and wait till you get settled—or till you change your mind."

"Don't bother. Just give me the key."

He slapped it into my palm, laying on a soul-brother handshake. "Good to see you, Tommy. Even if it does take something like this to drag you back home."

"Hey, you could always come see me. Planes fly in both directions."

"Not with my fat ass on them, they don't. Call you in the morning."

He kept his high beams lighted while I unlocked the front door. I waved to him that I was all right, but once in the house I wasn't so sure. The past enfolded me as if the intervening years, my wife and sons and our life in Rome, had never existed. Surrounded by familiar sounds and smells, I glided through the rooms like the ghost of the boy I had been in the weary body of the man I had become.

I had imagined Big Tom would be a miserable housekeeper, but the place was so scrubbed and spotless it looked uninhabited. Clean ashtrays and coasters were laid out on end tables. Crisp, white antimacassars protected the two morris chairs and the couch. Massive and uphol-

stered in maroon velour, the couch reminded me of a plush
seat in an old-fashioned train compartment.

In the kitchen, the linoleum floor and drainboard
gleamed, and the cupboard was crammed with canned
goods and boxes of instant mixes, as if Big Tom had turned
into one of those gun-nut survivalists who stock enough
food to outlast Armageddon. In the television room, next
to the kitchen, there was a sofa and a BarcaLounger, both
covered with blue Leatherette. A pair of scissors marked
a page in a magazine. The night he was shot, my father
must have been clipping discount coupons, preparing to
lay in more supplies. Framed photos of Buck and Peggy
and their brood, and Marisa and me and our boys, formed
a family shrine on top of the TV.

Upstairs, I paused in the door of my parents' bedroom,
debating whether to switch on the air conditioner and sleep
there. Snapshots of Mom and Big Tom were everywhere—
on the night tables, the chest of drawers, the walls. In this
collage of the couple's life, there was no chronological
order, no discernible sequence. The pictures bounced ran-
domly through time and space the way that scientists claim
radio waves do.

In many of the photos, my father held a bottle of beer
and a cigarette whose smoke narrowed his eyes. Mom's
characteristic pose was with her arms shyly folded behind
her back. There were shots of them in their twenties on
the boardwalk at Ocean City, in their fifties at Buck's wed-
ding, in their late thirties at my high school graduation, in
their sixties, no more than a few years ago, on the Skyline
Drive, autumn leaves blazing with smokeless fire on the
mountains behind them.

I couldn't stay here, not tonight. Instead, I climbed the
stairs to my old room in a dormer space under the eaves.
Like the rest of the house, it had the blurry-edged appearance of a dream memory, all the more haunting seen
through my haze of exhaustion. Posters of rock stars and
actresses long dead, pennants for teams that no longer ex-

isted—the Washington Senators, the Baltimore Colts—were tacked to a cork board.

Raising a window, I let in a faint breeze that brought with it an eddy of incomprehensible conversation. Somewhere people were speaking Spanish. I couldn't distinguish individual words, only accented syllables that reminded me of Italy. From where I stood, my Roman apartment, my privileged life, seemed not so much far away as falling beyond the range of the credible. I ached to be back there with Marisa, Kevin, and Matt—or at least to telephone them, if just to prove they existed. But it was too late, after four A.M. their time.

Not bothering to unpack, I stripped off my clothes, stripped the blanket from the bed, and stretched out on the bare mattress. When I put out the lamp, the room, the whole house, disappeared, and I hung suspended, not unlike my father snarled in a web of tubes and wires.

Compared to what I often described in my work, compared to chapters freighted with gory forensic detail, the scene at the hospital had been tame. Big Tom had taken a single round in the chest. No stippling, no streaking, no signs of a near-contact wound. No horrifying Rorschach of hair, teeth, and brain matter on the walls.

But because this victim was my father, I couldn't make any pretense of professional detachment. I wasn't interested in extenuating circumstances or the assailant's psychology or the childhood traumas that had built to a moment of murderous rage. I just wanted to catch the son of a bitch and quit feeling that if I had been a better son, none of this would have happened.

But it wasn't as if Big Tom had ever been easy to get close to. At an early age Buck and I learned to keep our distance and read the signs—his eyes, his complexion, the cadence of his speech. His breath was the one sure indicator of his sobriety, but when you were near enough to smell it, you were in danger. Whenever we made the mistake of wandering within his reach at the wrong time, he grabbed us by the hair and cracked our heads together.

Buck claimed it had been good training; it hardened his skull for football. The best I can say is it built in me a wariness, an instinctive suspicion, that has come in handy in my work.

The breeze had died, as had the staccato gabbling of Spanish. The night had a beat, a combination of beats—disco, reggae, rap—and in the distance there was a cacophony of car horns, sirens, and what sounded like gunshots or garbage cans banging to the bottom of stairwells. I should have heeded Buck's advice and gone to his house, cool and quiet near the Bay. If I didn't sleep soon, I'd be a basket case tomorrow.

Carrying a pillow and my clothes and shoes, I found a bottle of whiskey in the kitchen, downed a glass, then moved into the living room, onto the velour couch. Settling for the night, the house groaned like an old man, its timbers as brittle as bones. Eyes wide open, waiting for the whiskey to work, I lay on my side facing the window and watched a reflection of the venetian blinds expand and contract accordionlike as cars swept down the street.

Then I saw a darker shape slipping through the shadows outside. I sat up, prepared to believe I was wrong, prepared to bolt if I was right. The shadowy figure rounded the front of the house, then reappeared in the windows on the side. I pulled on my pants and pushed my sockless feet into my shoes.

With crooked, hobbling steps, the man headed toward the back door. Before I called the cops, I wanted to get a look at his face.

Crouched low, I hurried from the living room to the kitchen. He was black—I could make out that much and no more. He didn't see me. He was too busy jiggling the doorknob, trying to jimmy it open.

I withdrew to the wall phone on the far side of the refrigerator, then realized that if this joker was wired and carrying a weapon, he was liable to bust in and start shooting while I was babbling to the 911 operator. I needed help now, not in twenty minutes when my corpse was cooling.

"Drop it, asshole," I shouted. "You're under arrest. Hear me? Drop it or you're dead."

There was one metallic clank. Then another. The man leaned sideways as if ready to run. I was ready to run too.

"Don't move," I hollered. "I want to see both your hands flat against the window."

"I can't do that, man. I thrown down my crutches and I'm near to tumping over on my ass."

"Who's that? Is that you, Luke?"

"I hear you, Tommy. Don't shoot."

When I opened the door, Luke was poised on one leg like an egret. I flipped on the kitchen light. "What the hell are you doing?"

"Hey, you ain't got no more gun than I do." Smiling, he nibbled at the tuft of hair below his bottom lip. "I seen lights. Downstairs. Upstairs. Downstairs again. I speculated somebody broke in. Maybe the dude that drilled your daddy."

"Why didn't you call the police?"

"The less I do with them, the happier I am as a man."

"Sounded like you were breaking in."

"Just checking the door, whether it was locked. I don't need to break in. I got a key. Your daddy, he gave it to me. Sometimes I come over, watch the color TV, and see everything's all right when he ain't here." Bracing himself against the stair rail, he bent down and scooped up his crutches. "Well, seeing how you don't believe that neither, I'll go on home."

"Come in. You scared me. That's all."

"Hey, we all uptight around here after what happened." Luke lowered himself into a chair, eying the bottle of Johnnie Walker on the kitchen table. He was roughly my age, somewhere in his forties, but his skin had a dry, grayish tinge like a deflated inner tube that had been left outdoors too long. His right trouser cuff was rolled up and fastened with a safety pin at midthigh. He had lost the leg in Vietnam and now lived on a disability allowance.

"This neighborhood, you got your drugs," he said, "you got your gangs, you got your Rastas. People getting greased left and right." He chewed his mustache and his tuft of bebop hair, top lip, then bottom. "But I never expected it to hit my friend. Many's the night your daddy and I sat at this table, chillin' out with a few drinks."

I found that tough to believe, but no more so than that Big Tom had given Luke a house key. I fetched a couple of glasses, poured him a shot, and splashed in a little for myself.

"I know"—he drank off half his glass—"Big Tom had a bad mouth for black people. But last couple years, after your momma passed, we got on fine. Evenings I drop in, we talk. Two, three times when he still driving his truck, he take me along for company."

This didn't sound like my father. Although as he grew older he hired day laborers to help with his soft drink deliveries, he had never, to my knowledge, let them sit in the cab with him. He made them squeeze in among the bottle boxes, molding themselves to the splintery angles and edges as gingerly as a swami bedding down on broken glass.

I topped off Luke's drink. "Buck said you saw him get hit."

"No, I seen just after."

"Tell me about it."

"I already told the police. Not that they believe a fucking word." He was holding the glass so tight, his fingernails were pink as shrimp. "I was like, 'I seen this. I heard that.' The cops was like, 'We know you capped him.' Then they go, 'We know a friend to you did it and you're alibiing him.' They don't want to listen."

"I do."

"Well, it was like this. I hear loud voices, like arguing, which they got a lot on this block. I don't pay it no mind. I don't perk up till there's a pop. A definite pop." He extended a bony finger like a gun barrel. "A thing I know, I know a pistol shot. So I duck outside, stick my head between the hedges to study the why of what I heard. And there's this white dude with long blond hair motoring down the driveway."

"Motoring? He was in a car?"

"No. Running. Got the gun in his hand. End of the driveway, he cuts right."

"Did he get into a car? Was somebody waiting for him?"

"Didn't notice nobody else and no car. Soon as he's gone, I push through the hedges to help your daddy." He sucked at the Scotch, remembering. "Damned if he ain't on his hands and knees, trying to stand up. He's bleeding from his chest and he's cussing like a motherfucker. 'The bitch shot me,' he says. 'The bitch step up and shot me.' He's showing me where on his chest. Which anyways I could see on account of the blood."

"He said 'bitch'? You're positive it was a man?"

"That's what the cops keep asking—why Big Tom say 'bitch' and I say 'man.' They shine a light in my eyes. They're like, 'Up against the wall.' They go, 'Empty your pockets. Lemme see your hands.' I tell them, 'Make it simple for yourself, sucker. Ask my man am I the one smoked him.' Naturally Big Tom shake his head no."

"But you definitely saw a man?"

Luke set the glass on the table and smacked his index finger against the palm of his hand. "Let's go down the definites. It's definitely white. It's definitely blond hair and definitely long."

"How long?"

"Long so's it's bouncing when he run. Not to his shoulders or nothing like that. Looking at it a different way, it might have been a woman, a big one, but she didn't motor like no lady."

"How old?"

"Not old, not young."

"Can you describe his face?"

"Just white. Kind of thin. No meat on his bones."

"Anything else you remember?"

"Like what?"

"Did Big Tom seem worried lately? Was there anyone, anything, he was afraid of?"

"It's your daddy. That sound like him, being scared?"

"I guess not. Did the police check the house, see whether anything was stolen?"

"He had the key in his pocket. The door's locked. Nothing missing inside, nothing missing on him. His money's still in his wallet."

"Maybe this blond guy panicked before he had a chance to steal anything."

Luke shrugged his skinny, loose-jointed shoulders. "He didn't look like no robber to me. Had nice clothes, a good appearance."

"What kind of clothes?"

"It wasn't, you know, overalls or a T-shirt and jeans. More like threads on a man in a magazine."

"Any rumors going around?"

"Some folks say—not me, I'm just telling what they say—it must be a woman. Maybe Big Tom—I'm not running down his reputation now—but maybe he's been dipping his wick with this lady, then did her dirty, and she's getting back at him."

I had to laugh. "Jesus, Luke, he's sixty-seven."

"The older the buck, the harder the horn. But my opinion, it ain't no woman. It's a mistake. Big Tom's a mushroom, somebody crops up in the wrong place, wrong time. Maybe this dude's a dealer and comes looking for somebody sold him dope that's been danced on."

" 'Danced on'?"

"Cut with baking soda. Only he pumps down the wrong man. It happens." He poured me some Scotch and a belt for himself.

"Did the police process the crime scene?"

" 'Process'?" Luke lifted a hand to his hair.

"Block off the area, search it?"

"They poke around, pick up rusty bottle caps and cigarette butts. They didn't process nothing I noticed. Didn't even find the bullet."

I felt my pulse surge. Here was something I could do. "Tomorrow morning, you show me where he fell. We'll look for the slug."

"No need." Luke grinned and the gray-black skin stretched tight across the bridge of his nose. "I done that process already in the aspect of next day I notice a tear in the aluminum siding. Didn't seem like no bullet hole. But then, what I seen in Nam, those motherfuckers fly through a body, bullets don't look like bullets either. I fetch my hedge clippers and cut open that hole. Just clip the tin and there it is."

"Did you give it to the police?"

"Way they treat me, I'd as soon give them my dick."

"Where is it?"

"Got it right here." He pulled it from his pocket. "Figured Big Tom like to have it for a souvenir when he's home from the hospital. Hang it on a chain around his neck."

"Mind if I see it?"

"Help yourself." He handed me the slug. "Keep it. Give it to your daddy."

I rolled it between my finger and thumb. It wasn't badly misshapen—just bent at the tip and flattened on one side. It was easy to make out five lands and five grooves and a right-hand twist—the signatures of a .38 Smith & Wesson.

"Luke, when it comes to crime-scene processing, you're number one."

He fixed the metal crutches to his forearms, and as he hobbled toward the door carrying his drink, he said, "I'll bring your glass back when me and you can sit down and catch a football game. All's I got's an old Zenith. Black may be beautiful, baby, but black and white ain't no way to watch the Redskins. I come over here for color."

4

I finally nodded off and slept as if drugged, my dreams kaleidoscopic with menacing colors and faces. But when my eyes rolled open at daybreak, I came awake in an instant and knew I didn't stand a chance of falling asleep again. I showered and shaved, fixed a cup of instant coffee, and ate a piece of toast for which I had no appetite. I felt I should call Marisa, but wanted to wait until I had a surer grip on myself and the situation.

Sipping a second cup of instant, I watched the morning news, national, then local. The talk was of drought in the Midwest, the Republican convention, and Dukakis's lengthening lead over Bush. Medical waste was washing ashore in New York, New Jersey, and Baltimore harbor. There wasn't a word, of course, about my father's shooting.

When I couldn't stand it any longer, I lifted the car keys from the hook where Big Tom hung them next to the front door. His Toronado had a plush interior the same shade of burgundy as the paint job, the AC system could have chilled wine, and the radio was tuned to the twang of country-and-western music.

My father favored American automobiles, what he called Detroit iron. He admired the space and comfort of their front seats, and he had spent many an hour passed out there, sleeping off drunks. Miraculously he had never had an accident; he always made it as far as the driveway. Then frequently he fell into a stupor, draped like a dead man over the steering wheel or sprawled on the upholstery, until Mom sent Buck and me to carry him into the house. He must have been heavy, but I really don't remember. What I recall is the way I felt as we lugged him up the steps. It saddened me to see him like that—head lolling, mouth slack and drooling. But there was another part of me that wanted to let go, just drop him down the concrete staircase and let him slide out of my life, out of his. Long before I wrote books about it, I knew what it was to be tempted to murder somebody you love.

Driving through Hyattsville, seated as if on a mobile sofa in a sealed space as large as a living room, I cruised along streets where I had hiked as a kid, heading for the library to read and daydream. Back then, I had had no interest in murder mysteries or tales of crime, true or otherwise. They were too threatening, too reminiscent of home. I preferred escapist fiction, adventure yarns where everybody got out alive.

Now the library had been made over into offices for lawyers and bail bondsmen. Across the street, the County Service Building loomed over a parking lot full of squad cars shimmering in wavy rays of heat. A massive mock-colonial building, it had wooden pillars that resounded like empty barrels when you banged them with a fist. The narrow portico provided scant shade and was no more inviting than the picnic table bolted to a patch of grass near the entrance. In this weather, it was hard to imagine anyone's lounging there for a few contemplative minutes before going in to pay a traffic ticket or stand trial.

Inside, a heavyset guard was watching "The Price Is Right" on a portable TV. As he turned to me, his leather holster creaked like the harness on a horse. "Bet I know why you're here," he piped up in a cheerful voice.

"Bet you don't," I replied just as cheerfully.

"This hot spell we're having, I see suit, I see tie, and I think lawyer. You're here to spring a client."

"You think wrong," I said, peppy as a game-show host. "My father was shot the night before last. I'd like to talk to the officer in charge."

"Sorry. Step through the metal detector, over to the cage."

"The cage" was a reception desk screened in by heavy-gauge wire. A pregnant secretary in a pink muumuu sat there eating honey-dip doughnuts. She was pretty and had her hair in a ponytail. Granules of sugar sparkled on her upper lip.

"Hey, I know you," she said. "I recognize you from the picture on your books. I even recognize the suit."

"The guard thought it made me look like a lawyer."

"I read all the time. We hardly ever have any interesting cases in this dump. I just saw you on the 'Today' show—when was it?"

"Couple years ago." Flattering as some writers found it, I didn't like to be recognized, I didn't like having potential subjects and sources knowing more about me than I did about them.

When I explained to the woman why I was here, she brushed the sugar from her mouth. "Jeez! Lemme call down and ask is the detective available."

I strolled up the hall, wondering whether it mattered if she mentioned I was a writer. I didn't want this to deteriorate into the halting rhythms of a reporter-cop interview. Even in court, testifying against defendants they were dying to convict, policemen tended to be dry and laconic. Confronted by a journalist, they were apt to clam up altogether. Working words out of them was like extricating a barbed arrow from a wound.

There were no wire-mesh walls at the County Literacy Council, the Energy Assistance Program, or the State Program for the Aging. If these offices existed when I was a kid, I had never noticed them. All I recalled about the building were squad rooms, courtrooms, and cells. From time to time, I had come here to bail Big Tom out of the drunk tank, and as a teenager, back when local police were less punctilious about illegal searches and seizures, I had been scooped off the street during routine sweeps and hauled in for questioning.

On one occasion, as I was changing classes in high school, a plainclothesman collared me at the water fountain, and with no wasted breath about Miranda and Escobeda, he sped me to the station and stuck me in a lineup. Because the witness couldn't make a positive ID, the cop grudgingly drove me back in time for algebra.

So much of what I later wrote, so much of my personal and professional attitude, began in this building—a sense of violation, the realization that cops favor a rough justice rarely encumbered by much concern about rights and strict procedure. Some critics claim I have a bias in favor of defendants. I suppose I do. You couldn't grow up in this neighborhood without harboring a few hard feelings against men in uniform. That's not to say I haven't depended on policemen. Some of my best sources have been cops—and some of my most ferocious adversaries.

Leather heels clicked down the hall behind me. The man was in street clothes—a shortsleeve white shirt, blue tie, blue wash-and-wear slacks, and brown loafers. His thin black hair was carefully combed across a bald spot.

"Paul Gant." He shook my hand. "Real sorry about your father. I'm the detective on the case. How's he coming?" He had a faint Southern accent—Virginia, North Carolina, somewhere in there.

"Still critical."

"They save a lot of chest-shot victims. Didn't use to, but these days doctors get plenty of practice. Hell, around here we got military surgeons working in emergency rooms, training for battlefield conditions." Gant was nearly my height and had the top-heavy shape of a weight lifter, a big-boned guy battling in a gym to keep his arms and shoulders pumped. "Tanya tells me you're a reporter."

"Not exactly. I write books. But this is personal. I'd like to talk to you about my father."

"Sure. Downstairs." As he turned to lead the way, I saw the snub-nose .38 holstered on the back of his belt. "Tanya says you write about murder."

"Sometimes."

"Well, we got a bumper crop in P.G. County. Average volume's more than a hundred a year. On top of homicides, we catch a raft of cuttings, stabbings, and shootings. These computer jockeys, they'll show you the numbers. It's a thousand percent jump in ten years."

As I followed him down the steps, I could smell it, taste it, in the sour air. We were in the part of the building I remembered, the bowels, the business end. I felt at home here, reminded of police stations I had worked in all over the States. The hallway looked like a cattle chute with horn and hoof marks on the walls. The floors were institutional tile, stainproof because their pattern resembled permanent stains. The light fixtures were far out of the reach of homicidal or suicidal hands; the color scheme was khaki and gray-green; the desk tops were a collage of cigarette burns, chicken-scratched paper, and brown circles from coffee cups.

What I could never convince Marisa of was that I didn't mind jails, detention centers, prisons, even death rows. After being dragged down here as a kid, scared shitless, it gave me a rush to return to such places in a different role—not merely a spectator, but rather a participant in a fascinating game called Justice, a complicated charade in which cops and courthouse reporters, lawyers and prosecutors, all got their fondest wish—to live a life of crime without having to commit an indictable offense. No longer powerless, I knew the lore and the language, the slang that bubbled up out of the cells and percolated everywhere until eventually even judges were rapping away like cons. Simultaneously an insider and an outsider, I enjoyed a stereoscopic view, yet never had to show my hand to anybody, and—what I liked best—I got to have the last word.

When we reached a wire-mesh door, Gant punched in a code on the combination lock and walked me through a squad room where two detectives were rattling Spanish at a man whose head was wrapped in bloody bandages. In

the cramped, glass-walled cubicle that served as his office,
he said, "Coffee?"

"No thanks."

He sat behind a desk buried beneath drifts of paper-
work. I took a swivel chair in front of it, and he resumed
talking about the crime rate. "Weekends we'll have a
dozen shootings. Domestic violence. Drunks. Drug-related
incidents." He propped his feet on the desk and folded
his hands behind his neck, giving me a good look at his
biceps. "We got dealers been shot five, six times. 'Frequent fliers,' we call them. Their friends run them to the
emergency room. Don't even bother to stop. Just drive up,
roll them out, and take off. We go to the hospital, ask for
a statement. Give us some names and addresses is what
we're looking for. The victim says, 'I don't know nothing
from nowhere.' We go, 'Your choice,' and let those assholes work it out on their own. Some of my men, not me,
but some claim there aren't any innocent victims in Prince
Georges County. There's just cops and creeps."

"My father isn't a creep," I said.

A deepening rush of color rose from his shirt collar,
climbing the broad planes of his face. "That's what I'm
coming to. My guys don't get many cases with real victims. Typical thing, they get Kanawha Street on a Saturday
night with Rastafarians rubbing each other out. They get
Colombian cowboys. They get rich white kids cruising in
from Montgomery County to score crack. They love a
case like your father's, something they can jump on and
feel good about."

"What's your closure rate?"

"Over ninety percent on homicides."

"And nonfatal assault?"

"Thirty-five, forty percent. That doesn't mean we quit.
It's a question of resources, manpower."

"Any results from your crime-scene search?"

Gant shook his head. His wispy black hair stayed slicked
down.

"Fibers? Footprints? Hair?"

"Nothing so far." Although his voice was level and polite, and his blushing had subsided, the muscles of his neck were still corded. "Forensic evidence is fine—long as you got a suspect to match the fibers and footprints with. But we don't have a single lead—unless you know somebody who'd want to shoot your father."

"I don't." I saw no sense mentioning my suspicions about somebody from one of my books.

"The black fellow next door, he said it was a white guy with blond hair. We brought him, this one-legged fellow—"

"Luke."

"Yeah, Luke. We brought him in, had him look through mug shots. Negative. Then, our usual drill, we had him look at local high-school yearbooks."

"You're kidding."

"Not a bit. We make plenty of arrests that way. A witness'll pick a winner—another loser—right out of shop class or the pep club. We've had so much luck, the Future Criminals of America are wising up and staying home the day class pictures are taken. But Luke, getting back to him, he didn't see anybody that resembled the assailant."

"What do you do now?"

"Knock on doors. Talk to folks in the neighborhood. Hope the perpetrator ditched the weapon and somebody finds it."

I hauled myself to my feet. "Appreciate your talking to me." The .38 slug was in my pocket, and I had seen no reason why I should surrender it to Detective Gant. But then I saw something else. It flickered in and out of his eyes, over his smooth-shaven face. He didn't want me to walk out. He pushed back from the desk, digging in the bottom drawer.

"Got a minute? Sit down," he said. "Considering you're in the business, so to speak, I'll violate department policy and show you something, give you an idea what we do with our days. Some people seem to think we just dick around, don't follow through on investigations.'' He tossed a manila folder in front of me and flipped it open.

I had seen worse, much worse. The top sheet was a run-of-the-mill medical examiner's snapshot of what was referred to as ''the body of a well-nourished black man.'' He was on his back, naked, his chest neatly perforated by four small-caliber gunshot wounds clustered near his sternum. He had also been shot in the head. The entry wound had crushed his right temple. There was no exit wound, but his left temple had a lump the size and color of a plum—a plum with a metal pit.

''Tell me now,'' Gant said, ''your experience, your expert opinion''—even delivered in a perfectly neutral voice, his words had a venomous bite—''what do you make of this?''

''Looks like a very dead black man,'' I said breezily.

''And how do you reckon he got that way?''

''All those bullet holes, why do they make me suspect murder?''

''Because you're guessing, jumping to conclusions. Half the department, plus the coroner, spent hundreds of hours cracking this case.''

''I give up, Detective Gant. Tell me what the gentleman did to deserve so much of your attention.''

''He committed suicide.'' Gant allowed himself a satisfied smile.

I pursed my lips and pretended to study the photograph, biding my time, waiting for him to go on.

''The guy's girlfriend comes home from work, finds him in the living room, dripping wet, like he just jumped out of the tub and climbed into his clothes. There's blood from one end of the house to the other. Appears he took a round in every room, including the john. Naturally, the girlfriend screams murder, and naturally we have to operate on that assumption.''

''Naturally,'' I said, still waiting.

''We search the premises and locate the weapon, a .22 pistol. It's outside the house in the grass. We send it to the lab, have it dusted for latents, and they raise the dead man's prints. Nobody else's. We process the house. Looks like there's been one hell of a struggle—chairs and tables turned over, lamps and china on the floor. But again, all we pick up are the victim's prints. And nothing's missing. Nobody in the neighborhood saw anybody come or go.

"Finally the medical examiner puts together this jigsaw puzzle, and he does it with a terrific—I'm talking Ph.D.—dissertation on blood spatters, blood drips, and blood pooling. Turns out this pathetic son of a bitch"—he tapped the photo—"is depressed and decides to off himself. Maybe thinking warm water'll ease the pain, he fills the bathtub, takes off his clothes, hops in, jams the gun barrel against his chest, and pulls the trigger."

"Okay, that's one shot, but there's—"

Gant held up his hand, a professor requesting time to elaborate his theory. "First shot doesn't hit a vital organ. But now he's in deep pain and has another reason to want to die. So he squeezes off a second round. No luck again. He hits a rib and doesn't do much except spread the pain around. He crawls out of the tub and dresses. Who the hell knows why? Maybe he changed his mind and is heading to a hospital. Maybe he just doesn't want to die naked. He's in his pants and T-shirt, stumbling out of the bathroom"—Gant rocked his muscle-bound torso, mimicking a man bouncing off walls—"into the bedroom, the living room, the kitchen, splashing blood everyplace. Somewhere in there he pops himself two more times in the chest.

"You see our problem? We got four contact wounds—two on bare skin, two on top of the T-shirt. At some point he nicks a major artery. All the poor bastard needed was to wait and he'd have died. But he's thrashing around, he's, he's . . ." Gant started giggling. "I know, it's fucking awful, it's not funny. But the guy's so crazy to end his misery, he plugs himself in the temple."

"And the fifth shot punches his ticket." I too felt giddy listening to this Grand Guignol anecdote.

"No. He blows out his optic nerves, but he's still moving. He's blind and bumping around the house, knocking over furniture, climbing the walls. He must have flung out his hands for balance, and the pistol flew through a window. Then the sad-sack son of a bitch crashes and dies, and like I say, we spend the next four months trying to make sense of what happened.

"Any way you slice it, it's a great shaggy-dog joke," Gant said, "but legally speaking a complete piece of shit. Still, we stuck with it. That's the bottom line. If we stayed on a case like this as long as we did, you better believe we're going to keep hunting for whoever shot your father. I'm not promising miracles, but we'll pursue every lead."

"Hope you're half as good a detective," I said, "as you are a storyteller."

"Oh, hell, that one tells itself." He shut the manila folder.

When I extended a hand, he started to shake it. Then he felt the slug and frowned. The way his forehead furrowed, it looked as if he'd spent hours exercising those muscles too. "Where'd you find it?"

"I didn't. Luke did. He cut it out of the aluminum siding on my father's house."

"Somebody screwed up." He grumbled and took the bullet. "We're supposed to be the experts. We should have found it."

"Well, you have it now."

"Right." Gant tossed the slug into his left hand. "Thanks. This could help. But until we find the gun—"

"I know how it goes. I'll be in touch."

5

The telephone was ringing when I walked into the house, and I picked up the extension, an old-fashioned black model in an alcove off the living room. "Where you been?" Buck asked. "You had me worried."

"Dropped by the police station, talked to the detective on the case."

"Bet he was a study."

"He seemed pretty sharp. He swears he'll have—"

"Don't get a mad-on at me," Buck broke in. "But I'm not interested in anything cops do. I get enough of that at work. I'm more worried about Big Tom."

"You don't think I'm worried?"

"All I'm saying, Tommy, don't treat this like a book you're researching. Let the cops look after their own business. I want you with me, not off someplace meeting people, conducting interviews."

Buck had brought me close to boiling temperature, but I managed to keep my voice cool. "Sorry I wasn't here when you called."

"Why I phoned, I may be late getting to the hospital. I have to talk to a man about Big Tom's medical insurance."

"I'll be there whenever you make it."

I had planned to ring my agent and editor and let them know I was in the States and why. They liked to have a number where they could reach me at all times. But after Buck's crack, I didn't care to speak to anybody who might murmur a few pat phrases of sympathy, then remark that the situation was reminiscent of my books. Did I see a story in it? Should we put out a press release?

I did, however, think back over my books and jot a list of names—a couple of killers out on parole; a vindictive lady who sued me for slander and lost; a convicted child abuser who flew into a rage when I wrote his story; a drug dealer who was convinced I had dropped a dime on him with the DEA; a cop who struck me as the most psychopathic thug I'd ever met, on death row or off. Had one of them come stalking me and hit Big Tom Heller by mistake? For a couple of hours I called around the country, satisfying myself these people had been in jails or detox centers or on duty or had airtight alibis the night of the shooting.

Then I tried Marisa. The circuits were busy, and I had to ask the international operator for assistance. Waiting for her to ring back, I remained in the alcove, recalling a time as a kid when I had sneaked out of bed in the middle of the night and found my father here with Buck's sixth-grade arithmetic book open on his lap. Big Tom had just been promoted, and now, along with his deliveries, he had to keep his own accounts.

He caught me staring at him. "What the hell you looking at?"

"What are you doing with Buck's math book?"

"Correcting his homework."

"Mom does that."

"All right, smartass, I'm reviewing fractions. I was out of school by the time they taught that. Is that something to be ashamed of? Are you ashamed of me?"

I shook my head no.

"Then why are you all teary eyed?"

"I don't know." I backed away, scared he'd smack me.

"Don't cry. I can't stand a kid that cries. Go to bed before I boot your ass up over your shoulder blades."

Too young to understand his anger, I nevertheless knew that much as I feared him, I also felt sorry for him—and for myself for having such a father.

The phone rang, and Marisa's voice was clear and strong. Yet I had trouble connecting with her. Sitting here, I couldn't picture her there. Somehow it seemed simpler to tell her Big Tom was in stable condition, showing signs of improvement, and let it go at that. Anything I might mention about Buck or my childhood or this mausoleum of memories would only worry her.

"I watched the American news today," she said. She meant last night's "CBS Evening News" rebroadcast in Rome this morning.

"Hope you didn't expect a piece about Big Tom. In the U.S., you have to shoot the president to get on network news."

"No, but watching it made me feel closer to you. I wish I were there."

"Believe me, it's better this way."

Marisa passed me to Kevin and Matt, who promised they were obeying their mother. They missed me already, they said, and asked when I'd be back. "Soon," I swore, and gazing out the window at the harsh, vertical light of a summer day, I said good-night and hung up.

In the waiting room of the intensive care unit, a tiny, darkly tanned woman sat reading *Cosmopolitan*. More magazines and newspapers were strewn over the floor around her feet.

"What's this," I asked, "the Christian Science Reading Room?"

Peggy, Buck's wife, bounced up and hugged me. I kissed her on both cheeks.

"How continental," she said. "How charmingly Old World."

"Don't bust my chops. I haven't had time to adapt to local customs. What should I have done—shake your hand?"

She gave me the sort of playful shove—part flirtation, part warning—she must have been dishing out to men since she was a teenager. Peggy was beautiful, a perfect miniature. Buck described her as built like an automobile-hood ornament, her body aerodynamically sculpted, her hair brushed straight back as if to cut wind resistance.

Yet sleek and smooth as Peggy was in appearance, she could be as abrasive as any woman I'd ever met. Doughty daughter of a state trooper, she disagreed with me—and often Buck—about everything.

"Are we going to see you at the house? The kids are asking." She steered me to the upholstered bench where she had been, and we sat side by side. Over our heads hung a huge color photograph of an Alpine valley, complete with shepherd and chalets.

"Sure, I'll get down there eventually."

"Why not stay with us?"

"I think it's better not to leave Big Tom's place empty."

"But how can you stand it, that street, the noise?"

"You just don't like the neighbors." I tried to keep it light.

"That's right," she snapped. "Make me sound like a racist. It's easy to love blacks when you don't have to live around them. For you, breezing back from Rome, I bet it all looks like a scene from Uncle Remus."

It was wiser, I felt, to fall diplomatically silent. After a moment Peggy asked in a voice from which the acid had been leached, "How's Marisa? The boys?"

"Great. Just spoke to them. They send their love."

"It's a shame we never get to see them. When are you moving back? You don't do it soon, Kevin and Matt'll turn into a couple of zips."

"Zips?"

"You know. Zips?" Suddenly she seemed unsure of herself.

"No, I don't know."

"Maybe I made a mistake. Buck calls them that. Italians in general. Not your kids."

"Zips is cop shorthand for mafiosi. Kevin and Matt would be tickled. I don't think Marisa would."

"Jesus, don't tell her I said that."

"What you meant to say is they'll turn into wops." I smiled to show her I wasn't angry.

"No, all I meant, honest, was they should get to know the States. What the hell, get to know their aunt and uncle and cousins. Learn baseball, fall in love with Vanna White."

"I'm sure they could be persuaded. They're fascinated by everything American."

"That figures. You're the one that hates it."

"I don't hate it." I had a tough time holding the smile. "It's just easier for me to work in Rome."

"Who're you kidding?" She drew back her head and gave me a look. "Your books are all set in the States and they're all, I noticed, about murdering families ruined by too much money. That's the funny thing. You've gotten rich by writing about lousy rich bastards. Is that why you hide in Rome? So people won't know you're rich too?"

"You guessed it." I gave her a deadpan response. "I'm rich, corrupt, selfish, and sexually depraved."

Peggy doled out another of her shoves. "Now you're bragging. Look, I don't like to browbeat you, but you know Big Tom misses you. So does Buck."

"And I miss them. But I told Buck yesterday, planes fly in both directions."

"How are we going to get to Italy—four kids in school, Buck in court all day, flat broke most of the time? I know, I know, you offered us tickets. That's sweet, but we feel bad enough not paying back that loan—how long's it been?—since Buck got out of law school."

"It wasn't a loan. It was a gift."

"Still, you know . . ." She glanced at her wrist, at a red-and-green Swatch. "It's twenty minutes till visiting hour. Maybe we can sneak in. What do you think?"

What I thought was that for a change she didn't care to continue pressing at these sore spots any more than I did. "Yeah. Let's try."

In the doorway to Big Tom's room, a doctor was talking

to a nurse. When he noticed Peggy and me, he asked, "Can I help?"

"We're here to see Mr. Heller," I said, and something about his eyes, the slightest suggestion of uncertainty, set off a strange commotion in my stomach. "I'm his son. Is anything wrong?"

"Mr. Heller has congestion in his lungs. His temperature's been fluctuating." The nurse drifted away as the doctor spoke. "He's running a fever."

"Is he going to make it?" Peggy asked.

The doctor hesitated, and that told me more than his equivocal remark. "We're monitoring the situation."

"Can we see him?"

"Yes. But he's a bit confused."

Big Tom's coloring had gone from putty gray to brick red. If the doctor hadn't mentioned his fever, I would have viewed this ruddiness as a sign of renewed health. His eyes were wide and the pupils darted around the room. When he spotted us, he stretched out a hand, groping. I grabbed it and held tight.

Big Tom was talking, gabbling about his truck. Where was it? He had left the keys in it. Somebody had to take over his delivery route. He strained to sit up. "Have to work," he muttered.

"No, Dad. Lie down, rest."

He subsided as quickly as he had started up, his head sinking into the pillow. His eyelids drooped, fluttered a few times, then fell shut. He dozed off to fidgety sleep, still mouthing dreamy disconnected fragments of talk. Peggy smoothed his hair, touched a hand to his forehead, and whispered, "Hot."

We sat on either side of the bed and I was grateful for the silence. I can't say what fears flitted through Peggy's mind, but I was tormented by scraps of barely remembered medical lore, the debris of past research about gunshot wounds, respiratory ailments, thoracic traumas.

After an hour, Peggy had to start back to Annapolis, and I was left alone, listening to more hallucinatory gibberish about Big Tom's truck. In all his years of drunkenness, he had never been one to babble. For him, liquor wasn't a truth serum, it didn't loosen his tongue. At least it never led him to tell me what he thought about any subject more serious than the necessity of rotating tires every ten thousand miles. Today was probably as close as I would ever come to his unconscious mind, yet it seemed as severely circumscribed as it did during his waking hours. What had I expected? That feverish and full of medication he'd confess I was his favorite; he'd always loved me?

Abruptly he raised himself on his elbows. "Take the truck, Tommy," he said in an eerily distinct voice. It was what he had told me as a teenager.

During high school and on into college, Buck and I worked with Big Tom during holidays and over summer vacations. He pushed us hard, and I've never forgotten the backbreaking, fingernail-splitting labor of loading and unloading soft drinks. We lugged them up stairwells into airless attic storerooms; we stacked them in dank basements beneath restaurants where fat rats lived cheek by flabby jowl with cats that were supposed to kill them. When we moved too slowly, Big Tom ranted. When we rushed and broke bottles, setting off explosions of splintered glass and sticky-sweet effervescence, he docked our pay.

Worst of all, I remember my pitiful attempts to drive his truck. Big Tom was a great believer in baptism of fire. As soon as I turned sixteen, he stuck me behind the steering wheel and imparted in a single word the entirety of his wisdom as a member in good standing of the Teamster's Union: "Go!"

Nerve-stricken in anticipation of imminent catastrophe, I ground the gears like pepper mills, stepped on the brake when I went for the clutch, and rarely rounded a corner without colliding with a curb. On one bleak occasion I spilled hundreds of bottles onto Bladensburg Road, paving the asphalt with broken glass and blocking traffic for miles in both directions while Buck and I cleaned up the mess, sweeping to a chorus of catcalls, honking horns, and Big Tom's caustic voice.

What I dreaded most was parking. I lacked the reckless confidence that allowed my father and brother to wheel the rig around, slam it into reverse, and ram it into a spot at a loading dock.

"Stick it in that hole," Big Tom would bark.

"Come on, Tommy. You can do it," Buck shouted encouragement.

But I didn't dare try. Angry and ashamed, I'd slink down from the cab and let one of them do it.

One summer evening at the bottling plant, in front of a full audience of drivers and black day laborers, Big Tom roared, "I figured out why this boy of mine can't park. He won't stick it into any hole that doesn't have hair on it. Ain't that true, Tommy? There was a bush around this slot, you'd slip in easy as an eel."

Goaded on by their laughter, I got behind the wheel and gave it a rip. I stomped the accelerator and shot straight back, clipping off the mirror on the passenger side, but wedging the rig between two trucks with no additional damage. That won a round of applause from Buck and the rest of the men. From Big Tom I got a final taunt: "You'll look your whole life for a pussy that tight."

A nurse showed up and asked me to step outside while she checked on my father. In the hall, a man loitered near the waiting room. At a distance, he looked to be elderly, his head bald, his body arthritically shriveled. But as I got closer, I saw he was young, in his midthirties, with cornflower-blue eyes and a boyish, insinuating grin. He had appeared to be stooped and off-center because of his suit—a fashionable, loose-fitting number badly wrinkled at the elbows and knees. The material had a sheen to it, as did his freckled, sunburnt scalp. Despite the industrial-strength AC, the man was sweating.

"How's it hanging?" he said, flashing his grin.

I went past him into the waiting room.

After a moment, he sauntered in, blotting his head with a handkerchief. He slouched on the bench where Peggy and I had been and picked up a newspaper from the floor. The headline announced that Bush was reorganizing his campaign team. The fellow grimaced as if personally affronted.

"Why is it these days," he demanded indignantly, "everybody that looks like a weenie, the type guy carries his penis in a pocket holster, why is it the press makes him out to be tough? A no-nonsense guy, they say. Macho! Like all these government wimps are regular nut-busters." He glanced up from the paper, his grin a disconcerting contrast to his sandpapery voice. "Now you want to talk tough, my clients, they're tough. They grab a gun, go into a garage, pistol-whip half a dozen guys, come away with forty bucks for a night's work." He let the *Post* crumble to the floor. "Me, I'm tough. I win all these cases with guilty clients and nobody's making me campaign manager." He spat a wad of gum into an ashtray.

"I take it you're a lawyer."

"Righto," he said. "Got a client here. Ran a police roadblock in a Toyota—about forty pounds of pure tin. Nothing much left of it or him. You got a loved one in ICU?"

Before I could answer, Buck barged into the room, beard glistening with perspiration. The fellow in the accordion-pleated suit pitched to his feet. "Hey, what's this? A meeting of the American Bar Association?"

"How's it going, Curtis?" Buck introduced me as his brother. No name.

"Curtis Koontz," the bald man said to me. "You guys are here for what?"

"My father was shot the other night," Buck said.

"Gee, sorry." Koontz dug into his baggy-pants pocket for a plastic board of what looked like pills. Pressing out a lozenge, he popped it into his mouth and chewed. "Catch you later."

I leaned out the door, watching Koontz head for the elevator. "What's with him?"

"He's an ambulance chaser," Buck said. "Hoped you had a personal-injury case. You notice how he scooted when I showed up? Ashamed I caught him trying to get over on my brother."

"Weird guy," I said. "I had a feeling . . ."

"Weird's putting it politely," Buck said. "That grin, the way he dresses, he looks like a clown you'd hire for your kid's birthday. But Koontz, he'd eat your ass for lunch and save your face for dessert. He's always one step away from being disbarred—or slapped behind bars with his clients." He unfolded the newspaper he was holding. "You seen this?"

The headline of the *Baltimore Sun* read, "Andrew Yost and Grandson Murdered." The subhead said, "Daughter Discovers Bodies." There were three photographs above the fold—Andrew Yost shaking hands with Richard Nixon; Clay Farinholt, his twenty-one-year-old grandson, in a golf cart; and his daughter, Elaine Yost Farinholt, forty-two, wearing a long, low-cut gown, standing next to Nancy Reagan at a White House reception.

I had to sit down and steady the newspaper against my knee.

"Didn't you know these people?" Buck was plucking at his shirt, pulling the damp broadcloth away from his chest.

Unsure what my eyes showed, I kept them fixed on the blur of newsprint and searched for the right way to feel. My first reaction was one of irrational relief, very close to joy. It seemed impossible Big Tom would die now that these people had been killed. Then I was ashamed of the solace I took from another family's misery, appalled that a man toward whom I had harbored murderous emotions was dead.

"Tell you something," Buck said, "that lady, what I read between the lines, is up to her ass in alligators. Hope she's got a great lawyer. Jesus, don't I wish it was me!"

He was pacing the room, rambunctious at the thought of such a rich client. I should have settled him down, told him about Big Tom's fever, but I couldn't stop reading.

Late last night, the *Sun* reported, an assailant entered the Yost home and shot Andrew Yost and Clay Farinholt. Elaine Yost Farinholt found the bodies. She was said to be in shock and under a doctor's care. Her father and son had been DOA at Mercy Hospital.

The Yost house was on Syms Island, described as "a posh, exclusive community on the Chesapeake Bay between Annapolis and Baltimore." Since the causeway connecting the island to the mainland was patrolled by around-the-clock security guards, police theorized that the killer had come ashore by boat. In the past year there had been a number of burglaries on the island, all blamed on thieves arriving and escaping across the Severn River. A preliminary investigation had revealed, however, that nothing was missing from the Yost home.

Unnamed "authorities" and "sources" speculated that robbery might not have been the motive for the murders. Andrew Yost was said to have had enemies—a massive understatement likely to provoke amusement in many who had known the man. There was a single-sentence reference to recent death threats against the family.

The *Sun* identified Yost as a former state legislator and two-term congressman who had financed his career with an inheritance estimated at $20 million. When his wife, Delores, died twenty-five years ago, he retired from politics "to care for his daughter and only child, Elaine." According to economic analysts, he had more than quadrupled his fortune in real estate investments and TV stations. Long after he had withdrawn from elective office, he remained a substantial contributor and behind-the-scenes lobbyist for Republican candidates and causes.

Again I glanced at the dead man's photograph—the thatch of white hair, the cocky smile, the aggressive stance, leaning toward the camera. He was a crusty son of a bitch and could be every bit as crude and far ruder than Big Tom. "Only the middle class has to be polite," Yost used to brag. "If you have a lot of money or none at all, you can tell the world to kiss your ass. But nobody kneels down and osculates your buttocks if you're poor."

He once grabbed my hand and clamped it to his chest. In his fifties, he had had heart surgery. A tube the thickness of a garden hose throbbed under my fingertips, pumping blood through his body. "I let them crack me open like a clam and replace my innards with plastic," Yost said. "That's how bad I want to live."

His daughter, the story continued, was active in state and national politics. Her late husband, Townsend Claybourne Farinholt, had served as ambassador to Nicaragua and Ecuador. Elaine later ran unsuccessfully for her father's seat in Congress, and during the past decade she had "worked in the arts." There was a list of opera and orchestra boards, municipal theaters, museums, and dance companies she had raised funds for. "In recognition of her contribution," the *Sun* said, President Reagan had appointed her to a post as roving cultural ambassador, and since her travels took her to Latin America, "sources" theorized the killings could be linked to political terrorism.

"I don't buy that 'unknown assailant' bullshit," Buck broke in. "It's what we call the SODDI defense: 'Some other dude did it.' Half the 'unknown assailants' in this country were ever caught, they'd fill Grand Canyon."

Nodding not so much in agreement as simply to indicate that I heard him and didn't want to be interrupted, I studied Elaine Yost Farinholt feature by feature, examining the familiar contours of her face, the smooth-grained pores of her complexion. It amazed me that a snapshot, some hackneyed, out-of-date society portrait, could call back such a snarled train of emotional baggage.

Over the years I had seen her pictured in magazines, squired by this eligible bachelor or that widowed senator or industrialist, most of them nattily dressed walkers well-known for having no interest in women except as arm ornaments. Back when I knew her, Elaine's blond hair had been long enough to sit on. Sometimes she wore it pinned up in a chignon, an old-fashioned style her father preferred. With me she let it hang loose. Naked, she hid behind it—or half hid. Now her hair was shoulder length and a darker shade, although still streaked here and there by the sun or some beautician's art.

The high cheekbones and strong chin inherited from her father, the thin nose that looked best in profile—they were the same. In person, without makeup, she may have had crow's-feet at the corners of her eyes, puffiness at her neck or jawline. But through a camera lens, there were few traces of aging, no evidence that she wasn't the woman I had loved at age twenty.

Staring at her so intently the picture dissolved into grainy dots before my eyes, I realized that what had been hidden for decades might soon be revealed. Despite the journalistic blather about political enemies and international terrorists, I was aware of several more plausible suspects. I wondered whether Elaine would name them. I wondered whether I would be among them.

The boy, Clay, bore a marked resemblance to his mother—same cheekbones, same fine, long nose, and I would have wagered, same green eyes. But there was a spoiled pout to his mouth that changed his smile into a smirk. His hair had been hacked short in the kind of butch cut favored by athletes in my era and by punk rockers today. A jeweled earring studded his right lobe. It clashed with his check pants and golf sweater—as did the last few lines of the article. He had dropped out of Princeton, then Hopkins, then the University of Maryland. A part-time student at Anne Arundel Community College, Clay was said to have a juvenile record and three arrests—for possession of marijuana, for speeding one hundred and five miles an hour in a forty-five-mile-an-hour zone, and for aggravated assault.

"Seriously here." Buck was raking his fingers through

his beard. "Your lady friend did it, right? Whacked her old man and the kid."

What he suggested exerted such a disturbing grip on my imagination, I felt compelled to reject it. "You're nuts."

"Come on. There must be a humongous estate. She clipped her father for his money."

"Then why kill Clay?"

"Maybe to eliminate a witness. Maybe because she wouldn't inherit as much if he was alive. Maybe just, you know, the kid sounds like your typical rich fuck-up running naked through the streets with his hair on fire."

"So she snuffs him? Is this how public defenders operate? Spitballing theories from the bonzo zone?" To break off the discussion, I told him what the doctor had said about Big Tom.

"That's normal, isn't it?" Buck asked. "An infection, a fever—that doesn't necessarily mean anything serious."

Still, he hurried with me down the hall and took up vigil at the bedside, leaning closer to listen to Big Tom mutter, reaching out to feel his forehead. The shadowy light and faint murmurous whispering reminded me of those mornings when Buck and I had served Mass as altar boys, and for the first time in years, I prayed with something approaching that childhood fervor. I prayed that my father would recover and I would get a chance to be a better son.

But even as I clutched his hand and pleaded for his life, I thought back over my own. I thought about Elaine, Andrew, and Clay. I thought about murder, something I did quite often in my business. Maybe it was only the illusion of policemen and paranoiacs that at some elemental level all crimes are related, but as I made my way through a mind-rubble of memories, I was seized by a conviction that in thinking about one case, I was thinking about both.

6

After visiting hours, I followed Buck to College Park, and we ordered pizza at a carry-out joint where we had gone for lunch almost every day when we were students at the University of Maryland. As commuters cut off from normal campus life, we had enjoyed a social status just slightly higher than that of janitors, and we had been reduced to using this place as our surrogate fraternity house.

Tonight the pizzeria was so crowded, we ate outside, sitting in the Isuzu. Every few minutes, Buck switched on the ignition, and as the air conditioner cooled the truck, gum wrappers and stray papers swirled around our feet.

"Check in the glove compartment," he said, handing me a key, "see if there's paper towels we can use for napkins."

I checked all right, and what I found was four pounds of shiny metal in the form of a .357 Colt Python. "A surprise anniversary present for Peggy?"

"A man in my profession needs protection. Lock it back up and gimme the key."

"Jesus, Buck, why not just go nuclear."

"You dealt day in, day out with some of the freaks I'm around, you'd keep a bit of extra muscle handy yourself."

"A bit! That's a cannon you're carrying. Where'd you get it?"

"A client. He couldn't pay his bill. So he gave me what he had. I don't guess you ever get paid like that."

"No. But I work around some freaky people myself.

Crazy, isn't it? Mom wanted one of us to become a priest, but we both wound up in the same racket.''

Buck said, ''You lost me there.''

''Well, we both work with criminals and cops. But Mom got part of her wish. We hear a lot of confessions.''

''Maybe you. Not me. My clients keep their mouths shut and their asses tight. The protocol in my job, you don't ask. Questions are your deal, Tommy.''

It sounded as if he wanted to draw a line between us, distance himself from what I did. So I simply observed that he was right; I did ask questions and I heard a surprising number of confessions.

Buck finished a mouthful of pizza. ''I don't remember too many times you gave absolution.''

''What the hell,'' I wailed in mock horror. ''I hope you don't see me as a prosecutor.''

''More like a judge.''

I was sure he saw the hurt on my face. I didn't care to have him hear it in my voice. I pretended to be preoccupied with my pizza. A greasy mushroom oozed off the crust onto my pantleg.

Buck took off his tie and wiped up the mess.

''You'll ruin the tie,'' I said.

''Better that than your suit. This's why I suggested eating in the Isuzu. Drop pizza on Big Tom's upholstery and he'd rip your head off.''

''Were you ever really that afraid of him?''

''*Were*? What's this *were* stuff? He's still alive.''

''Okay, *are*.''

''Are I afraid of him? Hell, yes, I are.''

''I was thinking how strange it is to have a relationship with your father where fear's the primary emotion.''

''What were you expecting?''

''There are other possibilities. Love, for instance.''

''What's love got to do with it?''

''Goddammit, Buck, don't give me song titles when I'm trying to have a serious conversation.''

Turtling his head down, he stared through the windshield as if we were in heavy traffic and he had to pay strict attention to the road. "How long's it been we haven't talked?"

"Last summer."

"No, last summer you were promoting a book. We had dinner together at Duke Ziebert's with that publicity chick with big tits and the talk-show twink with hair like Liberace. I don't remember any intimate family chat."

"So let's talk now."

"Be my guest. But don't expect me to make like Merv Griffin. I don't know what you want me to say."

"Say why you're afraid of your father."

"Because he's big and belligerent, and case you forgot it, he drinks."

"Ever wonder why?"

"Not much. Peggy's always after me to read books about alcoholics, go to group meetings of children of alcoholics. She thinks we should do one of these interventions. You know, gather the clan, sit the old man down, tell him we love him, but he's an alkie and we're stashing him in some fancy drunk farm."

"I'd go along with that."

"Chrissake, we're talking about Big Tom, not a Norman Rockwell character. He wouldn't stand for that crap. Anyway, he hasn't been so bad the past few years."

I lowered the lid on my pizza. "Sometimes in the middle of the night when he's tanked, he calls Rome, says he's lost, asks me how to get home. That doesn't sound good to me."

Buck turned in the seat. "He's never called me. But then that figures. He's always been partial to you."

"You gotta be kidding. You were the athlete, the ass-kicker, the kind of guy he loves."

"Nah, you oughta hear him brag about you—your books, your Mercedes, your apartment."

"Far as I know, he's never read one of my books."

Buck laughed. "That's the kind of loving father he is. He doesn't need to read 'em to like 'em."

I shook my head.

"Come on," Buck said. "He's not such a tough nut to crack. He had to fight his way up from zero. He may not be all that much now, but for him it's been a battle every step of the way. Can you blame him for being such a hard dick?"

"No, I don't blame him. I just wonder . . ."

"What? Why you're so much like him?" Buck laughed again. "What you read, people that get knocked around as kids take it out on their kids. That's why I married Peggy. I ever touched one of our little monsters, she'd murder me."

"Luke tells me," I said, "the old man's mellowed. Claims he and Big Tom watch TV together, take rides and talk."

"Next thing you know they'll be campaigning for Jesse Jackson." He bit into the last slice of his pizza. "Going back to that other thing—that Yost chick. Were you screwing her?"

"What's this, stag night? Thought we were talking Big Tom."

Buck wouldn't be sidetracked. "I've always been curious what you were up to that summer you spent so much time on Syms Island."

I rolled my window down and sailed the pizza box into a trash bin. "I was getting a lesson in humility. Learn them from the right person at the wrong time, there are some lessons you never forget. As for your other question, it'd be hard to say who got screwed."

Buck flung his box, too, but missed the bin. He climbed out, picked up the carton, and slam-dunked it. Rolling his head on the thick column of his neck, he moaned, "Back's killing me. I regret all the times as a teenager I banged girls standing up in doorways." He slid in behind the wheel. "Okay, I admit it. Most times there wasn't a girl. Damn, those doorjambs are rough on a young boy." It was his way of apologizing for asking about Elaine.

* * *

Because I couldn't bear another night in the jungle heat of my room or cramped like a contortionist on the couch, I went to my parents' bedroom and set the air conditioner on MAX COOL. Still, I couldn't sleep. Much as I'd like to believe my insomnia was brought on by worry about Big Tom or loneliness for Marisa and the boys, I knew it was Elaine. Astonished by the rawness of my emotions, ashamed of the whiny way I had answered Buck, I couldn't quit thinking about her.

I've met people no more callous or controlled than I am who were married for decades, then divorced. Eventually they all seemed to forget the past or at least managed to leave it behind. But I continued to mull over my few months with Elaine, pondering the meaning of events that were—that should have been—no more than a curt postscript to adolescence.

She had been different from the girls I knew, so different she might have sprung from another species. She was the sort I usually saw from a distance, in a convertible speeding down Wisconsin Avenue, or up in the bleachers when I played basktcball in Bethesda, or at a restaurant in Georgetown when I helped Big Tom with his deliveries. Such girls all appeared to be blond, with caramel-colored tans, faultless complexions, and perfect teeth. They wore camel-hair coats and saddle shoes, plaid kilts, and cashmere sweaters with gold circle pins. None of them—not in the gauzy lens through which I observed them—had acne, smeared lipstick, or sweat stains under the arms of their blouses.

Given the mixed feelings they whipped up in me—I was somewhere between bewitched and bitched—I couldn't have said whether I loved them or hated them. I simply burned to have one.

In late spring of my junior year, I was working as a cashier at a Safeway in East Riverdale, a shabby patch of Prince Georges County once rural, now a slurb of Washington, once the domain of whites, now scalded by the discontent of blacks.

Why Elaine Yost stopped at that particular supermarket, I never asked. Wheeling a cartful of food toward my register, she was dressed for tennis—something you rarely saw in that neck of the woods—in white shorts and a white knit shirt with a green alligator crawling across her left breast. At the heel of her low-cut socks, there were bouncy pink pompoms.

Roast beef, mushrooms, steak, lamb chops—I shoved the merchandise along the counter and blindly stabbed at the keys on the register, keeping my eyes on her. After double-bagging her groceries, exercising elaborate care not to damage the perishables, I punched the TOTAL button. "That'll be two dollars and seventy-six cents," I said.

She gazed at me with deep green eyes, then glanced at the groceries—about fifty dollars' worth. "You sure?"

"That's what the register reads."

"I like your prices."

I let my eye rove the length of her legs. I assumed I'd never see her again and it didn't matter what I said. "I like your outfit, 'specially those little pompoms."

"Do you play?"

"Always wanted to learn."

"You should take lessons."

"Unfortunately, the pro at my club has been arrested for child molesting."

"What club do you—" She didn't finish. I thought I spotted the ghost of a smile hovering at her lips, but she left before I could be sure.

Next day she came back and set a carton of soft drinks on the counter, the kind my father delivered. I rang up twenty dollars.

"Sort of steep," she said, "for a six-pack."

I told her we lived in an arbitrary universe.

"Is the manager aware of that?" she asked.

"No, he's more concerned with whether the corn's fresh and the ice cream's hard."

"What do you do when you're not smarting off with girls and fiddling with prices?"

That led to a more or less normal conversation, and afterward it was easy, very easy. We seemed to coast through the summer on the crest of a slow-breaking wave. To the extent that I let myself question, not simply marvel at, what occurred, I concluded that apart from physical attraction, apart from the entire unstable chemical compound that carries the label of "love," she was interested in me for much the same reason I was entranced by her. Just as she wasn't remotely like any girl I had ever met, I didn't resemble anybody in her life except perhaps her family's servants.

There was so much I didn't know, so many people and places I had never heard of. Yet even this fascinated her. It wasn't that she enjoyed playing Pygmalion to my Galatea; the idea of molding me held no appeal for her. She wanted to see me as a sort of low-rent Byronic figure, mad, bad, and dangerous to know. This sounded more like Big Tom or Buck, but I didn't correct her.

If I sometimes felt like a specimen under a microscope, I couldn't very well object since I treated Elaine to the same close scrutiny. She went to Wellesley and had just returned from her junior year in Europe. She spoke of her father, Andrew Yost, as if he were the Grand Dragon of Maryland politics. I had never heard of the man and said so. She liked that.

Her stationery came from Pineider of Florence and her address book had a marbleized cover and watermarked pages. She had jewelry boxes made by Papyrus in Rome, and her shoes were by Charles Jourdan. She called rum and Coke "cuba libre," and when she ordered Martini, she meant an aperitif, not a cocktail.

But what intrigued me most about Elaine wasn't her stylishness or her mastery of brand names new to me. It was her willingness to cheat a little or a lot. A risk-taker, she was decorous and ladylike on the surface, reckless underneath. She seemed adventurous in bed, but regarded me as more experienced—or professed to, at any rate—and she incessantly asked questions: When did I lose my virginity? How old was the girl? Was she a virgin? Did she come? Had I ever slept with a black?

About her own sexual history she was considerably less loquacious, and she had a disconcerting habit of emerging from our hasty, hard-breathing encounters as though she had barely been touched. There'd be a slight blush to her fair skin and one vein on her forehead that darkened when she was excited.

She wore underpants so clean, so pale and fragrant, that I expected them to leave powder on my fingers like pollen from a flower, and she was the first girl I'd known who used a depilatory on her pubic hair. She'd bought it in France, she explained, where bikinis were commonplace, and she trimmed her bush into a tidy triangle. Despite the lip service paid to doing what comes naturally, it has seemed to me ever since that in sexual matters it is more often artifice that holds sway.

She also had a way of talking that struck me as deeply erotic. She *knew* things, she knew people and saw through them, down to the murky bottom. In her father she had a fount of gossip about celebrities and movie stars, and she knew which famous marriages limped along with the help of punitive prenuptial contracts or bizarre sexual arrangements or the tight fit of mismatched organs. She knew prominent politicians, their secret vices and prosecutable offenses. Years before it became fodder for the tabloids, she told me that Spiro Agnew was just another two-bit Maryland pol on the take, J. Edgar Hoover had lived for decades with a fellow FBI agent, and Nelson Rockefeller ran around on Happy.

The one subject she shied away from was her mother's death. The obituary—already an indefatigable researcher, I looked it up in the newspaper morgue—said it had been "sudden and unexpected."

Every day after work that summer, I shed my Safeway apron and black clip-on tie, shaved and slapped my face with English Leather, then drove through the lush green landscape, past tall cornstalks, tented tobacco fields, and roadside stands that sold live bait and crabs. Nearing the Bay, I crossed brackish creeks and estuaries, clattering over wooden bridges, feeling the first coastal breezes comb through the cattails, breathing the smell of shucked oysters and brine. I always sped down the last long stretch of state road, my tires popping bubbles that had boiled up in the tar during the heat of the day.

Where the asphalt ended, a causeway paved with crushed shells began. At the gate, an armed guard checked my name against the guest list, then slipped a permit under my windshield wiper, allowing me to pass over onto Syms Island, into something close to a royal enclave, literally a deer park. Plentiful and tame, the deer grazed on lawns and would have nibbled the leaves off trees if homeowners hadn't hung bars of soap in the branches.

During those fractious times, when the light at the end of the tunnel in Vietnam was obscure and the black ghettos of Washington and Baltimore blazed with Molotov cocktails, Syms Island was one of the few places in America where people still felt free to be ostentatiously rich and white. It was a place where, before the birth of the term *Eurotrash*, foreigners of requisite wealth and class were called jet-setters and were presumed to add cachet to any social occasion. Gristled Argentinean polo players, Italian yachtsmen, teak-colored Spanish tennis stars—with these and other exotic transplants I dipped into catered hors d'oeuvres and followed their example in the perilous order of forks.

Looking back, I'd like to say I was true to my upbringing and acquitted myself like a rough-hewn prince among bogus aristocrats. But I did nothing of the sort. Grateful to have gotten past the gate, I slunk onto the island in my dented, ten-year-old Dodge and cravenly submitted to lessons, not in humility as I had told Buck, but in humiliation worse than I had ever suffered from Big Tom.

No doubt these lessons were long overdue, and painful as they were then, some strike me as funny now, particularly those laid on by the heavy hand of Andrew Yost. I can't even claim that he singled me out. He insulted everybody.

At one memorable dinner party a lady in brocade brayed at numbing length about her love affair with France. "I suppose I'm a born Francophile," she repeated at the end of every anecdote about summers in Deauville and winters in Cannes.

"Is that so?" Andrew asked. "You're really a Francophile?"

"I most certainly am."

"Strange. These days, you don't meet many Francophiles that'll admit it."

"I assure you," the lady said, "I'm not reluctant to shout it from the rooftops."

"Well, here's to you." Yost raised his wineglass. "I'm on your side. Franco is one of the most maligned statesmen of the twentieth century. He's done wonders with Spain."

No one, not even the lady, dared correct him. Like everybody else, I lifted my glass, swallowing a little pride along with the wine.

It was harder to swallow when I was the butt of his barbed comments. Having since met my share of egotistical trial attorneys, power-mad potentates, and jailhouse sociopaths, I'll have to say Andrew Yost is still my candidate for world champion in the grand game of giving gratuitous offense. Almost as often as I've fantasized about how I'd do with Elaine if I encountered her again, I've wondered how well I'd cope with her father. Of course my picture of the man is more than twenty years out of date, and it was never altogether objective. But it's not just that I couldn't separate my feelings about him from my own youthful insecurities or from what ultimately happened. I never could separate Andrew from his daughter. Theirs was an extraordinary closeness that fed on the undercurrent of friction that flowed between them, and I can't forget how she talked to him; how he touched her hair; how an hour after we made love I'd see Elaine sitting in his lap kissing him good-night.

Still, I suppose the hardest thing to forget isn't what he or she did to me, but what I did to myself. I remember an evening on the terrace when Andrew was enthroned in a peacock chair surrounded by guests, gazing down a lawn that sloped toward the Chesapeake. He was watching a sailboat regatta, taking small satisfied sips of his vodka gimlet. Sighing at the sight of those sleek white triangles slanting against a color field of blue, he said, "You know, Tom, if poor folks ever realized how marvelous it is to be rich, they'd start a revolution."

"Some say it's started."

"Gangs of niggers running wild through the streets hardly qualifies as *le déluge*."

Sensing trouble, Elaine took that opportunity to tell Andrew that I had just been inducted into Phi Beta Kappa. What made the honor all the more remarkable, she explained, was that I had worked my way through the university, and she added, as if this clinched some unstated argument between them, my father was a truck driver.

Yost called for quiet and announced the news to his guests. Then he proposed a toast. "Here's to Booker T. Washington."

My blood, the flesh on my bones, felt as if it had turned into one excruciating sheet of flame. A high-pitched whistle shrieked in my ears as I watched the other guests laugh and look to Yost for approval. I knew what I should have done—what Big Tom or Buck would have done. They'd have whipped the man out of his chair and wiped the terrace clean with his ass. For a moment I imagined how it would feel to tighten my fingers around his throat, toss him aside like used toilet paper, and walk out of this house, out of Elaine's life.

It would be simpleminded to say that fear of losing her held me back. It was deeper than that, buried beneath protective layers that would require the combined efforts of a psychiatrist and an archaeologist to strip away. Even then I must have dimly recognized that everybody has to pay a price in self-respect to achieve the American Dream, the one of crossing over into a more vivid world. And in my defense, I did fight back, but I flailed out at Andrew Yost by becoming what he implied I was.

"Yes, like Mistah Yost say, I'm black." I spoke in the stentorian tones of an evangelical preacher. "I'm black and I'm from the ghetto"—I pronounced it *gâteau*—"and I'm proud to be the first member of my race invited to Mistah Yost's house to meet you good citizens of the People's Republic of Syms Island. At the end of this party there'll be a cup passed, and I beg you to be generous. Send this nigger boy to graduate school."

Elaine looked stricken, as did everyone except Andrew, who gave me a glance of what I took to be reappraisal. Then he broke into prolonged laughter. The others followed suit, and as I ran on with my rap, they seemed to find me genuinely funny.

What started as an evening's improvisation evolved into a long-running performance. Whenever a cocktail or dinner party sagged, Andrew cued me, "Booker T., how about some background on the black point of view," and I'd break into my routine. I did voices, I recycled tired racial jokes, I replayed major scenes from my life. With ever-increasing embellishments, I recounted what were regarded as hilarious fictions about a black father's heavy drinking, a shiftless family's scramble to meet the bills, a jive-ass younger son's ineptitude at parking a truck. I described a season of CYO basketball when Buck and I shared a pair of gym shoes and could never be in a game at the same time. We even took turns warming up. He'd shoot a few jumpers, then dash to the bench, kick off the sneakers, and send me out to practice lay-ups. Andrew loved that one and sometimes called me Shoeless Joe instead of Booker T.

Simultaneously sickened and exhilarated, I wanted to believe these half-true anecdotes served as an exorcism of

personal demons, and since I salted my monologue with
enough venom to sting the audience, I imagined I was
dishing out more punishment than I was absorbing. Like
a slaphappy prize fighter willing to take a dozen hard
punches in the hope of landing a haymaker, I consoled
myself that I'd have the last laugh. Soon Elaine and I would
be alone—if not in the house, then on her father's yacht,
in my car, or at some deserted cove where the summer's
lessons would continue, only with me in the role of full
professor and her the pliant student.

I fucked Elaine in her frilly bedroom, I fucked her on
her father's desk and in the great man's bed, out on the
terrace in his peacock throne, in the garden swinging in a
hammock, in the boathouse, and on the front lawn. Sometimes she begged me to stop. Then I acted so cold and
aloof she begged me to start. I thought I was in the lead
and she was swept away. Yet whenever I took the trouble
to notice, she was far out in front of me, headed in a
direction, toward a destination, I couldn't guess.

The summer's education ended with such abruptness I lost
my position as student and professor, performer and privileged interloper, all in the space of a few minutes. In
early September, when the air was freighted with the first
apple-scented hint of autumn, I stopped at the gatehouse,
and the guard checked the list and shook his head. "Your
name ain't here."

"You know me. I pass through every night."

He shrugged. "Your name ain't on the list, you don't
cross. That's the rule. I break it, I lose my job."

"Can I use the phone?"

"That's another rule. You have to drive back to the
booth on the state road."

The pay phone was five miles away, and in the five
minutes it took me to reach it I ran through the likely
reasons. There had been an emergency; Elaine was sick;
her father had dragged her off to some social obligation
and she hadn't had time to call me.

The phone booth was carpeted with dead crickets that crunched under my feet. Breathing in the dusty smell of their dried shells and the sharper odor of my sweat eating through the aroma of English Leather, I dialed her number. The metal disk, hot as a skillet, stung my fingertips. Andrew Yost answered, and it was reassuring that he sounded normal—which is to say gruff.

"I had a problem at the gate," I told him. "I think there's been a mistake."

"There's been a mistake all right. I'm looking after that. You look after yourself."

Was this a new wrinkle in the routine? Was I supposed to dance a buck-and-wing? "Elaine and I had a date."

"Elaine's dating days are over."

With a piercing sense of my own stupidity, it came to me that someone had seen us—a servant, a neighbor, a crewman at the boatyard. Finally, I had pushed my luck and Elaine too far. But I let on nothing to her father. "When does she leave for school?" I asked, thinking I'd reach her there.

"She doesn't. A bit of friendly advice, Booker T., white man to black. Forget about Elaine. You had a nice ride this summer. Now it's time to jump back on your father's truck."

What happened next was agony to relive even twenty-two years later, lying awake in my parents' bedroom, staring open-eyed into the darkness. For weeks I had telephoned Syms Island, praying Elaine would pick up. I called so often, Yost had the number changed. I wrote her. I sent registered letters and telegrams. There was never a response.

In desperation—no, derangement—I rented a boat and rowed across the Severn River, telling myself I had come too far to turn back. Like so many of the cons and condemned men I was later to interview, I wouldn't accept that somebody I loved had let me down. I didn't want to believe I had been a fool and was a bigger one now paddling across the river, my blistered hands aching to touch her. If I could reach her, kiss her, I was convinced she'd come away with me.

But I never had a chance. A security guard grabbed me as I beached the boat in front of her house. I told him to take his hands off me, and when he didn't, I swung wildly, missed his face, but knocked off his cap. He pulled his pistol and left no doubt he'd use it if he had to. Then he marched me at gunpoint up the lawn, around the terrace, past people peering through windows. I didn't see Elaine, but I saw Andrew waving good-bye.

It was then, long before I had my first murderer, that I grasped the full power of ignominy and its place in crimes of violence. If I had had a gun, I'd have killed the guard or Andrew Yost or anybody else who crossed me. I could, I realized, have shot my own father, for in my mind, skewed as my thoughts were at that moment, he was responsible for what was happening to me. Here I was being treated like trash and booted off the island because Andrew Yost imagined I was like Big Tom and the extravagant tales I had told about him. But my father treated me with much the same sort of contempt because we were nothing alike.

7

Next morning, I spun up out of sleep like a drowned man rising to the surface of a murky pond. I felt I'd been on a binge and was hung over from too much reminiscing. I needed fresh air.

Outside the temperature was already near ninety degrees and the sidewalks and streets quaked with mirages. At the corner market, owned by Koreans, the customers were mostly Rastafarians, their hair bristling with dreadlocks and swaddled in baggy wollen caps. Heading uphill toward the high school, I passed two pigtailed girls skipping rope with a strip of yellow crime-scene tape. Then I crossed a vacant lot paved with pulverized bricks, melted glass, smashed stereo speakers, scorched batteries, and transistor boards. It looked like a scene from Belfast or Beirut—or as if somebody had bombed an electrical appliance store.

At my alma mater, eight black fellows played basketball on the parking lot, skins versus shirts. The hoops jangled with nets of rusty chain. You didn't shoot a swish here. A clean shot was a clanker, and the ball resounded on the tin backboards like a mallet on a gong. A high fence marked the boundaries of the court, and I clung to it, the sun scorching my shoulders through my shirt as I watched them work it around, bumping and elbowing under the boards.

This was where I had learned the game. As a boy, I practiced every day, year-round. In winter Buck and I shoveled off the snow or cracked away the ice before we did one-on-one drills. We went at each other so long and hard our fingers blistered and our toenails turned purple.

These guys had put in plenty of practice too, but they played an altogether different game. No set shots behind screens, no give and go, no pick-and-roll patterns. They free-lanced and flew above the rim, jamming the ball. They stuffed an opponent's shot and flung it downcourt for a fast break.

They dressed differently too. Decked out like an urban dance troupe, they wore high-topped Nikes and Reeboks, slouch hats and knit caps, sunglasses and European bicyclist pants knee-length and tight-clinging as a second skin. Their hair had been buzz-cut into the Box Top or the Philly Fade, and they had tufts on the crown or rattails in back or razor-carved initials on the sides. The goal was to look bad, to look dangerous as we in our day thought we did in our ducktails and tight jeans, leather jackets, and stomping shoes. Nothing so frivolous as dressing for success, it was more a matter of survival.

When they noticed me, they hammed it up like the Harlem Globetrotters, dribbling between their legs, tossing behind-the-back passes, slapping high-fives. Then a big guy with a raised welt of scar on his belly heaved the ball into the fence in front of my face.

"What you looking at, whitey?"

"A basketball game."

"Yeah, but what you looking *for*?"

The eight of them took a breather. They reminded me of myself at their age. They thought they were tough and smart, and they played the part. But for all their posturing there was a shadow of bewilderment in their eyes. They had already had a lot of experience at losing and couldn't figure out how that had happened if they were such hard asses.

"I used to play on this court," I said. "My father's house is down the hill. He was shot a few nights ago and I—"

The big one with the scar said, "Any y'all shot his daddy?"

"No way." A few of them laughed and slapped hands. "Sorry, man. The killer ain't here."

"He wasn't killed. He was shot by a white guy with long blond hair."

"Sounds like you describing yourself," the big one said. "Anybody wanna play ball? Or you rather chew the rag with Mr. Honky Private Eye?"

"You got a reward out for this shooter?" It was a scrawny fellow with a café-au-lait complexion.

"You know something," I said, "I'll pay you."

"How much?"

"Quit jiving, Jamail. You don't know diddly shit. Next thing, he'll be accusing you."

"I got something to say to this man." He motioned me to a gate at the end of the court.

Jamail wore a pair of black spandex bicycle pants and red wristbands. Behind mirror-lens glasses, his eyes were invisible. His forearms bore a crude blue tracery of jail-house tattoos. "What kinda bread we talking about?"

"Depends on what you know."

"Sure, I talk and you take and don't pay."

I handed him a twenty-dollar bill. Behind us, the other guys were shooting around, shouting catcalls. "Hey, Jamail, who you snitching out for chump change? The man's dissin' you."

"It's worth more," he said.

"Convince me and you'll get it."

"Other night I seen a white man." He tucked the twenty down the front of his pants. "He's going up Varney Street holding his hand in his pocket like he's carrying a piece. He gets in a car."

"What kind of car?"

"Just a car."

"You notice whether it had Maryland tags?"

"I didn't notice they wasn't. It's California, Nevada, I'd remember. Thing catches my eye, the dude gets in the car and his hair—"

"What color hair?"

"Blond. What he does, he whips it off. It's a wig."

"You sure?"

"You think I make up some shit like a man wear a wig?"

"What was his real hair like?"

"He's driving away fast and I'm considering the fact of the wig, not what's under it."

"Anything else you remember?"

"I remember I want more bread."

"Tell me your last name."

"O'Rourke."

"Jamail O'Rourke?"

"You got something against Irish?"

I handed him another twenty, and he tucked it in with the first one. "Hope you find the motherfucker. But hey, better be careful out here. These niggers'll steal you blind."

Jamail was turning to go when I grabbed him by the back of his pants with both hands and yanked straight up. A wedgie is what we called it in school. Jamail's snug Spandex britches were custom-made for nut crushing. I had him up on his toes, moaning.

"Did you see a white man with a wig or didn't you?"

"I seen him. Swear to God."

I shoved him away, over toward his friends, who were hooting and laughing. I kept an eye out for the big one with the scar, but he was shooting fouls at the far hoop.

"Look at Jamail," someone said. "His ass cheeks is eating his pants."

He plucked at his privates, rearranging them and my forty bucks as I moved on around the fence, away from the court.

Without the makings for espresso or cappuccino, forced to settle for instant, I cooled my coffee with dairy creamer as I stood in the kitchen dialing Det. Paul Gant. "Got something," I told him. "Maybe it'll bring you a step closer. I bumped into a neighborhood kid who claims the night of the shooting he saw a white man with blond hair climbing into a car."

"He give you the model, the plate number?"

"No, but the thing is—"

"Could he identify the man if he saw him again?"

"I didn't ask." Greasy globules bobbed to the surface of my coffee. The dairy creamer had curdled.

"Did you get the witness's name?"

"He said—don't laugh—Jamail O'Rourke."

Gant laughed anyway.

"So he jerked my chain?"

"Not with his name he didn't. In this precinct Jamail's a household word—a word like Drāno or Sani-Flush."

"Let me at least tell you what he said."

"Sure. Go right ahead." With his sweet Southern drawl, Gant might have been calming some screwball.

"The blond guy climbed into the car and took off his hair. It was a wig. Why not send my father's clothes to the lab, check for wig fibers?"

"That's an idea." Then after a pause, "Appreciate what you're trying to do, Mr. Heller, but you go around asking these homeboys questions, it's more than your chain's liable to get jerked."

"I'll take care of myself. You take care of business at your end."

I hung up and drank the coffee. The hell with the curdled dairy creamer. It didn't taste much worse than instant usually does.

There was a knock at the back door, then Luke came in wearing a T-shirt that might once have been white—it was now egg-yolk yellow—and a pair of orange jogging shorts. The stump of his amputated leg showed an inch or two of seared flesh below the bottom of the shorts.

"You seen this?" He handed me the *Washington Post*. The Yost murders were on the front page with the same file photos of Andrew Yost, Elaine, and her son.

"That woman," Luke said. "Funniest thing, I can't verbalize it in my mind, but I'm thinking, that's the son of a bitch running down the driveway."

The hair on my arms stiffened. "You said it was a man."

"That's what's funny. I remember a man, but facialwise this woman reminds me. Up around the cheeks is where we're talking similar."

"Similar or the same?" I soft-pedaled the question, concerned Luke might tell me what he thought I'd like to hear. I wasn't certain what I wanted to hear.

"Similar. Say, you got more coffee?"

I spooned instant into a cup, and while the microwave warmed the water, there washed through me an urge to yield to my suspicions. Then the very thought of that emotion was what convinced me to fight it. I poured boiling water over the shiny granules and shoved the cup in front of Luke.

Holding his crutches in one hand, he inch-wormed his index finger over the photographs, blocking out this one's lower face, that one's forehead and hair. "Now I come to study it, the whole family's got those cheekbones and eyes."

"What about the boy? What if he wore a wig?"

"Could be."

"Was it somebody Andrew Yost's age?"

"No. He's too old. It's between the woman and the boy."

"The reason I mentioned a wig, I met a fella this morning, Jamail O'Rourke. You know him?"

"Everybody knows Jamail."

"Would you believe him?"

"It ain't hurting him, he'll tell the truth, maybe. Hey, you got something for my coffee?"

"The diary creamer's gone bad."

"I was thinking something to sweeten it."

"There's sugar somewhere." I turned to the cabinet, fumbling through Big Tom's larder of supplies.

"What I was asking, it ain't sugar. More like whiskey."

The bottle was on the drainboard where I'd left it last time. Luke splashed a shot into his coffee, nibbling the tuft of hair beneath his lower lip.

"In Italy," I said, "that's what they call *caffè corretto.*"

"Many's the day your daddy and me sat at this table correcting our coffee."

"At ten in the morning?"

"Mostly after supper. But there was times after your momma passed when we started early and kept at it all day."

We were at a fork in the conversation, and I wanted to know what lay in both directions. What had Big Tom told Luke? What had his life been like these last few years?

But the other branch led to Elaine, and I followed it, just as I had in the past. "These people"—I pointed to the photographs—"do you know who they are?"

"Only what they say on TV. Rich dead folks."

"No, the woman's alive."

"Yeah, and seem like she done it. Her prints on the pistol."

"Have you ever seen these people? Back before Big Tom was shot, did they or anybody that resembled them come to the house?"

"Never." He slurped at his cup, then topped it with Scotch. The color of the coffee was changing from muddy brown to amber.

"Tell me, Luke—think for a minute—could you give a positive identification?"

"Meaning what?"

"Could you swear the person you saw running down the driveway was this woman or her son?"

"Swear to who?"

"To the police."

"I ain't talking to no cops after how they treat me."

"Talk to me then."

"No, it's nothing definite. It's just these pictures remind me. And let's get real, I don't feature rich folks riding into this neighborhood, gunning down your daddy. Which anyway, in my own mind it was a man."

* * *

When Luke left, swinging across the driveway through phosphorescent sunlight, he forgot to take his newspaper, and for a few minutes I resisted reading more about the Yost murders. It was senseless to sift the debris of another family's problems when I had my own to deal with. But ultimately I justified it as professional interest. This was precisely the sort of case that served as raw material for my books.

The *Washington Post* repeated the essential points from the earlier story in the *Baltimore Sun*, only with fewer references to unnamed "sources" and "authorities close to the investigation." People were starting to speak for attribution. What they said might be inaccurate, might be errant nonsense, but it would shape perceptions from here on. Even the cops and the State's Attorney were talking to reporters, putting their spin on the evidence.

On the other side—already an adversarial situation had developed—the Yost family lawyer, a fellow named Whiting Pierce, did all the talking. He said Elaine was still in no state of mind to answer questions from the police or the press. She had, however, described events to him, and he passed her version along as though it packed the weight of a sworn deposition.

His client, he explained, had come home late and found her father and son dead. Period. New paragraph.

His client, fearing the murderer might be in the house, picked up the pistol at the scene. That's why her prints were on the murder weapon. Period. New paragraph.

Pierce acknowledged that a substantial portion of Andrew Yost's estate would have flowed to Clay had he survived his grandfather. Now that her father and son were dead, Mrs. Farinholt was the sole beneficiary. Period. End of paragraph, end of statement by family lawyer.

The State's Attorney wouldn't comment on Pierce's remarks or say whether an arrest was imminent.

The last paragraph of the article mentioned that the Yost family—presumably Elaine and her lawyer—had hired a P.R. agent to respond to further inquiries about the case. In a quote that came as no surprise to me, the agent said a number of authors, independent film producers, and network executives had been in touch. "But Mrs. Farinholt has no intention of turning her personal tragedy into a book or movie."

When Buck called, I thought it was to rag me that things were developing as he had predicted. "Okay, don't rub it in," I said. "I know family murder's easy. You just charge the last person standing. But if you knew Elaine—"

"Tommy," he cut in. "Tommy, listen to me. He's dead."

I didn't have to ask who. I felt it, yet didn't feel it. Like a man who's been injured so badly he can't make sense of the insult his body has suffered, I experienced a purely anticipatory pain. The hurt resided in a recognition of how awful it was going to be once I got over my numbness. "When?"

"This morning. I came out of court and there was a message."

"Why am I finding out so late?"

"They called the house. There was no answer."

"I went for a walk."

"From what they told me, it wouldn't have mattered. He was gone before you could have gotten there."

"What happened?"

"The fever, the infection. You know how he was thrashing around. Couple of those tubes popped out of him. He couldn't breathe."

It was sweeping over me now, the first waves. "Let me have a few minutes. Then I'll drive over and stay with him until you get there."

"He's gone, Tommy."

"I can still be with him."

"No, what I'm saying"—he too was having trouble— "they sent the body to Baltimore for the autopsy."

"Oh, Jesus."

"You wanna come down here? Be with Peggy and me?"

"I don't think I better drive. I better sit tight for a while. Is there any way I can help?"

"That'll wait. I don't like you being alone."

"I'll be all right. I have to call Marisa."

But long after Buck was off the line, I couldn't bring myself to do it. I wanted to talk with her, I needed her. Yet I knew she'd be upset, and there was nothing I could do and no response I could make if in her misery she mentioned my work and her long-standing worry that something like this was bound to happen.

My pain was compounded by knowledge. In almost every book I had dramatized the gruesome procedure on the theory that an autopsy was the essence of a homicide investigation and therefore an obligatory scene for any responsible journalist. But I couldn't bear to picture Big Tom laid out on a slab, reduced to a technical jargon that I could repeat verbatim the way I had parroted the Baltimore Catechism as a boy.

Using a Bard-Parker blade affixed to a palm-size handle—this scalpel was designed for tough cutting, not the delicate touch of surgery—a diener or morgue assistant would start at the shoulders and slice down to the sternum, then extend the line to the abdomen. With a crutch-shaped incision, he would open the body and remove the internal organs, examining and weighing each.

Slitting the scalp across the crown of the head, the diener would peel back the skin, preparing the skull for a Stryker saw. Originally invented to remove casts, a Stryker saw was pressure-sensitive and sliced through bone without destroying the underlying tissue. The drill-like instrument's oscillating blade would open the cranial cavity, and the brain would be removed, examined, and weighed.

Then the coroner would address the damage.

Significant internal injuries appear in the right ribs and right lung. No smoke, powder, or stippling is present in the skin surrounding the wound. A hemorrhagic wound perforated the skin and subcutaneous soft tissues and entered the right pleural cavity and the 10th intercostal space. The manner of death is homicide. The cause of death is a gunshot wound to the chest.

In the end, the coroner's report would reveal everything about Big Tom's death, nothing about his life. It was irrational, I realized, but I found myself growing furious at what the autopsy would ignore, and by the time I dialed Marisa, I had to force myself to move gingerly, fearful my anger would wash over her like sulfuric acid. When she said she and the boys would catch the next flight to the States, I begged her not to. "I don't want Kevin and Matt to remember their grandfather in a casket."

"If we don't come," she said, "they might not remember him at all. They've seen him so few times."

"I'll tell them about him. They'll know him through me. The way he died, I'm afraid it'll confirm their worst fears about America." I didn't add that it was as likely to confirm her view of the States, which was largely based on my books.

"I'll come alone," she said.

"Please don't."

"What are you saying? Don't you want me there?"

"Of course I want you. But Peggy and Buck have all they can handle. We can't stay with them and I wouldn't feel safe bringing you to the house."

"You're there."

"I grew up here. But I'd be worried about you."

"We'll stay in a hotel."

"No, if we leave the house empty, somebody'll break in. If you want to help me, Marisa, please stay home with the boys."

Finally she was persuaded that I was being brave and noble, but I knew better. I was protecting her all right—protecting her from the worst part of myself.

8

As played out on the front page and the lead story on TV, the obsequies for Andrew Yost and Clay had all the trappings of a state funeral. The Reagans sent their condolences, and George Bush interrupted a campaign swing to express his and Barbara's sympathy. Politicians, show business personalities, corporate executives, and sports celebrities acted as honorary pallbearers, and the faces of the famous and the familiar flashed in the camera's eye. The words "tragic," "inexpressible sorrow," and "senseless" recurred in every sound bite.

Flanked by motorcycles, a long cortege of limos advanced into the cemetery, past lofty monuments and massive tombstones. At the graveside, under a green tent, her face shaded by a broad-brimmed hat and further obscured by a veil, Elaine Farinholt listened to a sun-pinkened minister deliver a eulogy that left the curious impression that Clay had died after a life rich in achievement, while Andrew had been cruelly cut down before he reached his prime. Then the caskets were carried into a mausoleum that was nearly the size of my father's house.

Big Tom's murder rated a three-line paragraph in the *Post*'s Metro section. "The viewing" took place at Gasch's funeral parlor, but there was little to see. The coffin was closed. A couple of cousins, their necks red enough to stop traffic, flew in from South Carolina, and when Luke showed up with me at the requiem Mass, they cut their eyes in his direction, then turned away, bewildered.

Fortunately, Buck and Peggy and their four kids filled

a pew and gave the illusion of a crowd at the graveside. Mt. Rainier Cemetery baked in the heat, the grass brown, the trees sagging with wilted leaves. In the background, a chorus of cicadas buzzed like a ceaseless rotary blade sawing the day in half.

By the time Big Tom was lowered into the ground beside Mom, black clouds had boiled up on the horizon, and the temperature seemed to plummet ten degrees in ten minutes. Rain didn't so much fall as fly sideways in torrents that toppled trees and tore down telephone lines. While Peggy and the kids returned to Anne Arundel County and Big Tom's cousins scattered, I drove back to the house with Buck.

For an hour we sat in the kitchen drinking beer, listening to the storm, talking very little. The windows were open. The place was ours now and neither of us cared whether the drapes got wet or the floorboards warped or the paper peeled off the walls. We wanted air, we wanted to be distracted by the crash of thunder, the sizzle of lightning, the drumming of rain on the roof. I can't say what chain reaction of associations it set off in Buck, but the smell of summer rain drenched me in a nostalgia that I didn't dare indulge if I hoped to remain dry-eyed and get anything done today.

Buck switched from beer to Scotch and said, "I bet fifty dollars we don't find one."

"How could he have a lawyer for a son and not leave a will?"

"Don't think I didn't bug him about it. But every time I brought it up he told me he didn't plan to die. Not ever."

"It doesn't really matter," I said. "I'd rather you and Peggy keep it all."

"Ready to turn your back without taking a last look?"

"That's not what I meant. I just thought if it'd simplify things, I'd sign over my share."

"What about the stuff in your room? It doesn't mean anything to you?"

"Maybe the problem is it means too much."

"You're going to have to explain that, Tommy. It's too deep for me."

"Look, Buck, let's not pretend we're talking about one thing when you're talking about something else. If you're saying I don't give a damn about this place or the family, you're wrong. And if you think I'm passing my share on to you and Peggy to put you down, you're even farther off base. Don't do this to me. I don't want to end up arguing."

He drained the glass of Scotch. "Me neither. Let's get started."

In the TV room, we pulled the drawers from the breakfront and crouched on the floor as we had as kids playing Scrabble and Monopoly. There was a shoe box stuffed with discount coupons that Big Tom had never got around to using. Buck flipped through a dozen manila folders, then tossed them to me. They contained reviews of my books, filed in chronological order. "You don't think the old man doted on you?" he asked.

"If he did, why'd he save the bad ones?"

Buck laughed. "You're such an asshole."

When we were boys, the hall closet was strictly off-limits; that's where Big Tom stored his business records. We invaded it next, unlocking two Samsonite suitcases full of checkbooks and receipts wrapped in rubber bands. We also found copies of his last few federal tax returns. In his best year, Big Tom had grossed $27,000. He retired on a pension that totaled little more than $1,000 a month. No wonder he kept his eyes open for discounts.

Upstairs, Buck took the drawers from the dresser bureau and plunked them down on our parents' bed. The top two held Mom's neatly folded blouses, sweaters, stockings, brassieres, and underpants. Buck showed me stacks of airmail envelopes tied up in ribbons. "She saved your letters, going all the way back to when you were in the Army. When you settled in Rome, she loved the envelopes with Vatican stamps. She must have thought they were blessed and postmarked by the pope."

It embarrassed me to recall the rushed, empty-headed notes I had scrawled. If I had known how much they mattered to Mom, I'd have . . . What? Crafted them like poems? Maybe not, but I'd have put more of myself into them.

Buck said, "You should hang on to them. Kevin and Matt might like to read them someday. Get a different slant on their dad."

As we rifled through Big Tom's belongings—his "personal effects," as a police report would put it—I thought of how often I had poked around in the midden heaps of dead people's lives. With luck, pliable sources, and an occasional bribe, I sometimes came into possession of letters, diaries, medical records, psychiatric profiles, and confidential reports from prosecutors and parole boards. In many instances I knew more about people than they could have told me themselves.

But with Big Tom, we not only never located a will, we never discovered a single document that revealed more about him than was available to the H&R Block employee who prepared his tax returns. Except for his nearly illegible signature, there wasn't even a sample of his handwriting. As Buck and I continued the search, I had the sense I was attempting to identify a dead man, my own father, who was as large a mystery, as elusive and unfathomable, as his murderer.

"Is it possible he had a safe-deposit box?" I asked.

"I'll check at the bank. But I doubt it." Buck gestured to the mess we had made of the house. "I bet what you see is all there is."

"No, there was a lot more to him than this."

"You think so? Yeah, I seem to remember he had a good right hook and a great thirst. Speaking of which . . ."

We were leaning against the kitchen sink drinking beer when Paul Gant banged at the door, eager to get in out of the downpour. His sport coat bore a cape of wetness around the shoulders, and the sopping, summer-weight material was molded to an impressive high-relief of muscles. Rain had ruined the clever job he did combing his hair. He ran his fingers through it, coaxing the strands back over his bald spot.

"You off duty?" Buck asked. "Wanna beer? Something stronger?"

"Can't tell you how sorry I am about your father." He lingered next to the table, uncertain whether to sit down or just say his piece and step back out into the storm.

"Thanks," Buck said. "What about that beer?"

"I reckon I will." When he sat down, his wet shoes made a squelching sound. "I know how lousy you must feel," he said to me.

"I'd feel a hell of a lot better if I knew who did it."

"It's not going to bring him back," he said quietly.

I didn't like to take it out on Gant. But neither did I like counseling from a cop. "I'd settle for some results."

Gant stood up to it rather well. "We're still working."

Buck handed him a Budweiser and sat beside him, the two of them looking like a tight end and a tackle sizing me up at the sink.

"My experience," the detective went on, "whatever happens now, it's not going to be enough."

"You don't get satisfaction out of solving a case?" I asked.

"Not a whole lot. Not anymore." He draped his coat over the back of the chair. "I sorta lost faith you can solve a crime. A math problem, a puzzle, you can solve that. But a crime . . . Well, on a great day, as good as it gets in my department, I call up a lady and say, 'Hallelujah! We caught the cocksucker that hacked your husband to death.' Sometimes I wish I worked in robbery so every once in a while I could make somebody really happy by saying, 'Terrific news! We found that stereo of yours that was stolen.' "

"Believe me, you find out who murdered my father, I'll be happy."

"Like I told you, we haven't quit looking. The question is what you're going to do."

I glanced at Buck. I was beginning to get the feeling he and Gant had orchestrated this in advance.

"I plan to stick around," I said, "see what turns up."

"That's what I was afraid of. But if you're thinking, you know, of involving yourself in the investigation, it could boomerang. Better let us handle it."

"Like you handled the slug? Like you learned the shooter wore a wig?"

Gant concentrated on the keyhole-shaped opening in the top of his beer can.

"Paul understands you're an investigative journalist," Buck said. "But this is a different deal. Those books you do, it's strangers you're writing about. For you to get tangled up in Big Tom's case . . . well, you know what they say about a lawyer that represents himself."

"He has a fool for a client," Gant spelled it out.

"Say you pick up some clues"—Buck was crushing his beer can—"say you learn the true facts—"

"As opposed to what? False facts?"

"As opposed to true crime," he fired back. "As opposed to the shit you serve up like it's red-hot inside info."

"What your brother means," Gant intervened, "is you could have a lead on the murderer, but step in shit and track it everyplace and stink the case out of court."

"So you're advising me to do what?" Anger had started to drum against my skull like the rain on the roof.

"I'm advising you want to play the game, you better know about proper procedure," Gant said. "I'm advising you have to be able to prove that that slug was the one that killed your father. Seeing how it came to me through you, who claimed it came from Luke, who claimed it came from the crime scene, a judge might rule it's inadmissable. Or take Jamail O'Rourke."

"What about him? Have you questioned him?"

"Sure have, and what he told you about the white man and the wig could come in handy down the road. But then he told me something else. Said you paid him forty dollars and roughed him up. If the defense learned you bribed and intimidated a witness, they'd eat us alive.''

"Do you understand what he's saying?" Buck asked.

I did and I was ashamed—not for buttonholing people and pressing for answers, but for going at it in such an amateur fashion. I popped Gant a second beer and one for myself. "I'll keep out of your way. Buck and I have plenty to do. There's the furniture—"

Gant nodded, and thin, drying locks of his hair flopped down over his forehead. "Yeah, there's always too much to do when you're not in the mood."

"Got any food in the house?" Buck asked. "I'm hungry as hell."

"Don't just help yourself," I said. "Fix us all something. For days I haven't eaten anything except sandwiches."

"I can't believe my baby brother," Buck was rattling cans and cartons in the cupboard. "A real man cooks. I bet Detective Gant cooks. Any man with muscles, any man who's secure about his sexuality, he's not afraid to be caught in the kitchen. But a limp-wristed fella like Tommy, a writer with a thirty-two-inch waist, he fries an egg, a single egg"—he lifted a box of eggs from the refrigerator and began breaking them into a bowl—"and right away he's out of the closet and into eyeliner."

Gant and I nursed our beer while Buck scrambled an omelet and burned some bacon. We ate it and swore it tasted delicious. Then we switched to whiskey, got tight, swapped jokes, sang a few choruses of "Country Road," and held a proper three-man wake for Big Tom. Outside the wind dropped off, the thunder and lightning stopped, but the rain kept falling.

BOOK TWO

1

Two days after the funeral, Marisa phoned to say I had
had a call from an American lawyer. Since it made no
sense for anybody associated with Big Tom's case to contact me in Italy, I assumed this was another in the endless
line of attorneys with warped clients and ambitious book
proposals.

"Did he leave a name?" I asked.

"Yes. I'm not sure I got it right." Though her English
was excellent, she had trouble with names she had never
heard before. "Let me spell it for you. W-H-I-T-I-N-G
P-I-E-R-C E. What kind of name is that?"

"Pretentious."

The Yost family lawyer, whom I had seen on TV, was
a tall, lean fellow with a Tidewater accent and a frosty
patrician manner. Every time a correspondent referred to
him by his first name, Pierce paused as if debating how
to deal with such insolence.

"Did he say how he got my number?"

"I presumed your agent or publisher."

"Did you give him my number here?"

"You've trained me better than that."

"Did you mention Big Tom's murder?"

"No, I told him you were in the States on business and
I'd relay his message. He said it's urgent. Why? Does this
have something to do with your father?"

"I doubt it." In my own mind I didn't dismiss the idea,
but there were other, more compelling reasons why Pierce
might need to speak to me.

"What is it, then?"

"Old business," I said. "How are the boys?"

"They miss you. They ask when you'll be home."

"There are things that have to be settled here first. The will, the house . . ."

"Buck told me there is no will and you're not interested in the house."

I let a moment pass. "You talked to Buck?"

"Yes, I called with my condolences. I wanted Peggy and him to know my thoughts are with them even if I'm not."

"One reason I'm staying, I want to see what the police turn up."

"Tom, if you get mixed up in this, it'll only be harder."

"It's already hard, I'm already mixed up in it. He was my father." I couldn't keep the annoyance out of my voice. It was bad enough having Buck and Gant riding me. I didn't like hearing it from Marisa, knowing my brother had put her up to it. "Give me a little more time. Once I'm sure the cops have done everything they can, then I'll . . ."

"You'll what?"

"Then I'll know there's nothing left to do."

"So this is going to be another one of those summers," she said wearily.

We had been married long enough for me to have learned better than to ask. But I couldn't stop myself. "What sort of summer is that?"

"One where I never see you."

"Jesus, Marisa, don't make it sound like I'm running around with divorcées and dancing girls."

"I almost wish you were. I wish it was anything except another murder." And then, to my surprise, she was the one who dropped it. Saying it didn't make sense to discuss this long distance, she hurried through "love" and "good-bye" and hung up.

I waited awhile, mulling over Marisa's complaints. I couldn't dispute what she said. I did spend too much time away from home, and I had to admit there was something promiscuous about my profession. It was simply in the nature of a writer to form intense, yet evanescent, attachments to people who meant nothing more than a story. But even as I granted this and vowed to spend more time with Marisa and the boys, there wasn't any doubt I'd contact Whiting Pierce. However slim the lead, I always followed up. That was my guiding principle—I had to know.

Sitting in the alcove, I dialed the number, and a woman—it sounded like a maid—answered. She said Mr. Pierce would pick up on another phone.

"Mr. Heller." He paused until the woman hung up. "Are you in the area?"

"I'm in Washington."

"Then you're aware of the Yost family's tragedy."

"I read about it. Very sad."

"Yes, sad and likely to get worse. Mrs. Farinholt is devastated. You can't imagine what she's gone through."

Pierce waited for a response from me. When he didn't get it, he said, "I'm told you write books. Excellent books. I don't do much reading myself, but I know your reputation and I . . ."

As he nattered on, there crossed my mind one possibility I hadn't considered. Maybe he was about to suggest I do the authorized account of the murders. Over the years I had heard hundreds of these pitches, all prefaced by the same lawyerly gum-beating and throat clearing, the same lament that the real story remained to be written.

"My wife," I cut in, "said it was urgent to call you."

"Yes, Mrs. Farinholt tells me you and she were once close friends."

"I haven't been in touch with Mrs. Farinholt for more than twenty years."

"But at one point, you knew her well."

"I'm not sure I ever knew her well." That came out more barbed than I cared to sound. I tried to soften it. "It was a long time ago."

"That's when I'm referring to. A long time ago you were close, and that could be crucial to her now."

"Really? Is she looking for a character witness?" I drawled with deep disingenuousness.

"What Elaine's looking for is someone who can confirm that she had an illegitimate child in 1966."

"Who's the father supposed to be?"

"That's not relevant. The fact is she had a baby and you know it."

I didn't deny it. I didn't answer at all. The conversation was advancing along lines I had expected, but since I couldn't be sure where these lines converged, I waited to see whether Pierce would explain.

"Given the delicacy of the subject," he said, "I trust we can talk in person."

"I don't know how much longer I'll be in town."

"Could we meet this evening at the Yost house?"

"Will Elaine be there?"

"Yes, if the doctor feels she's up to it."

My instinct was to play hard to get. But then that might suggest I placed as much importance on the meeting as he did. "I suppose I could drive down."

"Do you remember the way to Syms Island?"

"Tell you the truth," I said, testing how much Elaine had told her attorney, "I don't have very fond memories of Syms Island."

"I understand. Nothing like that'll happen this time. I'll leave word with the guards."

It gave me sweet, if childish, pleasure to dress for the meeting. In contrast to my uniform of that long-ago summer—chinos, Hush Puppies, and a drip-dry shirt—I put on an Ermenegildo Zegna suit and a pair of B. Beltrami shoes. I considered renting a car, but decided Big Tom's Toronado was an inspired touch of insouciance—like wearing faded jeans with an Armani jacket.

I also considered calling Buck. It might be wise to have a little legal advice, maybe even bring him along. But I feared he'd try to talk me out of going. He'd say I was spinning my wheels, blundering down a blind alley in a futile search for Big Tom's killer. Worse yet, he might accuse me of kidding myself and jumping at the chance to see Elaine.

Well, he wouldn't be entirely wrong. It was a scene I had in a sense been preparing for over the years, and I wasn't about to pass up an opportunity to play it out.

The route to Syms Island no longer followed a glistening snake of two-lane blacktop curving through pine forests, over wooden bridges and swampy creeks. A system of interstates swept me past an all-but-unbroken landscape of shopping malls and subdivisions where the suburbs of Washington merged with those of Baltimore and Annapolis. The few remaining fields of corn and tobacco resembled decorative shrubbery, and the widely spaced barns and silos looked like quaint exhibits in a theme park, leftovers from life in Yesterday World.

Still, it was good to be moving, good to be on the road. This was what I missed in Europe, the exhilarating sensation of release, of hurtling off into the immensity of a continent that seemed to hold out incalculable promise. Even at my lowest, knocked flat by Elaine's disappearance, I had felt this way when I set out to find her.

After being strong-armed off Syms Island, I had hired an investigator, my first fleeting encounter with the shabby subculture that foreshadowed my later work. Far from the hard-boiled figure made famous by paperback mysteries and film noir, this private eye was a plump, middle-aged man with a wardrobe of polyester suits and a chronically upset stomach. He swigged milk of magnesia straight from the bottle the way Mike Hammer knocked back bourbon. When he realized I was talking about a girlfriend, a college coed, not a wife who had vanished, he advised me to take a cold shower and save myself some money.

But I insisted I'd pay his price, and he, with no clever sleuthing, no convoluted plots to worm information out of witnesses, quickly cut to the heart of the matter. He bribed the Syms Island mailman, who produced an address and phone number in Austin, Texas. Elaine had moved there, the dyspeptic private eye informed me, and she was pregnant.

The news came as a relief, offering both a plausible explanation of her disappearance, and a face-saving excuse for following her. Where I grew up, pregnancy was the final step of courtship. While it wasn't the way I preferred to get married, I was more than willing to do what in those days was thought to be the right thing. I went so far as to wonder whether at some unconscious level I had wanted things to work out like this. Why else wouldn't I have asked if she was on the pill?

As for why she had run off rather than confide in me, I blamed her father and his eagerness to break us up. And I granted Elaine credit for not making me feel trapped, for giving me a chance to show what sort of man I was.

I showed her I was the kind of guy who took his cues from the same hillbilly tunes and treacly ballads as Big Tom listened to. Quitting college and my job, hocking my car and kissing off my draft deferment, I headed west. In my mind, extravagant gestures were what the situation demanded. Even the decision to hitchhike was more symbolic than practical. Although a Greyhound bus would have cost next to nothing, I opted to cross half the country under the worst possible conditions, to prove to her and myself that I was willing to throw away everything and begin life again with her and the baby.

Flagging down truckers, I rode on the bouncing flatbeds of tractor trailers. For hundreds of miles I clung to an outboard motorboat towed by a honeymooning couple. I slept in garages and bus shelters and slogged through rain and wilting heat. I ate slumgullion in small-town diners, blinking under relentless fluorescent bulbs, and kept clean by sponging off in men's rooms where the mirrors were flecked with insects that had flown to their death by dashing against their own reflections. My traveling companions were bums, crackpots, religious fanatics, and sexual deviates who invariably observed, "I bet a big boy like you gets a lot of pussy."

On campus and on television, the times had an up-tempo beat, but out on the highway the tune hadn't changed since the Great Depression. Drifters lamented lost love, repossessed houses and cars, factories that had closed, breaks that had gone against them. "Born to Lose" was their anthem, the basic tenet of their theology.

When I mentioned what I was doing—chasing after a woman who had ditched me—it made perfect sense to these people. But there was divided opinion what I should do once I found her. Some counseled me to marry the gal and give her a second chance. Others admonished me to put my mark on her, leave her with a scar so she'd never forget that she'd fucked with the wrong man.

I sided with the sentimentalists. My feelings had altered in her absence, and now desire was only one of many emotions Elaine stirred in me. During the long days of that trip I realized how deeply I loved her; I couldn't bear to be without her.

Riding through Texas, I had the sensation of sitting on a vast, dull-green blotter that was slowly being dragged from beneath me. A soldier just back from Vietnam dropped me in Austin near the university. The fall semester had started, and students thronged the streets. While the heat was enough to unhinge me, the UT colors, burnt orange and white, suggested an East Coast autumn.

I checked into a rooming house on Lavaca Street, showered, and changed clothes. Although I knew her phone number, I had no intention of calling Elaine and telling her I was in town. I was afraid she'd disappear again. For all I knew, her father or some relative was with her and might force her to leave before I saw her.

I decided to find the address on foot. Until that day my one goal had been to get here. Now I needed time to formulate an attitude, a face that reflected my changed feelings.

Crossing a creek that trickled along a bed of pale lime-stone, I climbed steadily into a residential district where the scrubby land was broken by slabs of crumbling rock. Cactus and yucca plants sprouted on suburban lawns. No one was out on the street except black maids trudging toward bus stops, and in the dense silence it struck me how foreign this was, how far I had traveled.

The house was in a cul-de-sac shaded by live oaks and pecan trees. It reminded me of the mansions on Syms Island, but a brass plaque identified it as the Creekmore Agency, and I rightly assumed it was a home for unwed mothers. Although abortions were illegal back then, I was surprised Elaine hadn't had one. A man of her father's influence could have found a willing doctor or else flown her to Europe.

Ringing the doorbell, I heard chimes play the first few bars of a show tune I couldn't name. The woman who answered was short and trim and wore a miniskirt and a sleeveless jersey. Her sunglasses were shoved back on her head like an outlandish barrette holding her brown hair in place. When she smiled, fine lines gathered at the edges of her eyes.

"Can I help?"

I told her my name and asked to see Elaine Yost.

"Is she expecting you?"

I figured, Why not? "Yes."

"I'll buzz her room." She motioned for me to come in. "Hot out there, isn't it? I'm Diane Kershner." Her smile had the same lacquered fixity as her hair.

She led me to a parlor furnished with folding chairs and card tables. I might have been back at the University of Maryland, at a sorority, waiting while the housemother went to call my date.

She couldn't have been gone more than two minutes, and I remember every second. I remember the frigid rush of air from the AC ducts; the lemony light slanting through chintz curtains; the busted flush somebody had left laid out on a table. Fiction writers claim that when they get the details right, they're sure a scene will be charged with emotions they need not name. I don't share their confidence. How could air or light or a poker hand convey the woeful turbulence of those last minutes alone?

Diane Kershner came back with Elaine. "Tom, how nice to see you," she said in a voice that sounded nothing like hers.

I wanted to kiss her, but because the woman stayed with us, I settled for a hand on her bare, cool arm. She was wearing a cotton dress with brightly colored flowers embroidered on the bodice. It looked Mexican and was loose at the waist. I wouldn't have guessed she was pregnant.

"Can we take a walk?" I asked.

"Show him around the property," Diane Kershner suggested.

Once we were outside, Elaine sagged against me. "You shouldn't have done this."

"You knew I'd come." I took her hand, which in my memory is no larger than Kevin's or Matt's.

Her face was in profile—the long, straight nose, the prominent cheekbones, and deep green eyes. She had her hair pinned up the way Andrew preferred it. Perhaps in the fierce Texas heat, she preferred it that way too. I was tempted to pull out the pins, let it unfurl over my fists, spill down her back.

We stepped off a sidewalk onto grass that looked as firm as a putting green, but felt spongy underfoot. Behind the house, the oblong of a swimming pool sparkled in the sun, giving off a powerful whiff of chlorine. No one was in the water or in the chairs around it. Nobody except us appeared to be outside for miles around. On a bench under a live oak, we sat in leaf-patterned shade. I was looking at her, she was looking down at her lap.

"I want you to come away with me," I said.

"I can't. Don't you see?" She turned to me and what I saw were eyes clouded with a confusion as profound as my own.

"I love you. I thought you loved me."

"I do."

"That's all that matters. We'll get married."

"No, Tom, that's not all that matters."

"Look, Elaine, the important thing—"

"The important thing is I'm pregnant."

"It's not a fatal disease. Happens all the time."

"Not to me it doesn't."

"What's the problem? Your father? He furious at me?"
She pulled her hand from mine. "It's me. I don't want
to get married like this."

"You'd rather what? Give the baby away? Don't I have
any say in this?" I found myself giving in to questions I
knew were useless to ask. "I had to hire a detective to
find out the truth."

"You didn't get your money's worth," she said. "You
didn't get the whole truth. Because the reason I left . . .
Isn't it obvious? It's not your baby."

I used to kid myself that if she hadn't broken down and
cried then, I could have left, packed my bags and gone
home. Much later I admitted that although I stayed partly
out of sympathy, there was also my incessant need to
know. As soon as she calmed down, I asked, "Whose is
it?"

"What good will that do you?"

"I want his name."

"You've never met. His name'll mean nothing to you."

"How can you be sure he's the father?"

"I'm sure."

"How?"

"I'm more than four months pregnant. It happened before I met you."

"Why'd it take this long to find out? You should have
known before."

"Before what? Before I slept with you?" she said
sharply. "You're right, I should have. But I didn't."

"This other guy, does he know?"

"What does it matter? I'm here and I've made up my
mind what I have to do."

"You kids okay?" Diane Kershner walked toward us on tiptoes to keep her heels from sinking into the grass.

"We're fine," Elaine said. "Tom was just about to leave."

Stung by her curt dismissal, I crossed the lawn and went down the driveway without looking back. That's how it should have ended. In a novel or movie, that would have been the final scene, the fade-out. Even writing true crime where facts resist tidy conclusions, I've learned strategies for cropping the frame and closing on a dramatic tableau, coercing shape out of chaos. But much as my pride and my narrative instinct rebel, there's no way I can make sense of the jumbled events that followed.

I stayed on in Austin, got a job waiting tables in a restaurant near the UT campus, and kept in touch with Elaine. I wrote letters full of sentimental slop, and it sickens me to think she might have saved them. If memory serves, I also sent poems some the cloying fruit of my imagination, others copied out of an anthology. Each line shrieked with self-pity and ended with a plea for her to let me see her again. Sometimes she replied; sometimes weeks went by. Whenever I was sure she had cut me off for good, she called and we'd meet for a movie or a meal as any college-age couple might. We cheered at Longhorn football games, we ate *huevos rancheros* at Cisco's on Sunday mornings, we took trips on a paddle wheeler along Town Lake. Then when the mood struck her, she returned to my rented room.

The first time she saw it, she said, "This is really very nice," and she paced it from wall to wall, as if measuring for a carpet. "Too bad you don't have your own things here."

What things? I wondered. I didn't have things. Yet rather than glory in the freedom of having nothing to tie me down, I felt unhelmed, adrift. I thought that must be what she found lacking in me, what I needed if I hoped to have Elaine—possessions, a rich history written in objects.

* * *

A different history was being written on her body. When she undressed, I couldn't conceal my amazement at the changes. Her breasts had swollen and were marbled with blue veins. The aureolas of her nipples had darkened, and the tiny pink bud of her navel had turned inside out. I was reluctant to touch her, afraid I'd hurt her.

"I'm ugly," she said.

"No, you're beautiful." My keenest, most poignant recollections are of Elaine pregnant. Afterward, in my worst moments, I half-hated the flat-tummied girl I had romped with in her father's house. But I went on loving the woman I remember from that bare room in Texas.

In bed, I placed my hands on either side of her shoulders and straightened my arms, holding my weight up off her belly. It wasn't just her body that had changed. Some elemental chemistry had altered, and the previous summer's headlong grasping pleasure slowed down, turned tentative. Nothing simple or direct seemed possible; with each caress, I was asking a question and waiting to read an answer in her reaction.

Satisfied with what I thought I saw on those nights we spent together, I said I wanted to marry her and keep the baby; I didn't care that it wasn't mine. She turned me down and begged me not to ask again, but I didn't believe she had made up her mind. Otherwise, I reasoned, she wouldn't have come back to my room. I felt her wavering. I felt this as surely as I felt the baby kicking against my hand.

She began to talk about the future—what she'd do, where she'd go after the baby was born. I didn't believe she'd discuss this unless the future included me.

She said she intended to travel and asked if I was interested in going to Europe. When I mentioned a slight problem, a matter of money, she said, "Are we rich or aren't we?" It was what I had heard her ask Andrew when he bitched about her spending. The question made him laugh—maybe because he, unlike me at the time, realized she was quoting Clare Boothe Luce, who had snapped the line at husband Henry when he crabbed at her for dropping $20,000 on lingerie.

In the Vuitton overnight bag Elaine always brought with her, there was a tube of cream covered with German script so minute it was barely decipherable. A mixture of animal enzymes, hormonal extracts, and herbal essences, it wasn't on sale in the United States, she explained, not even with a doctor's prescription. Andrew had bought it for her to prevent stretch marks.

Handing me the tube, she lay facedown on the bed and asked me to massage her with the floral-scented ointment. Still tan from the summer, the mounds and declivities of her body gleamed as if glazed with shellac. When she rolled over onto her back, she kept her eyes shut and her arms rigidly at her sides. She might have been a statue, a piece of mortuary art from a sarcophagus. But when I touched her, she smiled, her nipples tensed, and the rest of her relaxed. "That feels good," she said.

Between her legs, there was a sheath of muscle as flawless and slippery as a silk scarf. That's where I went next to the final, the best, stroke of the treatment.

It's tempting to remember those months in Texas as a time when life flowed with the same smoothness as my hands gliding over the swells of her body. But there were days when nothing worked and no movement seemed possible without monumental effort; days when Elaine mercilessly found fault with herself or with me. In her situation, it couldn't have been easy being around me, listening to my dreamy, impractical plans one moment and my defensive prattle the next. The maladroitness that had amused her early on must have grated now, and she had to wonder what it would be like to spend her life with a rube, a gangling, overgrown boy who had little to offer except what he imagined to be a literary sensibility and the certainty of his future greatness—what Buck called my "trailer-park pride."

In her blackest moods, Elaine let up on me and railed at her father. She resented his devouring egotism, his nonstop attempts to control her life. He paid for everything, she said, and wired her money as if she were at a resort. But then he told her how to spend it and insisted she account for every penny. He phoned day and night, often two or three times, and was enraged when she wasn't there. "He's jealous," she said. "He's beginning to get suspicious."

"Does he know I'm here?"

"Of course not."

Late in her ninth month, she showed up after a doctor's appointment and said he had advised her it was best that we didn't make love again. At least not as we had been doing.

Elaine went over and lay on the bed. "It doesn't mean you can't touch me," she said. "Or am I too cowlike for you these days?"

I kissed her mouth and her breasts, her high, rounded belly, both thighs, then between them.

Afterward, she rolled onto her side, turning her back to me, and spoke in a quiet, faraway voice. "Have I ever told you how my mother died? He killed her."

I had been about to touch her. I held back. "Who?"

"Daddy."

"You don't mean that," I said. My hand hovered above her shoulder.

"Yes, I do. She was sick and upset, and Daddy had no patience with her. He treated her like he treated everybody else." Her words were unhurried, uninflected. She wasn't trying to sway me. She was simply telling me, trusting me. "Mother said if that's how he was going to be, she'd kill herself. She didn't want to live that way. Daddy said— we were sitting at the dinner table, and Daddy said, 'I don't give a goddamn what you do.' That night she swallowed a bottle of Seconal. Daddy had the whole thing covered up. He didn't care if she committed suicide. But of course he didn't want anybody to know about it. She didn't even get the satisfaction of taking him down a peg or two.''

I stroked her hair and her face, which weren't wet with tears as I had expected. ''That's terrible. I'm sorry.''

Yet ''terrible'' and ''sorry'' didn't tell the entire truth of my feelings, for at some level not far from the surface I felt a strange exhilaration, partly because she had shared such a secret, partly because I didn't believe that she would have done so unless she had made up her mind that her deepest loyalty lay with me now, not her father.

Next day we had a date for lunch, and when Elaine didn't show up, I called the Creekmore Agency and got Diane Kershner. Without preamble she said, ''Elaine left this morning. Her father flew in and they left together.''

''Where'd they go?''

''They told me not to tell you.''

''They? He's the one calling the shots.''

''*They!*'' she repeated. ''I know you're upset, Tom, but you and I have to talk.''

''Just tell me where she went.''

''We need to discuss the baby's father.'' She trolled the right bait.

It was a cold day, the first one of winter. A blue norther, as Texans call these clear bursts of arctic air, had blown all afternoon, buffing the sky till it glowed like scoured aluminum. I caught a cab and struggled during the ride to make sense of my emotions. Stuffed to the point of exploding with rage at Andrew Yost, I was also furious at Elaine—why had she gone with him?—and full of self-loathing. I had had a second chance and had blown it.

At the Creekmore Agency, Diane Kershner met me at the door, hugging her chest, flushed with high spirits as if I were here to pick her up for a hayride. She wore a pair of patterned stockings and had her sunglasses shoved back on her head, just as she had all summer.

''On the radio,'' she said, leading me to her office, ''they predict a hard freeze in the hill country.''

She sat at a desk, and I took the only other chair, shifting it out of the sunlight that flooded through a window behind her. On the window ledge were a dozen dolls in national costumes. "I collect them," she said. "A lot of the girls travel after they give up their babies, and they send me dolls from all over the world."

"Is that what Elaine's doing? Traveling? Shopping for dolls?"

She reached into a drawer of the desk. "She hasn't had her baby yet."

"Where is she?"

"I'm not free to say where." She pulled out a sheaf of papers. "As for why she went, I think she was feeling a lot of pressure."

"From her father. Not me."

"I can't quote what she told me in so many words. But the substance was you followed her here, you wanted her to keep the baby and marry you." Mrs. Kershner crossed her legs, and her stockings made a faint rasping sound as though they were woven of fine steel mesh. "She had a hard time coping with the stress. Last night she called her father. Next thing I knew he was in Austin."

"Does he know I'm here?"

"Yes. She told him. Look, Tom, I'm sorry you and I haven't had a chance to talk. You could probably use a sounding board."

"What I could use is a telephone number. If I could talk to her, I could—"

"What?" Diane Kershner picked up a pencil and ran the eraser over the sheaf of papers. "I think the problem is Elaine realizes what a serious matter marriage is for you."

"Isn't it serious for everybody?"

"Yes, but you're Catholic. You can't blame Elaine. A woman doesn't have to be a religious bigot to think the Catholic attitude toward birth control is a bit, shall we say, antiquated."

What I did then is something defense attorneys coach

their clients never to do. I leaped ahead to where I thought she was leading me and volunteered information that hadn't been asked for. "My attitude toward birth control had nothing to do with Elaine's getting pregnant."

She broke into a smile. "So she told me. She swore you're not the father." Her stockings hissed as she recrossed her legs and pushed the papers toward me. "I'd like you to read this and sign it. It states what you just said—you're not the father and you have no claim on the baby or Elaine or her family."

"Wait a second. Say I was the father, she doesn't need a release. I've known guys that got girls pregnant and—"

"We're not talking about guys and girls, Tom. We're talking about prominent people. The Yost family needs to protect itself and the adoptive parents."

"Protect against what?"

"Against confusion. Against future claims."

"Monetary claims?"

"Are you looking for money, Tom?"

"I'm looking for the truth. Is there some reason you don't believe Elaine? Are you sure I'm not the father?"

"Of course. We simply have to complete our records."

I flicked the papers with my finger. "You tell me where Elaine is and I'll sign."

She shook her head. In the failing light, her sunglasses flashed a random semaphore.

"Then it's no dice," I said.

"Tom, listen to me. If I tell you where Elaine is, it won't help. You'll get there and she'll go someplace else. It's over."

"I want to hear it from her."

"Why? You like to be hurt?"

However it was intended, the question stopped me dead, and I cut Diane Kershner off before she could ask another. Leaving the unsigned papers on her desk, I ran back to the rooming house. The running warmed me on that raw, windy day. It made me look like a jogger, a health nut, not a bum floundering along the roadside. The running kept me from thinking, from crying, and left me too exhausted to chase after Elaine.

Next morning I stopped at an Army recruiter's office and volunteered. Stationed in Germany and assigned to the serviceman's newspaper, *Stars and Stripes*, I didn't have an easy time getting over Elaine, but I didn't die either, much as I felt I might a year later when I noticed on the Associated Press wire that she had married a diplomat named Townsend Claybourne Farinholt.

Several months before my enlistment ended, a U.S. Army colonel based in Garmisch-Partenkirchen was shot and killed by his fifteen-year-old daughter. I covered the story and quickly realized there was more to it than I cared to report for a PFC's salary. On the basis of an outline and a sample chapter, I got a book contract and began pursuing the dead man's wife. Gradually, I won her confidence and learned that her husband had been sexually abusing their daughter since she was eight. According to medical records smuggled to me by an orderly, the girl had had a baby and given it up for adoption shortly before murdering her father.

A person would have to be purblind and terminally obtuse to miss the parallel between this story and what I had gone through with Elaine. Although no reader or critic was in a position to make the observation, I hadn't come out of the relationship empty-handed; I emerged with the theme of my life's work—betrayal. For what is crime after all but a form of betrayal? Whether he kills or robs, cheats or embezzles, a criminal is somebody who violates the trust of others. And what is a true-crime writer if not somebody who makes a career out of betraying betrayers? Since my first book, I've been busy conning con men, cozying up to, then exposing, crooked cops, listening to the self-incriminating ramblings and outright confessions of killers—and it was Elaine Yost who taught me how to harden my heart and do it.

* * *

After my discharge from the Army, I felt no urge to return to the States. Financially free, launched in a profession, I didn't care to live in places that reeked of failure or to seek the approval of people who had rejected me in the past. Perhaps as Peggy had said, I was hiding from success as well as failure. So be it. I feel no shame in admitting that I wanted to escape, wanted like a fugitive in one of my books to assume a new identity, wanted to remain in foreign cities where I could always explain away my estrangement as the inevitable price paid by an expatriate. Better that, I thought, than feeling like an alien in your hometown.

Following a few years in France, I landed a contract for a book about the Red Brigades, moved to Rome, and hired Marisa as my interpreter. In some ways, she has played the same role ever since.

When she first visited the apartment I rented near Trajan's Forum, she said something remarkably similar to what Elaine had told me in Texas. "This will be wonderful once you have your things here." But it was her things, her radiant presence, her family and their history, and our two boys that transformed the light-splashed, anonymous space into a home for me, a counterweight to the house where I grew up and to the room in Austin where I came of age.

This is not to suggest that Marisa was a replacement for Elaine, some sort of runner-up prize. I love her as much as I ever have anybody. But driving to Syms Island for the first time in twenty-two years, it occurred to me that I might have married a woman so completely different from Elaine and lived a life so detached from my family not because I wanted to forget the past, but because, in my fashion, I was bent on remembering it. The two women— the tall, lean blond, the dark, buxom Italian—would never blur in my mind, and I could go on loving the palpable reality of the one and the painful memory of the other without feeling unfaithful to either.

2

At the Syms Island gatehouse, a guard checked my name on the guest list and gave me a temporary permit. As I drove across the causeway, sea gulls took flight from the bulkhead, rising from splintery pilings, resettling after I passed. Out on the Bay, sailboats bobbed idly, waiting for a breeze. Farther away in the channel, enormous oil tankers, riding high and empty, chugged south from Baltimore.

Returning to a place after decades of absence, people are apt to remark that things look smaller. But here the houses looked larger. In fact, they *were* larger. Now that Baltimore and Washington were within commuting range, many summer cottages had been expanded into year-round residences.

At the clubhouse, a classic example of carpenter's gothic, I parked between a Volvo and a Saab and strolled the grounds. It wasn't a delaying tactic; I wasn't attempting to prove to Elaine or myself that this appointment was a trivial matter and I could care less about punctuality. I wanted to see whether anything except the size of the houses had changed.

The same couples, dressed in obligatory whites, seemed to be playing doubles on the clay courts. The same dowagers and doddering gents seemed to be sitting in wicker chairs on the clubhouse porch, sipping iced tea or something stronger. The same teenagers swam laps in the pool— tan buds and bucks, all with braces on their teeth. The island was still an orthodontist's dream of heaven.

Nobody took particular notice of me. I was simply a man in a suit and tie, somebody's husband or father home from work early, debating whether to have a dip before dinner. The strange thing was, I didn't feel ill at ease or out of place. Overlooking superficial differences, this could have been Capri or Cap Ferrat, Marbella or Costa Smeralda, resorts where Marisa and I had summered.

I didn't hate these people. I didn't have to hate them. I repeated this mantra as I set off to meet Elaine and her lawyer.

For the last mile I followed a leathery old lady who steered a golf cart down the middle of the road, serenely unaware of me right behind her. I didn't dare lean on the horn and risk short-circuiting her pacemaker.

Pulling onto the Yost property between tall stone pillars, I approached the house from the rear. Even from that angle it was an impressive pile of lumber and brick surrounded by boxwood hedges. But you had to see it from the front, from a boat, to get the full theatrical effect of the fluted columns, mullioned windows, and mansard roof.

In the white-pebble driveway, half a dozen foreign cars were arranged like a graphic demonstration of what had gone wrong with Detroit. A Jaguar XJ6, a Citroën-Maserati, a Range Rover, a Maserati Biturbo, a BMW 633, and a Mercedes station wagon formed a luxury flotilla into which I intruded Big Tom's tugboat.

A black maid had the door open before I knocked. "They waiting on you in the sun-room," she said, leading me down a long corridor to what used to be a screened-in porch. It was now glassed-in, air-conditioned, and furnished with rattan chairs and floral-patterned cushions.

Whiting Pierce was on his feet to welcome me. Elaine remained seated behind him on a couch. I had an urge to step around him and go straight to her. Instead I stuck to the caveat that an investigator should never start off where he intended to wind up.

Pierce wore tan pants and a pink, knit polo shirt with a club insignia and turned-up collar. His salt-and-pepper hair was damp, as if he had just been swimming or had dashed out of a shower.

Elaine looked . . . Actually, to dwell on a lady's appearance a week after her father and son have been murdered is a dangerous proposition for a supposedly neutral reporter. If you say she looks terrible, it sounds callous, catty. If you say terrific, it sounds as if you don't believe she's sufficiently upset. I've covered cases where a defendant first came under suspicion for not looking as the police thought he or she should.

Still, I have to say Elaine was holding up well. Subdued, a bit pale and distracted, she nevertheless looked splendid in a black linen dress. Compared to pictures I'd seen of her, she might have lost a little weight, but she didn't have that flat-chested, frail-shanked build of women who starve themselves to be stylish. I'd wager that she kept her figure by riding, swimming, playing tennis and golf, just as she did in our day.

"I can't tell you how sorry I am," I said.

"It's kind of you to come down." The hand she placed in mine felt warm, almost feverish. I was near enough to smell her perfume. Estée Lauder. Once when I saw the name on a vial in her purse, I pronounced it *Esty Louder* and she instructed me to read her lips—this was before anybody had heard of George Bush—and repeat after her. *Estay Lawder.* I watched her lips all right, then kissed them. But I also noted the name and have remembered it ever since.

Although there was room on the sofa beside her, I took a chair next to Pierce. I needed the distance. Behind Elaine, through the room's glass wall, I noticed a doe and two fawns amble over the lawn, their presence no more remarkable here than cats in the Colosseum.

"Whiting tells me you live in Italy," Elaine said. "In Rome."

"Yes, for the past fifteen years."

"Must be marvelous. You're married?"

I nodded.

"An Italian?"

"Yes."

"Kids?"

"Two sons."

"Marvelous," she repeated.

I was less impressed by the marvels of my biography than by the extent of Elaine's apparent ignorance. The basic information had been printed on several hundred thousand hardbacks and millions of mass market paperbacks. Maybe she didn't read and never watched talk shows. Then again, maybe she didn't like me to think she had deigned to notice anything I'd done in my life.

"How are your parents?" she asked after a couple she had never met. Given the scant coverage of the crime and her understandable preoccupation with her own problems, it was likely she had heard nothing about Big Tom's murder. For the time being I preferred to keep it that way.

"They're dead," I said, and this prompted an expression of polite sympathy from her.

Pierce leaned forward in his chair, elbows on knees, cuffs hiked up over his hairy ankles. He wasn't wearing socks with his Top-Siders. He probably hadn't worn them anywhere outside his office or a courtroom since he graduated from Gilman. Fifty years old and still a preppie.

Elaine asked whether I wanted a drink. I said no. I meant to keep this cordial, yet not allow the slightest pretense that it was a social occasion. This seemed to suit Pierce, who got down to business with a briskness that contradicted his country-club casuals and yachtsman's tan.

"Elaine is in an awful position. The Anne Arundel County State's Attorney has his own agenda. Sam Gaillard, you've heard of him?"

I hadn't.

"A local figure with national aspirations. He's using his office as a political launching pad. For him the Yost murders are the chance of a lifetime. He'll drag it out in the media as long as he can. He'll drag the family name through the mud. He'll play the trial like vaudeville and—''

I barely listened. I had been through it too many times before—this predictable set-piece from defense attorneys who professed to be indignant about a system whose delays and ham-handed appeals to public opinion they invariably profited from. Instead, I stared at Elaine—or rather at the top of her head, at the neat part in her hair. She must have sensed I was watching her. She glanced up, her green eyes so naked and full of pleading I had to turn away. I had seen that expression long ago and had flattered myself that it meant there was something enduring between us.

''Gaillard would love to indict Elaine,'' Pierce said as though he were sharing a choice secret. ''He'd love to put her through the third degree, put her on the stand and—''

''And you'd like to keep her off the stand and out of jail,'' I interrupted.

Pierce paused a moment and struck an admonitory pose, making stern use of his strong, close-shaven jaw. ''I didn't realize you were in such a rush, Mr. Heller.''

As a rule I'm never rude without a reason. With Pierce's type you always have one. ''On the phone you said you had something urgent to tell me.''

''I thought you'd get a clearer picture if I summarized the facts.''

''That's my problem. I don't know what the facts are.''

''The fact is Elaine didn't have a damn thing to do with the murders.''

''I'll take your word on that. But going by what I've read, she was at the scene, her prints were on the pistol, and the police figure she had a motive. If you've got facts that prove something else, you shouldn't waste time on me. You and she should be talking to this fellow Gaillard.''

''In the present climate of opinion, there's no point letting a prosecutor abuse Elaine with a lot of inflammatory questions. We want to cut this witch-hunt off way before that. Maybe you've read the family received death threats before the murders.''

"He's referring to some letters," Elaine spoke up. "They came from somebody who knows I had a baby that time in Texas. He, this person, demanded money.''

"It's painful to think about," Pierce said, "but we've got to face it. Elaine's child could have written the letters. That's the most logical hypothesis. He'd be in his early twenties. He might have learned that the family's wealthy and decided to blackmail her.''

"You keep referring to a 'he,' " I said.

"I had a boy," Elaine said.

"You don't say." I flattened every emotion out of my voice except mild interest.

"It's possible this boy, this young man," Pierce went on, "is the maniac who murdered Andrew and Clay. We're afraid Elaine was his primary target and he'll come back to finish what he started.''

"Did you see him?" I asked her.

"I think so. I saw someone running across the property.''

"Do you remember how he was dressed? What he looked like?''

She raised a hand to her sun-streaked hair. "Just that he had long blond hair. Long for a man.''

My heart was stammering. It was what Luke had said. "Did he look like your son?''

She squinted. "Like Clay?''

"I mean, did it seem he could be your son?''

"Oh, Tom, how can I say? I was too far away and I saw him for a few seconds.'' Her eyes brimmed with tears.

"The police should be out searching for this lunatic, not hounding Elaine.'' Pierce passed her a clean, folded handkerchief.

"Where'd the letters come from?" I asked.

"Texas," Pierce said. "They had a Dallas postmark. It's preposterous for Gaillard to go on posturing for the media when—''

"If it was blackmail," I said, "there had to be a return address or contact point where Elaine could pay off."

"There was a postal box." Pierce continued to do the talking. "The police say it was rented under a fictitious name. Nobody in Dallas remembers who paid for it. Gaillard claims Elaine did it all herself—rented the box, wrote the letters, killed her family. I pointed out she's the target, the person in danger. We requested police protection. Gaillard refused. We had to hire a security guard. He's in the house around the clock."

Oozing self-righteous indignation, Pierce moved over next to his client and held her hand, soothing her. It occurred to me that he might do more than service Elaine's legal interests.

"I don't want to believe it." She had begun sobbing. "I don't want to believe my son—even if I did have to give him up—I don't want to believe he killed them."

The tears were an effective touch. They didn't appear to be forced or phony. I tried to imagine how moving they'd be during a trial. I tried to imagine how her kid might have learned my name, the same name as my father's.

When she recovered her composure and Pierce quit his consoling pats on her shoulder, I said, "One thing I don't understand. If somebody was blackmailing you, why would he kill Andrew and Clay?"

"Because she wouldn't pay off," Pierce said. "She didn't even answer the letters."

"Okay, but what purpose would it serve to shoot her father and son?"

"I told you," he snapped, "he was probably after Elaine."

"That doesn't make a lot of sense either." I acted quizzical, not inquisitorial. "Isn't it more likely somebody after money would keep tightening the screws, threatening to go public with her secret, backing her into a corner until she had to cough up or be exposed?"

"He did write Clay," Elaine said, and Pierce plainly wished she hadn't.

"The same letters?"

"More or less," Pierce said.

"Did you and Clay discuss it?" I asked Elaine. "What was his reaction?"

After a glance at her attorney, she said, "I don't think he took the whole thing seriously. You have to understand, Tom, in this family—maybe because of politics, maybe because our picture was in the papers too much—we get loads of hate mail. Squeaky Fromme, Charles Manson, that type of thing. It's not like Clay wasn't accustomed to having me and his grandfather badgered for money or called awful names or even accused of crimes."

"Clay was more interested in girls, cars," Pierce said. "You remember what it was like to be his age."

Indeed I did. I remembered meeting Elaine at his age. "You say the cops haven't zeroed in on this letter writer. I don't get that. It shouldn't be hard to trace Elaine's son."

Pierce returned to his chair, his knees cracking like kindling as he sat down. His voice had fallen into the instructional mode he assumed whenever he was reiterating the obvious as though it were a hard-won discovery. "Policemen are limited people, Tom, and they have limited budgets. And a political creature like Gaillard has limited appetite for evidence that doesn't advance his ambitions."

"That didn't quite connect with my question. Did they find the boy or not?"

"That's the problem. That's why we called you." Elaine twisted Pierce's handkerchief around her fingers like a tourniquet.

"I'd rather be the one to explain," he said, and she sagged back on the cushions, a splash of black against the bright floral pattern. "My policy has been to cooperate with the investigation. Once I had Elaine's approval, I confided in Gaillard about the baby she put up for adoption twenty-two years ago. He did the easy thing. He has his men contact the Creekmore Agency in Austin. As soon as they hit the first hurdle, they quit.

"The agency went out of business ten years ago,"

Pierce said. Although I didn't react at all to the news, he assured me, "It's not so surprising. Because of the pill and abortion and more and more unmarried women keeping their babies, that kind of private adoption outfit naturally shriveled to nothing. The disturbing thing—from a legal point of view it's unforgivable—the agency's files have been lost. There's no proof Elaine was there."

"What about the staff?" I mused like a man eager to help, not challenge. "The other girls? They knew she was there."

"Sure, but how do you locate them after all this time?"

"I don't remember a single name," Elaine said. "I have an absolute mental block. It's not the sort of experience you go through, then stay in touch with people."

"There should be other records," I said. "Like a birth certificate. Even after an adoption, they'd keep the original birth certificate. Gaillard could get a court order."

"A *ducus tecum* decree," Pierce volunteered.

"Right. And with that they'd open the files, find out who adopted the baby, run him down, and question him."

"The police did what you're suggesting." Pierce wagged his natty barbered head. "But they never came across a birth certificate."

"Strange." Again I acted no more than politely puzzled.

"Yes, it is strange. But instead of pushing on with the investigation, Gaillard decided Elaine was lying—lying about an illegitimate son, therefore lying about the threatening letters, therefore lying about the night of the murders."

"I've been wondering . . ." Elaine started off as if an idea had just occurred to her. "Daddy couldn't bear to have anybody know I was pregnant. That's why he hushed things up and got me away from Syms Island to a place where no one would find out."

"I found out," I reminded her.

"Yes, and once you did, what happened? As soon as Daddy heard you were in Austin, what did he do?"

"Beats me," I said. "I was out of the picture by then."

"He took me away. What I was thinking, Daddy had connections in Texas. He knew Sam Rayburn, he knew LBJ. Maybe he cashed in a favor and had the birth and adoption records destroyed."

"What it boils down to"—Pierce folded his legs and let a Top-Sider dangle from his bare foot—"Elaine needs somebody to confirm that she was pregnant, went to Austin, and had a baby."

I looked beyond Elaine at the lawn, as if absentmindedly waiting for the deer to return. Inside I was steaming, but realized that if I blew up, I wouldn't learn what I needed to know.

"Will you do it? Sign an affidavit?" He scratched his ankle as if what he asked were no more consequential than an idle itch. "A straightforward statement of what you know of your own knowledge."

"Know of my own knowledge." I lingered over the legalism. "Well, I know she was at the Creekmore Agency and I know she was pregnant. But I can't swear she had a baby. I never saw it. Like I said, I was out of the picture by then."

"But Tom." Elaine let out a wounded little wail. "You were with me right up until a few days before I went into labor."

"That's all right," Pierce assured her. "It's a big help that he can establish you were pregnant."

"As for the rest of what I know, well, I wonder, how personal do you want me to be?"

The skin reddened at the delicate flanges of Elaine's nostrils, and the vein, the one I remembered, lifted near her left eyelid and darkened toward her hairline.

"This isn't a personal matter," Pierce insisted. "It's a judicial issue."

"It's personal with me."

He shoved his foot into his shoe and placed it flat on the floor. "I'm sure you're aware there are other ways we could go about this."

"Yeah, I can think of a much more effective one."

"I could subpoena you," he said.

"That wasn't what I was thinking. But sure, you could go that route. Of course, you'd play hell trying to serve me, and I doubt your client has given you any idea what I'm in a position to say under oath."

"Are you suggesting you'd lie?" He was working himself into a self-righteous sweat.

"I'm not suggesting anything. I'm saying you're not in full possession of the facts." I struggled for the right tone, the note that would punish even as it conveyed perfect indifference. "The best way to get what you're after is go to the source. Get an affidavit from the father."

Elaine's face went nearly as dark as the one pulsing vein. "After all these years, do you think he'd risk his marriage, his career, his reputation?"

"Like the counselor said, you could subpoena him."

"And ruin a man's life because you don't want to be bothered?"

"What about my life? My marriage? The risks to my career?"

"What risks?" Pierce asked. "You're just a college friend who knows Elaine was pregnant."

I glanced at her. "Oh. Is that what I was?"

"It's nobody's business. The point, as Whiting told you, is you know about the baby."

I laughed. "No, for me, the point is what the cops'll do if I sign an affidavit."

"They'll take those letters, those threats, seriously," Pierce said. "They'll search for whoever sent them."

"But what'll they do first?"

He fell silent, his jaw set at an imperious angle.

"Since this seems to be beyond your area of expertise, I'll spell it out for your client. They'll haul me in," I told Elaine. "They'll slap me under oath and ask how I know you were pregnant. What do I tell them?"

"You tell them the truth," Pierce said.

"Great. I'll tell them I was sleeping with Elaine that

summer. Then she disappeared and her father refused to say where she went. I learned she was pregnant, I'll tell them, and followed her to Texas, and we resumed our sexual relationship until she ran off again. I'll tell them I had no idea where she went or why, and I never heard from her again until her father and son were murdered when I just happened to be in Maryland. What'll they make of that? Come on, Whiting, don't sit there with your thumb in your ear."

His cheeks turned as pink as his polo shirt, and his wiry arms tightened. If he'd been holding a tennis racquet, he'd have been a dangerous man. "For a short time, they'll regard Tom as a suspect."

"That's ridiculous," Elaine said.

"No, they'd have to determine whether he's the baby's father. And they'd question him about his feelings toward you and your family. Is there ill will? Does he bear a grudge? They'd obviously hear about the time he trespassed and your father had him run off the island at gunpoint."

"But that was decades ago." She appealed to me, hoping I'd agree that the past was so much water under a bridge that was no longer standing. I said nothing.

"I appreciate your concerns," Pierce told me, "but they're groundless. Sure, the police'll interrogate you, and for a few days there'd be lurid stories about you, your fling with Elaine. But you'd soon convince people that you had nothing to do with the murders and you'd be a hero. An old boyfriend who came to the rescue."

"I've lost my appetite for being a hero."

"You really hate me, don't you?" Elaine demanded. "You're so full of spite you'd like to see me convicted of murder."

"Hate you? Who could keep that up for twenty-odd years? I'm just—how did Pierce put it?—an old college boyfriend. One of several, if I'm not mistaken."

She met my gaze with green eyes that had hardened to

chips of jade. "Where do you find a barn big enough to stable this high horse of yours?"

I had to laugh. She reminded me so much of her father. I had forgotten how bitchily funny they could both be. "I'm a quick study. I watched you and Andrew for a few months and followed the blueprint."

"This has gone far enough." Pierce made as if to push to his feet.

I waved for him to stay seated. "I didn't say I wouldn't do it. Tell me, what's in it for me?"

"Do you expect to be paid?" He was prepared to show how distasteful he found this.

Elaine was more pragmatic. "What's your price?"

"No," he warned her. "You pay a witness and his testimony is worthless."

"I don't want money. I want the exclusive rights to the story, up to and including the trial, if there is one."

She whipped her head back and forth so emphatically her hair slapped her cheeks. "Absolutely not. That's been my response to all the scavengers who've come snooping around."

"I didn't come snooping. Your lawyer called me. If he knows his business, he'll tell you I don't need permission to do a book. The case is in the public domain."

She turned to Pierce. He nodded.

"The best you can hope for," I said, "is an accurate account. I'll guarantee that."

"And what else do you guarantee?" Pierce asked.

"Once I'm satisfied I have the facts straight, I'll sign an affidavit."

"What sort of financial and editorial involvement will Elaine have?"

"None. For the same reason you don't pay witnesses, I don't pay sources and I don't grant anybody editorial control."

"Frankly, I don't see why she should accept such an arrangement."

"She shouldn't—not unless she wants that affidavit."

"This is about at the level of those blackmail letters," she muttered.

But after a moment, Pierce said, "I suppose you should have your lawyer or publisher contact me."

"No, for the time being, this is between us."

"To the contrary, even if there's no financial consideration, I'd insist on something in writing."

"Later. It's premature to draw up an agreement now. Like I said, I'm not signing anything until I'm sure I have the facts straight."

"What facts?"

"You claim there've been threatening letters from her son."

"Him or somebody who knew about the adoption," Pierce said.

"Somebody like the father."

"No." Elaine whipped her head again. "He has no reason to blackmail me."

"Maybe he isn't after money. Maybe he's out to get even."

"Some people have better things to do than carry grudges all their lives."

"Yeah, well, some other people carry the kind of king-size grudge that got your father and son clipped."

Pierce had his legs crossed again and the Top-Sider dangling from his toes. "You want the father's name?"

"Yes. So will the police."

"There's a difference between speaking in private to the police and having his name published in your book."

"If he's not involved, I'll give him a pseudonym or let him remain anonymous. But to protect myself, I need to know."

"Protect against what?" Pierce asked.

"Against getting used. I'm not going to supply an affidavit and find out afterward Elaine was holding back information."

"You're not very trusting."

"Not a second time."

"Wanting the father's name, wanting to root around in my personal life," Elaine said, "are you positive this is for a book and not for your own perverse pleasure?"

I smiled. "All my books are for my perverse pleasure. Why don't you two talk it over and let me know? But keep in mind, no matter what you decide, I might go ahead and write about the case. You've really primed my interest."

As I got up to go, I thought Elaine was searching for something final and wounding to say, but she simply murmured, "You've changed."

"You bet," I said. "But not you. You look great."

3

For symmetry or symbolism I'd like to say I sped away from Syms Island to the same public phone I used years ago. But I can claim no more than that I stopped at the first one I saw, a stifling glass-walled booth overgrown with honeysuckle.

At this hour of evening, I assumed Buck would be home, but Peggy told me to try the courthouse. I caught him there as he was leaving.

"We've got to talk," I said.

"Meet me at the house. I'll pick up some beer."

"What I have to say, I don't want to tell you in front of your wife and kids."

"So tell me now."

"I have a hunch who killed Big Tom."

He groaned. "Tommy, please, I know you're torn up about this. So am I. But you gotta give it a rest. I been in court all day copping pleas like some men sell Tupperware. I'm wasted and I'm damn sure not driving up to D.C."

"I'll meet you in Annapolis."

"Okay, at Fran O'Brien's. I'll be the bleary-eyed fat one at the bar."

On Ritchie Highway commuters were locked bumper to bumper with vacationers heading to the Eastern Shore, and it took forty minutes to reach the Severn River Bridge. By then the domes and campanile of the Naval Academy appeared inlaid with gold leaf and looked vaguely Venetian in the fading light. From this vantage point, Annapolis seemed to be the same small, lovely town I remembered exploring with Elaine—a nest of narrow streets, colonial row houses, and red-brick government offices. Before I moved to Europe, I couldn't imagine a place more steeped in history and atmosphere.

But once I crossed the Severn and cut through the campus of St. John's College, I noticed the changes. The streets were curb to curb with cars, and many of the row houses had been made over into boutiques, fern bars, candlelit restaurants, and souvenir shops. The economy seemed to be booming, and about 25 percent of it was based on T-shirt sales. Annapolis was still a lovely town, even if it was cluttered with cute signs and sunburnt tourists. But where had they hidden the oystermen and blacks who used to live along Fleet and Pinkney streets?

Rounding Church Circle, I found a parking place near the courthouse, then strolled downhill past the Maryland Inn. Traffic on Main Street was at a standstill, and people stuck in cars, steaming on the rugged brick pavement, had worlds of time to window-shop at Laura Ashley and Britches of Georgetown. The only establishment I recognized from the old days was Chick and Ruth's Delly.

Fran O'Brien's smelled of bourbon, beer nuts, and Bain de Soleil. Buck was crammed between two couples arguing whether condoms should be advertised on television. I told him to drink up and meet me outside.

"Crissake, Tommy, it's too hot." He wore a black corduroy suit, like some burly Basque peasant dressed for a funeral.

"I'm not going to talk in this zoo."

He growled, but downed his draft and came away with flecks of foam in his beard. We crossed Main Street through the milling crowd on Market Square, then over to City Dock, which was almost as boisterous as Fran O'Brien's. I was put in mind of Portofino, St.-Tropez, spruced-up, picture-postcard villages paralyzed by success. The channel was choked with schooners and sloops, rubber dinghies and Boston Whalers. Muscle boats snorted and backfired, cruising the circuit like the low riders that rumble along the boulevards of East L.A.

"Welcome to Ego Alley," Buck shouted into the din. "Everybody in sunshades and gold chains and tans one step short of skin cancer. All these assholes dying to look like drug dealers, and here I spend every day defending dildos who *are* dealers and are fucking desperate to pass as businessmen."

I pulled him down beside me on a concrete bench. A woman in shorts and a crocheted halter glided by. Buck smacked his lips. "See nipples and die. Isn't that the motto of your adopted land?"

"Jesus, how many have you had?"

"Not enough. Not by a long shot. Now if I looked like you, all icy cool and blond and neatly pressed, I wouldn't need to drink. I'd be off on assignment for *Gentlemen's Quarterly*, modeling underwear. But hey, ease up." He nudged me. "Don't get mad. I'm listening."

"Elaine Yost's lawyer called me."

"Name of the lawyer?" He removed his coat.

"Whiting Pierce."

"Ah, yes, Whiting old boy." He did a passable British accent. "My colleague and coeval. Does 'coeval' mean we're equally evil?"

"It means the same age."

"He's a helluva lot older than me and evil enough for both of us. He's the type guy provides the rare occasion to really sink your teeth into the word 'prick.' "

"What'd he do? Win a case against you?"

"I ever got a chance against him in court, I'd kick his ass. But Pierce, his firm does mostly corporate stuff. It's a white-shoe outfit. What I hate, he always has this look of, Where's my limo? What he'd call for—restaurant tips in Rome?"

I hoped if I stayed patient, he'd eventually settle down. "There's a lot about Elaine and me you never knew."

Buck grinned. "Ah, so you *were* banging her!"

"Problem is, I wasn't the only one. She was pregnant

when I met her." His grin dissolved by slow degrees as it registered on him that I wasn't joking. "That time I went to Texas, she was there to have a baby and give it up for adoption."

"Jesus, Tommy, I'm sorry. Why didn't you tell me?"

"Too ashamed of myself, I guess. Anyway, what could you have done except call me a damn fool for chasing after her?"

"You positive it wasn't your kid?"

"That's what she told me. She was living at an adoption agency in Austin. We spent a lot of time together. I thought we'd get married. Then her father showed up and off she went. I never saw her again until today."

"What did she want?" I had his total attention now.

"She and Pierce think the boy she gave up years ago came gunning for her and nailed Andrew and Clay by mistake."

"Fat fucking chance. Even a limp dick like Pierce should know better than to peddle an alibi like that."

"Hold on and hear me out. It's not so farfetched. Right before the murders they got—Elaine and Clay got—threatening letters from somebody that knew about the adoption. It might have been the illegitimate kid."

Buck scratched his beard, ruminating while I went on. "Pierce tells me there's this State's Attorney, Sam Gaillard, that doesn't believe Elaine had a baby. Because, you see, the cops can't locate any record of the birth or adoption."

"I get it." He was grinning again. "They need you to testify she had a kid nobody's been able to trace."

He let his hand fall to my knee and squeezed hard. "Tell you something, little brother. Stay the hell clear of these people. Hop on a plane tomorrow, fly home, and don't look back."

"No, wait. There's more, Buck."

"Damn straight there is. They're setting you up."

"I've considered that."

"Consider it again. Sitting here half ripped to the tits, my brain cells in brownout, I'm picturing all kinds of possibilities, every one of them god-awful for you."

"I know, but there's one possibility—"

"No, you don't know. Dammit, Tommy, for once in your life listen to me." He squeezed tighter. "She may not have had a baby."

"She was pregnant. She was out to here."

"Did you ever see the kid?"

I admitted I hadn't.

"She could have miscarried," he said. "It could have been born dead. Why else wouldn't there be a birth certificate?"

"Elaine thinks her father had the documents destroyed."

"No. What it sounds like to me, she wrote those letters and planned to blame this mystery boy who's dead. She figured the cops couldn't shoot down her story because adoptions are supposed to be ironclad confidential. But Gaillard got a court order."

"A *ducus tecum* decree."

"Congratulations! You haven't forgotten your altar-boy Latin. So the cops accessed the files, found zip, and suddenly your old flame is stuck with a bum alibi and decides to dump this double homicide on you. Believe me, suspicions are bound to arise, due to you were humping her back then."

Now I grabbed his knee. "If we were just talking about her troubles, I wouldn't give it a second thought. I'd be gone. But Big Tom was shot by somebody Luke described as having long blond hair. Two nights later, Andrew Yost and Clay are killed, and Elaine says she saw a prowler with long blond hair."

Buck hit the side of his head with the heel of his hand. "I'm missing something. You got a murder in one corner of Maryland, then a couple murders in the next county, thirty, forty miles away. The only connection, aside from blond hair, is one victim's your father, the other two are folks related to a girl you fucked in college."

"No, don't you see, I'm the connection. The old man and I have the same name. Elaine's kid might have mistaken Big

Tom for me. Because—wait! Please don't break in—there was a strange scene at the adoption agency. A woman there wanted me to sign a release swearing I wasn't the baby's father. When I refused, that might have convinced her I *was* the father. Or maybe Elaine put my name on some document to protect the identity of the real father.''

''You said nobody found any documents.''

''The cops came up empty. That doesn't mean this kid didn't get lucky.''

''You know, you want to speculate, Tommy, just spitball theories with nothing to back them up, you could as easily say Elaine shot Big Tom to point the finger at her alleged long-lost son.''

''That's what I've been driving at. Whether she did it or the kid or the kid's father, there's a link.''

Buck stretched mightily, then rolled his shirtsleeves to the elbow. His wristwatch was nestled in curly red hairs. ''I'm damn near sober. I don't know what to say except give up and go home. You're clutching at something not even as strong as straws.''

''I can't leave until I'm sure.''

''You like to trot up the street, talk to the cops?''

''They'd toss me into the rubber room.''

''Damn right they would, unless you had evidence.''

''That's what I want to do—get hard evidence. I was hoping you'd help. The two of us could poke around, crack these murders on our own.''

''Tommy, Tommy.'' Buck sighed. ''Listen to yourself. You sound like Nancy Drew, kid detective. I don't mean to insult you. Your books, I read them and enjoy them most of the time. But this investigative journalism deal, it may be journalism, but it's not investigating. It's second-hand stuff. You had to do an investigation on your own, you wouldn't know where to start.''

I had to ride this out. It would do no good to fight back, defend my honor and the integrity of true crime. Save that for talk shows and op-ed articles.

''I could open your writing to any page,'' he went on,

"and tell you where you stole your material. Same with all these books that claim to deliver the 'inside story, the sensational truth never known until now.' " Suddenly he sounded like a TV shopping-channel barker. "That's bullshit, pure and simple. The author shows up *after* some dumb cop cracked the case and the defendant's convicted, and he—the fucking writer—rides on the public record, the police reports, coroner's notes, pretrial depositions, and trial testimony. Half the time he's handed a story on a silver platter. The other half he goes and pays for information—which to me is like paying for pussy and pretending you're Warren Beatty."

"I don't pay sources," I broke in. "Not anymore. Look, Buck, I understand what you're saying. That's why I need you. I want to piggyback on your experience, your contacts at the courthouse."

"You need me? That's a switch. I never thought I'd hear you ask for my help."

"You want me to get down on my knees and beg?" I made as if to slide off the bench.

He grabbed me. "Stay put. People'll think you're a homo for sure. You serious? You plan to write a book about the Yost murders?"

"I might. From what I've seen so far, it has the elements I look for in a story."

"Another best-seller," Buck mused. "But what about Big Tom? What if there's no connection?"

"I'm convinced there is. That's what I have to find out. I can't go back to Italy or on to anything else until I know the truth."

"The truth?" He let out a mirthless laugh. "You're around as much lying as I am in my job, you start to count on it, factor it in on your decisions. Truth ain't part of the equation."

"It is in this case. It's the old man we're talking about."

Buck laughed again. "You wanna hear something true? When Big Tom got shot, first thought I had—I hate to admit it. Just popped into my mind—I thought somebody finally did what I was tempted to do as a teenager. Can't tell you how many times back when he was hitting the bottle hard and hitting us harder, I thought about shooting him. Makes me feel like shit now.''

I confessed I had indulged my own murderous adolescent fantasies, and later, that summer on Syms Island, I had tried to kill Big Tom off in a different fashion—by making fun of him. ''At this point,'' I said, ''it's hard to put in words how I feel about him. But I know one thing—I wish he weren't dead. And I want to find out who killed him.''

He shook out his coat, then refolded it. ''I don't suppose it'll hurt me to give you a hand.''

''I don't expect you to work for free. I'll cover your costs, and we'll split the jackpot, if there is one.''

''Won't lie to you, that'll help.'' He stood up. ''Let's move off this bench before I catch arthritis of the ass cheeks.''

We shouldered our way through a mob of guitar-pluckers, backpackers, and panhandlers. A new class of plebes had arrived at the Academy, and they marched along with their families and girlfriends, stiff as rigor mortis in their starched whites. ''Always hated those bastards,'' Buck whispered. ''You ever see a single one that isn't handsome?''

At the Old Customs House, we hiked up Green Street to Duke of Gloucester. Buck was carrying his coat over one arm, jingling the change in his pants pocket with his free hand. ''Since we're teaming up on the research, is there any chance of doing the rest of the book together?''

''You mean write it together?''

''Yeah. What's the matter, you think I can't spell?'' He was about to bridle.

''Hell, it'd be fun to have both our names on the cover. But first we have to find out if there's something to write.'' The book, in my mind, was a distant second to solving Big Tom's murder.

He bumped me with his shoulder. ''This works out, Peggy won't believe it.''

"What is it? She the one that thinks you can't spell?"

"Promise you won't get pissed off?"

"Go ahead, shoot," I said despite my better judgment.

"She thinks *you* think I'm a dumb shit. As for you, she thinks you're a stuck-up prick."

We had stopped under a streetlamp whose globe swarmed with insects, their wings magnified in shadows on the sidewalk. Hurt, I tried to joke it off. "That doesn't sound like Peggy—calling me a prick."

"She left it at 'stuck-up.' I tacked on 'prick.' " He had hit me with both barrels and didn't appear to feel good about it.

I felt worse and was afraid I might break down and bawl. "Buck, I'm sorry. You know I don't think you're dumb. And I apologize if I gave you and Peggy the wrong impression."

"It wasn't an 'impression,' Tommy. It's a fact—you haven't set foot in our house since you got here. At the funeral, you didn't know the kids' names. Peggy asked, 'How can he be a hot-shit investigative reporter and he can't even remember his nieces and nephews?' It's like you're ashamed of us," he said. "Not just Peggy and me, the whole family, what we are, where you come from."

My eyes and throat ached. "No, I'm ashamed of myself. I love you guys."

This embarrassed Buck. "I'm sure it's partly our fault. We're jealous you've made a mint and live at an address we can't pronounce."

I yanked at his beard the way I had seen his kids do. "I'll make it up to you. I'm looking forward to working with you."

Once we were walking again, he asked, "Where do I start?"

"In the prosecutor's office there must be somebody that owes you one, somebody who'll bootleg information. I want what doesn't get into the newspapers."

"Heard something today. You know what MUD records are?"

I did, but said no to allow him a chance to shine.

"Message unit details. It's a record the phone company keeps of every call from every number. The MUD on the Yost house showed that after the murders, the first call from Elaine wasn't to the cops or the rescue squad. It was to Whiting Pierce. He's the one dialed 911. By the time the detectives hit the scene, Pierce is there claiming she's too distraught to give a statement."

"In his place, what would you have done?"

"Same thing. No client of mine's making a statement at the scene. But you see the problem—she's cool enough to call her lawyer, then too upset to talk to the cops. Juries gobble up that kind of contradiction."

"Pierce says Sam Gaillard is hounding her"—I hurried to keep pace with Buck—"to get his name in the papers and his kisser on TV. How ambitious is he?"

"Scale of one to ten, he's a fifteen. The man never met a microphone he didn't love. Still, it's tough to understand why he'd do this for publicity."

"Isn't it every prosecutor's wet dream—a high-profile case involving a prominent person? What Tom Wolfe called the Great White Defendant."

"Maybe in books it works that way." At Church Circle he led me under a bank arcade, down South Street toward his Isuzu and Big Tom's Oldsmobile. "But in what passes for real life, nobody likes to pick a public fight he could easy as hell lose. I mean, Andrew Yost's daughter— Gaillard's gotta know every time he turns around there's a chance she'll take a bite out of his ass.

"The normal tendency"—he leaned against the front fender of the Toronado—"is to stick to the double standard. We bang hard on blacks in Cherry Hill and the housing projects. But when it's a white lady pumping a few rounds into her relatives, it's always, you know, a distressing domestic incident that oughta be dealt with in a mental institution, not a courtroom. Which is what makes me think Gaillard must have the goods. A witness or a piece of evidence that'll fry her."

"Or maybe he's making a career-ending mistake."

"I wouldn't bet on it. Sam, type of guy he is, he'd rather have root canal than go to trial with a case he hasn't already won. Most of us, we look at plea bargaining as the Ex-Lax that keeps the shit flowing from the holding pen to the state pen. But Sam loves to try cases where the defendant is begging to cop to a lesser charge."

Buck switched his coat from one arm to the other. "Tell you another thing. She has Pierce as her attorney, she's definitely going down the tubes."

"You just don't like the guy. You think he's a stuck-up prick, like me."

"No, Pierce, he's an arranger, someone you hire to write a will or structure a real estate deal. Murder one calls for a man that doesn't mind getting his pants dirty."

"Sounds like you're ready to audition for the job."

"I'd jump at it. And at her." He was patting his pockets for his car keys. "Or are those pictures of Elaine airbrushed?"

"No, she's aging like fine wine."

"Yeah, well, Ripple's my brand and Isuzu is my ride. But I do wonder about you, bro. You can bullshit me and I'll never know. But be honest with yourself. Sounds like you have as big a hard-on for this case as Gaillard. Is it because you're hot to catch Big Tom's killer? Or you still have a sweet tooth for Elaine Farinholt?"

"I want the killer."

"Good. So do I." He held out his hand and we shook. Then he climbed into the Isuzu and coasted down South Street.

It was a lousy feeling to have lied to Buck. But as he had urged, I was at least honest with myself. If my interest in the Yost murders was strictly their link to my father's death, I would have called Paul Gant, asked him to check for a match between the bullets in the two cases, and let him carry it from there. But first I intended to get answers to questions I had waited twenty-two years to ask.

4

Returning from Annapolis, I drove in a state of distraction so deep I scarcely noticed the road or the traffic around me. I was worried less now about my lie to Buck than about the astuteness of his observations about true crime. Fortunately he had stopped short of the rancorous complaint that I manipulated people, won them over with promises I never intended to keep, misquoted what they said, betrayed their trust, and worst of all, violated their memories of the dead. "You wrote that about my father, my sister, my son, my wife, etc., etc.," the standard accusation ran, "just to sell books."

Often compared to a prison informer who listens sympathetically to his cellmate, eggs him on to recount his life's story, then rats him out in return for a reduced sentence, I was regarded as not all that far removed from the criminals I wrote about. At best, people accepted that I was akin to a spy. My ear to the ground, my eye to the keyhole, I occasionally came up with valuable, even life-saving information. But there was always a moral taint to my means.

It made me wonder how readers and reviewers—hell, how my own family—would react if I wrote about the Yost murders. This time the cost of exposing the killer would include exposing myself, stripping under a microscope for the amusement of millions of book-club members, bored travelers, and languid ladies buying a page-turner for the beach. It would all come out—my pitiful, puppylike pursuit of Elaine; the nonchalance with which she picked me up, then dropped me; the possibility that I had got her pregnant and it was my son who had killed Andrew and Clay and Big Tom.

It was easy to picture how it would play in the tabloids: "Bad Seed Comes Back to Haunt Family." Even the legitimate press would lick its chops, and literary critics would delight in drawing the least flattering parallels between my life and my career.

Having had plenty of practice, I was confident I'd survive the skin-shriveling publicity. But how would Marisa and the boys fare?

The question lingered all during the drive, and I was still fretting over it when I reached Hyattsville. In book after book, I had rationalized the pain my revelations caused people with the thought that the truth was its own reward. How could I back down now?

Bouncing over the unpaved stretch on our street, I went by the black kids listening to their boom boxes and was pulling into the driveway when I heard the sharp *crack!* I thought my tires had thrown a stone up off the road, or one of the blacks had heaved a rock.

The bullet smashed through the window on the passenger's side, buzzed past my nose, and shattered the glass on my side before I understood what had happened. Even then I was too stupefied to do anything except sit straight up behind the wheel, headlights on, motor running, a perfect target.

The realization arrived in slow motion; whoever it was, he might take a second shot. Cutting the ignition and the lights, I rolled out of the car and crawled for cover, tearing the knees of my pants. Hidden in a clump of hollyhocks beside the front steps, I strained in the darkness for any movement, any strange sound. There was nothing.

After what seemed an hour—my watch said it was five minutes—I slipped out of hiding and up to the door. From there I had an unobstructed view of the yard and beyond it, the street. Still nothing—nothing except the thudding of my pulse, the beat of the boom boxes.

I couldn't decide who to call first. Buck? He'd never believe the killer had come back.

Dialing the County Service Building, I asked for Detective Gant. The man who took my call had a calm and reasonable voice. He said Gant was off duty. He said he could send a squad car and have a couple officers inspect my windshield. Oh, it was the windows, not the windshield. Okay, they'd write up a report, snap a few photographs if I insisted. But he felt sure I didn't need to go through that aggravation. Usually you filed your claim, he said, got an estimate, and nine times out of ten your insurance company paid up, minus, of course, your deductible.

"And if somebody was shooting at me?" I asked.

"No insurance against that," he said with admirable equanimity. "This neighborhood somebody's always shooting at somebody. You wanna stay outta the middle."

My knees bloody and the palms of my hands pebbled black with asphalt, I hung up half-convinced the man was right. What was Luke's word for it? A "mushroom"— that's what I was. But the other half of me wondered who'd be home if I rang Syms Island.

Pierce answered. When I asked for Elaine, he passed her the phone without any pleasantries.

"Tom," she said, "Whiting and I were just talking about you."

"I bet you tell that to all the guys."

"There aren't many 'guys' around these days."

"Did I leave my sunglasses at your place?"

"I didn't notice you wearing sunglasses."

"Oh, well, another pair lost. Let me hear from you when you make up your mind."

I went to bed that night reassured by the notion that she hadn't tried to kill me. Not personally anyway.

Next morning I ran the Toronado over to a garage in Mt. Rainier and had the windows replaced. "What'd you do?" asked the owner. "Rob a bank?"

I told him a stone flew up from the street.

"Yeah. Got a lot of that around here, stones flying straight through cars. Careful, man, stay outta the middle."

"That should be a bumper sticker or the motto on Maryland license plates."

He laughed. "Beats 'America in Miniature.' "

Back at the house, I double-checked an idea that had nagged at me since yesterday afternoon. It seemed a stretch. Still it was worth making sure that the private eye I hired decades ago hadn't figured the time was ripe to get rich off his knowledge that Elaine Yost had been pregnant and unmarried.

His name was listed in the yellow pages, but a receptionist said he had retired and moved to Immokalee, Florida. He was listed in that directory too, the long distance operator told me. But from his wife I learned he had been dead for two years.

After pawing through our parents' belongings, neither Buck nor I had much stomach for deciding what of theirs should be kept and what discarded. But while I waited for word from Elaine, I went up to my room and started gathering things to give to Goodwill. It surprised me how reluctant I was to part with the Colts and Senators pennants, my high school team jacket, and a copy of a campus literary magazine that had published my first short story. It made no sense to ship them to Italy, and once the house was sold, I couldn't see storing things in the States. But I wanted to hang on to them a little while longer.

Maybe Matt and Kevin would be interested in this stuff. It seemed doubtful. It all related to a life, to a person, they had heard about only in the autobiographical yarns I spun after dinner when I was tipsy with wine. Although they urged me to talk about my childhood, I suspected that they regarded these tales as the sort of fantastic realism that South American authors are famous for.

Thumbing through my high school yearbook, I recognized names and faces and recalled what had become of them. It was stunning how many of my classmates had wound up with Buck and me in the crime business. Although he was the lone lawyer and I was the one true-crime writer, a slew of kids had become cops, and almost the same number had done time. Maybe I should take the annual to Paul Gant and test how many of his colleagues and culprits he could identify out of the class of '63.

I turned to my picture—a shot of a thin, towheaded teenager with a black bow tie and a white formal jacket. My face, it pains me to admit, had the pinched wistfulness of a romantic. Back then I had read Hemingway as if he wrote self-help books, and I had yearned for adventures in foreign lands. But what I had found overseas was more mundane—a wife, children, a kind of stability. This neighborhood, this house, was still the most exotic place I had ever been.

Now that Buck knew about Elaine, I wondered whether Big Tom had ever told Mom. It hadn't occurred to me how much it might have hurt her when I left for Texas. Whenever she referred to that time, she made it sound like a cagey career move. "He wanted to be a writer," she would say, "and he wasn't getting any inspiration at the university."

I wish I had confided in her. Or what I really wish is that we had been a family capable of confiding. A clutch of secretive souls, all of us were rendered mute by alcohol. When Big Tom was roaring drunk, we didn't dare speak up, and when he was sober, we tiptoed around for fear that the wrong word would send him skidding back to the bottle, bellowing in rage at some unarticulated anguish that he shared with us the only way he knew how—by spreading the pain around.

Yet on my last night of leave before I shipped out to Germany, he had climbed the stairs to my dormer room and asked, "What happened to the girl?"

I laid it out for him in two words. "She left."

"Well, whatever else you're feeling, at least you'll never feel it might have worked out if you'd tried."

"What I want to know is when I won't feel anything."

"Shit, that's easy. When you're dead." Then he handed me a hundred-dollar bill. "Hold on to this. Don't spend it over there on beer and poontang. Save it for something special."

Years later, when I phoned to say Marisa and I were married, I told him I was calling with his money.

"Remember the night I gave it to you?" He was exuberant at the news and at the notion that I had used his hundred bucks to announce it. "Remember how sad-assed you were? Some girl dumped you and you acted like your life was over. But nothing ever ends."

Well, he was right about that, although not in the way he intended.

Late that evening Elaine called, her voice as crisp as a recorded announcement. "I accept. If the only way to get a signed affidavit is to give you the right to do the story—"

"I've got that right. Any hack can do a book. What I want is a guarantee of your cooperation."

"I accept," she repeated. "Let's start. What do you need to know?"

"Not over the phone. In a day or two we'll get together."

"Look, Tom"—her voice went from crisp to querulous—"any minute now Gaillard's liable to move for an indictment."

"Sorry," I said, "there are things I have to do before I get to you."

"I suppose I should be grateful I'm on your long list of appointments."

"Oh, you're way up near the top. Good night, Elaine."

I went to bed thinking about Marisa, missing her, aching for her, and I fell asleep, passing from conscious reverie into an erotic fantasy that commenced with shimmering clarity. Marisa was beside me; I recognized the curve of her belly and breasts, the dense, fragrant, close-grained feel of her flesh. Then by some dizzying dream logic my hands carved another shape, a different person, out of the darkness, and I was holding Elaine. There was no mistaking the lightness of her bones, the trim inverted delta of hair between her legs. I wanted to stop. I went on.

Next morning when the phone rang, I thought that through some process of mental telepathy Marisa might have been moved to call me. But it was Buck.

"Spoke to Sam Gaillard, and he agreed to meet you. 'Agreed' is an understatement. He's foaming at the mouth. For him, meeting a writer proves these murders must be almost as important as he believes."

"When can I see him?"

"We'll huddle at my place, Tommy. Go through the info I collected. Then you, Sam, and me'll have lunch."

As I was coasting down the driveway, I spotted Luke in the rearview mirror, waving a crutch. I nudged the Toronado into reverse and lowered the window on my side. He leaned his gaunt, gray face toward me. "What's happening?"

"Going to see my brother."

"The thing of Buck, he's a lucky dude having a house near the water."

"I'd take you with me, but I have a meeting later."

"Shee-it." Luke grinned, lifting his lips above bad teeth and blue gums. "You ain't fooling me. You ain't taken no nigger to no beach in your whole life."

"You've got me mixed up with somebody else. I don't call people niggers."

"You call them what?"

"Blackamoors."

"Blackawhat?"

"Come on, Luke. You didn't call me back to discuss racial attitudes."

"Got a preseason game on TV this week. Skins versus Steelers. Wanna watch it in color? I'll bring a bottle."

"Thanks. I'll be there if I can. If not, you have the key."

"You ain't afraid I'll steal everything?"

"I'm petrified. Stand clear while I race down and warn Buck."

My brother and his family lived in a development of modest beach cottages and retirement homes now inhabited by year-round commuters. Few houses had a view of the Bay, but everybody could feel it in the briny freshness of the air, and they could smell it. It was the smell of summer—salt water; swimsuits drying on the clothesline; pungent creosote-covered piers; varnished boat decks baking in the sun.

Buck's was a sturdy cinder-block structure, painted pale green, its window ledges laden with old-fashioned AC units. Under the carport, a boat trailer was draped with damp beach towels, and on the front lawn a passel of kids played an improvised game with badminton racquets and Nerf balls. They were busy flailing away at one another until I pulled up.

Four of the kids were my nieces and nephews, each a dead ringer for Peggy. Ranging in age from six to twelve, they had tans that would have shamed a Sardinian fisherman. I had brought a Madonna tape, a book of Farside cartoons, and jerseys from the Roma soccer team. Because I couldn't recall which faces went with which names, I tried to disguise my ignorance as I doled out the gifts.

"You've all grown in the last week," I lamented. "Line up and let me guess. Now I bet you're Megan. No, you are! And you're Brendan. You're . . . Hermione."

"No, I'm Beth." She giggled.

"I knew that. And you're Lum."

They were all laughing, even the neighborhood children. "I'm Marty."

"Okay, so there's Megan and Brendan, Beth and Marty.

I should be able to remember if you don't grow any more this summer.''

"When are we going to get to see Kevin and Matt?'' Megan, the oldest, asked.

"When you visit us in Rome.''

"You should bring them here. They don't even know what Nintendo is.''

"Yes, but they know what spaghetti *alle vongole veraci* is. Do you?'' This struck them as sidesplittingly funny.

Peggy came out of the house and kissed me on both cheeks. "I decided I liked it like that—double your pleasure, double your fun.''

She was barefoot and wore a T-shirt and the bottom half of a bikini. "We've been swimming. Buck's getting dressed.''

We went inside to the TV room where the set was tuned to a twenty-four-hour-a-day weather channel. Toys littered the floor ankle deep. I sat in a canvas deck chair with CAPTAIN stenciled on the back. Peggy folded a towel on the couch and planted her firm little rump on it.

"Sorry about the air conditioners,'' she said. "We don't switch them on unless it's boiling. This book you're doing with Buck, is it a gimmick to give us money to fly to Rome?''

"I'm beginning to believe it's a gimmick to keep me in the States longer.''

"It'd be nice to have your family here. And it'd make sense while you're researching the Yost murders.''

There was no indication Buck had told her my interest in that case was connected to Big Tom's killing.

"I want you to know we're grateful,'' she said. "It's more than the money. It's your belief in Buck. But promise me you won't get him in over his head.''

"What the hell, Peggy, he knows his way through the woods. That's why I asked for his help. Most of the time he'll be leading me.''

"Sure, he knows his job,'' she said. "But he can be like a kid taking a dare. He'll want to prove something to you and it's liable to blow up in his face. You can go back to Italy. We've got to live here.''

"What's this?" Buck entered the room roaring. "A casting conference? I catch my wife on the couch in her underpants and my brother breathing hard through his open mouth."

Brandishing a fistful of yellow legal-pad pages, he was kicking dolls and slot cars, Whiffle balls and Legos, out of his path. As usual, he was dressed to kill—to kill himself with heat prostration—in a tweed jacket and flannel pants. "Gaillard told me, show you what a modest guy he is, he's not the Robert Redford type. He'd be happy to have Clint Eastwood play him in the miniseries. But I don't see a role for Peg, not as long as Pia Zadora's available."

"Pia Zadora my ass." She got up and snapped her towel at him.

"Keep the kids outta here. We writers need privacy." He sent a Cabbage Patch doll flying with his foot. "Welcome to my study."

"It's no messier than mine."

He handed me the sheets of legal-pad paper. "There it is, the whole ball of wax. Whatever Gaillard's got, you've got. Couple guys in the computer room arranged to leave their machines on and the door unlocked. They couldn't risk letting me print out, but I made notes on the lab reports, autopsies, statements from investigating officers and crime-scene processors. They should bring you up to speed before you see Gaillard."

"And before I talk to Elaine again."

"Handle her however you like. But with Sam, do me a favor. Don't refer to this stuff, don't even hint what you know. For the time being, use it for background. Otherwise he'll sure as hell guess where we got it."

"Has your opinion changed? Or you still believe Elaine's the shooter?"

"Tough call." He drew a breath, as if about to tell me everything in a rush, but then he spoke slowly, formulating his thoughts. It always surprised me how thorough and methodical he was in his work. "Old man Yost, he wasn't universally loved. Fact is, he wasn't locally loved. Some claim he wasn't even loved in his own house. Had this habit of pissing people off, friends and family alike. But Clay's the one struck everybody as the leading candidate to cork off and ice his grandfather. Apparently they had fights, regular humdingers, where Andrew yelled, 'Over my dead body,' and Clay came back, 'That can be arranged.' "

"Elaine and Pierce seem to think the boy was just high-spirited."

"High he was. Check the coroner's report. Night he died, Clay was smoking crack. Look at the hair samples. They tested positive, which means he'd been using over a long period. This was no one-shot deal. He'd had a couple of arrests for possession, and once when he was cracked out, he got busted for assault and battery. Beat up a girl-friend so bad she wound up in the hospital. He pled to disorderly conduct, paid a fine, and did a stretch at some sort of psycho-ward detox center where rich families stash their heirs when they start raping the maid and shooting down chandeliers. Clay was still alive, he'd be suspect numero uno."

While I shuffled the pages, skimming his notes, Buck said, "A scenario I toyed with—was there a chance Clay capped Andrew, waited for Elaine, went to kill her, and got plugged in the tussle?"

"Why wouldn't Elaine tell the police? Why would she concoct a tale about threatening letters and a guy with blond hair?"

"That's one reason I shelved that theory. Other reason, the coroner believes Clay checked out first. It's not a huge time difference—couple hours between deaths—like maybe the murderer did the boy, then waited for the old man."

"This girlfriend Clay beat up, I don't see much on her."

"She got a settlement, left the state, and stayed away.

The cops interviewed her by phone and are satisfied she's clean.''

"From what I read"—I rattled a page—"Clay put up a struggle. There's no sign that Andrew did. Maybe the murderer was somebody he recognized, trusted.''

"The question's whether Andrew would have recognized himself. His blood alcohol content was way over the line for legal drunkenness. He was so crocked, he never knew what hit him.''

I found myself glancing up from the notes, following the numbers on the TV screen. Temperatures from European cities streamed by like a stock-market ticker tape.

"A scenario that intrigued the cops,'' Buck said, "Clay had some raunchy friends. Did one of them smoke too much rock and get a chemical message to take out the Yost family? I mean, this guy ran with a gang they wouldn't let onto Syms Island to clean septic tanks. And you know where most of them live? Our old stomping grounds—Hyattsville, Riverdale, East Pines. Clay's last squeeze, she's got a brother that's done a bit of everything—possession, burglary, dealing, simple assault, felonious assault.

"As for the chick herself, she's not your typical Syms Island socialite either. More like something you'd buy in a doughnut shop—a sugar bun with a hole in the center. Doreen Perry's her name, and Allah only knows how Clay met her. But it looks like she won the lottery. Her lawyer just filed a paternity suit. Claims Clay's knocked her up and her kid should inherit his share of the estate.''

I swung my eyes away from the TV. "Where'd you hear that?''

"Courthouse.'' With his index finger, Buck was absentmindedly sketching a circular pattern on his cheek. It was a gesture Italians made when a dish was delicious. "Her lawyer's that sleazeball you bumped into when Big Tom was in the hospital.''

"What sleazeball?''

"Curtis Koontz—remember, the guy with the choirboy grin and the chrome dome?"

"Yeah, the one that was hustling me. Any chance it's a legitimate claim?"

"Who knows? The baby hasn't been born yet." Buck laughed ruefully. "Hard to believe anything Koontz does is legitimate. He's got a reverse Midas touch—it all turns to shit in his hands. But if Doreen's telling the truth, that slut-muffin's carrying a multimillion-dollar bun in the oven."

"What does the baby figure to inherit?"

"Depends how Yost's will was written. I'm no probate expert, but the standard boilerplate is for the money to pass down to the lineal descendants. Assuming Koontz is working on a contingency fee of thirty or forty percent, that little fuck'll skim off a fortune."

"Can we do without this?" I got up and switched off the television. "I keep watching for the temperature in Rome." I sat down and went back to Buck's notes. "I see the murder weapon was a .38 Smith and Wesson."

"I know—same as Big Tom. But there must be millions of trey-eights floating around the country."

"How many times had it been fired?"

"It's in there. Four times."

"They find four slugs?"

"Found three. One in Andrew. One in Clay. One in the wall."

"And the fourth round?"

"Could be the cops never located it. Those mothers will bounce around on you. Then again, that round might have been fired weeks, months, ago."

"What about prints?"

"They got Elaine's on the pistol. That's all the cops seem to care about. But the crazy thing is, they got Clay's and Andrew's too. Maybe Andrew did struggle. You know, grab at the gun."

The room was warming up; Buck began to perspire. "They also picked up an unknown partial print on the

Smith and Wesson. Doesn't match anybody at the scene or anybody that works at the house. I lay money Gaillard doesn't mention it today.''

"You think it's significant? Or just an arguing point for the trial?''

"What I understand, it's not on the pistol grip. It's on the barrel. Could be somebody that handled the gun months ago.''

"Have they traced the Smith and Wesson?''

"Not yet. The search always spiderwebs in directions you don't expect, then generally dead-ends with the last registered owner, who ninety-nine times out of a hundred says it was stolen.''

"Maybe the gun trace is what's delaying an indictment.''

"That and the fact that every piece of evidence cuts two ways. It's going to come down to which side does a better job of drawing a pretty picture. Actually, forget pretty. None of it's pretty. Know what the buzz is about Elaine's late and beloved husband?''

When I had first read about Townsend Farinholt's marriage to Elaine, and for years afterward whenever I spotted their picture on the society page, I had despised the man and felt I was entitled to. But now that he and his son were dead and I had an inkling of the chaos of Clay's life, I found it impossible to stoke up any animosity toward him. "Unless it's relevant to the murders, I'd rather not hear it.''

Buck did a histrionic double take. "Whatever happened to 'the devil lives in the details'? What about innocence being ignorance?''

"I'm stuffed to the gills with details. I'm so bloated with being in the know I can hardly climb out of bed in the morning.''

"You're bloated?'' Buck smacked his belly.

"This is good work.'' I folded the pages into my coat pocket. "You saved me weeks of wheel-spinning. Let me buy lunch.''

* * *

Going to meet Gaillard, I recognized little of the landscape Buck drove us through, and as we neared Annapolis, my geographical amnesia became complete. Forests and cornfields had been bulldozed and shopping centers built. At every cove and inlet, there were clusters of new town houses and condos with nautical names—Lazyjack Court, the Bowsprit, Chandler's Dock.

We turned in at a community called Chesapeake Harbor. It had security guards every bit as officious as those at Syms Island, but Buck knew them and sped through the gate, over a sun-warped parking lot, past four-story apartments of gray, faux-weathered wood. So many speedboats swarmed the marina, I could have crossed it on foot, clambering from bow to stern, bow to stern.

We parked next to a restaurant, an ornate heap of jigsawed lumber that resembled a lighthouse. As we climbed out into the gathering heat, he asked, "Remember this place?"

"What's it supposed to be? An imitation Nantucket? Martha's Vineyard?"

"No. I mean, remember what it used to be?"

I didn't.

"Carr's Beach," Buck exclaimed, as amused by my disbelief as by the idea that one of the county's few black resorts had metamorphosed into a subdivision of quarter-of-a-million-dollar condos. In high school and college, imagining ourselves hip and daring and racially enlightened, he and I had driven down here for rock 'n' roll acts that seldom played in white clubs—Joe Turner, the Eldorados, Big Mama Thornton, Bo Diddley.

"Now that it's officially integrated," he said, "you never see a black. Even us white trash can't afford it."

A stripped-down Ford swung in beside us and two men got out—one tall and gangly, the other thickset and swaggering.

"Shit," Buck said. "I thought he'd be alone."

The tall fellow introduced himself as Sam Gaillard and

locked his eyes on mine in that moment of intense counterfeit personal contact that American politicians imagine voters expect. He had an impressive head of hair that had been styled to soften an angular face.

The broad-shouldered swaggerer said nothing—it was Gaillard who introduced him as Det. Mike Quinn—and when he shook my hand, he stared through me, dead-eyed and stone-faced as a prizefighter before the bell rang for the first round. He looked as if he had gone to a military base and paid a quarter to have his hair mowed short.

"Mike's in charge of homicide," Gaillard said. "I brought him along to keep me on track." He grinned. "A lot of times, I blab too much."

Quinn headed into the restaurant, a strutting bantam cock in wheat-colored jeans and a check sport coat.

"I'm a great fan of yours." Gaillard latched onto my elbow as we followed the detective. "I've read all your books. Regardless how high you rise in this game, you can always learn something from a long-ball hitter like Tom Heller."

I didn't dare glance in Buck's direction for fear he'd blow me a loud lip-fart.

Inside, the ambient air temperature was that of a meat locker; I almost expected plumes of frost to form when I breathed. Quinn still led the way; even the waitress trailed in his wake. He wanted a table with a view of the marina, and once seated, he said, "Know what I'd like?"

"Hold it a sec," the waitress said. "Lemme bring you a list of the specials."

"I'd like to search those Cigarette boats without having to show probable cause." He spoke with a Baltimore accent, all nasal vowels and chewed-over consonants. "I guarangoddammtee you, more than half are holding drugs."

As the waitress passed around menus, I considered how to get Gaillard talking without Quinn's sticking in his two cents' worth. "Any chance there's a drug angle to the Yost murders?"

"How's that?" Gaillard gave the appearance of preter-
natural interest.

"Clay, from what I hear, was a user and ran with a
rough crowd. Rumor has it he might have burned the
wrong guy and things got out of hand."

"We looked into these rumors, Tom, and we don't see
anything to them. Do we, Mike?"

Quinn was rubbing his chin, rasping a thumbnail along
his jawline. He hadn't gotten a close shave this morning,
and reddish whiskers bristled on his pebbly skin. "You
realize who's floating all the rumors? Elaine Farinholt's
lawyer. That's all he's doing—sending up trial balloons.
Nothing but hot air."

"What sort of smoke has Whiting been blowing your
way?" Buck asked.

When Quinn didn't answer, Gaillard jumped in. "It
changes every day. He started off saying the killer could
be a political opponent of Andrew Yost. A celebrity hater.
An ex-business associate. Then he says Mrs. Farinholt has
an illegitimate son. The new line is we should look at
Clay's girlfriend and her brother."

"Have you questioned Doreen Perry?" I asked.

Quinn expelled a ragged breath of exasperation. "I got
a problem here. It's nobody's goddamn business who we
questioned."

"Now, Mike, now, Mike," the prosecutor nattered.
"Mike has mixed feelings about the media. I respect his
position, but I like the press and they've been good to me.
I'm a believer in the First Amendment. I think people have
a right to hear my views so they can judge for themselves
whether I'm doing the job I was elected for. But Mike, he
makes a contribution when he keeps me from straying out
of bounds."

The waitress stood with her pencil poised on her pad
until Gaillard ran out of gas. "Y'all ready to order?"

Quinn wanted a bacon cheeseburger, french fries, and
coffee. Buck and I had crab cakes and beer. Gaillard, the
razor-thin one, asked for the Dieter's Special, a fruit plat-

ter. But when the food arrived, it seemed the State's Attorney was determined to pack on weight, not lose it. His platter was the size of a trash can lid and was heaped with bananas, sugared strawberries, pineapple in syrup, scoops of sherbet, and mounds of cottage cheese. His meal had more calories than our three combined.

"I'd like to clarify something, set your minds at ease." I launched into a spiel I'd often recited to distrustful cops and prosecutors. "I'm not a journalist, not in the usual sense. I'm not sniffing around for a scoop that'll break on this evening's news or in tomorrow morning's paper. I'm researching a book that won't be published for a year or two, maybe longer. Nothing you tell me today is going to affect the course of the investigation or blow back on you during the trial. If there's material you'd rather discuss off the record, we can do that too."

"What about him?" Quinn aimed a bent french fry at Buck. "How do we know he won't leak something to the defense?"

"Only thing I'd leak to Whiting Pierce," Buck said, "is something I'd do on his shoe. And who are you kidding? We know you're not going to prosecute with secret evidence. Whatever you have, pro or con, you gotta turn over to the defense before the trial. All Tommy's asking is to be brought into the picture early."

"I don't want to be part of his picture."

Given how Quinn looked at the moment, mustachioed with catsup, his flat brown eyes dark as squashed beetles, I was willing to cut him from every scene, including this one. "Your privilege," I said. "You rather stay out of this, you won't offend me. But like Sam said, it's to everybody's advantage to let the State's Attorney educate his constituents about the legal process."

Quinn glanced at Gaillard; Gaillard focused on his fruit platter. It couldn't have been clearer that his boss didn't care if he took a hike.

"Will you be interviewing Elaine Farinholt?" Gaillard asked.

"I spent a few hours with her the other day."

"No kidding." He didn't bother feigning indifference. He was caught up in the ballet, the intricate adagio of give-and-take I had danced with many prosecutors in the past. Once they realized I was in a position to provide more than publicity—I had information to trade—even brass-balled detectives like Quinn sometimes dropped their guard. "What did she have to say?"

"We covered quite a chunk of ground. She gave me her version of events on the night of the murders. Naturally I intend to go over that again and branch out into other areas. We'll be meeting on a regular basis."

Since neither Gaillard nor Quinn had exchanged two words with her, this had to rankle. The detective fell back into his prefight stone-face. The State's Attorney continued spooning up cottage cheese and pineapple, speaking between bites. "I hear she's not exactly prostrate with grief."

"No, she's plenty upset. She can't understand why you don't believe she has an illegitimate son."

"Because there's no proof," Quinn said.

"She thinks her father may have thrown his weight around, had friends in Texas destroy the documents."

"More bullshit," Quinn said.

"Well, if she's lying—and you might be right—it does raise a fascinating question."

Quinn refused to tumble. Gaillard waited with his spoon in midair. A dollop of pineapple dribbled from it before he finally asked, "What's that?"

"Why would she invent such an embarrassing alibi?"

"Hey," Quinn said, "to keep her ass out of the electric chair, she'd swear she had triplets by Mike Tyson."

Gaillard shot him a look. "Under pressure, Tom, perps, even superintelligent ones, do illogical things. When she wrote those letters and left them lying around for us to find, she didn't realize we could run down her story and disprove it."

"No, what Tommy's saying," Buck chimed in, "it's not

a question of her alibi having holes in it. It's a question of considering her family, her community standing, et cetera, et cetera, why concoct that story? Screwing around as a girl, giving birth to a bastard, that's an alibi for a cocktail waitress. No Syms Island widow's going to admit to an illegitimate kid unless it's true.''

"Okay, have it your way." Quinn was gnawing on his cheeseburger. "Personally I don't buy this business about some cockamamie kid coming back to kill her. Her only crazy son, you ask my opinion, is dead, and she killed him. But even say it's true, say she put a baby out for adoption and somehow—who the hell knows how?—but somehow the records got lost and still her kid tracked her down over a trail that's clean as a nun's cunt and wrote those letters—what the hell's that prove?''

"It proves he had a motive," Buck said. "And he made threats.''

"Her and her lawyer call them threatening letters. But you like to get down to fine strokes, they don't threaten to kill her or anybody else. They say—read the fuckers—they say, Come across with serious dough or I'll spill your secret. What that shows, it shows she's the one with the motive. She was scared she was going to be exposed.''

Buck rolled his eyes in theatrical disbelief. "So she whacks her father and son? Then exposes herself with her alibi?''

Gaillard glanced at Quinn as if the detective had let him down. "I think what Mike's saying—''

"I said what I'm saying. It's all there—her in a room with two stiffs and her prints on the pistol.''

"I think what Mike's saying," Gaillard began again, "Elaine Farinholt had a motive—she wanted the estate for herself. She had the means—the .38 found at the scene. And she had an opportunity. Whiting Pierce claims she wasn't there when Andrew and Clay were killed, she came back afterward. But the guards at the gate swear she never left the island. The dock keeper swears she didn't go out on a boat. No witness saw her anywhere off the property. It all adds up to an overwhelming presumption of guilt.''

''Sounds like the lady has a serious problem.'' I dipped a chunk of crab meat into the tartar sauce. ''Only thing I don't understand.'' I shoveled in the crab and chewed it thoroughly. ''If the evidence is as convincing as you describe it, why haven't you arrested her?''

''First good question you asked,'' Quinn said.

Blood rushed to the bony ridges of Gaillard's face; his forehead and hollow cheeks remained pale. ''When you go to the grand jury, Tom, it's a great responsibility. Before I move to indict, I need to be sure I know all the facts on both sides of a case.''

''Which facts are you unsure of?''

''You answer that,'' Quinn said, ''you oughta have your head examined.''

Gaillard set down his spoon. ''Wait outside, Mike.''

''Glad to.'' He shoved back from the table, knocking over his chair, and grubbed in the pocket of his jeans.

''I'll cover it,'' I said.

''I pay my own way.'' He tossed down a ten-dollar bill and left.

As the color slowly drained from the bladelike edges of the State's Attorney's face, the waitress cleared away the dirty dishes and cutlery. Gaillard ordered coffee, sweetening it with Equal. ''Mike's a good cop,'' he said at last. ''Buck will back me on that.''

Buck did no such thing. ''I worry about his eating habits. All that red meat and grease, on top of his temper and a tension-packed job''—he shook his head solemnly—''it's a recipe for a heart attack. Even the man's hair looks too tight.''

''What Mike sometimes fails to comprehend is a prosecutor and a policeman play different roles.'' He sipped his coffee. ''Call me a demon for procedure, call me a perfectionist. One thing I promise you, I know I have a credible case and I know I have the support of the department, Mike included.'' He laid his hand on my arm; his eyes honed in on mine as if on a Minicam. His phoniness was of such magnitude he managed by some curious reverse English to sound sincere.

"You see, Tom, we don't BS each other in this district. Do we, Buck? We all have to go on living together. So why pull stunts? When I tell you there's probable cause with Elaine Farinholt, I mean it. We're moving ahead."

He climbed to his full clumsy height. "I'm counting on a signed copy of your book."

"We'll see each other long before then."

"Good, good." He buttoned his suit coat. "Anything you need, just let me know." He shook hands with me, with Buck, with the waitress, the busboy, a couple of customers. Searching for someone else to shake with, he performed an awkward pirouette, then reoriented himself and headed for the exit.

I waited until he was gone before asking, "What's he like in a courtroom?"

"Dynamite," Buck said. "He acts like a dimwit, but he never gives anything away."

"He certainly didn't give us much."

"Juries love him because he's smart enough to know he's a nerd and doesn't have any choice but to be himself. By comparison, the defense attorney comes off like a con man. You attack him, he's got this routine where he reacts like a wounded fawn."

"What happens when you attack Quinn?"

"He goes ballistic. Fucking guy, once a narc always a narc. In a way, you gotta feel sorry for him. You spend ten years on the street staring up the ass end of humanity, you develop a proctologist's view of the world. But Gaillard wasn't wrong. He's a helluva cop."

"Any other redeeming merits?"

"He's good with dogs. They get a pit bull emergency, they call Mike out to coax the animal away from the mangled corpse. You having coffee?"

"Sure, if you are."

He signaled to the waitress. "This is fun sitting around

with you, shooting the shit, not having to prove anything. That's when life is pure hell—when you have to plead a case and prove it. That's the problem Gaillard's up against.''

''He sounded confident to me.''

''No. I come away feeling Quinn and Sam are a couple boys playing pool with bad breath.''

''Meaning?''

''Guy goes into a pool hall with empty pockets and hustles a game, he's playing with bad breath. He wins, he gets a stake and goes on playing. But he loses that first game, he gets his ticket punched and his hands broken.''

''You figure Gaillard and Quinn have empty pockets?''

''Half empty. Something's missing. You pulled the right lever. If they have the evidence, why not arrest her?''

''I notice they didn't bring up the partial print.''

''Told you they wouldn't.'' Buck lifted his coffee cup and clinked it against mine. ''The literary life, I love it.''

5

The following days I spent indoors, up in my parents'
bedroom, laved by the cool air of the window unit, preparing to interview Elaine. During breaks for meals, I
skimmed the *Post* or watched television for updates on the
case. There was nothing new. At least nothing dramatic
enough to keep those homicides in the headlines when so
many others were going down every day. The nation's cap-
ital had become a killing ground; every twenty four hours,
regularly as rent, someone else was murdered.

Much as I missed Marisa and the boys, much as I missed
Rome, the press of people in the streets, the random
snatches of organ music resonating from churches, I
shrunk the focus of my life to what was in front of my
eyes. Reminded of times in college when I had holed up
to cram for tests, I studied Buck's notes and occasionally
called him for clarification. I jotted lists of questions and
rehearsed my lines. Like an actor, I had to memorize a
script, master it by rote, but then play it with such spon-
taneity it sounded like idle chatter.

Having acquired as a child a knack for dancing clear of
my father's roundhouse swings, I normally had no trouble
choosing which role to play. Whether questioning a cop
or a convict, a housewife or a hooker, I knew the tone to
strike, the distance to stake out between us, and during
the course of the same conversation, I could come on as
an affable uncle, the Grand Inquisitor, then a sympathetic
father confessor. While I was no longer willing to trade
money for information, I paid in other currencies; I paid

court, I paid with time and patience, I paid fawning attention.

But this time I was after a larger story, the one that would tie up the loose ends of my life. To get it I'd have to be smarter and tougher than I'd been before, and if that meant putting the torch to some of my most cherished notions . . . well, I believed it was worth the risk of going down in flames.

When I called to set up the meeting, Elaine insisted Whiting Pierce had to be there. I didn't object. "If you're comfortable with him around," I said, "it'll be easier for us to talk."

"It's not going to be easy at all, Tom."

"That's why I don't blame you for wanting to have a friend with you."

"It's not like I think of you as an enemy," she said.

I let that sink in. "Good. See you in the morning."

Assuming Pierce would wear his summer-camp uniform—polo shirt and Top-Siders without socks—I put on a pair of slacks and a shirt open at the collar. After a last-moment debate, I left without my microcassette recorder. Something about a taped conversation spooks people, especially at the start. I made do with a notebook and pen.

At this hour, in midweek, the roads to the Bay were nearly empty, and I arrived at Syms Island just as late commuters were leaving for work. Boats bobbed offshore, their sails slack in the humid air, their halyards beating faint musical chimes against aluminum masts. The golf course was wet with dew, and carts had made silvery wheelmarks as distinct as snail tracks through the grass.

In the driveway behind the Yost house, the Mercedes was missing. The other five foreign cars, waxed to a high gloss, shimmered with beads of condensation. The same bl--- servant opened the door before I knocked and --- me away from the glassed-in porch, toward the far

"What's your name?" I asked.

"Mary Beth."

"Is the security guard here?"

"Yes, indeed."

"Where?"

"I ain't supposed to tell."

"Tell what?" Elaine asked as we stepped out onto a deck. She sat under an umbrella, an immense white one like the kind that shade Italian cafes.

"Where the guard is," I said.

Elaine set her mug of coffee on an end table. "He moves around. He's almost invisible." She held out her hand. "Hello, Tom."

Mary Beth left, and I settled onto a wrought-iron chair. Elaine was in white today—white slacks and an off-white blouse. Maybe this signaled an end to mourning. Or simply that she didn't care what I thought; the widow would wear what was cool and comfortable.

"Where's Pierce?"

"I decided I'd rather talk to you alone. Even if none of this"—she gestured toward the house—"had happened, you deserve answers. I've owed you an explanation for a long time."

This didn't strike me as the predictable product of Whiting Pierce's coaching; I couldn't dismiss the possibility that it was sincere. But I had spent enough time plotting strategy to suspect that she had done the same.

"What's to explain?" I opened my notepad.

"Why I left Austin without telling you. Where I went, what I did."

"We'll get to that," I said, as though the subject were of no great interest to me.

She retrieved the coffee mug, holding it in both hands. "Shall I have Mary Beth fix you some?"

"No thanks. I understand Clay had a girlfriend. Doreen Perry. You know her?"

"I've met her. Can't really claim I know her. We haven't

exchanged a dozen words. But maybe that's the poor girl's entire vocabulary.''

"An airhead?'' I smiled, showing her how easy and amiable I could be. "Why do men fall for them?''

"Sex.'' She was smiling too. "That's what Clay said— they had terrific sex.''

"Sounds like you and Clay had a nice open relationship.''

"Yes, there wasn't much we couldn't talk about.''

"I guess he told you she's pregnant.''

"I'll let the lawyers look after that. They're the ones who are going to get rich off it.''

"Actually, Doreen and her baby figure to get rich if her paternity claim sticks. And you'll get rich—*richer!*—if the estate stays intact.''

"That's a lot of ifs. I'm sure Whiting would be delighted to explain our position.''

"I'll have him do that. Meanwhile, I'm curious what Clay told you. Did he say she was pregnant? And how long was that before his death?''

"Look, Tom''—she went on smiling, keeping it light— "I don't want to say anything that Doreen's lawyers'll clobber me with in court. And I don't see how this relates to your book.''

"It could be the key. If Clay got her pregnant and refused to marry her—''

"What? Doreen might have murdered him and Daddy? Is that what you're saying?''

"According to police reports, she has witnesses who were with her at a disco. But—''

"She could have hired somebody. She's got this revolting brother. The police should be investigating him.''

"Do I gather then that Clay did tell you Doreen's pregnant?''

"Yes.''

he admit the baby was his?''

bt he knew. I doubt either one of them knew. All she's pregnant and pressuring me to marry her.''

"What did he plan to do?"

"You're asking questions, but I notice you're not taking notes."

"Before I put anything on paper, I want to be sure you understand what I'm saying. Doreen could claim she and Clay planned to get married. You knew it and murdered him to prevent her from getting his money."

"That's absurd. All you have to do is look at his bank statement." She set aside the coffee mug and started to fold her arms, but changed her mind. It was too hot to sit tied in knots. "Clay didn't have any real money. Except for a few thousand dollars from a trust fund, he wasn't going to get any until Daddy died."

"I see." And what I saw was the basis of Doreen's suit. "After Clay and Andrew were killed, Clay's share passed to the baby."

"That's Doreen's line. She'll have to prove it," Elaine said in a voice that recalled her father's fighting spirit.

"I expect Pierce has been doing his homework."

"That's what he's paid for."

"How long's he been the family lawyer?"

"I don't know when it became official, but he's been on Syms since I was a teenager."

"He have a wife, kids?"

"Yes. His oldest daughter's about my age."

"Come on, the guy can't be more than fifty."

"He turned fifty-eight this past spring. But you caught me in a fib. His daughter's ten years younger than I am."

"His family still lives on the island?"

"The children have grown up and gone away. And his wife . . . well, she spends most of her time at their place in Maine."

"They're separated?" I asked without any special emphasis.

"More or less," she answered in the same fashion.

I started doodling on the pad. "Let me see if I have this straight. When Clay told you Doreen was pregnant, did

Andrew do anything about changing the provisions of his will?"

"Suffice it to say he didn't regard Doreen as sterling material for a daughter-in-law, the mother of his grand-children."

"Did he ask Pierce to draft a new will, cutting Clay out or reducing his share?"

She was fiddling with the coffee mug just as I was with my pen. "Whiting was aware of Daddy's feelings."

"Was Clay?"

The question splashed into the green pools of her eyes and slowly sank toward bottom. She couldn't disguise the care with which she calculated her answer. She had to consider what I might have heard from someone else. And was there a scrap of paper that had drifted into the wrong hands? How much might Pierce reveal under oath? "You know Daddy," she said. "He didn't believe in mincing words."

"So Clay knew the score, but none of this got written down?"

"There wasn't time. A few days later they were both dead."

Above us, the broad canvas umbrella baked like a sail in the sun, the smell reminiscent of lazy hours Elaine and I had spent lying becalmed on Andrew's yacht, drowsing on the deck after sex, the bottom half of her bikini rolled down and dangling from her ankle. "What was your atti-tude toward Clay and Doreen? I mean, you'd been in a similar predicament."

She laughed a rich, throaty laugh as she sometimes had when she kicked that scrap of cloth from her foot and goaded me on again. "Call me a cockeyed optimist, but even at my worst moments I've never noticed much sim-ilarity between Doreen and me."

"Weren't you once pregnant and unmarried and wor-ried about what to do?"

"If you're asking whether I feel sympathy for Doreen, of course I do. I feel more sympathy for the baby. Okay,

I know what you'll say. If I'm so concerned, why not let it inherit? But that's a different matter."

"Oh? How?" I kept the notepad on my knee and continued doodling.

"It was Daddy's money and he had every right to do what he wanted with it. He made it clear he didn't want it going to Doreen and her brother. If a blood test proves Clay's the father, I'll set up a trust fund for the child's education. But it doesn't make sense to fork over millions of dollars to those people."

"Yeah, they'd fritter it away on coke, flashy cars, and kooky friends."

Elaine leveled her eyes on me. "Listen, Tom, if you're insinuating I was a lousy mother and Clay was a spoiled brat, I won't argue."

"I don't want to argue either. And I don't want to hurt your feelings. But you had to know the question would come up. What went wrong with Clay?"

"Wrong?" She tilted her head back, as if lost in thought, but in fact hiding her face—her resentment—from me. "My understanding of substance abuse—trust me, I've talked to plenty of experts—is there's no right or wrong. It's a sickness, a chemical dependency."

"So it was drugs, pure and simple. No other problems?"

"Don't make me sound like a fool, Tom. Of course Clay had other problems, and drugs made them worse. Now you'll ask about the other problems."

She was still studying the tented underside of the umbrella. "There was Townsend's death. Clay never got over that. He missed a man's influence. Daddy was too old and impatient, and I was busy—traveling, running for Congress, doing committee work. If I had it to do over . . ." She let her voice trail off, a little too theatrically for my taste.

"If you had it to do over, what would you have done that time he punched out his girlfriend and put her in the hospital?"

"That's easy. I'd have made him stay in therapy. Right before the murders, I was trying to get him into a—into what they call a structured environment where he'd have psychiatric help. But how do you control a kid today? How do you reach him once he's dabbling in drugs? What would you do with your sons, Tom?"

I didn't reply. It was one of the unassailable advantages of my job. I asked the questions. Somebody else had to answer them.

"There's no way of saying this without your accusing me of interfering," Elaine said. "So I'll admit it, I'm begging you. Don't make him out to be a monster. Clay was a warm, lovely boy. There was a side to him people didn't see when he was on drugs."

"You have my word. I'll show both sides." I flipped a page on the notepad and drew two parallel lines. Now that she had asked a personal favor, I risked one myself. "Did Andrew threaten to cut you out of his will when you got pregnant? Did he threaten to disinherit you if you married me?"

"Look, Tom, you said you don't want to hurt me. I don't want to hurt you either."

"Don't worry about that. I'd like to know."

"All right, he did say he'd cut me off. The next thing you'll ask is whether that's why I left you. The answer is no, but I'm sure you don't believe me."

It was useless to discuss what I did or didn't believe. If we blundered into that marshy terrain, we'd never make it back to the murders. I closed the pad. "I think I will have a cup of coffee."

"Let's go inside. It's too hot out here."

With its broad, clean working surfaces and bright lights, the kitchen resembled an operating theater. Everything—tile floor, stainless steel pans, copper pots, and silverware—sparkled. Mary Beth watched a "Wheel of Fortune" rerun while she brewed me a pot of coffee.

En route to the glassed-in porch—Elaine seemed to restrict herself (or was it me?) to the wings of the house—

we passed through halls and rooms of a sort I saw nowhere in Italy. The pegged, wood-plank floors were bare and polished. The walls were hung with nineteenth-century nautical maps, prints of hunting parties and horse-jumping competitions, sooty oil paintings of ancestors who belonged to no branch of the Yost family tree. The spindly furniture, poised on dainty brass hooves, appeared not to have borne any weight in centuries.

The porch was blessedly cool. Elaine sat on the couch and smoothed her hair away from her face.

"Was Mary Beth here the night of the murders?" I asked.

"No, she leaves at six."

"I'd like to talk to her."

"Help yourself. But I hope you're not under the same delusion as one Baltimore TV station. They grabbed her as she left the island, shoved a mike in her face, and put her on live. You could tell they thought they had a real scoop, an exclusive with the faithful old family retainer— somebody like Dilsey in *The Sound and the Fury*, somebody who'd moan, 'I seen the beginning and I seen the ending.' Instead Mary Beth said, 'I been working for Mistah Yost, oh, it must be, I reckon when I look back, it adds up to almost two months. Came to the island as a temp and just stayed on and on.' "

I laughed and watched Elaine laugh with me. Was she steering me away from something Mary Beth knew?

"Do you still write short stories?" she asked.

"No."

"What about poems? I remember the ones you sent me."

"These days I send faxes."

"A pity. I liked what you wrote way back when." She kicked off her sandals and folded her legs up under her. "I liked it a lot better than what you do now. Of course I haven't read all your books. I've just skimmed a few in the past couple of days. Parts of them are fascinating. Repulsive but fascinating."

"That's crime for you," I said. "Never less than fascinating, rarely more than repulsive."

"What I don't get is the point. I suppose there must be money in it."

"I'd do it for free."

"Would you? Why?"

As she leaned into the subject, I leaned back, went limp, showing how little I cared to debate the value of my work. "There are certain satisfactions."

"I don't see it," she said. "It's not like you're solving crimes. The police do that. It's not like you're punishing criminals. Prisons do that."

"Sometimes they don't. And sometimes even after a case has been tried, there's no real explanation. That's where I come in."

"Come in and do what? Can you honestly say it helps anybody to have you rummage around, analyzing their childhoods, dissecting their motives? My God, when there's been a murder in a family, people want to get on with their lives."

The phrase set my teeth on edge. I heard it over and over and hated it more every time. "I want to change people's lives," I told her. "I want them to recognize what's really there."

"You mean rub their noses in it."

"Whatever's there."

My refusal to get riled seemed to rankle Elaine. "I feel sorry for you, I honestly do, if all you see in life is violence and corruption."

"Oh, I see other things too."

"You must. You wouldn't live in a city like Rome if you didn't." Settling back on the couch, smoothing a wrinkle from her blouse, she asked in a milder voice, "Why do you live there?"

I gave her the abridged version. "My wife's Italian."

"What's she like?"

"Lovely."

"At least tell me her name," she said in mock-petulance, as though I were hiding a high school flirtation she had a right to hear about.

"Marisa."

"And your sons, do you raise them as Italians?"

"They go to international schools. They're bilingual. They have the best of both worlds." To my own ears this sounded fatuous, and I was relieved that she didn't ask what the best of both worlds was.

"I've been to Rome a few times. I loved it. We might have passed each other in the street."

I didn't care for this line of conversation and Elaine's pretense of interest in my life. The full strength of her attention was a disorienting experience; it was like basking in a warm spotlight. When that light was on you, you felt you were the center of the world. When she switched it off, you were left out in the dark.

I said, "I'd like to see where it happened. You don't have to come. Mary Beth can show me."

"No, I'll do it."

We retraced our steps through the halls, past the foxes and hounds, the mounted riders in livery and the anonymous nonrelatives in waistcoats and snoods. Elaine was in front of me, her shoulders broad, but not so much as the cut and padding of her blouse suggested. Her back nipped in at the waist and flared nicely at the hips and bottom.

When we reached the double doors to the library, she threw them open, then let out a scream. I grabbed her and heard what sounded like a pistol shot. I was about to drop to the floor, dragging her with me, when I saw what had frightened her.

A man was at the desk. A uniformed security guard, he was holding a book as fat as a dictionary and had slammed it shut when she cried out. Now he was on his feet, blinking, unsteady, bewildered. "I was taking a peek at this here manual on duck decoys. You all right, ma'am?"

She nodded, but I could feel her trembling. I helped her to an armchair.

"Guess I better roost someplace else." The guard hurried off.

"He surprised me," Elaine said. "I didn't expect anybody to be here."

"We'll do this later."

"Just give me a minute."

I took a slow turn of the room. The library had been the site of one of our more memorable sexual escapades—those puerile attempts to put my mark on everything that belonged to Andrew Yost. I might as well have been a puppy peeing on the stern of an ocean liner, convinced that that staked a territorial claim.

Behind the desk, on rows of shelves rising from floor to ceiling, there were more duck decoys than books. They must have been worth a great deal of money. Andrew wouldn't have collected them otherwise.

A rogues' gallery of photographs hung on the other walls—Andrew at Congressional Country Club with Jack Nicklaus and J. Edgar Hoover; Andrew in a tent at Persepolis with the Shah and Princess Soraya; Andrew in the winner's circle at Longchamp with a wizened jockey and a well-fed Aga Khan. The man knew everyone—or so it had seemed to me. Once when Elaine and I were alone in the house I had spun through her father's Rolodex. I can't say what impressed me more—that he was in touch with Johnny Unitas or Henry Kissinger, with Madame Nhu or Ben Bradlee. Viewing that directory as a talismanic source of power and privilege, I attempted to arrogate a portion of it to myself. I wouldn't have dared call anybody, but like some primitive tribesman, I believed I was carrying away their aura by copying down their numbers and addresses.

French doors gave onto a patio and beyond it, about fifty yards away, the Bay. In the doorjamb a hole the size of a dime had been circled in red.

I wondered whether Elaine remembered the night we had sneaked in here. She wanted to lower her panties and lift her skirt. She wanted to spread a towel on the desk to protect its lacquered surface. I wouldn't hear of it. I stripped her to the skin and laid her back on the polished wood. Standing, I pulled her legs up over my shoulders and drove deep into her.

"How do you feel?" I asked.

"Much better."

"Can you tell me where Clay was when you first saw him?"

"In front of the desk, on the floor. Daddy—I can't explain why, but the instant I saw him, I knew he was dead. It was the way he was twisted in the chair. But I couldn't believe it about Clay and I went to help him. That's when I noticed the blood all over his face. He was dead too."

"The gun, where was it? Did you touch it?"

"Yes, it was on the desk. I grabbed it and ran to the door and saw the man with blond hair out on the lawn. I should have gone after him. I had the pistol. But that's not how my mind was working. I was terrified he'd come back and kill me too. I slammed the door and locked it."

"Did you notice which way he went?"

"Toward the water."

Leaning against the desk, I slowed down the pace of my questions and her answers. I didn't want her to feel she was under cross-examination. But then she began speaking on her own, without my prompting.

"I can't tell you how horrible it was." She lifted her hands, staring at them, transfixed. "There was blood everywhere. It was streaming out of Clay's ears and mouth. It was running down my arms."

This sort of emotion would never move the cops, and if she stood trial, Sam Gaillard would trample on her lines before she warmed up her act. But for the time being I was a judge and jury of one, and she may have thought that if she managed to convince me, she'd never have to play the scene for anybody else.

"How long was it before you called for help?" I asked.

"A minute or two."

"Who did you call?"

"Whiting."

At least she had the brains not to lie about that. "Why not the police?" I asked. "Why not the guards at the gate? It's going to strike people as peculiar that your first call was to your lawyer?"

"I wasn't phoning a lawyer," she protested. "I was calling a neighbor, a close friend. I knew he'd get here quicker than the guards. And Whiting has a cellular phone in his Mercedes. He called the police and an ambulance on the way over."

"Backing up a bit, you said the man you saw had long blond hair. Could it have been a wig?"

"There *was* something strange about his hair. It didn't lie right—maybe because he was running. But it could have been a wig."

"Do you ever wear a wig?"

"No."

"You don't own one?"

"No."

"What did you do after you called Pierce?"

"Sat right where I am." She patted the arms of the chair. "I thought, Everything will be okay as soon as Whiting gets here. Then it came to me—Daddy's dead, Clay's dead. Why am I sitting here like a damn fool? There's nothing anyone can do. That's when I lost it. By the time Whiting came, I was hysterical."

Tears trembled on her lashes, then trickled down her cheeks. One fell to her lap, leaving a grayish mascara stain on her white slacks.

I didn't want to feel sorry for her. I didn't want to feel anything at all. I especially didn't want to be suckered by a masterpiece performance. But I was moved. Having just lost Big Tom, I could appreciate what she was going through. Having listened to the confessions of condemned killers, I could understand the agony Elaine was in even if she was guilty.

I laid a hand on her shoulder. Her stylish shoulder pads prevented any close contact until she reached up and

squeezed my fingers. "If you're finished," she said, "I'd
rather get out of this room."

Mary Beth served lunch on the glassed-in porch and offered beer, wine, or Perrier (Peareer water, she called it).
Elaine asked for wine and I uncorked a bottle of Pinot
Grigio, and while making vapid remarks about Italian vin-
tages, I downed two glasses. After that I drank slowly,
afraid I'd be worthless for the rest of the day.

I like to believe I've trained myself to recall conversa-
tions verbatim and recreate interviews without benefit of
notes. But during that meal Elaine talked a lot, I listened
closely, and I couldn't quote a single sentence. What came
back to me later wasn't words. It was the sense of her as
a mesmerizer acting out another scene like the one I'd
witnesssed in the library. Not that she had to be an Academy Award winner to rivet my attention. Her mere presence was charged for me with all the electricity of a live
wire.

After a dessert of fresh raspberries, she said, "Why
don't we go for a swim?"

I was tempted. Cold water was what I needed to jolt me
back to business. "The Bay?"

"No, it's teeming with jellyfish. The pool."

I didn't care to be around a crowd of club members and
their kids—the boys courting girls by shoving them off the
high dive.

"How about the pond?" she said.

I remembered nights we had swum there naked like
aquatic creatures whose skin was sheathed in phosphores-
cence. That she had mentioned it made me question how
much of this was impromptu, how much purposeful provocation. "We've got work to do."

"Let's at least go for a walk," she pleaded.

"Does the guard have to come along?"

"No. We won't tell him."

We left by a side entrance and padded across the lawn.
There rose to my nostrils a familiar smell of Rome—the

sweet scent of straw on Via Sediari where the ships sold raffia baskets. At the shoreline the sand was damp and firm, and we headed south.

"The night of the murders," I said, "you weren't in the house."

"That's right."

"Where were you?"

From her pocket she pulled a rubber band and tied her hair up in a ponytail. "I went for a walk. It was warm and I was aching to be outside."

"Did you leave the island?"

"No. I hiked to the pond and wound up skinny-dipping."

"Anybody see you?"

"You mean paddling around in my birthday suit like Susanna and the Elders?"

"At any time while you were out of the house did anybody see you? Did you see anyone?"

"Not a soul."

"Some people—Sam Gaillard—might think it's a tad too convenient, that spur-of-the-moment walk."

She let a frown slide over her face as idly as she might let a silk scarf slip through her fingers. She didn't respond in any other way.

"This morning," I said, "you were about to tell me what happened after you left the Creekmore Agency."

"There's not a lot to tell. Daddy flew in and took me to a ranch. When I went into labor, a doctor and nurse came and delivered the baby. I never saw him again. What the agency did with him, the identity of the adopting couple, all that was kept secret from me. I just signed some papers and left." She had her eyes fixed on her feet as if she were squeamish about stepping on beached jellyfish.

"The papers you signed," I said, "did you get copies?"

"Daddy may have. I didn't."

"Were they in his files?"

"We haven't found anything there."

"What about records related to the adoption? He must have paid the agency and bought plane tickets to and from Texas. Did he keep the canceled checks, the receipts?"

"Does anybody save them more than twenty years? He didn't."

"This ranch, where was it?"

"In the hills near Austin. I don't know exactly where. I wasn't in any frame of mind to read maps or road signs."

"Did it have a name?"

"Not that I remember. We're not talking about Tara. There was a nondescript house, a couple of trailers, and miles and miles of scrub land."

"Could it have belonged to a friend of your father's?"

"No. I think the agency owned it. There was a delivery room. The doctor and nurse knew their way around."

"You still don't remember any of the people—other girls? the staff?—at the agency?"

"I've tried. Faces come to mind, but no names."

I was beginning to get a headache from the glare off the Bay. Or maybe the headache came on because I remembered Diane Kershner and couldn't believe that Elaine didn't.

"Where'd you go after Texas?"

"Latin America. I traveled for a few months. Then I met Townsend in Managua."

"During that time, didn't you have to visit a doctor for postnatal care? He could corroborate that you had a baby."

"No. I was disgustingly healthy."

Syms Island tapered to a spit of land, and on its leeward side stood a screened-in summerhouse. People flocked here in the evening to watch the sunset, then stayed on at night to see star showers. Without a word, we headed for it, anxious for shade. Its benches had been carved with hearts and entwined initials, some jagged and new, most polished smooth by weather and time and the buttocks of generations of islanders.

"I haven't been here for years." Elaine roved from bench to bench, reading graffiti. "Surely somebody at some point carved a heart with my name in it. Didn't you ever do it, Tom?''

''My switchblade must have been broken.'' I sat down, pulled off my shoes, and poured out enough sand to fill an hourglass.

She sat beside me and extended her legs, staring at her feet and sandals powdered with dust. ''You don't believe me, do you?'' She spoke without any rancor; she simply sounded disappointed. ''You think I killed them?''

''I don't know what to think, Elaine.'' I slapped sand from my socks, stinging the soles of my feet with each swipe of the hand. ''You're a bright woman. What would you think of somebody who lived for months with a group of people, then forgot everyone's name? Somebody who had a baby delivered by a doctor she didn't know at a ranch she can't remember in a place she can't quite pin down.''

''I'd say it's understandable. I'd say she had amnesia about a very painful period in her life.''

''Selective amnesia. The past isn't blank. You only forgot those details that could undercut your story or break down your alibi.''

''Maybe some things are too awful to remember. You don't have any idea what it was like to give up the baby, to lose someone you love and have no hope of ever holding again.''

I underplayed it, delivering the line with no work on it at all. ''I think I do.''

''Sorry, I suppose it was a terrible time for you too. God, don't we pay for all the things we do.''

''Look, Lady Brett, spare me the melodramatics. The girl I used to know was a tough cookie. She wouldn't hide behind this damsel-in-distress, forgetful-fairy-princess routine. She knew what she wanted, went ahead and did it, and never made excuses.''

''They're not excuses,'' she shot back. ''And don't kid yourself. You're the one playing a role—Bob Woodward, I presume, ace reporter, asking such clever questions, hoping I'll contradict myself. Where's the guy I fell for? Sure, he had a chip on his shoulder, but he'd tell you what was on his mind. Now I'm with this very arch, very ironic, world-famous author who knows all about Italian wines and nothing about human nature.''

''We're getting off the subject.''

''Which is what?''

''Which is double murder and your lousy memory.''

''No, that's only your excuse to badger me. You're still furious I left you.'' She herself sounded more and more furious. ''Well, let me tell you why I did. I left because the rest of our lives would have been like this—nonstop bickering about things that are over and done with. Constant reminders that I was wrong and you were right and nothing was your fault.''

I chucked my ear as I had seen Buck do a few nights ago. ''I must have missed something. How did we get from your legal problems to my faults?''

''No, no,'' she was shouting. ''Nothing's ever your fault.''

''Okay, let's hear about these faults of mine. But first, tell me, weren't you the one that got pregnant? Weren't you the one that informed me of that fact by disappearing? And when I found you and said I wanted to marry you and keep the baby, weren't you the one that answered me by taking off again? Whose fucking fault was that?''

In the silence that stretched between us, it came to me with a kind of stomach-curdling clarity that I had spilled my guts just like the sorry, sentimental punk I used to be.

When she spoke again, Elaine's voice had lost its combativeness. ''What you'll never understand, Tom, is I loved you more those last weeks in Texas than I ever did before. But I knew if we got married, we'd be miserable. That's why I called Daddy. I knew he'd put an end to it.''

''Why? He hated me that much?''

''He liked you about as well as anybody I dated. And he admired your guts. Years later he still talked about the way you wouldn't quit and he had to have the guards kick you off the island. He just didn't want you marrying me.''

''At least you two agreed on that.''

''Yes, for different reasons.''

There was no sense holding back. I gagged up the rest of my bile. ''I don't suppose your reasons had anything to do with thinking I was poor white trash?''

''No, the terrible thing, what ruined any chance for us, was *you* thought you were white trash. That's why I had to get away.''

She covered my hand with hers. ''I'm sorry, but it's true.'' I tried to shake off her hand; she held tight. ''That summer before I went to Texas, you acted so resentful and defensive. Sometimes even when we made love it was like you were retaliating, taking a pound of flesh.''

I shook my head.

''You deny it?'' she asked.

''No, I just never knew I hurt you.'' I felt woozy from the heat, the wine at lunch, the zigzags of our argument. Mine was also the grogginess of a man gazing into a mirror and not recognizing himself. Or rather getting a glimmer of his true self for the first time. In my case it was the second time. The first came the other evening in Annapolis when Buck informed me that my opinion of myself wasn't necessarily shared by others.

Elaine lifted her hand from mine. ''We'd better start back.''

We returned on a road of crushed oyster shells. Under my feet, they felt like eggshells, and I crunched over them wondering, What next?

The road wound through a swamp where amid reeds and cattails a heron stood on one leg and rotated its head, tracking our passage like a radar device. When we reached higher ground, a few cheerful retirees on three-wheel bikes pedaled past us, heading toward the summerhouse. Two of the men had picnic hampers balanced on their handlebars. They called out, ''Hi!'' but didn't slow down.

"Now that I've told you everything," Elaine said, "will you sign an affidavit?"

"We're a long way from finished. There are things we haven't even touched."

"For instance?"

"Who's the father?"

"Do you really need to know?"

"Yes. To write a book about the case I—"

"That's the other question," she cut in. "Do you really have to write a book?"

"Have to? Are we going to argue about that again? It's why I'm here."

She scuffed at the road with her sandals. "It's cruel to crash into the man's life after all these years."

"This fella whose privacy you're so concerned about— if the police believed your story, they'd be searching for him. First to size him up as a suspect, Then to warn him."

"Warn him what?"

"Say your son is the killer, he might go after his father next."

"He'd never find him."

"He found you. Don't you think the man deserves fair warning?"

She didn't answer.

"Look, Elaine, there's another reason I need to know. There's a rumor going around. Some people say Andrew is the father."

She whirled on me. "Who said that?" She grabbed my arm. "That's despicable. Tell me who said it."

"More than one person." In fact, no one had said it. But the possibility had occurred to me as I recalled Andrew's smothering attention, his possessive pawing at his daughter.

"Is this the sort of garbage you'll write?"

"Not if it's untrue. It's one rumor you can kill right away. Tell me the father's name."

She kicked at a shell; it skipped like a flat rock across

a pond. "Don't tell him I told you. Let him think you learned some other way. Promise me that, Tom."

"You have my word."

"Peter Babcock."

"Where's he live?"

"I don't have any idea. I haven't been in touch with him since I told him I was pregnant."

"Where was he then?"

"In school. Yale."

"Where was he from?"

"His family had a place in Lakeville, Connecticut."

"Do you know what he became? His profession?"

"He wanted to be a lawyer. He was applying to law schools."

We had entered an abandoned apple orchard overgrown with pines and oak saplings. Deer pranced from tree to tree, nibbling at low-hanging branches, heedless of us.

"You won't believe me," she said, "but I didn't know Peter very well. It's not another memory lapse. We didn't have much of a relationship. I met him at a party. We smoked a little dope—take notes, Tom. Aren't these the racy, down-and-dirty touches your readers crave?—then we did it. Not a lot of foreplay, not a lot of afterglow. This was the sixties. You remember what that was like."

"You and I may have a different take on that decade."

"Don't act like such a prude. You never did before. I was thinking of that today. Is there anyplace in the house where we didn't have sex?"

"You mean, anyplace I didn't retaliate?"

"All right, I was letting a bit of retaliation out of my system too. Remember the hammock? Remember the hood of Daddy's car?"

"I'm too old and creaky to be reminded of my youthful indiscretions. I'd rather hear about your experiences as a flower child."

"Hate to disappoint you, but I was sort of square. I didn't sleep around that much in college. Not compared to some people, not compared to my time with you. I saw

Peter a few more times. Fucked him a few more times, if that's the kind of frankness your fans prefer. As for clinical measurements, anatomical stuff, I don't remember anything special. If I hadn't gotten pregnant, I probably wouldn't remember him at all.''

"You weren't on the pill?"

"No. There must have been a dozen American coeds that year who weren't.''

"When you told Babcock you were pregnant, what did he do?"

"His first question, come to think of it, was, 'How can you be sure it's mine?' Then he asked if I wanted to get married. He didn't exactly propose. It was more of an exploratory conversation.'' Her voice dripped sarcasm. "He offered to arrange and pay for an abortion, but I didn't want that any more than I wanted to marry him.''

"Why not?"

"I couldn't believe he'd get anybody who wasn't a butcher. When Daddy found out, he said he knew a doctor in Baltimore, but I couldn't go through with it.'' She shrugged. "Now it seems normal, the practical thing. Then it was grubby, criminal.''

We walked in silence, advancing from sunlight into a copse of trees, then back to sunlight. It was after six o'clock and heat still radiated from the road.

"There's something I've always been puzzled about,'' I said. "After you left the agency, I was called in by a woman.''

"Do you remember her name?"

"No," I lied.

"Too bad.''

"She asked me to sign a document stating that I wasn't the father and had no claim on the baby or on your family. What was that about?''

"I don't have a clue. Did you sign it?''

"No. But think it over. Did you ever see my name on any papers?''

"What kind of papers?''

''At the agency.''

''I told everyone, Tom, I stressed that you didn't get me pregnant. As for your name being on something, I don't see how that's possible unless one of the counselors kept notes on our sessions.''

''You talked about me with people at the agency?''

''Obviously. They saw you. They asked who you were.''

''Did they keep notes?''

''Not that I noticed.''

As we stepped off the crushed shells onto the pebble driveway of the Yost house, the sound of our crunching feet changed timbre, turned hushed. I stopped next to Big Tom's Toronado, an anachronistic hunk of metal set squarely amid the sculptured, futuristic shapes of the foreign cars.

''You're leaving at a bad time.'' Elaine removed the rubber band from her ponytail, letting her hair down. ''You'll hit rush hour. Why not stay and have a drink?''

Again, as with the invitation to swim, I was tempted. ''I've got to be somewhere. Thanks anyhow.'' Then after a moment, ''You were right about one thing. I did think I was white trash. On a bad day I guess I still do. But I didn't know it stuck out like such a sore thumb, and I sure never meant for it to jab you in the eye.''

''Thanks.'' She touched me lightly on the cheek, then walked toward the house where there was no one except her security guard.

6

Modifying your picture of the past is like renovating a skyscraper. Any revision on the lower floors requires long thought and close study. Once you fiddle with the foundation, moving the basic building blocks around, you risk bringing a pile of rubble down on your head.

As I drove off Syms Island, my mouth was dry and gritty with the taste of crumbling mortar. The familiar edifice hadn't collapsed, but it was teetering dangerously. I had always prided myself on casting an implacably cool eye on my own and everybody else's actions. Now Elaine's version of events challenged me to take a closer look at myself, to consider whether I had pushed her, had punished her, into leaving. Half-fearful, half-furious that I didn't deserve her and was bound to lose her anyway, had I behaved in a fashion that made the loss inevitable? And if I had punished her when I loved her, was I doing the same now by refusing to believe her?

Elaine had been on target about the rush-hour traffic. Soon fed up with inhaling exhaust fumes on Ritchie Highway, I set off over backcountry roads, searching for a shortcut. But absorbed in thought and beset by questions, I wound up wandering along unmarked stretches of heat-buckled blacktop. For miles I was unaware of other cars. Then suddenly there was one behind me, riding my bumper. At a curve, it pulled out to pass. I moved over to let it by, but I didn't have much room and the car kept pressing for more. By the time I decided it was trying to run me off the road, there was only an instant to glance left for a glimpse of a slim face surrounded by a wind-whipped swirl of blond hair.

The Toronado rumbled off the asphalt and onto the shoulder, rattling through billows of airborne gravel. Weeds and brambles raked the paint. The horn seemed to be blowing; it was me screaming. I let up on the brake and steered into the slide. That straightened me out and brought me to a stop at the lip of a concrete drainage ditch.

The motor conked off, and I sat there in the abrupt silence, sunk deep in the hollow where my feelings should have been. The engine block began to tick as it cooled, and I thought, Elaine. She tried to cut me off, kill me. Yet even as I thought this, I knew it wasn't true. The blond hadn't really resembled her, hadn't been at the wheel of one of the Yost-family dream machines, and I wasn't convinced it had been a murderer. More likely a drunk driver or somebody like me, too preoccupied to watch where he was going.

Clammy in the palms, parched in the throat, I drove on until I spotted a tavern. A low-slung log cabin with a cedar-shingled roof and a stone chimney, it was the kind of place my parents came when Buck and I were boys—a roadhouse with a rippled mirror behind the bar, a dance floor not much bigger than a tabletop, and a chubby waitress who called all customers, regardless of age or sex, "hon."

I drank a beer at the bar, then moved to a booth for dinner. To insure that the experience was a total 1950s retro, I ordered steak, baked potato, sour cream, and onion rings—a meal any dietician or Italian housewife would dismiss as swill. But it tasted terrific, as did four more full-octane bottles of National Bohemian.

The tavern had a jukebox that played old songs, not the Golden Oldies of my teens, but tunes I had heard Mom hum and had watched her dance to with Big Tom, who, despite his bulk and his preference for country and western, was astonishingly nimble on his feet. "Goodnight Irene," "Nature Boy," "Tennessee Waltz," "Old Cape Cod"—the schamltzy music and the alcohol left me susceptible to reveries I didn't like to indulge. There had always been a flip side to those family evenings—my father falling over the edge from amiable drunkenness into misdirected rage, moments when the waltzing wasn't so easy and he struck out at Mom, Buck, or me.

I sat there sipping a sixth National Boh, surmising what my life might have been like had things worked out differently. What if, for instance, Elaine had married me and we had raised her son as our own? Could we have made it? Or would we be miserable, as she maintained? And if we had managed to stay together, would Andrew Yost and Big Tom be alive today? Fumbling with this question as awkwardly as I wielded the silverware with my slow fingers, I asked another: If I was to blame for our breakup, was I partly to blame for the murders?

I didn't want to believe that. I ordered more beer and fed the jukebox a few quarters and tried again to imagine a life with Elaine. But I couldn't do it. I guess that's why I no longer wrote short stories and poems. I could recall what had happened. With effort I could recapture the rough contours of past experience. What I knew, I never forgot. But "what might have been" remained lost in realms of speculation beyond my scope. In the end, I was reduced to dealing with facts. The difficulty in this case was figuring out what they were.

The waitress poured me refills of coffee until I was sufficiently clearheaded to hit the road. Following her directions I reached Hyattsville just as the reggae and rap music clicked on like an electrical appliance controlled by a timer. Once inside the house, I noticed a lighted lamp in the TV room. I was positive I hadn't left it on. The wisest move would have been to back out the door and call the cops. But I rushed forward—and found Luke dead to the world on the couch. The television set, switched on without sound, cast a purple glow over an empty whiskey bottle and his metal crutches on the floor. Lying on his back, sleeping with his mouth open, he had his hands curled on his concave chest, his pantleg dangling like a wind sock in dead air.

I hated to wake him. If I knew he would sleep until morning, I'd have let him be. But I didn't want him waking in the night, stumbling around the house. I had had enough heart-stopping surprises for one day.

When I snapped off the TV, Luke lifted his head. "Yo, man!" He pitched to a sitting position; his foot hit the floor with a thud.

"It's me, Tommy."

He knuckled his eye sockets, then brushed at his mustache and the tuft of hair beneath his lower lip. "Thought you and me had a date to watch the Skins."

"I got lost down in Anne Arundel County. Then I stopped to eat. What about you? You had dinner?" I lowered myself into Big Tom's lumpy, Leatherette-upholstered BarcaLounger.

"Ain't hungry." He picked up his crutches, but stayed put on the couch. "Skins won themselves an exhibition. Doug Williams done a number—couple numbers—on the Steelers. 'Course the Steelers ain't what they was, but I see us in another Super Bowl come January." He sized me up with heavy-lidded eyes. "You ever play ball?"

"Not much. Football was Buck's game. Basketball was mine."

"What position?"

"Forward. Sometimes center."

Luke laughed soundlessly, his skinny shoulders twitching. "You shitting me? Okay, you're tall, but a white boy like you, even one-legged, on crutches, I'd outrebound you."

"You think so? Where'd you play?"

"Spingarn High School. Home of Elgin Baylor and Dave Bing."

"We played you every year," I said.

"Yeah, well, you was on some honky team around here, I bet we took you turkeys apart and left the bones on the floor. Ain't that some shit though? Probably we played against each other." Luke was deeply pleased by the idea, so pleased he didn't care to ruin it by asking where I went to school or when I graduated. "You still go out there, toss up a few?"

"No. My boys play soccer. That's the big sport in Italy."

"Too bad. Me, I dream about hoops almost every night, which I'm not surprise, in the aspect of I played so much since I was little. After high school, I sign up in the service, thinking to be on some Army team. My mama and me, we argue back and forth, she screaming they going to send you to Nam. Me saying, No, I'll be playing ball. But sure as hell, she's right."

I didn't know what to say. "Whoever listened to his mother when he should have?"

"Ain't that the fucking truth?" He dabbed at his bebop tuft. "These dreams of mine, I'm the Elevator Man, King Kangaroo, and Mr. Windex all mixed together. I grab the ball off the glass, go coast to coast and slam it down like Doctor J. Pretty soon I'm not running the court anymore. I'm flying. Never touch wood. Airborne all the way. I make Michael Jordan look like he's got white man's disease." This time when he laughed, there was a leathery honking from his lungs. "I was you, I'd be out there playing, maybe coaching."

"I'm sorry you're not."

He gave a loose-limbed shrug. "At least I didn't leave my nuts over there is my way of looking at it. Plenty dudes did, you know."

I had half a mind to crack open another bottle, pour Luke a drink and one for myself. But bag of bones that he was, he needed food, not whiskey. "Why don't you let me fix you a plate of bacon and eggs?"

"Another way of seeing it"—he wasn't listening to me. He was moving his fingers rhythmically up and down one crutch as though he were playing a reed instrument—"It was almost worth losing my leg to get a chance to watch Doug Williams quarterback the Skins last year."

Luke saw the dubious expression on my face. "You think in a million years they'd ever let a nigger call the plays in the Super Bowl unless a whole mess of us died over there? No way! You remember what it used to be like in this town? You remember the all-white, uptight, no-talent, drag-ass slow, fumble-fingered Mr. George Preston Marshall Redskins?"

I laughed and assured him that I did.

"Eddie Lebaron at quarterback. A fucking midget," he exclaimed. "I ain't saying he was bad, but what kinda chance you got with a dwarf throwing passes? It wasn't till—what?—the early sixties they traded for Bobby Mitchell. They still lost, but they were showing some style."

"Sure you won't have something to eat?"

"You starting to sound like the nurse at the VA office, which her name escapes me, but she's on my ass all the time about am I eating right, am I sleeping good, am I making friends."

"What do you tell her?"

"Doing fine, I say. Doing fabulous. I ever find a woman, one doesn't want to dance and run around, I'd be a happy man. But she, this nurse, she wants to know why I don't appreciate the plastic leg they give me. I go, I appreciate it. I just don't want to wear it."

"Why not?"

"Hurts my stump. And I don't like how it sounds. Know what I'm saying? I walk around my house and it sounds like I got a bucket on my foot. I rather stick with the crutches. You hit your stride on these mothers, you can motor." He hauled himself upright, as if for a demonstration. But then he paused.

"Ain't none of my business," he said, "but I'm wondering do you got a problem?"

"Me? Why do you ask?"

"In other words of saying it, I'm worried about you.

That's why I'm over here tonight—get you to kick back and watch a ball game.''

"I'm fine.''

"That's what I tell the nurse lady when she asks am I all right in the head to go on living alone one-legged. But you ain't okay, Tommy. Otherwise why you hanging on, not flying back home where you live at?''

"Buck put you up to this?''

"Ain't nothing to do with Buck. I got eyes, which I guess I should keep my mouth shut. But after what I seen your daddy go through, I hate to watch it again.''

"You're trying to get rid of me. Don't you like having a neighbor?''

"It's nice with you next door. It's just you oughta chill out a little. Even a cop, even the chief, takes a day off every now and again.''

"Don't worry about me.''

"Your daddy warned me. Said you're one stubborn motherfucker.''

"That's Buck, not me.''

"No, he said Buck was like his mama. Gets mad, blows up, but he bends. You and your daddy, you tough it out till you brook.''

"Is that what happened when Big Tom started getting lost? He snapped?''

Luke grinned. "I promised not to tell.''

"I already know about it. He used to call me and ask where he was.''

"No, Tommy, the promise was I wouldn't tell you he was teasing. He wanted to trick you into hauling your ass back to America. He wanted to see his grandkids.''

"Why didn't he say so?''

"Hey, it's your father we're talking about. He could be bleeding in the street and he ain't asking no favors of nobody.''

"Let me get this straight. He wasn't lost any of those times?''

"Not him. He was right here in the house.''

"And he thought what? I'd come home to check on him?"

"Something like that. You better get on to bed," he said as though I had suggested we party. "I'll let myself out and lock up."

"Thanks, Luke." I squeezed his emaciated arm as he went by. Hard as it was to believe he had ever been an athlete, I was glad he could relive past glories in his dreams, gliding coast to coast, weightless as a paper airplane.

BOOK THREE

1

According to those in the full-time business of tracing bail jumpers, bigamists, and alimony evaders, it's difficult to disappear in this country unless you're willing to sink below the poverty line and live an off-the-books, cash-only existence. From the little Elaine had told me, Peter Babcock didn't fit that category.

Next morning I dropped in at the legal offices across from the County Service Building and asked a receptionist for a look at *Martindale-Hubble*, the Who's Who or Who's Anybody of American lawyers. Peter Babcock wasn't listed.

The rest of the morning I spent on the telephone. Although readers imagined otherwise, many of my working hours passed in this unglamorous sedentary fashion. When I wasn't at a word processor, I had a phone glued to my ear or I was in the Hall of Records combing through files. In my experience, the Department of Motor Vehicles could be a better source of information than an interview with an eyewitness or an arresting officer.

Naturally, the reality of my research, like the drone labor of most detectives, held little excitement for publishers or moviemakers. They insisted on quirky, violent characters, breath-catching chases and shoot-outs, shattering discoveries of evidence at the last instant. But the truth is that murders are more often solved at typewriters, computer terminals, and over the telephone.

Contacting directory assistance in Lakeville, Connecticut, I learned that the Babcock family still had a home

there, but the number was unlisted. Rather than catch a
flight to Hartford and race off to the western corner of the
state only to discover that son Peter resided in Florida, I
made a few more calls.

The registrar's office at Yale confirmed that Babcock
graduated in '67, and although it was against university
policy to reveal more without permission, a helpful gentleman explained that I might get the info I needed from
the alumni magazine. The magazine, while refusing to
give Babcock's address or phone number, told me the name
and number of the class secretary, the fellow who drafts
an annual report chronicling the adventures of Yalies
who've been promoted to regional vice president or are
recovering from surgery.

I wound up talking long distance to Wickie Karsh, an
agent at International Famous in Los Angeles, and as his
voice echoed against the acoustical cologne of Muzak, I
realized we were on a speaker phone and he was mean-
dering around his office, maybe putting a golf ball on his
carpet.

"Do I know you?" Wickie asked. "Your name, it's
familiar. What spook were you in?"

He lost me there, and as usual when I'm caught off base,
I answered a question that hadn't been asked. "I live in
Europe. Just got back and wanted to look up Peter Bab-
cock."

"I don't recall you from our class. Did you make it to
the twentieth reunion?"

"A different class," I said. "I met Peter through mu-
tual friends. I have an urgent message from somebody
very close to him."

"Sorry to be the one to break it to you, but Peter's
dead."

"Jesus!" I didn't have to fake my shock and distress.
"How'd it happen?" I half-expected to hear that Babcock
had been gunned down.

"Heart attack," Karsh said.

"When?"

"April."

"You're sure about the cause of death?"

"Absolutely. It was in the alumni magazine. Aren't you getting your copy? Better gimme an address."

I took a blind stab. "What about his wife, his kids?"

"What I hear, they're holding up okay. It wasn't like he hadn't been warned to slow down. But you know Pete."

"I know he did his share of hell-raising," I said, embroidering on what Elaine had told me. "Great guy, but even as an undergrad he was a heavy drinker and he smoked a lot of weed."

"That's Pete. Lately, of course, he cut out the smoking and went heavier on the booze."

"You kept up with him over the years?"

"Best I could." It sounded as if Karsh had stopped roaming and was standing next to the phone. "My job, I travel east two, three times a year."

"His family—the wife and kids—they in Lakeville?"

"That's his parents' place. Pete and Moira lived in New Jersey. Way to hell and gone to Peapack."

"I feel terrible for not keeping in touch. Do you have an address, a phone number? I'd like to send Moira some flowers."

Karsh gave what I asked for, then said, "You know, getting back to that, your name is definitely familiar. Don't you write? I put together a package and I think you were one of the elements."

"Damn shame about Pete. Makes you wonder about other people you partied with in college. Are you in contact with his friends?"

"Some. As class secretary, I get lots of letters. I was always warning Pete to stop and sniff the roses. But anytime he stopped to sniff, it was some quiff."

He waited for the laugh track to kick in. I obliged him with a chuckle. "We used to double-date," I said. "His junior year he was running around with a girl named Elaine Yost. Went to Wellesley, came from Maryland. Rich. Her father was a former congressman. Remember her?"

"Sounds like I should. Matter of fact, I wouldn't mind meeting her now. I'm sort of between wives."

"Pete never mentioned her?"

"Keep in mind who we're talking about. Line up all the chicks he drilled, you'd have one long tube of spare tires from here to Las Vegas."

"But Elaine Yost, she's not someone you remember him with?"

"Can't say I do. Why?"

"Good to talk to you."

"Hey, before you hang up, what about a pledge?"

"Sorry. Like I said, different class."

Mrs. Babcock, when I called her, was considerably less gregarious than Wickie Karsh. After offering sympathy, I asked if she and Pete ever heard from Elaine Yost, and the lady barked, "I have no interest in anybody my husband hung around with in college. I don't know what you and this woman are after, but he's dead and I don't have to put up with this kind of crap any longer."

I sat at the kitchen table, gnawing at the subject like a rat nibbling a stale crust of bread. Unless I got lucky, there was no chance I'd learn whether Elaine and Babcock had actually been lovers, and even less chance I'd find proof that he was the father. Now that he wasn't a suspect or potential victim on his son's hit list, I'd never convince Elaine to tell me more about him.

It occurred to me that Babcock's illegitimate son, if he had one, might have been anxious to find his father for some of the same reasons I had—curiosity, an urge to confront him and force him to talk, a basic compulsion to fill in the blank opening page of one's life.

I felt a sense of kinship with Elaine's son. If he had searched for his father, painstakingly gleaning clues, drawing closer and closer, determined to get the truth . . . well, then discovering Babcock was dead and that that door was forever shut might have been what set him in motion toward Syms Island, thinking it was too late for talk. It was time to take it out on somebody.

When I telephoned with the news of Babcock's heart attack, Elaine wailed, "That's horrible. He was our age."

"You've been taking better care of yourself than Pete."

"How did you find out?"

"Through an old friend of yours." I waited for her to supply a name, any name. When she didn't, I said, "Wickie Karsh."

"Who's he?"

"Yale, class of '67."

"I don't know him."

"He's a Hollywood agent. Kept in contact with Babcock ever since college. He didn't remember you either."

"Since I've never met him, that's not surprising."

"Maybe I'll talk to Pete's parents. Think they'll remember you?"

"I never met them either. He might have mentioned me. But then, how much did you tell your parents about the girls you slept with?"

"It's tough for me to feature Andrew Yost's daughter being a casual fling—somebody a fellow never discussed with his friends or family."

Elaine didn't take me up on that. "The funny thing is, much as I hated the idea of you barging in on Peter, I feel let down. I feel he got off easy."

"You think being dead is getting off easy?"

"I know it sounds awful. But he never had to face the past. What'll you do now?"

"I'll fly down to Austin and see whether I have better luck than the Anne Arundel County Police Department."

"I'm sure you will," she said with far greater confidence than I felt. "Maybe I should come with you. That might trigger my memory. What do you think?"

I thought it was wise not to field the question. I told her we'd talk later.

Still at the kitchen table, I considered what she suggested. The concept had size and shape, as Wickie Karsh might have said. In Hollywood terms, it was fascinating casting, a recipe for fireworks. But even if traveling to Texas with Elaine might make a certain sense, I'd hate to have to explain it to Marisa.

Buck banged at the back door, and when I let him in, he growled, "This weather, screw it. I'm ready to slap on the snow tires and fight slush for six months. On top of everything, the Isuzu's air conditioner is on the fritz."

At the sink he doused his face and neck, then drank from his cupped palms. Straightening up, he shed water like a spaniel. "I tried to call, but the phone's been busy."

"What's the emergency?"

"No emergency. Just a run-of-the-mill storm warning. The cops are keeping Elaine Farinholt under close surveillance. This morning Gaillard buttonholes me in the hall, lays on this word-to-the-wise number. Says you're getting too chummy with the defense side of the situation."

"There's no defense side. Nobody's been indicted."

"Tommy, let's not fall out over definitions." He tore off a paper towel and blotted his beard. "The nature of cops, they're paranoid. They spotted you on the beach with Elaine and went haywire."

"I was interviewing her. I told Gaillard I intended to meet with her on a regular basis."

"It's how you were interviewing her that excites them. Gaillard claims, I'm quoting, 'The two of them looked like models in a mouthwash ad.' "

"Where were they? In a boat, spying on us through a telescope?"

"Wouldn't put it past them. They're bird-dogging her real tight. You might want to steer clear for a while."

"Your advice or theirs?"

"Weigh the thing in your own mind. You're getting good stuff, keep going back for more."

"I'm not sure what I'm getting. I don't see her as a killer, but I have a hunch she's lying."

"Maybe she's covering for an accomplice. Why lie, why stonewall the cops and risk an indictment unless you're protecting the perp or yourself?"

"Could be she's protecting something more important to her." I fixed a cup of instant—my third of the day, all together equal in strength to a single espresso. Buck refused coffee and fetched a beer from the refrigerator.

"You're making this too complicated," he said. "You been around enough killers to know when you're talking to one. I defend them every day. I never pin them down and ask, 'Did you grease the guy?' But I goddamn well *know*. You feel it. Do something like that, smoke your kid and your old man, you gotta be one sick bitch. Does that describe Elaine?"

"No. But without insulting your clientele, it's safe to say she's a lot smarter and has more acting ability."

Buck swigged his beer. "Bumped into your buddy Whiting Pierce. In ten years we haven't exchanged twenty words. Now it's like I'm his long-lost friend from New Haven."

"Pierce went to Yale?"

"Yeah, as he never tires of reminding us guys who had the privilege of matriculating—or is it micturating?—at Agnew U."

It fit so neatly I hesitated. Was it that obvious—Elaine leafing through Pierce's alumni magazine to the obituary page, feeding me Peter Babcock's name, knowing I'd hit a brick wall?

"I need a fill on Pierce's relationship with Elaine," I said. "There must be rumors. Is he more than her lawyer?"

"I'll ask around."

"Keep it, you know, discreet."

"That's me, Mr. Discretion." Gripping the neck of the bottle between his index and ring fingers, he tilted it to his lips and chugged down the beer.

"I had another heart-to-heart last night with Luke about Big Tom."

"We should've had him on the payroll years ago," Buck said. "Family therapist. What'd he tell you now? Big Tom was about to sign on with the Peace Corps in Africa?"

"Those late-night calls, the ones where he'd ask me how to get back home—seems he wasn't lost. He thought I was. He was hoping to coax me back by subliminal suggestion, I guess."

"Doesn't surprise me. It bugged Big Tom, your living abroad. He didn't believe anybody could be completely happy except in the USA."

"I don't recall him ever being 'completely happy.' And according to Luke, he thought I was like him. A mean, stubborn motherfucker."

"You are." He smiled to soften what he said. "You may not be the ass-kicker he was, but you're hardheaded and you want to have things your own way. Trouble is, like with him, it isn't easy to tell what you're after. Both of you are shelled-in people. Me, I'm more like Mom—out-front, in your face."

"I see you've had your sessions with Luke too."

"Don't need them. I know who I am. Sometimes I don't like it, but I can live with it. I cut myself a lot of slack. You oughta cut yourself more."

He chucked his bottle into the trash can. "This is hard work, this sitting around like a fat-ass Buddha sharing my wisdom."

"I was thinking of going over to East Pines," I said, "making a run on Doreen Perry and her brother. Like to come?"

"Sure. Long as you drive the Toronado. Pull up in an Isuzu with a busted air conditioner, they'll take us for Mormon missionaries or encyclopedia salesmen."

Although it was cradled in the rumbling intersection of Riverdale Road and the Washington–Baltimore Parkway, East Pines had the forlorn look of some blighted holler in rural West Virginia. Roads were potholed, and weeds sprouted from cracked sidewalks. In some yards the grass grew waist high and the shrubbery had gone wild. In others the ground had been scraped bald as it would be in a jungle village where the natives feared snakes. Houses no better than shacks were surrounded by wrecked cars, rusty engines, blown-out tires, and inner tubes. Car seats, the upholstery stinking of mold, decomposed on front porches.

The scattered trees that gave the development its bucolic name looked scabby with decay; the people hunkered in the shade beneath them appeared to have contracted wood blight. Its primary symptom seemed to be terminal torpor. The only folks moving were a few motorheads tinkering with cars and one old man in Bermuda shorts pushing a grocery cart with three kids in the basket.

Recently with Elaine I had had a sense that time past had overtaken the present and I had reverted to late adolescence. Now I reentered another compartment of my childhood. Until I was ten, we had lived here, and Big Tom regarded our getaway from East Pines as one of the major triumphs of his life. He hated it whenever Mom joked that we'd have to move back unless business got better.

"What's the name of that writer," Buck said, "the French cat that ate the cookie and had his whole life flash in front of him?"

"You've fooled everybody all along. You're not a lawyer. You're a grad student in comp lit."

"Proust. Marcel Proust." He answered his own question, pronouncing the name Prowst—on purpose, I suspected. "It's like I bit into a Twinkie and time-warped back to when you and I were kids."

The style in dress and hairdos hadn't changed. The men favored grimy blue jeans, undershirts—no T-shirts with smart-aleck quotes—and hair slicked back in ducktails. The women wore pedal pushers and plastic curlers or spray-hardened beehives.

The asbestos siding on the Perry house, once white, was

now grayish-green with mildew, and shingles had fallen off, showing a checkerboard pattern of tar paper. Under the weight of a derelict refrigerator, the front porch sagged and the steps had rotted away and been replaced by three cinder blocks. At the curb sat a Chevy Impala, its hood raised and a human body stuffed into its maw as if into a shark's gullet.

I parked near the Impala, and as we started for the house, a fellow who looked as if his hair had been snarled in the fan belt reared up out of the Chevy. His eyes were the dazed whirlpools you see on speedfreaks; his chest appeared to be welded out of wire coat hangers and doorknobs. A rawboned, rope-muscled country boy, he was chewing gum or tobacco or his own sunken cheeks. There was a beeper clipped to the waistband of his jeans, and he had a lug wrench in his hand. "Y'all looking for somebody?"

"Could be. Who are you?" Buck took a tone that struck me as wrong.

"We're here to see Doreen Perry." I moved forward, friendly, nonconfrontational. "You must be Darryl."

"Yeah, and you and your buddy must be pigs. You got a warrant?"

"We're not cops." Buck fell in beside me.

Darryl waggled the lug wrench. "You ain't, then clear the hell outta here. I'm busy."

"I'd like to interview your sister," I said.

"You don't listen good, do you? You got wax in your ears? What you better do, you better get back in your car and go."

"Or what?" Buck demanded. "You threatening us with that wrench?"

"I'm not threatening nothing." His mouth twitched as he spoke. He jabbed at it with his free hand and left his upper lip mustached with motor oil. "Any trouble, it's you bringing it on yourselves."

"Oh, I know your type," Buck said in a soft, saccharine voice calculated to rankle rather than soothe. "Kind of guy, any problem you cause, it's never your fault. It's always the other fella.''

His freaky eyes flicked back and forth between us as he debated which one to hit first. Then Doreen stepped out onto the porch. She looked to be seven or eight months pregnant and was carrying the baby high, her swollen breasts resting atop her rounded stomach. She had on tight black shorts and a pink maternity blouse, and her dark hair hung down over one shoulder. "What is it?" she called.

"Couple assholes from the newspapers.''

"No,'' I said, "I'm not with a newspaper. I'm—'' As I pushed past Darryl, a fork of pain flashed up my left arm. He had cracked my knuckles with the lug wrench.

When I heard a second *thwack!* of metal against meat, I assumed he had hit Buck too. But Darryl was the one screaming. The wrench sailed out of his hand, spinning end over end, knocking another shingle off the house. Buck had him bent back into the Chevy and was banging his head against the air filter.

"Stop!'' I shouted, but I couldn't have dragged Buck off one-handed if Doreen hadn't bustled down from the porch and helped me.

"Fucker's crazy.'' Darryl ran his greasy hands through his greasier hair.

"All you have to do is make up your mind,'' Buck roared, "you rather eat that wrench or let us talk to your sister?''

"No! We're here to *request* an interview, not give him the rubber-hose treatment.''

Doreen walked Darryl around to the opposite side of the Impala and propped him against a fender. "Look, if all this is over an interview''—she sashayed back to us—"I'm sorry, but my lawyer won't allow it.''

She was one of those radiant wild cards that crops up in the grubbiest genetic decks. She had essentially the same features as her brother, but where his deep-socketed eyes and slack mouth left him looking sullen and submoronic, Doreen was sultry and even eight months pregnant, very sexy. Her lips had a bee-stung pout, a look now so popular women were paying plastic surgeons to inject them with collagen, and her eyes hinted at secret knowledge or a smutty joke she might share if you pressed the right button.

She moved so close to me I could feel her body heat. She touched my arm as she talked. "Hope you're not hurt bad. Darryl's only doing what Curtis Koontz told him to—saving me from my big mouth. The best thing for both parties," she said, "you don't press charges and we don't."

"What would you charge us with?" Buck asked. "Denting his wrench?"

"You hurt his head."

"That boy's head's been hurt from day one. His head needs fixing."

Doreen raised a hand to her hair and stroked it with her fingers the way a child might rub a scrap of silk to calm down at nap time. "Please don't talk nasty about his head," she whispered. "Darryl hates that worse than anything—talk of there's something wrong with his head."

"All I want is to ask a few questions," I said. The pain from my hand seemed to settle into a sick pool in the pit of my stomach.

"Mr. Koontz gives me the go-ahead, I'll be glad to. Otherwise, well, he's a strange ranger, but he's the boss."

"I'll speak to Koontz later. But since I'm going to be writing a book about the case, we might as well get acquainted. This is my brother, Buck. He's a lawyer, a friend of Mr. Koontz." I was careful not to look at Buck when I coupled him with Koontz.

She said, "You don't look like brothers."

"He bleaches his hair," Buck told her.

"I doubt that. It's just, you know, you got different builds."

"Which one do you like better?"

"Can we go inside?" I said.

"The place is a mess, and Mr. Koontz'll be mad."

This time I touched her arm, gripping it gently at the elbow. "We don't have to tell him." When I felt resistance, I added, "I'll forget what Darryl did—what do you call it, Buck? Assault and battery?—if you'll chat for a few minutes."

Doreen and I climbed the cinder blocks to the porch, which rocked under our feet like a raft in rough water. When Buck stepped on it, nails screeched in the joists.

The living room was furnished with lawn chairs and a gray sofa that looked as if it had been swiped from a government office. There were no drapes or blinds on the windows and nothing except streaked yellow paint on the walls. Somewhere in the house a drain had backed up, and every random breeze carried a smell of bilge.

"I told you," Doreen said. "A mess. We'll be moving soon."

"Where are you going?" I sat on an aluminum and plastic chaise lounge. Buck stayed near the door, standing guard in case Darryl decided to take another crack at us.

"California." Doreen stretched out on the sofa. "I mean to raise my baby far away from the hassles me and my brother had. Before I was always like, 'Where's the party?' Now I got responsibilities is how I feel."

Despite the bargain-basement furniture, the Perrys had top-of-the-line electrical appliances—a color TV, a VCR, a compact disc player, stereo speakers the size of foot lockers—all arranged on the packing crates they had arrived in.

"How'd you meet Clay?" I asked, balancing my hand in my lap, searching for a position that would deaden the pain.

Doreen elevated her legs on the armrest at the far end of the sofa. "The doctor told me to do this. There's days my ankles are like sausages. It was Darryl introduced Clay and me, and it took off from there." She shot out her hand in a steep trajectory, showing how their rocket-burst romance had accelerated.

"How'd he know Darryl?"

"Cars. Clay had all kind of cars, but didn't know beans about them. That's where Darryl came in. He's a genius with tools."

Buck laughed and shoehorned himself into a lawn chair that hugged his bottom like a vise. "Yeah, he's hell with a wrench all right."

Doreen laughed too.

"What kind of guy was Clay?" I asked.

"Real sweet." She was rubbing her hair again, and her eyes had a dreamy look. "He was rich, but he wasn't stuck up one bit. Fit right in with my friends. Said he felt more at home here than with his family. Said having a big house and a buncha cars isn't everything."

"You believe that?" Buck asked.

"I'm fixing to find out once my money comes through. I know what it's like not to have a pot to pee in or a window to throw it out of. Now we'll see how the other side lives."

"Did you ever meet his mother and grandfather?" I asked.

"Just to say hi. They didn't like me."

"That's too bad."

She pursed her lips and proudly lifted her chin. "We had our life. Most times we mellowed out here listening to music or partying with friends."

"Is that where you were when he and his grandfather were killed? With friends?"

She let her hand fall from her hair. "I told the police. Plenty people saw me that night. I was never anywhere near Syms Island. That's all I have to say about that, okay?"

"Have any idea who might have committed the murders?"

"Seems like it must have been his mother. Going by what I've seen on TV and what people say."

"What do they say?"

"Just, you know, she wanted the money and she wanted

me and Clay and the baby out of her life. And she was totally stressed because of those letters.''

''The letters had to have upset Clay too.''

''You wouldn't believe how upset. What he told me, he always knew there was something missing in his life. Then *whammo!* He learns what it is. He's got a brother that his mother's hiding and won't talk to him about. Her and his grandfather, they'd rather bury it all under the rug. Clay was like, Who is this guy? Where is he? Why did you give him away? He wanted to meet him and send him money. But his mother was like, No way José. We're not answering the blackmailing bastard.''

''And that caused trouble between Clay and his mother?''

''Absolutely, because, you see, all his life he'd been drifting around searching for something to plug into. Finally, he finds me and he's feeling centered, 'specially with the baby on the way. Then he discovers there's another chunk of his life floating out there and he can't understand it.''

''There's no one else you suspect?'' Buck broke in, less patient with Doreen's maundering. ''Did he have any enemies?''

''Not a one in the world.''

''What about his old girlfriend, the one he landed in the hospital?''

''If it's the same person we're talking about,'' she said, ''I met her at a roller rink. Is she the one—red hair, flat chested, bad complexion?''

''Could be,'' Buck said.

''The night I saw her, she's wearing, it looks like leather, but you get real close, it's rubber. A miniskirt and tube top out of rubber. No taste, no class, but I don't feature her as a killer.''

''He tell you why he beat her?''

''She gave him a disease. That's how he found out she was slipping around on him. He came down with clap. Can you blame him?''

"What about your relationship with Clay?" I asked.

She smiled and crooked her knees, raising her legs from the sofa. There was a ripping sound as her damp skin lifted away from the Leatherette. "You mean what was he like in bed? You better speak to Mr. Koontz. That's a subject he doesn't want me dipping into until there's been negotiations."

"Negotiations about what?"

"Money. The book rights. The movie. You like me to describe our sex life, there's gotta be a deal up front."

"I wasn't asking that. Were you two planning to get married?"

"Yeah."

"Was the baby part of the plan?"

"A big part. It wasn't easy getting pregnant. I have what they call hostile mucus. So we had to be careful to, you know, get it on when the time was right." She giggled. "Clay'd be reading a book or watching TV, and I'd take my temperature and *bingo!*—time for bed."

"What about drugs?" Buck cut in. "Or is that another subject we have to negotiate with Koontz?"

"You mean fertility drugs?"

"I mean coke."

"I don't do that anymore."

"When did you quit?"

"When we decided to have a baby."

"What about Clay?" Buck pressed her.

"What he did, you'll have to ask somebody else. It's not like he was ever so deep into it he was toxic."

"Should we ask Darryl?"

"I don't think you better. Please, don't. He'll wig out."

"I noticed his beeper," Buck said. "Does he deal? Or does he deliver for Domino's?"

"Look, this is stuff I don't want to talk about. Okay? You said we'd have a little get-acquainted visit. We've had it."

It occurred to me that she didn't know my name.

"Among Clay's friends and the people he talked about, did he ever mention Tom Heller?"

I saw no sign of recognition on her face, in her eyes. "No."

"You've never heard that name?"

"Not till now. Look, I gotta run. These days I'm tinkling all the time. Can you guys let your own selves out?"

As we came down off the creaking porch, Darryl had his head in the innards of the Impala. He didn't look up until we drove off. Naturally, he gave us the finger. My hand was still throbbing or I would have returned the favor.

"What kind of candy-ass simpleton have you turned into?" Buck demanded. "Living in Rome seems to have dulled your survival instincts. Rule number one—there's somebody holding a lug wrench, you don't take your eyes off him. Rule number two—your questioning technique reminds me of something I'd hear in a singles bar. It's fine you want to get friendly with Doreen, but what about following up on leads, asking about Darryl?"

"I'm not a cop, Buck. I can't force people to talk. I have to gentle them along. You notice how she clammed up soon as you mentioned drugs? And I don't need to ask about Darryl to know he could be the killer."

"He was stoked up, I suppose he could cap somebody," Buck said. "But he's bulletproof against a murder charge. Doesn't have the gray matter for premeditation."

"He may be smarter than he looks. Think about it. He crosses over to the island by boat, does Clay, hangs around eating pills to keep his edge, then nails Andrew."

"Motive?"

"Doreen's pregnant and—"

"And he's defending her honor? Don't make me laugh. That chick wrote the book on trash."

"She's pregnant and her kid's in line to inherit a fortune if Clay and the old man die."

Buck tilted an air-conditioning duct in his direction. The current was stiff enough to ruffle his beard. "He'd have to know the provisions of Yost's will. He'd have to under-stand *per stirpes*.''

"Clay could have told him. Or Doreen."

"You think she's in on it?"

"Why not?"

He wagged his head, not in agreement, but to get a better angle on the air jet. "The two of them together don't have the brainpower to pack sand up a rat's ass. She's Good & Plenty. Melts in your mouth, not in your hands.''

"That's M&M's."

"You catch my drift. Where do they come from, the Doreens of this world? Raised on fatback, peanut butter, and Popsicles. Never ate any fiber or bran in her life. And she grows up to look like that.''

Because I knew better than to tax my brother's patience more than I already had, I drove home, dropped him next to his Isuzu, then headed for the shopping center where Curtis Koontz had his office.

In the late fifties, this strip mall of department stores, supermarkets, and fast-food carryouts had represented the acme of suburban convenience, a refuge for middle-class white folks from the heavy traffic, high crime rate, and racial discord of downtown D.C. Now the area was a free-fire zone. Those few merchants still in business had bar-ricaded their windows with heavy-gauge wire or sheets of bulletproof Mylar, and rent-a-cops patrolled their turf like private militia. Rather than the heady scent of batter-fried all-American fare, the air was aromatic of souvlaki, hum-mus, kimchi, and burritos. A movie marquee advertised films in four languages, but the livid posters all had the same tits and pistols, car crashes and ripped brassieres.

At Koontz's office, the front window had been bricked up and the glass door—it looked to be three inches thick—was locked. I rang a bell and was buzzed in by an elabo-rately made-up lady wearing hoop earrings. She asked if I had an appointment. I told her I didn't.

"Who should I say?"

"Thomas Heller."

"Mr. Koontz knows you from where?"

I saw no reason to remind him of our one glancing encounter at the hospital. "He doesn't."

"This is regarding?"

"I spoke to Doreen Perry. She said speak to her attorney."

"One minute, please." When she raised the telephone receiver to her ear, it rang the gold hoop like a gong. "A Mr. Thomas Heller to see you."

There was an unintelligible squawking on the other end. Then the receptionist told me to have seat, it would be a minute.

I waited on a sofa not unlike the government-surplus model in the Perry house. Doreen and Koontz must have hired the same interior decorator. I assumed there was a table beside the sofa. All that was visible was a mound of magazines, a midden heap of clues about Koontz's clientele—*Car and Driver*, *Guns and Ammo*, *Biker Babes*, *Soldier of Fortune*.

When a buzzer sounded, the receptionist motioned me into the next room where Koontz was at his desk, holding out a hand for me to shake. Dressed in a pale beige suit with padded shoulders and wide lapels, he looked more like a lounge lizard than a lawyer. His bald, freckled head was peeling from a bad sunburn, and his nose was running. He sniffed and treated me to the insinuating grin that brightened his blue eyes.

"I heard the name and couldn't figure who it was." His voice was a lively reminder of what New York cabdrivers used to sound like before the Russian and Haitian émigrés arrived. "Then it hits me. I been reading books and one's by you."

I waited for him to mention Buck, Big Tom, the ICU waiting room. When he didn't, I wasn't convinced his memory had failed. Now that he represented a multimillion-dollar client, he might not care to recall how recently he'd been beating the bushes for personal-injury cases.

"What can I do for you?" he asked.

I told him I wanted to interview Doreen.

"Yeah, she called, said someone came around." Koontz drummed a pencil against the shade of his desk lamp. On the wall behind him hung a law degree form Nova University and a framed plaque with a quote from Shakespeare, *King Henry VI*, Part IV, "First thing we do, let's kill all the lawyers." "What'd your answer be," he said, "talking hypothetical, if I suggested you cut me in for a slice of the royalties on your next book? I got a hunch you'd ask, 'What's in it for me?' "

I knew where this was headed. "I don't pay for interviews."

"Nobody's talking 'pay' *per se*." He went on waggling the pencil, but was no longer striking the lamp. The pencil looked to be alive—a skinny yellow eel writhing in his fingers. "I'm not interested in building a turnstile around Doreen, running writers in one at a time, fleecing them for a few bucks apiece. We're looking for a global deal."

"I don't make deals for interviews."

"Nothing personal. But no deal, no interview. Which I regret on account of I like your work."

"With or without Doreen, I can write the book."

"Feel free. But without her, what do you got?"

"I don't regard Doreen as a major player in the case."

He broke into gravelly laughter. "Don't bullshit a bullshitter, Tom. Old man Yost had, what? Round it off, say eighty million dollars. Doreen's kid's going to inherit every dime of it. That's not a major player in your league, then you're hitting for higher numbers than I guessed."

"As I understand it, Clay's share was a minor portion of the estate. How do you figure your client's kid's going to get it all?"

He dropped the pencil and jabbed at his nose. The fidgety gesture reminded me of Darryl—reminded me of anyone with an allergy or a problem. He shifted his shoulder pads like a quarterback loosening up before a game. "You smoke?"

I told him I didn't.

"Me neither. I chew this shit." He pressed a lozenge into his hand and popped it into his mouth. "Nicotine gum. Two years I been on it. My lungs are pink as a baby's ass, but my guts . . . well, picture swallowing three packs of Camels a day. Ever hear of the slayer's statute?"

I said I had.

"Basic concept," Koontz explained it anyway, "you kill a person, you can't inherit from him. Elaine Farinholt chills her father and son, she loses her seat on the gravy train. The entire estate flows to the sole survivor, Clay's kid."

Jawing on his gum, he slung a leg over the arm of the chair. It was hard not to be swept up in his roguish high spirits. He was the real American Dream—not hardworking Horatio Alger, but the two-bit angle-player who miraculously finds himself holding all the cards. I often gravitated toward Koontz's type—not to represent me, God forbid—but to liven up my grim chronicles of mayhem and murder.

Still, I had to let a little air out of his balloon. "The cops may get around to indicting Mrs. Farinholt, but that's not a conviction."

"Doesn't matter. I'm considering action in other vicinities besides the paternity suit. Say she beats the criminal rap, we haul her ass into civil court and sue her for wrongful death on account of she murdered the baby's father, depriving it of a happy childhood, parental love, et cetera, et cetera, and depriving Doreen of Clay's dick. What they call consortium. We depend on the same evidence the prosecutor dug up, but the beauty part is we don't have to prove it beyond a reasonable doubt. In civil court it's enough that the preponderance of the evidence indicates she killed them. Any way you stack it, this lady'll be spending the rest of her life in litigation."

"Which means your life too. Off the record, aren't you really after a settlement?"

"I don't want to hear settle." He cupped his hands over his ears. "They offered a settlement ages ago."

"Before the murders?"

"Yeah, weeks before. Their attorney proposed this miserable buyout for a sum that fell a mile short of chicken feed. I told him to fuck off until he was ready to get serious."

"You have a record of that offer?"

"Right in my files."

"Did it acknowledge paternity?"

"Didn't deny it."

Although I concealed it from Koontz, I felt a fiery spurt of resentment at Pierce and Elaine for not informing me about the settlement offer. "Where'd Clay stand in the dispute?"

"Hell, he was hot to marry Doreen. Of course he didn't have any money or a job or means to support a family." He flashed his impish grin. Then his nose began itching again.

"So you counseled your client to calm her foolish heart and forgo matrimony for the time being."

"Let's leave it I laid out her choices. She could marry Clay, have him move in with her and Darryl, and they could all three live with the baby happily ever after in East Pines." He paused a beat. "Or she could let me discuss the matter with old man Yost. I was recommending a number with six zeroes behind it."

"I happen to know Yost was one hell of a negotiator."

"Never had the pleasure of talking to the gentleman. I had to deal with that tit-head, Pierce. You met him?"

"Yeah. You don't like him?" I feigned surprise, which was all it took to provoke Koontz. He was like a self-cleaning oven—flip the right switch and he radiated heat, shedding the accumulated grievances of a career of defending penny-ante crooks. In his obstreperousness he reminded me a bit of Buck—only his compass had been knocked cockeyed by nose candy and the prospect of a big score.

"Let me say about Pierce, he's carrying himself like a prince representing a queen. But you ask me, he's the queen. He couldn't find his own dong unless he had a string tied to it. I most of the time like people and people like me. Your common man, the guy in the street, even a sick pup like Darryl Perry, I get along great. But me and Pierce never came to a meeting of the minds."

"How'd you get to handle this matter for Doreen?"

"That's a short short story." He was eager to get back to bashing Pierce. "I represented Darryl. He brought the loving couple into my life."

"I hear Darryl has a record."

"Nothing to write a book about."

I showed him my swollen fist. "He's got a hell of a way of saying hello."

"The boy can be aggravating, I grant that. Sometimes you look at him and it's like you're in touch with an unmanned space vehicle. I also grant he's got a rap sheet full of arrests. But he never took a serious fall or did serious time."

"Thanks to you?"

He couldn't suppress the grin. "I plead guilty to keeping him on the streets. Some nights, I gotta be honest, I don't sleep good knowing he's out there. But hey, he referred his sister to me, and my family will be grateful to him for generations to come."

"Don't get me wrong, Curtis." I spoke in a friendly, confiding manner. "On a level field, you'd maul Pierce. But back before the murders, I don't see where you had any leverage to pry money out of the Yost family."

"Oh, we had a few things." He swiveled in the chair, so delighted by his cleverness he seemed to have forgotten I was a writer—which is what every journalist dreams of. "I knew from the old man's will he could write Clay off. There was no irrevocable trust."

"You read it?" I asked, betraying none of the importance I placed on this.

"Sure, Clay slipped me a copy. So I knew Yost controlled the purse strings. But there's always, how do you say, moral pressure. Picture this: Doreen has the baby and right away goes on welfare. I top off a few TV types that this is Andrew Yost's great-grandchild. Here he's a multimillionaire, ex-congressman, adviser to presidents, his daughter's a patroness of the arts, a socialite, and they're ready to let a relative live in a rat's nest. But then we got lucky."

"Yost and Clay were killed."

Koontz's grin faded. Suddenly he was furious. "Hey, that's not funny. What the hell do you think I am, a hyena?" For an instant I feared I'd lost him. The little lawyer was like a log you cut into, sawing smoothly toward its soft core until you hit something jagged inside him, an iron spike that spat shrapnel. But then a moment later he was back to being charmed by the cadences of his own voice. "We got lucky when Clay receives this letter saying, 'Your mother had a kid and abandoned him.' It's perfect—the timing, just perfect.

"Here the Yost family's hounding him to repeat his mother's mistake—ditch the kid, dump the person he loves. Believe me, to keep that story out of the papers, they'd have popped for a million. But that's when the murders went down. I guess the widow—what? Was feeling the heat is how I figure it."

"You think she felt threatened?"

"Let's get this clear. There were no threats from me. I never talked to the lady."

"What about Clay?"

"Well, Clay, what I understand"—Koontz was bobbing his bald head in tune to a quickening internal beat—"he confronted his grandfather and mother with the letter, told them all the people that'd find it fascinating reading. I mean, it stands to reason. For years they treated him like a prize fuck-up, a freak of nature. Now he has proof he's part of a family tradition.''

"Do you believe Mrs. Farinholt has an illegitimate son? The police don't.''

He spat the wad of nicotine gum into a wastebasket. ''Personally, I think she does. But if you're asking do I buy this kid tracking her down and bumping off Clay and the old man, there I draw the line. She's the killer.''

"Did you mention that Pierce made another settlement offer after the murders?''

"No, I didn't mention it. And yeah, he did. He raised the ante, but I stuck to my standard screw you. He's reputed to be this hot-shit lawyer, but he's dreaming if he thinks he's gonna lowball me.''

Koontz smoothed a hand over his scalp as if over a mop of phantom hair.

"Any chance Clay isn't the father?'' I asked.

"Doreen tells me no. I got Clay on tape swearing they timed their screwing to make sure they'd have a kid. You and I know what the other side'll do. Pierce'll parade the NBA All-Star team into court and have them testify they passed her around like a party favor. But if the blood test proves the kid's Clay's—which it will—it's going to inherit.'' He slung a leg over the arm of the chair again and swiveled contentedly.

"The Yost estate is just the start,'' he said, "I see a major best-seller and a major major miniseries. I see Doreen like that chick Nicole in Mailer's *Executioner's Song*. My opinion, Nicole, not Mailer's what made that project go. It reads like a beat-off book, but it wins the Pulitzer Prize.'' As Curtis Koontz pronounced it, the award was the Pullet Surprise.

"Remember the chapter where Gilmore shaves Nicole's pussy and she has the Big O for the first time? Remember her visiting him in prison with suicide pills stuffed up her snatch and him finger-fucking them out?'' He beamed with literary appreciation. "That's the type material I'm talking about. Doreen told me things that Mailer'd trade his left nut to write. Make us a deal and they're yours."

"Thanks. But I'll pass."

I went to a pay phone and dialed Paul Gant. If Clay had had a copy of the will and discussed it with Doreen and Darryl, even those two dimwits might have realized how much more he was worth to them dead.

When Gant came on the line, I didn't waste time with prologues. "Do you know Darryl Perry?"

"Sure do. Got a sister, Doreen. Got a passel of friends known better by numbers than names."

"You have any idea where he was the night my father was shot?"

"Matter of fact I do," he said in his down-home drawl. "These days all kind of folks are curious about Darryl. Couple weeks back, I got a call on that double murder in Anne Arundel County."

"The Yost-Farinholt murders?"

"Exactly. A Detective Quinn asked me to check Doreen and Darryl out. Didn't take much doing. She was with friends the night of the murders. He was here on an assault charge, waiting for his buddies to bail him out."

"You're sure he was there that night?"

"Positive."

"And the night of my father's murder?"

"He was in a whole week," Gant said.

"Shit!"

"Something wrong?"

"Me. I was wrong."

"Mistakes, I make them every day. That's why they put erasers on pencils."

"During my father's autopsy—"

"Come on, man, I don't want to discuss your daddy's autopsy."

"Just tell me whether they rolled a set of his finger-prints."

"Yeah. Standard procedure." Gant's loose, rumbling

drawl turned tight as the leash on a junkyard dog. "What the hell is this? You promised to stay out of it. You step in shit and track it—"

I hung up and stood there in the sweltering booth, boiling mad, feeling foolish. I thought I had been so close.

On the parking lot, two Vietnamese boys were twisting the Mercedes emblem off the hood of a metallic-blue station wagon. They split when I walked over for a closer look. The Mercedes had a Syms Island resident sticker on the rear bumper.

It didn't take long to locate Whiting Pierce. He was skulking in the shade of a Pepsi billboard. In his green Izod shirt and Scotch-plaid slacks he would have been perfectly camouflaged at a country club, but at a P.G. Country strip mall he stuck out like a carnival barker.

Circling behind him, I jammed a knuckle into his spine. "Hand over your socks or I'll shoot."

He stiffened and hunched his shoulders.

"Hey, you're not wearing socks," I said. "You're dead meat."

He whirled on me. "You damn fool, what are you doing? I saw you come out of Koontz's office."

"I was interviewing him. What's your excuse?"

"I thought some of Clay's friends might contact Koontz, somebody involved in the case."

"The murders? Or the paternity suit?"

"Hasn't it occurred to you they could be connected?"

"Sure has. But the nature of that connection looks different from where I'm standing. Koontz told me a few things you and Elaine forgot to mention."

"Can we carry on this conversation somewhere else? I don't care to have Koontz see us together."

I didn't either. "Get your car. I'll lead."

I didn't believe Pierce. He was shadowing me, not Koontz. With Darryl and Doreen eliminated as suspects, I was back to the original cast, and it included Pierce.

After all, as executor of the will, he was in a position to pick up a million bucks in legal fees.

We drove down East-West Highway, through the campus of the University of Maryland. Deserted during the dead weeks between the summer session and the fall semester, its colonnaded buildings were locked, the windows glinting in afternoon sunlight. On a sun-scorched lawn, a solitary coed in cutoff jeans was tossing a Frisbee to a dog.

I stopped at the University Dairy, one of the last reminders that this campus, now hemmed in by suburban sprawl, had started off as a cow college, a glorified agriculture school that won the national football championship in the early fifties, then as an afterthought decided it was about time to buy a few books for the library.

We darted from our cars, across the parking lot, as if ducking for shelter from a thunderstorm. Even a short dash through the clammy heat was enough to leave us drenched. Inside when I ordered a scoop of strawberry, Pierce clucked about butterfat and cholesterol. Then he got a look at my cone and asked for a double scoop of chocolate.

Sitting in a booth, we spoke in voices pitched too low to be overheard by other customers. With his world-class tan and well-barbered good looks, Pierce might have been the varsity tennis coach here to sneak a high-calorie snack. I didn't flatter myself that I looked like anything except what I was—a middle-aged alum back on campus to test whether the ice cream was still tops. It was.

"I have a very distinct recollection," I said, "that you and Elaine told me when Clay got those letters, it was no big deal. He was used to the family being on the receiving end of nut mail. You said he was too caught up with cars and girls to give it a second thought."

Neat as a cat, Pierce continued licking his cone.

"Koontz tells me a different story. Tells me Clay was bowled over to learn he had a half brother. Doreen says the same thing. He had it out with Andrew and Elaine."

The pink tip of Pierce's tongue darted at the chocolate.

"Whatever Clay's state of mind before his murder, I hardly think it's material."

"Maybe you don't. But I bet a jury would if Gaillard convinced them to see things in context."

"It's this context of yours I can't quite envision."

"You're too modest, Whiting. Or do I need to draw you a chart? In the last few weeks of his life, Clay had a problem. His girl was pregnant and he wanted to marry her."

"There's no proof of that."

"Koontz tells me there is. Tells me he has a tape of Clay acknowledging paternity and saying he planned to marry Doreen. He also by the way—this is something else neither you or Elaine got around to mentioning—Koontz also has a file on your settlement offers."

"They may or may not be pertinent to the paternity suit," he said between bites. "They have no relevance to the murder."

"To the contrary, Gaillard'll tie it all together and tie a noose around Elaine's neck. Because according to Koontz, Clay made it clear what he meant to do unless Andrew advanced him some money on his inheritance. He was angry enough to go public, pass around the letters, let the ladies in the Junior League read about Elaine's other boy. But he never got the chance. Somebody shot him. A fair-minded party might conclude that Elaine had a mighty persuasive motive for murder."

Although his mouth was smeared with chocolate, Pierce managed a passable poker face. "This is all very interesting, this speculation and hearsay. But I'm not sure how much of it is, strictly speaking, accurate and admissible. I'm confident we can limit Mr. Koontz's testimony."

"You worry about the long-range legal strategy. I'm in for the short run, and I'm warning you again, I'm not signing an affidavit until I have the story straight."

Finishing the cone with a last crunching bite, he wiped his face and fingers with a Wash'n Dri from his wallet. "While you've been interviewing Koontz, investigating Elaine, I've been doing some information gathering myself. You contend you don't pay people for their cooperation," Pierce said, "but that hasn't always been the case, has it?"

"I learned better."

"You learned at other people's expense. In your first book you bribed an Army medical orderly. He was court-martialed. It ruined his career."

What could I do except repeat, "I learned better."

"But not right away. You signed an exclusive contract with a witness in a murder case and caused a mistrial. The judge wanted to cite you for contempt."

"He didn't." My ice cream was beginning to taste rancid.

"Then there's the question of the libel suits. How many have been filed against you? Six? Seven?"

"I've never lost a libel suit."

"Yes, but you've settled."

"Give me a break, Pierce. The schmuck sued for six million. Three years later he'll settle for ten thousand dollars. Should I go to trial and spend fifty thousand more in fees? What would you advise a client?"

"I don't have any advice, Heller, only an observation. You're a user. You use people, then throw them away. All of which makes me wonder what Elaine can expect from you."

With a flimsy napkin I tried to clean my hands, but wound up leaving my fingers flecked with paper. "She can expect the truth."

"How marvelous it must be to imagine you alone are the judge of the truth." He shook his handsome head. "I'm against this. I have been since Elaine mentioned calling you. Doesn't that tell you something? That she's the one who suggested contacting you. If she had something to hide, why would she want you around, a man who bears her a grudge?"

Why indeed? Was she playing a cleverer game than Pierce gave her credit for?

"It's preposterous to think Elaine could kill anyone,"

he said. "You never knew the Yost family. Not really. Of course, Andrew could be a monster. He had an immense ego. But Elaine respected him, and he adored her and they both loved Clay. Can you honestly hold it against them that they didn't want him marrying Doreen? If I could have arranged a sensible settlement—not the millions Koontz is demanding—and gotten Clay back into therapy, he might have had a chance. But the poor kid was behind the eight ball all his life."

The emotion remained in his voice when he started in about Elaine. "Don't you understand how dreadful this has been for her? What's the sense of subjecting her to more torment? All she asks is that you corroborate a single fact—that she had a baby in Texas."

When I didn't respond, he balled up the Wash'n Dri he'd been holding and tossed it into a trash barrel. "She thinks you won't help because you hate her. I think it's something else."

I stared at his face, the hazel eyes, the strong jaw, and I steeled myself to show nothing. I was afraid he had found out about Big Tom's murder and had guessed I was searching for evidence to convict Elaine and maybe him as well.

"You don't hate her," he said. "You love her and you're furious because you can't have her."

I laughed at him. "That's sweet. I better not eat any more ice cream. Too sweet and too rich."

"You identify with Doreen Perry. You'd like her to get the revenge you never got."

There was no point in admitting that if I identified with anyone, it was with Elaine's illegitimate son. "Yeah, I identified so closely with Doreen's brother, I came away with this." I showed him the welt on my hand.

Pierce wasn't impressed. "You don't fool me and you don't fool the police. They were watching you and Elaine the other day."

"Did they tell you I banged her on the beach? We went at it like bunnies. Top and bottom, flagpole and Mexican basket trick. She'll never be satisfied with missionary style again.''

He flinched, but bounced back. "Do you actually believe she'd be satisfied with you?"

"Something on your mind, Whiting? Something been eating at you all these years?"

"I was on Syms Island that summer. I'm not blind. Neither was the rest of the community."

"You sure you don't have this switched around? Sounds to me like you're the one carrying a torch for Elaine." I was conscious of how much I sounded like Buck—taunting, jeering, trying to goad him into an outburst, get him to tip more of his hand. "Makes me wonder what you were up to in those days . . . I mean, besides praying to catch us with our pants down."

"If you're accusing me of caring for Elaine, you're right. I don't want to see her hurt because of something that happened decades ago."

"What seems to hurt you, Pierce, is your client and I were fucking decades ago. Are you afraid we'll start again?"

For an instant, I thought I'd pushed him too far, I thought he'd slug me. But he said, "Just give me a time frame. How much longer do we have to tolerate this abuse?"

"I'm flying to Texas tomorrow. Talk to me when I get back."

2

I expected the flight to Texas to be quicker, more comfortable, and less idiosyncratic than my first trip there—those days of hitchhiking west, listening to a litany of folk wisdom from lonely servicemen and long-distance truckers. But I hadn't reckoned on the eccentricities of air travel in the age of deregulation.

The plane was three hours late, and nobody except me seemed to have checked a single piece of luggage. Passengers staggered aboard dragging carry-on bags big enough to accommodate cellos or armoires. After the first wave was seated, the terminal was still thronged with angry travelers brandishing confirmed reservations. Over the intercom, the captain regretted to announce that the flight had been overbooked, and this prompted a bargaining session as spirited and cutthroat as an Arab bazaar. As one batch of ticket holders was exhorted to yield to another, the bribes rose in value, the cabin temperature climbed, and tempers frayed. We were first offered a free ticket on the next flight. Then a free ticket anywhere in the United States. Then a trip for two to the Caribbean. Beside me a teenager whooped with joy at the prospect of Puerto Rico and sprang from his seat.

A woman in a beige linen dress, sunglasses, and a wide-brimmed hat promptly took his place. A moment passed before it registered on me that it was Elaine. "I remembered something," she said. "I think it'll help."

"You should have called. Or waited till I got back."

"I did call. There was no answer."

"You shouldn't be doing this." I could as easily have been speaking to myself. It was foolish to risk traveling with her, yet I didn't leave.

Lumbering away from the terminal, the plane eased into the takeoff line. The runway looked wet and it rippled with mirages. We might have been aboard an amphibious craft, bobbing on a lake of mercury. When it was too late to do anything about it, I said, "Look, Elaine, I'm going there to work."

"What do you think I have in mind? A sentimental journey?"

As we gathered speed, then lifted off, she spun her sunglasses by the earpiece. Soft whorls of hair at the nape of her neck trembled with the plane's vibrations.

It must have been Pierce who had told her I'd be flying today. With a few phone calls, she could have found out my flight number. Whether he had put her up to this was the troubling question. The man was behaving more and more like a suspect, a coconspirator.

The seat-belt sign blinked off, and a stewardess pushed a drink trolley up the aisle. I ordered us both a Bloody Mary. "Okay, what did you remember?" I asked.

She set the plastic glass on the fold-out tray. "Last night I took down an atlas and looked at Texas, the towns around Austin. Finally, it clicked—a simple word association. When Daddy took me away from the agency, we drove through a town called Blanco, and the ranch where the baby was born had the word 'white' in it. The White Rock Ranch. White Creek. Something like that. Maybe it's still there."

"Worth a look." Although I had little faith we'd learn anything about her son or the murders by finding a ranch, I thought in the search for it I might discover what she was up to.

Lunch arrived in lukewarm foil containers. I skipped the meal and squeezed past Elaine, strolling toward the tail section. There was a queasy dip in my stomach as the plane hit a pocket of clear-air turbulence and I spotted

Mike Quinn, sitting rigidly upright, his usually dead brown eyes wild with panic. Afraid of no man on solid ground, the detective had his seat belt fastened and his fist wrapped around a bourbon and soda. On the fold-out tray in front of him an unidentifiable lump lay under a blanket of tomato and cheese sauce.

"Drinking on duty?" I asked.

"Sorry to ruin your honeymoon." His lips compressed each time the plane hit a rough patch. "Whenever you and your lady friend look around, I'll be watching."

"You think she's fleeing to Texas?"

"I don't think anything. My orders are to maintain surveillance."

"If you've been tailing her, you know we didn't come to the airport together, didn't board together. I didn't realize she'd be on this flight."

"Bullshit. I warned Gaillard—anything arranged by that brother of yours was bound to be a jerk-off." As the tough talk streamed out of his wincing, terrified face, I had the giddy sensation of watching a foreign film with the wrong sound track dubbed in. "She's going down on this murder, Heller. You keep going down on her, you'll go with her."

"Officer Quinn, you're offending your seatmate."

"Get out of my face. Get back to your friend and play stinky-pinky."

I jostled the fold-out tray, nudging his lunch into his lap. The tomato and cheese sauce skated over the crotch of his wheat-colored jeans, down between his legs. He was grappling with his seat belt, screaming, when a stewardess came to the rescue—my rescue. I retreated to my seat.

"There's a cop following you," I told Elaine.

She glanced back at the commotion. The plane had hit more turbulence, and the stewardess had little trouble controlling Quinn.

"Whiting warned me they were watching us. What do they think they're going to see?"

"They'll take what they get and hope you make a mistake."

"Isn't there a law? Don't they need a warrant?"

"Nothing illegal about following a person," I said. "No law against slipping away either."

When we landed in Austin, I waited at the baggage-claim chute while Elaine rented a car and started for town. Under orders to tail her, not me, Quinn set off in his own rental car. I collected her luggage and mine, leased a car from a different agency and headed out of the airport, bore right, and passed three service stations before I spotted a Pontiac with its hood raised and a mechanic monkeying with the engine. Quinn was in a Ford at the next gas pump, gazing toward the rest rooms.

He didn't notice me swing around at an intersection and pull up on a parallel street behind the station. From where I parked with the motor running, I could see the rest room doors fenced off from Quinn's view. Elaine came out, crossed an expanse of hard-packed dirt, and jumped in on the passenger's side. Her smile was one I recognized—the smile of a risk-taker.

"This is fun," she said. "I've never been a fugitive before."

Speeding into town on side streets, I kept an eye on the rearview mirror. I figured we had a few more minutes before Quinn caught on. Then he'd have to circle back to the airport and find out what kind of car I rented.

Even living in Rome, I had read about hard times in Texas. The floor had fallen out of the oil and real estate markets, state savings and loan associations had racked up billions of dollars in bad debts, bankruptcy was rampant, and Austin ranked number one in the nation in unrented office space. But the city concealed its misfortunes well, and regardless of its current setbacks, it had flourished since I'd last seen it.

Studded with skyscrapers, the downtown resembled Dallas or Houston, if not New York, and its mirror-faced buildings glinted in the sun like unimaginably large jewels. Both shores of Town Lake had been developed; Armadillo World Headquarters, the celebrated night spot, had been demolished and replaced by a bank tower; and the University of Texas looked massive and monumental, its new classrooms designed with slotlike windows as if to thwart barbarians.

We crossed Lamar Boulevard, then a land fault where the ground began to break into rocky ledges and promontories of bleached limestone. We couldn't have been far from the former address of the Creekmore Agency, but we pressed on toward Blanco. For a few miles the road ran beside a steeply banked river where a water-skier—from this distance he seemed the size of a water spider—slalomed from shoreline to shoreline. The air was drier here and cooler than in Maryland, and it smelled of cedar, sage, and mesquite.

Elaine dredged in a deep breath. "That brings back memories."

She took off her hat and tossed it into the rear seat. Her sun-streaked hair fluttered in the wind that sluiced through the open windows. Wearing sunglasses, she was a handsome woman even with her best feature, her eyes, hidden.

"You want the air conditioner?"

"God no," she said. "I'm sick of it. This is like being a teenager again, riding around in a convertible with the top down." She lifted the hem of her dress and let it fall loose around her legs. "I don't suppose they televise 'Austin City Limits' in Rome?"

"Afraid not. What's that?"

"A country-and-western program Clay used to like. Sometimes I watched it with him and thought about our stay here. I remember one night when you and I stopped for a beer at this dinky club—it was in a renovated gas station—and listened to a singer with a ponytail and a scratchy voice. Turned out it was Willie Nelson. What do you remember?"

What I remembered was what Curtis Koontz had said and what I'd told Whiting Pierce—Elaine was lying to me.

I remembered Diane Kershner and didn't believe Elaine had forgotten her.

"I remember my room," I said, "and the oleander bush outside the window. I'd never seen an oleander before I came to Texas."

"Yes, your room." She curled sideways on the seat. "You wore a medal in those days, a religious thing on a chain around your neck. Once when we were in your room, it hit me in the mouth. I don't know how. It must have weighed as much as a silver dollar. It nearly knocked my teeth out."

My recall was more precise. I suspected hers was too and that she was daring me to supply the subtext. I wouldn't do it.

The medal had hit her when we were making love. Raised above her on the strength of my arms, I had moved, and as she moved under me, the medal swung from my neck like a pendulum. When it struck her, she opened her eyes and they had a curious expression, not so much as if she were hurt or frightened, more as if she was alert to new possibilities.

"Don't stop," she had said.

In Blanco, we dropped by a country store that had garden tools, rifles, and fly rods hanging from the rafters, and hunting and fishing trophies mounted on the walls. Inevitably, a rack of antlers was hooked to a jackrabbit's head and advertised to tourists as a jackalope. Elaine charmed the professional codger who ran the place, and he let us leaf through his phone directory looking for ranches with the word "white" in their names. Then he sketched an itinerary with a Magic Marker and launched us into the thorny cedar brakes of the Hill Country.

In her exuberance, Elaine appeared to regard this as a game, a sort of rally or motor cross in which sporty people race around matching checkpoints against dots on a map. We rattled across cattle guards, up rutted lanes, over posted roads to shotgun cottages, to pillared mansions, to

austere gray stone houses constructed by German pio-
neers. We were offered glasses of iced tea, cans of beer,
and on one occasion, a joint. We listened to stories about
crops and weather that had the plangency of ballads, and
other times we were assailed with salty phrases of dismissal. "Get the hell off my property. Come closer and
I'll sic the dogs on your ass." We spoke to blacks who
seemed unaware of the Emancipation Proclamation, and
an equal number of whites who had remained willfully
ignorant of the same document. We visited at length with
a homosexual couple who were restoring a hundred-year-
old grist mill, and we blundered upon a lost tribe of
hippies who lived in a commune on the banks of a
snake-infested lake.

What we never found was the ranch where Elaine gave
birth to her baby. Far from displeased in fact, she was
eager to go on with the game/search—she said, "Maybe
it was the doctor whose name had 'white' in it." She suggested we backtrack to the country store and thumb
through the phone directory again.

But it was late, and I was hungry, and we stopped at a
barbecue shack that was even more self-consciously rustic
than the country store. The booths were built like horse
stalls, the light fixtures were fashioned from wagon
wheels, and the waitresses were dressed as cowgirls. The
food was plentiful, the beer was cold, and the jukebox
played Patsy Cline, Hank Williams, and Conway Twitty.
Elaine said she loved the place. Whether she was buoyed
up by the hope of better luck tomorrow or by the idea that
she had led me in circles today, I could only guess.

"About the baby," I said to bring her back to ground
zero. "Was Pierce involved?"

She shoved her sunglasses up to the crown of her head,
like Diane Kershner. "Involved how?"

"If he was doing legal work for your father, he might
have drawn up the adoption papers."

"The agency took care of that." She poked her fork at

a dish of coleslaw. "Daddy would never have told Whiting I was pregnant."

"Still, I get the impression he had his eye on you in those days. He said yesterday he wasn't blind, he knew what we were up to that summer."

"Who didn't? We weren't very circumspect."

"Did your husband know about the baby?"

"Of course. You can't live with someone and keep a secret like that. I told him all about our time together. What about your wife, does she know?"

"She has the European attitude."

"Which is what?"

"Which is sex is one thing, and marriage and family another."

"Who's talking about sex?" Elaine said. "I just meant did you ever tell her about us?"

"She's not interested in what I did as a bachelor." This wasn't true. Marisa had a keen, if controlled, interest in everything about my life, my childhood, my family, the women I had known before I met her. Although she didn't ask many questions, that was mainly because I was so closemouthed.

"I couldn't live like that." Elaine poured Lone Star beer into a blue plastic glass. "I realized that right after the baby was born. I needed somebody to confide in."

I sat there recalling the hours we had talked, wondering whether Elaine had ever really confided in me. Was she doing so now? And I thought about Marisa. Suddenly it troubled me that I had never mentioned Elaine and the baby.

"Townsend was older," she went on, "and he'd been through a lot. I could tell him anything and never shock him. You see, he was the sort of man—" She reached across the table and patted my hand. "I'm sorry. I'm boring you with all this babble about Townsend."

It has been written that the capacity to hold conflicting ideas in mind is an index of maturity and intelligence. If so, I should have felt during dinner like a ripe old genius. But I didn't. I felt callow and cynical—simultaneously ashamed and proud of my ability to think one thing and do another. Although I believed very little of what Elaine said, it pleased me to pretend that I did, just as it prompted a different and more disturbing pleasure to have a premonition of what was going to happen next and to suspect that she did too.

After dinner, we decided to stay in the Hill Country and get an early start tomorrow. At a franchise motel whose one distinctive feature was that it was owned by Indians— East Indians, not Americans—a languid lady wearing a sari greeted me at the check-in counter. Her husband, a heavyset Sikh in a turban and beard bib, sat in the lobby with a child on each knee watching a TV broadcast of the Olympics in Seoul.

I asked for two rooms and assured the lady that it didn't matter whether they were adjoining or near one another. Out in the car, Elaine unsnapped her purse and insisted on paying her share. I told her to forget it, handed her a key, and tossed mine onto the dashboard. Then coasting to a halt at her door, I left it up to her. I sat and let it sink in—if she wanted something, she was going to have to ask for it.

"Like to come in?" she said.

I brought in both our bags, and by the time I set them on the shag carpet, Elaine had lifted the sunglasses from her head and was stepping out of her shoes, removing her earrings, reaching around to unbutton her dress. I took off my coat and tie. She mumbled something about a shower. I said, "Later." Then we said nothing at all, simply went on undressing, staring open-eyed at each other with what I thought was a kind of defiance. Take it or leave it, this is what I look like now; that seemed to be the unstated sentiment as our clothes fell away.

The smile returned to her face—the risk-taker's, the hell-raiser's, the daredevil who did as she pleased. I had forgotten how slim she was, how fine boned. The cage of

her ribs and the cradle of her hips pressed against taut
skin. From her tan line, curving high on her flanks, I
could see that she wore a one-piece swimsuit these days,
not a bikini. The trim triangle of hair was darker.

Even as I moved forward and touched her, even with
her mouth on mine, one corner of my mind remained as
sharp as a splinter of ice. I recalled how I felt when she
left me the first time. Then how I felt the second time,
running back to my room through the cold wind. For
months afterward, I had felt a bitter sting on my face
whenever I thought of her or heard a stray bar of music or
smelled a particular perfume. The pain was as close, as
palpable, as the vein that darkened and pulsed on her forehead.

I lifted her and laid her on the bedspread. She was light,
almost frail compared to Marisa. Time had worked
changes on her body, but my hands sculpted from her flesh
the girl I had known. I went on touching and kissing that
girl, all the while thinking of this woman. She's a liar,
likely a killer. She may have murdered my father.

The thought didn't give me pause. It spurred me on.
Maybe this had always been the electrical charge between
us, this idea that she was capable of anything, that there
was a core of corruption and danger to Elaine that I felt
compelled to be near, to be inside.

I rolled over, holding her on top of me, my hands running down the smooth notched column of her spine. She
pressed her hands to my chest and raised her head, then
her upper body. Her eyes were shut, her lips half-parted.
She sat up straight, arching her back as though searching
for something inside her.

Then she stretched, reaching deeper, and when she got
where she wanted to go, I was with her. There was no
thought, no subterfuge to hide behind, no barrier between
us but skin.

Minutes passed before she stirred, extending a hand to
switch off the lamp. She touched my chest, my throat.
''You've changed.''

"I'm forty-four. I should jog or something."

"Not that. Your body's the same, down to the hair on your arms and the small of your back. What's different is your face, your eyes." Her fingers traced my jawline, the curve of my mouth. "When we first met, the way you talked and acted, you reminded me of a truck driver."

"Son of a truck driver."

"A handsome truck driver, a smart one. And that summer on the island, that's how you were in bed—rough, aggressive."

"You make me sound scary."

"No, it wasn't until you came to Texas that I got scared. You were so tender, it terrified me."

"Why would tenderness terrify you?"

"You were asking more than I could give. I was afraid I'd end up hurting you." She sat up. In the dark I could see her silhouette against the window blinds. "Now you're more like when we met—tough looking, detached. I'm not sure I could reach you."

"You reached me all right." I wrestled her down beside me. I didn't want to talk. I didn't want her sounding my eyes and reading my bones. I didn't want to think about what we had done, what we were going to do again.

Afterward she fell asleep, or seemed to. I was wide-awake and reminded of a month I had lived in Belfast doing an article on the IRA. The hotel where I stayed had had signs in every room advising guests that no amount of vacuuming had succeeded in sweeping up the millions of minute glass slivers blown over the carpet by bombs. "Always wear shoes," the signs warned. Every night I went to bed with that admonition in mind, yet I woke each day and made the same mistake—bloodying my bare feet again.

Lying beside Elaine, listening to the rhythm of her breathing, so different from Marisa's, I felt the same sense of inexorable failure as I tried to rationalize what I had done. With jesuitical reasoning I could claim that it was part of my investigation. In movies and novels didn't detectives always do a great deal of their sleuthing in bed?

But if I had learned anything from this bit of undercover work, it was less about Elaine than about myself. Whatever her aptitude for deception, regardless of her guilt, I was her equal. There was no treachery, no betrayal, I wasn't capable of. The realization frightened me, just as the look on my face had scared her.

Next morning, after we had showered and dressed and like hearty campers repeated how hungry we were, we walked out to be greeted by the glare of the sun and the flash of a camera. The photographer managed to squeeze off four shots before Elaine ducked back into the room and I rushed over to where Mike Quinn stood sipping coffee from a Styrofoam cup. Behind him the creep with the camera clambered into a Texas Department of Public Safety vehicle.

Quinn had on black stone-washed jeans and a cowboy shirt with blue piping and mother-of-pearl buttons. His eyes burrowed in wrinkles of weariness. He must have staked us out all night.

"Let me guess," I said. "You've joined the Texas Rangers and your new beat is eyeballing motel rooms."

"No, my job is maintaining surveillance on a murder suspect, which you're fast becoming one of. What I hear, Elaine Farinholt's getting it from her lawyer on the side. Probably the back side. Does that make you and Pierce bunghole buddies by proxy?"

"Fuck you, Quinn."

With a flick of the wrist, he splashed his coffee down the front of my pants. "That should keep your dick red-hot for the rest of the day."

I made the mistake of raising my fists. He didn't wait to see whether I'd use them. He caught me with a right to the jaw and a left hook to the forehead and knocked me down. "Get up, asshole, and let me do it again."

Staying low, I lunged at his legs. He drove his knee into my chin, flattening me.

"Picture what a dumb prick you look like crawling around down there. Don't disappoint me, don't pussy out. Let's go for the hat trick."

I obliged him, flailing out with my foot, kicking at his kneecap. He pounded me on the back of the head.

When I felt up to moving again, I scuttled clear of Quinn before I got to my feet.

"Too bad. Fun's over," he sang.

As I reeled into the room, Elaine was screaming, "I saw him. I saw what he did." She slammed the door, chaining it behind me, and I collapsed and listened to the loud belling of my head. "I'll call the police," she said.

"He *is* the police."

"From Maryland. I'll call the local police "

"They're helping him. That's how he found us That's who took the pictures."

"But he hit you."

"My own damn fault." I experimented with a shaky walk around the room, then glanced into the mirror. My face looked lopsided. For a second I thought Quinn had injured my eyesight. But it was the rapid swelling of the right side of my jaw.

"What'll they do with the pictures?" Elaine was growing more agitated as I calmed down enough to understand how badly I had fouled up.

"Make trouble."

"How?"

"Put them in the papers and on TV. Say I'm a suspect and they're looking for witnesses who can place me at the crime scene that night. You better fly home. Quinn'll follow you. That'll leave me free to work here."

On the drive to Austin and east to the airport, Quinn idled along behind us, and I made no effort to shake him. I wanted him on a plane and out of here. There was some small, woefully inadequate enjoyment in imagining him airborne, in acute agony, white-knuckling it for the next few hours.

"About last night," Elaine started. She had her sunglasses and broad-brimmed hat on, and she seemed as self-contained and remote as I must have looked to her in bed. "I was wondering where this leaves us. It could change a lot of things."

I doubted she had a clue how much it might change— everything from the murder charge to my marriage, the disposition of her father's millions to my professional future. "We'll have to talk when I get back," I said.

"Meanwhile, what should I tell Whiting?"

"He's your lawyer." I waited for her to correct me, admit there was more. "Anything you say is privileged."

We rode the rest of the way without speaking. At the terminal I should have gone in and waited with her. But I couldn't bear to have Quinn leering at us, admiring his handiwork on my face. Elaine and I wished each other good luck and good-bye, but didn't touch, not even to shake hands.

3

At the Villa Capri Motel, close by the concrete bunker of the Lyndon Baines Johnson Library, about as distant from the Mediterranean as can be imagined, I spent the better part of two days with a telephone at my ear and an ice pack on my lumpy, discolored face. I should have called Buck. Even if by some fluke the photographs hadn't yet been pounced on by the press, he was likely to have caught flak at the courthouse, and he deserved to hear what I was up to. But I couldn't bring myself to speak to him until I had something except feeble excuses to offer in explanation of this trip.

For the same reason, I postponed calling Marisa. The pressure was on me to produce the goods. I couldn't come back empty-handed.

I dialed every Kershner in the Austin directory and asked for Diane. To no avail. Then I fanned out to surrounding towns and counties. She might have married or moved to another state, she might have had an unlisted number or none at all. But I needed to eliminate obvious possibilities and let my bruises fade a bit before I made the rounds of municipal and state offices and tried to trace the woman through tax rolls, utility records, or voter registration files.

At the outset of each call I referred to an inheritance worth millions of dollars. Although I stopped short of lying, I left the impression that the right person was about to become a very rich lady. People were guarded, disbelieving. A few sounded fearful, but nobody hung up.

A surprising number claimed they had worked in 1966

at the Creekmore Agency. Several swore they were still on the staff. When asked to describe the services the agency performed, they nattered on about land management or life insurance or executive training. Impressed by the summer's drought, a few suggestible souls maintained it was an irrigation company that channeled more creeks to arid farmland. One lady caused me a heart-clot of excitement when she said, "I was a placement adviser."

"What did you place?"

"Pets, mostly dogs, but cats and horses too. I placed animals with children who loved them."

Late on the second day, I rang a D. Kershner in New Braunfels. A man answered, and when I asked to speak to Diane, he demanded, "What for?"

"It's a matter of a large amount of money."

"Hey, Mom," he shouted without moving the receiver from his mouth. "Somebody about money."

A woman came on, and when I tossed her the line about the inheritance, she calmly inquired, "Who died?"

"I'd rather not say until I'm sure I have the right party."

"Who are you?" She had a sweet, pleasant manner and not a hint of a Texas accent.

"Richard Hodder," I said on the off chance she had read my books or remembered my name from our dealings decades ago. "Were you ever employed at the Creekmore Agency?"

"Yes."

"Where's it located?"

"In Austin." She volunteered the address, then added, "It's been closed for years."

Lightheaded, lighthearted, I rose from the chair where I'd been rooted, floating to my feet as if helium filled. "Why did it close?"

"There weren't enough babies available for adoption."

"What did you do at the agency?"

"Counseled pregnant women."

"We'd better discuss this face-to-face."

"Aren't inheritances generally handled through attorneys, Mr. Hodder?"

"I'd prefer to explain things in person."

"I don't mean to make your life difficult, but you'll have to go through my lawyer." She supplied his name and number. "You appreciate my predicament. I arranged hundreds of adoptions and I have to be cautious about what I say to strangers. For all I know, you could be somebody searching for his biological parents, or a father looking for his child. There are legal ways of locating biological parents. A lawyer can advise you. But if you're looking for your child, I'm afraid that's out of the question."

"Thanks. I'll contact your attorney."

The simplest and smartest move was to pass on her name to authorities in Maryland and let them subpoena Diane Kershner, then pursue Elaine's son through his adoptive parents. But I couldn't quit until I got answers to questions that were unlikely to interest either the prosecution or the defense.

Heading north on I-35, I recalled Diane Kershner as a pert, compact woman with a nonstop smile. Although then in her midthirties, she had dressed and acted more like a roommate than a counselor to unwed mothers. Given her closeness to the girls and her scrupulousness about confidentiality, I didn't delude myself it would be easy to coax information out of her. Still, there was one pressure point she might have no choice but respond to.

The interstate sped through an undulating countryside where the grass was dun-colored and the vegetation stunted. Cattle shouldered into scattered patches of shade, huddling under billboards when there were no trees. Set amid miles of sunbaked land, New Braunfels caught me off guard with its touches of German kitsch. There were shops styled along the lines of Bavarian chalets, windows full of beer steins, restaurants called the Hofbräu and the Rathskeller, posters advertising a Wurstfest in autumn.

On a plumb-line-straight road leading out of town, a mobile home was anchored to a plot of ground overgrown with weeds. The mailbox had a decal of a duck and the name KERSHNER stenciled in red letters. I parked beside a beat-up Subaru, and when I knocked on the trailer, it reverberated as though I had rapped the lid of an oil drum.

A woman in a motorized wheelchair opened the door. Her right arm and the wavering stalk of her neck were capable of movement; the rest of her looked dead. Draped in a tent dress, her hair gone coarse and gray, she was recognizable only by her smile and her sweet, beguiling voice. "Can I help you?"

"I'm Thomas Heller."

"If I'm not mistaken, you were Richard Hodder an hour ago. Have you spoken to my lawyer?"

"Sorry. I'm not one of your lost children or searching fathers. I'm investigating the Yost murders."

Diane Kershner's expression didn't change, but the timbre of her voice did. "Why didn't you tell me you're a policeman?"

I didn't correct her. "I have to ask you a few questions."

Still smiling—maybe her face was paralyzed in that attitude—she nudged the reverse button on her chair and made space for me to come in. The room was warm and close, but as neatly ordered as a ship's cabin. The wheels of her chair had worn grooved patterns in a green carpet. We stayed in a minuscule alcove furnished with a love seat and an end table. A breakfast bar separated us from the kitchen where a big blubbery man was perched on a stool, wolfing down a sandwich and a bag of Doritos chips.

"This is my son, Jimmy," she said. There was no sign of a Mr. Kershner or of the collection of dolls in international costumes that had decorated her office at the Creekmore Agency.

With his mouth stuffed, Jimmy said nothing, but he nodded and never took his eyes off me. Although the size of a sumo wrestler, he had the smooth, round face and hairless skin of an infant—an infant with a mild case of jaundice. He looked to be part oriental, part black, with curly reddish hair.

"It might be better if we spoke in private," I said.

"I have no secrets from Jimmy." Working the switches with her good hand, she swung the wheelchair around to face the love seat where I sat.

"Have you heard about the Yost murders?" I asked.

The question didn't dent her frozen smile. "It was on the evening news. Back east somewhere, wasn't it?"

"Yes. The surviving daughter, Elaine, lived at the Creekmore Agency in 1966. You remember her?"

"As I told you on the telephone, I'm not free to discuss my job." Her head wobbled as she spoke. "We guaranteed the girls complete confidentiality."

"You realize a court order could force you to talk?"

"Do you have one, a court order?"

Conscious of Jimmy staring at me, I found myself talking to him as much as to her. "The Maryland police have a *ducus tecum* decree that allows them access to all the documents concerning Elaine and her child."

"Then you don't need me, do you?" she said.

"Wrong. You're needed more than ever. And if you don't cooperate, I can promise you'll be subpoenaed." I was stretching the limits now. It was one thing to encourage her to think I was a cop. It was a lot worse to threaten her with a subpoena. I backed off and briefly described the killings and the disappearance of the birth certificate and adoption records.

"That's a shame," she said. "But whatever dealings I might have had with the woman—and I'm not conceding I worked with her, I'm not responding to that at all—I don't see how I'm involved."

"You were Elaine's counselor and—"

"That hardly makes me responsible for the loss of the agency's files."

"No, but it makes you somebody—maybe the only person—who can verify the contents of the files."

"Even if I could, what do they, what does her baby, have to do with the murders?"

"Her son's in his twenties by now. There's evidence he could be the killer."

"What evidence?" she asked, and Jimmy stopped chomping the Doritos, waiting for my answer.

"There were some letters."

Jimmy stepped away from the breakfast bar, wiping his hands on the seat of his pants. "Mom told you she can't talk about this."

"About what?" I didn't put much into the question. But I had a sudden urge to stand up and brace myself. Better yet, get the hell out of here, let the police question these two.

"She can't talk about this girl and her problems." Jimmy closed the gap between us in three strides. It was too late now. I was blocked in by this immense butterball and his mother's wheelchair.

"Let him finish," she told Jimmy. "What was in the letters?"

"Threats from somebody who knew Elaine had an illegitimate son."

"I dare say plenty of people knew." She clenched and unclenched her right hand. "The agency had dozens of employees, and lots of girls were living there then. And have you considered the baby's father?"

"Somebody from Texas was blackmailing Elaine. Then two members of her family were murdered. Probably by the blackmailer."

"How does that make her son a suspect?"

I hung my hand over the arm of the love seat and got a grip on the end table. "It makes whoever wrote those letters a suspect."

Jimmy telegraphed his punch, swinging from his heels. I went to block it with the end table, but he smashed that to kindling, then caught me with a left cross. My head banged against the wall, setting off a thunderous reverberation. It sounded as if we were battling inside a bread box.

I ducked a couple of wild swings and dug a fist into his gut. But I couldn't hold him off. Jimmy swarmed over me with his weight, punching down, hammering like a pile driver at my head. Pain flashed out of my eye sockets, and I screamed. Jimmy was screaming, too, and so was his mother. He hit me again and again, hollering louder each time until abruptly he reared back, wringing his fist. He had busted a knuckle on my skull.

Still holding a leg of the end table, I hurled it at him as he hurried for the door. It bounced off his rump, harmless as balsa wood. He scrambled into the Subaru and spun off across the field of weeds, spraying gravel against the tin panels of the mobile home.

Diane Kershner kept on screaming, wordlessly at first. Then she wailed, "Why? Why?"

When I stood up, glowing spokes of pain exploded somewhere in my head, and the room shattered into a gleaming shower of confetti. I must have blacked out for a moment. When I came to, the woman was saying, "He didn't mean it. He didn't mean it."

Scrabbling at the wall for balance, I staggered out of the alcove, over to the breakfast bar. The wheelchair hummed along at my heels. "Wait," she begged. "Listen to me."

I found the telephone in the kitchen, but had trouble with my fingers. I couldn't fit them into the right holes; the numbers on the dial were jumping around. When I managed to get 911, Diane Kershner reached out and cut the connection. "Please, let me explain."

"What's to explain?" I leaned over the sink and splashed my face with water.

"Jimmy didn't do it."

"The hell he didn't. You and he wrote those letters."

"I wrote them." The urgency in her voice showed nowhere on her sad, shapeless body except in the corded veins of her neck. "All he did was drive to Dallas and mail them. He didn't murder anybody."

"Tell it to the police."

"Please listen." She groped for me with her good hand, grabbing my pants pocket as my boys had done when they were small and wanted me to slow down. "Jimmy's been with me every day. He can prove he never left Texas. When we heard about the killings, we were afraid they'd blame us. But I swear we didn't do it."

Diane Kershner obviously couldn't be the killer, and Jimmy didn't fit the description given by both Elaine and Luke. It would take more than a blond wig to disguise that behemoth. Still I said, "Why should I believe you?"

"Because it's the truth. I'll tell you whatever you want to know. I'll tell you about Elaine's baby. Just don't blame Jimmy."

"Why'd he try to tear my head off?"

"He's afraid of losing me. He spent his whole childhood in refugee camps. He's Amerasian, one of the kids abandoned by GIs in Vietnam. By the time I got him, he was thirteen. He's the only thing that kept me alive when I learned I had MS. Now he's afraid I'll die in jail. Please don't arrest him. He only did what I told him to do."

I couldn't mislead her any longer. Sick of conning sources, ashamed of my strategies for emotional extortion, I didn't care to restrict myself to the kinds of questions a cop would ask. "I'm not with the police. I can't arrest anybody."

She made a weak, bewildered motion with her hand. "I don't understand."

"I'm a writer. I'm doing a book about the murders."

"Does Elaine know?"

"Yes. I was in Austin when she lived at the agency. You and I met back then."

Again she made a groping gesture. Then her head canted to one side as if she were seeing things from a new perspective. "Of course. You're the friend who followed her. The Catholic boy. Have you stayed in touch with her all these years?"

I shook my head and wished I hadn't. My eyes swam. "She called me after the murders."

"She had very special, very deep feelings for you."

I didn't want to get sidetracked and let her regress to her role as counselor. I didn't want to hear about Elaine's feelings. "If you and Jimmy hope to stay out of jail, you better have an alibi. Why not run it by me?"

But she went on mooning about relationships that survived separation and emotional attachments that endured. "Elaine is one girl I never forgot. Such a lovely, level-headed person. I was heartsick when I read what happened to her family."

"You liked her so much, why'd you write the letters?"

Her head bobbed as if I had belted her. I was ashamed of my outburst until I realized she was nodding—to her body, to her wheelchair, to this tin box of a trailer.

"Living like this, knowing it's going to get worse, I thought, well, she has a lot and we only need a little."

"Why her? Weren't there other girls you worked with who were easier marks and almost as rich?"

"No. Elaine was the most vulnerable. These days the stigma's gone. Lots of women are admitting they have illegitimate children. They're out looking for them, reestablishing a maternal bond. I needed somebody who'd pay anything to keep me quiet."

"So you figured Elaine was a pushover because she has a reputation, a prominent name to protect."

"She has something more important to protect."

"The identity of the father?"

"I'm sure she's anxious to keep that secret. But it's not the big one."

"The baby was born dead?"

"No, no. How could I blackmail her about a dead baby? It's something so obvious. It's why there aren't any adoption records."

"Don't turn this into a guessing game."

"There was no adoption."

Maybe Jimmy had punched out my reasoning powers. I didn't get it. "She's admitted it. It's been in all the papers."

"Does that make it a fact?"

When the light finally flashed on, it set off the same splintered kaleidoscope of colors as Jimmy's roundhouse rights. I should have seen it coming a month ago, a thousand miles ago. "She kept the baby."

Diane Kershner was nodding again. "That's what she's desperate to hide."

"Clay, he's the son she had here?"

"Not here."

The next leap was easier. "He was born someplace in Latin America?"

"Yes. When Andrew Yost came to Austin, he and Elaine left the States. It was too late for her to fly. He drove her south."

"Do you know why she didn't go through with the adoption?"

"Not really. My guess is it wasn't entirely her decision. Mr. Yost seemed to regard her and his grandson as personal property. He didn't like to let go of anything. As torn as Elaine was at the time, it wouldn't have taken much to sway her. I gather he arranged a nice marriage for her, and she and her husband raised the baby as their own."

I leaned over the sink again and swallowed some water. There was an ugly taste in my mouth. Dumping the blame on her own kid, Elaine had sent me off on a snipe hunt, searching for a dead man, one she had murdered.

There was a last thing I needed to know. "Do you recall the papers you asked me to sign?"

Diane Kershner peered at me with her perpetual smile. "I'm sorry. What papers?"

"A document swearing I wasn't the baby's father and had no claim."

"Oh, yes. That was Mr. Yost's idea. He was convinced you were the father."

"Was I?"

"Elaine said you weren't. She said it was an older man who worked for the family. She worried that it would ruin him if anybody found out. He had a wife and children and wasn't free to marry. And of course she was afraid what her father would do.''

I hadn't felt like such a goddamn fool since my last meeting with Diane Kershner. But I couldn't blame her for my blindness. I clasped her good hand as I passed on my way toward the door. "Take care," I said. "And thanks.''

"Don't be hard on Elaine," she called after me. "Anybody would have a horrible time with a father like that.''

"All God's children got fathers," I said.

Jimmy was sitting in the Subaru, a baby-faced Buddha awaiting his fate. Keeping a careful distance between us, I said, "Go on inside. Your mother needs you.''

"Are you okay?''

"Tip-top shape." I continued on toward my car.

"You're not going to arrest us?''

"No.''

"I'm sorry I hit you.''

"So am I.''

4

I had told nobody about my return flight from Texas, but clearly someone had a source at Continental's reservations desk. When I landed at BWI and walked down the ramp, a crowd was waiting. The reception committee included Buck, Sam Gaillard, Mike Quinn, a dozen reporters, and teams of men with Minicams and sound booms. A clump of onlookers converged around the press and the police. The flashbulbs hit me first, then the hollering. "How long have you and Elaine Farinholt been lovers? Are you the father of her illegitimate son? Are you in contact with him? Do you expect to be indicted? How does it feel to be an investigative journalist under investigation?"

Above them all, I heard Buck bellow, "Don't say a word."

Thumbs hooked through his belt loops, Quinn treated me to a taunting smile. Dressed for a photo opportunity in a blue suit and red tie, Gaillard stood beside him, a dour and disgruntled turkey next to a preening bantam cock.

"Gentlemen," I said, "I'm honored."

"Shut up, Tommy." Buck bulled his way over to me.

Seeing my newly swollen and discolored face, assuming it was damage he had done, Quinn sighed in spurious sympathy. "Looks like somebody tattooed you with a tire iron." In his nasal Baltimore accent it came out "tar arn."

The reporters milled closer, jostling for elbow room, eavesdropping with sound booms. Some shouted questions. Others screamed, "Shut up so we can hear."

"Like to have a word with you," Gaillard said.

"If he's under arrest, read him his rights," Buck demanded. "He's not, then fold this circus you set up."

"We're not here for an arrest." Gaillard was speaking to the reporters, not to me; his blade-sharp face angled for the cameras. "But we have some questions."

"Forget it," Buck said. "You got something to ask, get a court order."

"Wait," I said. "I'm willing to talk. But in private."

"What happened to your face?" a reporter hollered.

"Detective Quinn is a failed candidate for the Olympic boxing team. He took out his disappointment on me."

"Are you charging police brutality?"

"He's keeping his options open," Buck said.

"I know a place." Quinn grabbed my arm. On camera, it might look as if he had me in handcuffs. I yanked free.

Engulfed by the crowd, we moved, amoebalike, down the corridor, around the corner. The room was a lost-and-found office. Quinn shoved his badge in the custodian's face, and the fellow cleared out. The four of us went in and shut the door. There were chairs, but nobody sat down. We huddled on the industrial carpet like captains of opposing teams meeting at midfield before the kickoff.

"I want some ground rules," Buck said. "Anything he says is off the record and can't be used against him."

"Fine. This isn't just professional," Gaillard said. "I have some personal feelings to express."

Quinn couldn't get enough of my face. "Jesus, look how bulging around the cheekbones, look how black and-blue. What happened, Elaine Farinholt forget you were down there and cross her legs?"

Gaillard had his eyes locked on mine in a look of pure loathing. "I am a basically, I hope, ethical person. I trusted you. I'm always ready to meet the press halfway. So I don't appreciate people I talk to in good faith trying to get over on me."

The State's Attorney had a bad case of razor burn and his face flamed with anger. "Because your brother requested it, because I respected—past tense—your books, I agreed to discuss the Yost murders. You presented yourself as a journalist and I treated you as such, with all the privileges that pertain. I'm a great believer in the First Amendment.''

"Now I see," Buck said. "Quinn's here to wise off, you're here to practice a campaign speech.''

Gaillard powered on. "But you abused the privilege. Don't imagine for a minute you're going to shield yourself with a press card. Don't even dream about claiming you have a right to protect the anonymity of your sources. From now on our dealings are strictly as prosecutor and defendant.''

"How can he be a defendant?" Buck demanded. "He hasn't been arrested.''

"We're not in any rush," Quinn said. "We see him as a cinch as an accessory. But we're working like hell to tack on a heavier charge.''

"Are we talking about some violation of journalistic protocol?'' I asked.

"Don't play punch-drunk," Quinn said. "We're talking about murder. You and Elaine Farinholt were in it together—just like you were in bed together in Texas. She wanted her old man's money, you wanted her.''

"I'd never have talked to you," Gaillard said, "if I was aware of your relationship with the suspect, if I knew you hated her father and bore a grudge against him since he kicked you off Syms Island.''

I couldn't help smiling. "Who told you that? Pierce?''

"We're not naming names yet.''

"Didn't these nameless sources mention why Andrew kept me away from Elaine?''

"She was pregnant.''

"Thought you guys didn't buy her story about an illegitimate son?'' Buck made my point for me.

"What we don't buy," Quinn said, "is the kid committed the murders.''

"You think Tom did? You gotta be desperate on top of dumb."

"His girlfriend pulled the trigger. The question is whether he was in on it from the start or came in later to suborn the investigation. That's what we'd like to discuss."

"Discuss? Am I hearing right? Is that what this burlesque boils down to? You'd like to discuss what he learned as an investigative journalist?"

"Investigative my ass," Quinn said. "He couldn't track a menstruating elephant through snow."

"I'm prepared to consider a plea bargain," Gaillard said. "How generous I am depends on how forthcoming he is with us. I'm not offering a free ride, but I'll make sure he gets a fair shake."

"You guys are throwing shit at the wall and seeing what sticks. You haven't charged him and you're already squeezing him to cop."

"The charge we're flexible about," Quinn said. "At the light end, could be obstruction of justice. He'd rather play hardball, we'll book him as an accomplice."

"Look, you two enjoy fishing expeditions so much, why not buy a pole?" Buck took me by the arm. "We're out of here. My record's intact," he shouted back at them. "I never met a prosecutor or cop yet believed the Bill of Rights was any better than ass wipe."

He led me from the lost-and-found office, through the gauntlet of cameramen and reporters. Shouting and shoving, they followed us as far as the sculpture of the Chesapeake blue crab, where Buck turned to them. "Okay, I'll give you a statement. Then give us a break and quit trampling on our heels. My brother is doing a book about the Yost-Farinholt murders. Everybody he's interviewed, including State's Attorney Gaillard and Detective Quinn, was advised of that fact. Mrs. Farinholt and he dated when they were in college. Before the murders, they hadn't seen each other for twenty-two years, and their present relationship is that of reporter and source. Period. He has no other involvement in the case.''

''What about the picture of them coming out of a motel room?''

''He was doing research in Texas. Mrs. Farinholt was there to introduce him to people from her past. She's a central figure in the case, and naturally Mr. Heller will be spending a lot of time with her.''

''All night in a motel?''

The crowd broke into laughter.

''The Anne Arundel County police and the State's Attorney started this campaign of rumors to cover up their own failures,'' Buck said. ''Because they haven't been able to solve the case, they're trying to coerce my client into sharing his journalistic information with them.''

''What information?''

''Read the book.'' He waved his chunky arms, signaling he was finished.

The questions came down then like a cloudburst, and they continued as we left the terminal and crossed the parking lot: Do you deny you were intimate with her? Isn't it true you were lovers around the time she had an illegitimate child? How would you characterize your relationship with Andrew Yost? Is there a legal reason why you live in Rome? How much were you paid to do the book? Have you sold the movie rights? Who do you see in your role? When do you expect to be arrested?

Once we were in the Isuzu, they scrambled for their cars and vans and trailed us for a few miles, shooting more footage. Then they peeled off toward their stations and newsrooms.

I waited until we reached the Parkway before I asked, ''How bad is it?''

''Shit, Tommy, what can I tell you?''

''Tell me the truth.''

''The truth is you're a stupid prick and you're in deep trouble.''

"Has it been in the papers, the picture of Elaine and me?"

"Not yet. Gaillard just released it this afternoon. It was all over the courthouse in about three minutes. That's when I learned they were planning this Welcome Wagon at the airport. I was afraid they'd collar you."

"If they had anything on me, they wouldn't be willing to cut a deal."

"Listen, their deal, case you didn't understand, it's not the kind your agent puts together at the Polo Lounge. They want you to do time."

"That's ridiculous."

He rammed the Isuzu into low gear and lumbered past a line of cars. "Terrific! When they arrest you, that's how we'll plead you—ridiculous."

"What is this? You've made up your mind and it doesn't matter what I say?"

"Hell, no. Happy to hear your side. Now tell me you didn't fuck her," he said. "Go ahead and tell me!"

"All right, I did."

"I hoped—my mistake—you were in this for professional reasons, not pussy. We were supposed to be doing a book together—"

"We are."

"—finding out who killed Big Tom."

"We will."

"Funny way of going about it, playing drop the salami with the suspect. Now you've got zero credibility as a writer and a witness. And what about me? What about the people that passed us information?"

"Everybody'll believe me when they hear what I have to say."

"Which is what?"

"Elaine did it."

His foot slipped off the accelerator, and the Isuzu back-fired, its speed falling steeply. Beer bottles and soft-drink cans rolled forward, clanking at our feet. There was the sensation of plummeting in an airplane whose engines have conked out. Then he stepped on the gas. "What's your proof?"

I repeated what Diane Kershner had told me—how Elaine kept the baby, and Andrew arranged for her to marry Townsend Farinholt and raise Clay as their son. "This Kershner woman admitted trying to blackmail the family," I said, "but she couldn't have been the murderer and there's no reason to believe she had somebody else do the job. But her letters were what triggered it. Elaine couldn't afford to let the whole truth come out."

I expected Buck to insist that I define "the whole truth," identify the father, explain why Clay and Andrew both had to die. But he took off on a tangent. "I mentioned there was gossip about Farinholt. You didn't want to hear it. But it fits. Word was he was gay. He and Elaine had a hands-off relationship. His death certificate reads cancer; rumor says it was AIDS."

"Jesus, the poor bastard. Poor both of them."

"You figure, what?" Buck said. "She needed a husband for camouflage, he needed a wife for his career, and they both needed Yost's dough?"

"Some variation on that theme. Then after he died, she moved back to the island and had Andrew leaning on her around the clock. Plus there was Clay and his problems. Even before he knocked up Doreen and the letters came, Elaine must have been ready to crack."

"So she decided to wipe the slate clean."

"And she started by shooting Big Tom."

"I'm still not with you a hundred percent on that," Buck said.

"You will be."

"Why didn't you let Gaillard in on this?"

"I need a few last pieces to pin things down. And I'm not ready to turn it over to the cops. I want to be the one that puts it to Elaine."

"I can't let you do that, Tommy."

"I'm not asking permission and I'm not asking you to be there. But that's the way it's going to be."

"No, listen, I know you feel you got burned way back when. And maybe you feel she jacked you around again, asking for an affidavit. But you're not going to change anything by making a worse mistake."

"You don't have any idea how I feel. Quinn can have her for killing Andrew and Clay. But I want to tell her to her face I know she murdered my father."

5

Eventually Buck did ask about the baby's father and the part Whiting Pierce had played. He hounded me to describe the last pieces of evidence and how they linked Elaine to Big Tom. But I told him nothing, had him drop me at the County Service Building, and refused to let him come in.

Although it still struck me as too hot and muggy to sit outdoors, three construction workers in hard hats and mud-spattered pants were at the picnic table near the entrance. They had parked their butts on top of the table and planted their dirt-caked boots on the bench, and as I walked by toting the suitcase from my trip, one guy hollered, "You got the wrong place, buddy. This ain't a motel."

I winced. Had they seen the photographs? No, I was probably safe on that score until this evening's news.

Leaving my suitcase with a guard, I passed through the metal detector, over to Tanya, the pregnant receptionist who worked in a cage. When I tapped the wire mesh, she poked two fingers through the screen and shook my hand.

"You must be due any day," I said.

"Yeah, I'm tired of waiting." Then seeing my bruised face, "Hey, is there a problem? You have something to report?"

"I'd like to talk to Gant."

"You know where he's at. I'll call, say you're coming down."

I descended into the cooler air, the stronger smells, the louder clanging of metal against metal. Gant met and walked me through the squad room to his fishbowl of an office. A short-sleeve shirt showed off his pumped-up arms. He looked as if he had just finished a hard set of reps on a Nautilus machine. It dawned on me if I were a suspect and Gant was on my case, I wouldn't care to chum up to him any more than I did to Mike Quinn.

Thumbtacked to a cork board behind his desk were mug shots of six Rastafarians. Each had a face as battered and lopsided as mine. Their bedraggled dreadlocks called to mind the broken antennae of insects that had been stomped on. Gant said, "Those boogers got a bad habit of resisting arrest. What's your story?"

I had no intention of telling him about my run-ins with Quinn and Jimmy. "You look happy, healthy," I said.

"Just cracked a million-dollar coke ring. You might say it's the first coke case in this district where we're satisfied we caught the whole gang."

I nodded at the Rastas. "Those fellows?"

"Nah. White boys, college kids." He clasped his hands behind his neck, flexing his biceps, right, then left. "It's a little different than your average coke bust. They were ripping off Coca-Cola machines, cracking open the change dispensers. Like I say, it's the only coke case we can close the book on."

I gave him the laugh he was looking for. "Seeing how you're in such a great mood, mind doing me a favor?"

"Do what I can."

"The slug from my father's murder—pass it on to Mike Quinn, have him send it to the lab and check whether it matches the ones from the Yost-Farinholt murders."

Gant's feet, crossed at the ankles and propped on his desk, started a steady rocking. "You been playing detective again? That how your kisser got mashed?"

"If the slugs match, they might want to cross-reference the prints. They lifted a partial from the barrel of the pistol they found on Syms Island. I think it's my father's print."

His expression barely altered, but the rocking of his feet slowed. "I don't mean to take the position of as long as

my ass is covered that's all I care. But a guy like Quinn,
I make a request, I gotta give a good reason.''

"Say you received an anonymous tip that all three murders were committed by the same person with the same
:38 Smith & Wesson. Point out that in both cases a man
with long blond hair was spotted at the scene.''

"There better be a damn sight more to it than that.''

"There is.''

"Any idea who was holding the gun?''

"There's no sense talking till there's a lab report. I'd be
grateful if you didn't mention my name or my father's.
Just send the slug and the prints and see what the lab
says.''

"I don't know. I'm flying blind here. Is this going to
blow back on me?''

"How can it hurt? If I'm right, you and Quinn and I'll
sit down and have a long talk.''

Lugging my suitcase like a Fuller Brush salesman, I hiked
through Hyattsville past pawn shops, shabby offices of bail
bondsmen, used-car dealers, boarded-up buildings, and a
junkyard where a mound of discarded tires had been baked
gray and wrinkly as elephant hide. With rush hour over
and the sidewalk to myself, I was reminded of summer
evenings when I had walked this route as a boy, returning
from baseball practice. There were the familiar feelings of
hunger and fatigue and a needling disquiet, a sense of
anticipation bordering on fear.

Back then, I was always on edge until I found out
whether my father was drunk and I was in trouble again.
But even at the worst times, there had been another, not
altogether unpleasant level of anticipation as I waited for
my life to begin and looked for the escape hatch, the loop-
hole, that would let me get out of this place. In my fantasies, not much different from Luke's dreams, I had
imagined I would accomplish miraculous feats, soar above
the crowd, shake off crippling flaws, and in my own style,
fly coast to coast—rich, loved, applauded.

Yet despite the distances I had traveled since then, despite a wallet full of credit cards that could fly me still farther, I felt earthbound. Normally at this point when researching a new project, I would have luxuriated in the conviction that I was a step or two away from learning the truth. But I wasn't looking forward to what would unfold next. I was at the end of something, not the beginning. I was going back to my father's house, waiting to learn who had killed him, convinced it was a woman I had loved and in whose schemes I had often seemed to serve as the ignorant go-between.

Buck jolted me awake the next morning with a phone call. "You read the newspaper?"

"Nope."

"Don't bother. What about TV? Seen it?"

"No, I've been concentrating on my stamp collection."

"You better stick one of those stamps on an envelope and send a long letter to Marisa."

"That bad?"

"Let's say it's a great likeness of you and Elaine enjoying quality time in Texas. Seriously, Tommy, how are you? Anything I can do to help?"

"Yeah, write that letter to Marisa."

"Not me, buddy. But I'm keeping my eyes and ears open at the courthouse. Yesterday Gaillard was tilting toward an indictment. This morning they're on hold."

"Gant got in touch with them."

"With what?"

"I'm waiting. You wait."

To kill time I washed a week's dirty dishes, vacuumed the TV room, changed the sheets on my parents' bed, and finished two loads of laundry. Although the flurry of housekeeping was reminiscent of my days as a bachelor, I didn't forget for a minute that I was married and needed to talk to Marisa—to apologize, to negotiate a plea bargain. Still, I stalled, telling myself I'd better leave the line clear for Gant. Telling myself it was senseless to speak to Marisa until I had all the facts.

The phone rang that afternoon, and a voice I couldn't place asked, "This Thomas Heller? I'm talking about the writer."

"Who's asking?"

"Curtis Koontz." He chuckled as if amused by his own name. "Been seeing your snapshot with the widow Farinholt and I gotta ask up front, you in this with her?"

"In what?"

He cackled again. "Not in bed. That's none of my business and she's not my type. Looks like it'd take a jump starter to get her motor running. But hey, different strokes. Thing I need to know, do you have an exclusive with her for a book and movie?"

"I told you, I don't pay for information."

"That's how I remembered it. What I been considering, maybe I took the short view the other day. Maybe it'd be to Doreen's advantage to cooperate with you. Just to talk, what if I let you interview her, what would you ask?"

"That's another thing I don't do. I don't hand out questions in advance."

"Like you, I got no time these days to play it cagey. Which is why I'm grateful you're being blunt."

"Is something on your mind, Curtis?"

"Like always! Rust never sleeps. The subject that pops up over and over is whether to consolidate my gains."

"You and Pierce discussing a settlement?"

"That's this world we're living in, Tom—discussions and deals. Let's be in touch."

When the phone rang again a little later, I heard the subaqueous echoes of a transatlantic connection. "I was just about to call you," I lied.

"But you didn't," Marisa said.

"A lot of things have been happening. Some of them aren't clear yet."

"Yes, people have been phoning me all day. They weren't

too clear either.'' There were pauses between her words and strange stress patterns to her sentences. She spoke with the deliberateness of a diplomat—or of a woman left in the dark.

''It'd be better,'' I said, ''if we talked about this when we're together.''

''When will that be?''

''I should know something soon. Then I have one last meeting. Then I'll . . . I'll know.''

''Know what? Is it because it's long distance and you don't want to run up the bill? Is that why you're talking in shorthand? If you have something to say, tell me now, Tom. The boys are in bed. There's no one to interrupt or overhear. I can take almost anything except this vagueness.''

''I don't know what to tell you that won't upset you.''

''You don't think I'm already upset?'' Actually, she didn't sound upset, but it was the affectless tone of her voice that indicated exactly how distraught she was. ''People have told me about the newspapers, the film on TV. Who is this woman?''

''Somebody I knew a long time ago.''

''And now you know her again ''

I could have denied it. I could have told her, as I had Pierce weeks ago, that I wasn't sure I had ever known Elaine. I could have been honest and asked for forgiveness. But I attempted to steer the conversation onto a different track. ''The woman in the picture—don't tell this to anybody—but she's the one who murdered Big Tom.''

''I suppose you think that explains everything. I ask who she is and you tell me what crime she committed. Can't you hear yourself talk, Tom?'' Her words came quicker now, her voice climbing the scale. ''Are you that big a fool? Do you believe I am? Or do you really define people this way?''

''I thought you'd want to know.''

''What I want to know is what she is to you.''

''*Was* to me. I dated her in college.''

"The newspapers say that you were lovers. That she had a baby—perhaps yours—and gave it away."

"No. She was pregnant when I met her. I wanted to marry her. But she disappeared, and—this is what the papers, even the police, don't know—she married a man and raised the baby as their son. A few weeks ago—are you with me?—she shot Big Tom, then her father and son, and is trying to pin the murders on the dead boy. Do you understand?"

"Of course I don't understand. Because once again you're talking about a crime, the plot from one of your books. You're not saying how you feel or what this woman means to you or why you were in a motel with her."

"It's hard to explain over the phone. Please, wait and let me do it in person. The important thing is I love you. Not Elaine Farinholt."

"What hurts me, Tom, is you never confided in me, never mentioned this person or her baby or that time in your life. How can we be married for so many years and you never even said her name?"

"I guess I was afraid to talk about it."

"Afraid?" she asked, incredulous. "You're the man who papers his office with morgue photographs. You're the one who sits on death row and holds the killer's hand, the one who doesn't care about being arrested for contempt or sued for libel or called a scavenger. And this woman frightens you?"

"Look, it's a long, long story. When we're together, I'll start at the beginning," I said, wondering where that might be. "Until then, please take my word that I love you. Trust me and this'll work out."

"It's hard to trust you, Tom, when I feel I don't know you anymore. You keep so much of yourself from me and the boys. It's not just this woman, whoever she is. It's not just this time with Big Tom's murder. For you there's always another case, another excuse to leave us or to lock yourself in your office."

"Look, it's my job. It's how I support us."

"No, it's more than a job. It's how you choose to live. It's like you're a policeman. No, a priest. Someone who's taken a vow."

"You're exaggerating. You know I'm only doing research."

"No, I don't know," she said. "We have enough money. There must be other things to write."

"But that's what people love," I said. "True crime."

"I don't," she said. "I love you, not your books. The question is how much you love me."

"Of course I—"

"No, don't answer. Think about it. Do you love me and the boys enough to change? Because we can't keep on going like this." And to drive her point home, she hung up.

Hours later, when the phone rang, my first thought was that Marisa had stayed awake stewing and was calling back to raise the stakes of her ultimatum. But it was Gant. "We've got a match," he said.

"The slugs? Or the print too?"

"Both. Tell me who the shooter is."

"Why are you phoning at midnight? You and the fellows in Anne Arundel County been working overtime to figure it out on your own?"

"This late, I don't have a lot of patience. Neither does Quinn. Let's cut the shit and say what you know."

"I'll drop by tomorrow morning."

"Now. Gimme a name now."

"It's not that simple," I said. "I'll need to tell you more than a name. Let's talk when we're not half asleep."

"Okay. Quinn and I'll be at the station at eight-thirty sharp. You be here too."

As soon as he hung up, I bolted the house behind me and raced off in the Toronado. My hunch was that Gant had no intention of waiting until tomorrow. When I heard a squad car, siren blaring, head uphill in my direction, I knew my hunch was right. He meant to take me into custody and subpoena a statement if he had to.

Swinging into an alley, driving without lights as I'd often done as a teenager on these back streets, I barreled over the rutted pavement, bouncing garbage cans against garages, rattling gravel against my wheel wells. Dogs and cats and a couple of kids clutching crack pipes scattered before me. Low-hanging willow branches buggy-whipped the car roof; shoals of leaves eddied behind me. I could hear the cruiser, but couldn't see it and was sure it couldn't see me. At Bladensburg Road I switched on my lights and was soon lost in traffic.

My instinct was to head straight for Syms Island. But there was no chance of getting past the guards at the gate unless I let Elaine know I was on the way, and I didn't want her to have any warning.

From a Burger Chef in Cheverly, I phoned Buck, who was fuddled with sleep. "Did I wake you?" I asked.

"Oh, hell no. After midnight, Peggy and I lock the kids in the closet, break open the K-Y jelly, and play leapfrog all over the living room."

"I need to borrow your boat."

"Slow down. Don't hit me with everything boom, boom, boom! What's this about a boat?"

"I just got word—the gun that killed Big Tom is the same one that killed Andrew and Clay."

"Got word from where?"

"Gant. I'm going to Syms Island."

"Not in my boat, you're not."

"You want me to swim? I'll damn well do it. Swear to Christ I will."

"Okay, okay. Cool your jets, Tommy. Come to my place."

At this hour, Route 50 was deserted; I floored the accelerator and made the trip in half an hour. At Buck's house, the porch lamp illuminated the patchy front lawn and about a thousand dollars' worth of baseballs, basketballs, badminton racquets, and dirt bikes. Standing at the screen door staring out through a blizzard of moths, my brother wore a brown terry-cloth robe with loose threads at the cuffs and hem. He looked more bearlike than ever, his beard as disheveled as the robe.

"Get dressed and let's get started," I said.

He grabbed and dragged me inside. "You ain't going anywhere."

I tried to twist free. He tightened his grasp.

"Don't fight and wake up the kids." He strong-armed me into the TV room and plopped me down in the canvas sling chair. "The Bay's overcast tonight—no visibility and three-foot swells. Wait till morning and I'll run you over there. Only thing I ask—insist!—I don't drop you on the beach. I stay with you every step of the way."

"No. I'm going in alone."

"You're not going anywhere without me."

I started to stand up. He slammed me down and clamped his hands on my shoulders. "This is another casebook example, Tommy, in how far you're ready to push it to prove a point. Only problem is, nobody, 'specially not me, understands what your point is."

"It's a private matter between Elaine and me."

He shook me so roughly he rocked the chair on its creaking legs. "You're ignoring the fact I got feelings about this too. Even leaving out we're supposed to be working together, leaving out you made a horse's ass of yourself with this lady and are liable to do it again, don't forget he was my father too," Buck roared. "I'm fucking well coming with you."

Brendan, wearing blue Underoos, blundered into the room, yawning and scratching, and flopped onto a bean-bag chair. "I had a bad dream. Can I have a cup of apple juice?"

"I told you not to argue," Buck shouted. "Now you woke the kids."

The other three stumbled in. The oldest, Megan, had on a Naval Academy football jersey that hung down to her knees. "What are you two doing?"

Someone switched on the television and tuned it to MTV. Tom Waits rasped "Downtown Train."

"Turn that damn thing off." Peggy, in a T-shirt, strode over and punched the power button. "You jerks want to fight, take it outside."

"We're not fighting," Buck said.

"Then pipe down and let the rest of us sleep."

He released his grip on me. "Come on, team, back to bed." He bundled the three little ones into his arms and carried them off toward their rooms. "See you in the morning," he called to me.

"You staying or going?" Peggy demanded.

It was useless to try to reach the island alone. I also recognized Buck had a right to come along. "Staying."

She fetched a pillow and sheet and flung them onto my lap. "Sorry, Romeo. Maybe you're accustomed to better accommodations and classier company, but in my house you're bunking on the couch or the beanbag. What'll it be?"

"Give me a break, Peggy. I admit I made a mistake."

"A mistake? That's what you call it?" Fists on hips, she stood there in her T-shirt, her brown arms and legs so tight with rage they would have resounded to the touch like harp strings. "If I was Marisa and saw that picture, I'd—"

"Please." I raised my hands, surrendering.

"Really, Tommy, how could you?"

"It's a long, long story," I repeated the line I'd given Marisa.

"Bullshit! It's a short story. It's the same old story. Now you've got Buck caught up in it—both of you chasing around like damn fools, writing about this rich bitch and her family problems when you should be worrying about your own."

"Didn't Buck tell you? We're looking for Big Tom's killer."

"I wish you'd cared about him half as much when he was alive."

"You don't know what you're talking about. I always cared."

"No, he didn't count for much until he was dead and you saw a way to use him in a book and get even with your old girlfriend."

"Like you're getting even with me now. You've been waiting years for this chance, haven't you?"

"If I'm wrong, prove it," Peggy said. "Call the cops and let them handle Elaine Farinholt."

That shut me up.

6

The sofa was too short and narrow. I beat the beanbag chair flat and curled up on it, convinced I'd never sleep. For a long while I lay on the sack of Styrofoam bubbles, floating amid an ocean of metal robots and Micro Machines, sizzling with grievances and regrets, realizing too late what I should have said to Peggy, wondering how I'd ever make things right with her and Marisa. But it didn't take long for my sorrow and shame to yield to deeper obsessions, impatience with the passing hours, eagerness to tear away the final gauzy veil.

When I dozed off at last, it was to dreams that so accurately mimicked a waking state I couldn't conceive that I was asleep. For hours, it seemed, I did nothing but argue with a succession of faceless figures.

In the morning when Buck shook me awake, he marveled, "You can make it through a night on this sucker, you're ready for a bed of nails."

I was anxious to leave at once; he insisted on breakfast. Lumbering around the kitchen in cutoff jeans, a sleeveless sweatshirt, and a clunky pair of Nikes, he hummed as he fixed waffles and coffee and listened to a shortwave radio. I could do no more than listlessly push food around my plate.

When he shoved a pair of jogging shoes at me, I shook my head no. He dropped them on my lap. "Those loafers of yours'll make scuff marks on my boat. Not to mention you'll slip and break your ass."

At the dock, on a brackish creek scummed over with

algae, Buck led me aboard a Boston Whaler powered by an outboard engine. It was seven A.M. and already the sun burned down to the roots of my hair. As he threaded the boat through a channel clotted with cattails, he mused, "Why don't I call Gaillard, lay the evidence out for him, and—"

"Don't start."

We had reached the Bay and our fiberglass bottom was spanking against a light chop, cooling us with spray, when he spoke again. "Ever occur to you, assuming you're right and she is a killer, she might not sit there sweetly while you saddle her with triple homicide?"

"I'm sure she'll fight back."

"Forget about fighting. What if she starts shooting?"

"If you're worried, don't come in."

"No, I'm coming. It's just, Jesus, Tommy!"

We headed north, hugging the shoreline, watching people in modest beach cottages, baronial mansions, and weather-blistered shacks wake to the summery September morning. Little kids in pajamas sat on a porch swing and waved. An old black woman with yellow-white hair was on her knees at the end of a pier, pulling crab pots. Men with briefcases paused in their suits and starched shirts, peering at us before turning to their cars and the long commute to the office. Clumps of toenagers at a school bus stop eyed us enviously, imagining what fun it was to be grown-up, to be free.

"All I ask," Buck said, "is keep it short. Say your piece, then let's split before we get busted."

On Syms Island, a lifeguard was dipping leaves out of the swimming pool with a long-handled net. It was much too early for the trees to turn, but after months of drought, the leaves were brittle and curled at the edges, and the faintest breath of air sent them spiraling down into the water.

I didn't have to give Buck directions to the Yost house. For weeks there had been shots of it on the evening news. Its fluted columns and mullioned windows were now stock footage every bit as familiar as the logos of the local network affiliates. Coasting on gentle breakers the last few yards to the beach, nosing the Boston Whaler into wet sand, we jumped out and hauled the boat up near the high-water mark, mooring it to a boulder.

"This is state property," Buck said. "Theoretically, they can't impound my boat. Now we're trespassing." He caught up to me, striding across the cropped grass, our shoes dampening with dew. He was so fidgety I decided not to mention the security guard.

A doe and two fawns sauntered out of a copse of trees, alert and twitchy, but not frightened. Buck muttered, "What the hell?"

Rounding the house, I rang at the rear entrance and hoped the maid, not the rent-a-cop, would answer. I got my wish. But then Mary Beth took a look at Buck's burly arms and bare, hairy legs and reacted as warily as any guard.

"You remember me," I said. "We're here on business with Mrs. Farinholt."

"I'll call her."

"That's all right. I know the way."

She and Buck followed me over the pegged floors, past the antique furniture. He swiveled his head, drinking it in—the heirlooms, the hunting scenes, the découpage tables.

Puffing to keep up, Mary Beth said, "She ain't expecting company."

Seated amid the potted plants on the glassed-in porch, Elaine wore a green silk kimono with a floral pattern that matched the cushions. She had combed her hair, but hadn't applied makeup, not even lipstick. Her eyes were puffy as if she'd had a rough night.

Whiting Pierce, in a wine-colored robe with an Yves Saint Laurent monogram, sat beside her on the couch, finishing a breakfast of croissants and coffee. If they were shocked to see us, they didn't show it. Maybe they had watched us walk up from the beach. Maybe they'd been waiting for me.

Buck was still taking it in—the commanding view of the Bay, the massive feel of the house, the silverware and china, the single rose in a slender crystal vase, Elaine rising to the occasion with an insouciance that verged on arrogance. I waited for him—wanted him—to cut loose with a wisecrack, but he was cowed into silence.

"The gentlemen, they say they have business," Mary Beth said, "and they bust on in."

"That's fine," Elaine told her. "You can go."

"You know, of course"—Pierce was wiping marmalade from his mouth—"there's an armed guard in the house. All I have to do is call him."

"Why don't you? Be good to have him as a witness." I found myself falling into the broad mocking tone I expected from Buck.

Elaine lifted her coffee cup with both hands—to keep them from trembling, I thought.

"This is my brother," I said. "Buck. He's a lawyer. Pierce knows him."

"You never mentioned you had a brother." She made him a gift of her green-eyed smile. "Would you like coffee, Buck?"

"No, thanks." He settled into one of the rattan chairs. I sat next to him facing Elaine. "You interested in hearing what I found out in Texas?"

"In recent days," Pierce said, "Mrs. Farinholt has been reassessing her interests. She's concluded her interests are no longer compatible with yours."

"Is that true?" I asked her.

"Actually, it's your interests that appear to have changed," she said. "Otherwise you'd have called me when you got back. You wouldn't have brought a lawyer."

Like me, Buck was watching Elaine, admiring her aplomb, the composure I had seldom seen her lose anywhere except in bed. I meant to smash it now. "Yeah, things have changed," I said. "I never did find a ranch with the word 'white' in it. But I met a woman who worked at the Creekmore Agency. Remember Diane Kershner?''

"I can't say I do.''

"She hasn't forgotten you. Fact is she remembers everything. What you did with the baby. Why there aren't any birth or adoption records. How you came to marry Townsend Farinholt.''

She set the coffee cup on the tray, and no, I was wrong. Her fingers weren't trembling. She laid one hand on the arm of the couch and slid the other up behind Pierce. Tucking the robe between his knees, he folded his bare legs and put on a bland professional face.

"Her memory's so good,'' I said, "there's no doubt you did it. You killed Andrew and Clay.''

Having witnessed plenty of police interrogations and courtroom cross-examinations, I realized it was rare to see a dramatic moment of revelation. At most a suspect might suck in his breath or experience some involuntary facial tic. Still I expected Elaine to do more than quietly ask, "And why would I do that?''

"When Clay got the blackmail letters and threatened to turn them over to the press, that was enough to rattle you. But you understood if that much came out, so would the rest of it. You didn't want people to know Clay was illegitimate. You didn't want them to know Farinholt was a homosexual and your marriage was strictly a matter of convenience.''

"Oh, is that all it was?'' she asked, arching her eyebrows. " 'A marriage of convenience'? Sounds like something from a gothic romance. Are you switching genres, Tom? Borrowing from your literary betters?''

It surprised me that that hurt. "Too bad you can't beat a murder rap with book criticism.''

"Tell me,'' she said, "why would I kill Daddy too?''

"You mean besides the fact that he bullied you for years?'' I moved more cautiously, perplexed by what was for someone of her temperament a tepid reaction. "He ruled your life with his money, ruined it. I bet he loved rubbing your nose in mistakes you made as a girl. But the main reason you killed him was he believed I was Clay's father. He never guessed it was you, did he, Whiting? You and Elaine couldn't afford to have him find that out.''

Like Elaine, the dapper attorney scarcely seemed concerned. Holding down the hem of his robe, he recrossed his legs. ''Legally speaking, I'm a 'private figure.' You've been sued for libel often enough to understand that term. If you write about this, if you invade my privacy or Elaine's, I intend to make you very sorry you did.''

''Hey,'' Buck spoke up, ''I'm no expert in libel, but unless I'm miles off base, you're not going to make much headway against a homicide charge by claiming to be a private figure.''

''Are you accusing me of murder? First it's my client. Then it's her attorney. This is reckless disregard.''

''Don't get all Frank Lloyd Righteous.'' The old Buck was rousing himself. ''Before we showed up—correct me if I'm wrong—you were here in a personal capacity. This appears to be in the nature of an intimate relationship, unless you two are in your robes cooling off after aerobics.''

''Whatever our relationship, it doesn't make me a murderer,'' he said.

''Yeah, but if you're Clay's father, it sure gives you a shitload to explain.''

''You're right about some things.'' Elaine skipped the lawyerly bickering and spoke to me. ''That's always been your problem, Tom. You're right up to a point. Then you go on pushing and pushing until you're blind to everything except your need to punish people, to prove you're just as good as they are.''

''I'm listening.'' I leaned back in the chair, taking a stab at her sort of sangfroid. ''Tell me where I'm wrong.''

''She isn't going to tell you a damn thing,'' Pierce said. ''She isn't going to dignify these accusations.''

Elaine ignored him. ''Of course I didn't want people to

know about Clay and Townsend. And I didn't feel any obligation to tell the police all my business and have them leak it to the press. Clay had every right to rest in peace and Townsend had a right to his reputation. Whatever he did in his private life, it was nobody's affair but his own.''

''You still haven't said where I'm wrong.''

''When the police found the letters,'' she went on at her own pace, ''I let Whiting admit that I'd had an illegitimate son, and Sam Gaillard drew his own conclusions. I just didn't explain it was Clay. I didn't think I'd have to. I thought they'd go after the blackmailer and catch the killer.''

''Diane Kershner wrote the letters,'' I said.

''Why didn't you tell us?'' Pierce demanded. ''Have you informed Gaillard of that fact?''

''She's not the murderer. She has multiple sclerosis, she's confined to a wheelchair.''

''She could have an accomplice,'' Pierce said, ''someone she hired.''

''She had no reason to have Clay and Andrew killed. They were no good to her dead. She wanted money. You two wanted them out of the way.''

''This is all very fascinating, these theories of yours.'' He regally gathered the wine-colored robe around himself. ''But I don't believe you've got any more evidence than Sam Gaillard.''

Buck swung his eyes, the full weight of his attention, over to me, and I sensed that he, almost as much as they, remained to be convinced.

''The night before Clay and Andrew were murdered,'' I said, ''my father was shot. All three killings were committed with the same .38 Smith & Wesson. The link between the cases—the only person who had a reason to shoot those three people—is Elaine.''

Shaking back the sleeves of her kimono, she let the green silk slide up her slender arms. Except for the dark vein on her forehead, she was icily calm. ''And why would I murder your father?''

"You were establishing a pattern. That's why you had Pierce call me. The affidavit was secondary. You knew sooner or later I'd see the connection and point it out to the police. You counted on me to convince them to keep chasing after a dead man, the illegitimate son you had already murdered."

Returning to her two-handed grip on the coffee cup, she raised it to her lips and grimaced. Maybe the coffee had gone cold. Maybe she was pantomiming her distaste for me. In fact, her behavior ever since we arrived struck me as a pantomime, a kind of disappearing act. I had been wrong to warn Buck that she'd fight back. That's not what people of wealth and position did with their social inferiors. Instead, they withdrew, disappeared, as she had done with me twice before, as she was doing now.

"We were warned what you were up to," Pierce said. "We knew about your father's murder and how you were using this business about a book to frame Elaine."

"Who told you?" Buck asked. "Quinn? Gaillard?"

"They'd hardly help us. It was Curtis Koontz."

"He doesn't know his ass from his elbow," Buck said.

"I share your estimate of his legal ability. But he does have excellent sources of information."

"How long have you known?" I asked Elaine.

"Weeks."

"Then why'd you come to Texas with me?"

"I didn't want to believe it. I wanted to give you a chance to prove you weren't framing me."

"I don't suppose it had anything to do with leading me down a blind alley."

"Naturally, you'd see it that way. You've always imputed the worst possible motives to me. But you've never been good at examining your own."

"My motive's simple—finding out who murdered my father."

"Is that why you spent the night with me. Did you think I'd talk in my sleep?"

It wasn't her bluntness or the fact that she spoke up in

front of Pierce that caught me by surprise. It was something in her eyes, a look of betrayal, a bitter glint I had seen in my own mirror. For an instant I wavered, wondering whether I might be mistaken. But the lab report was irrefutable. "I didn't want to believe it about you either. I wanted to give you a chance to prove me wrong."

She laughed. She laughed so hard she had to steady her coffee cup. "You always have such noble intentions, Tom. You never do anything for yourself, do you?"

"I presume," Pierce said, "that you think the same person who killed your father murdered Andrew and Clay."

"I'm sure of it," I said, although suddenly I wasn't.

"Then what you've done," Elaine said, "with all your— what do you call it? Your research? Your scab-picking—is prove I'm innocent. Because, you see, the night your father was shot I was in Connecticut."

"Be glad to show you the plane tickets. The receipts for the hotel and meals. I was with her," Pierce said to cut short any conjecture that he had taken care of Big Tom while his client was out of town.

"We flew up together with Clay to look at a detox center," Elaine said. "We met the director, the doctors. We hoped if Clay got back into therapy . . ."

As she continued her coldly polite explanation as if to a servant she was about to dismiss, I couldn't listen. I couldn't bear to look at her, couldn't stand up to her poisonous stare. I felt my bones melt, my mind turn to mush. I had felt this way before both times that I lost her. Now I was losing something more essential, some long-held image of myself.

Pushing to his feet, Whiting Pierce tightened the belt of his robe and told Buck, "It's up to your brother to take this new evidence to the State's Attorney."

"Tommy'll do the right thing."

"I hope so. He once insinuated he'd flee to Italy to avoid a subpoena."

"I said he'll do it and he will. Come on, Tommy."

Buck didn't wait. He didn't want to face me yet—no more than I cared to face him. Pierce followed him, leaving me alone with Elaine.

Head reeling, I hauled myself upright. I had a sense of reaching for something that retreated, dreamlike, just beyond my bobbling fingertips. It had seemed close last night, securely in my grasp. Now it was gone.

I started to touch Elaine, but didn't dare. I was afraid I'd hurt her, just as I had been afraid when she was pregnant that my weight was more than she could bear.

"I'm sorry," I said.

"Whatever you think of me, no matter how much you hate me, I'll never understand how you could believe I killed Clay."

"You should have told me. You should have told me the truth from the start."

"You wouldn't have believed me. You probably don't believe me now."

"I do. Just one thing. Did you ever mention me to Clay?"

"No, never."

"What about Andrew? Could he have given Clay my name?"

"How would I know?" She was fed up with my questions. Still, I had to ask a final one.

"Was I his father?"

"No. How many times do you have to hear it? He was Whiting's son." Her voice had started to quaver. "One thing I want to make clear. Whatever your reasons for sleeping with me in Texas, I did it because I still had feelings for you. You were a happy memory from a horrible time in my life. Now you've destroyed that too."

"I'm sorry," I said again, then withdrew down the echoing halls, past the portraits of stern-faced and peruked ancestors of some stranger's family.

As I walked from the house, over the springy grass, I was reminded of the day the security guard had marched me at gunpoint up this lawn, and my blood had seethed

with murderous rage, with a desire to get even. Back then
I couldn't imagine a deeper, more shattering ignominy
But this was worse, and there was no illusion of an enemy
a deserving target. I was on my own, wondering how many
other times, about how many other people, I had been
wrong.

At the boat, Buck was being berated by an elderly gentleman in pressed white ducks and a panama hat. "You're
trespassing on private property," the man ranted.

"Sorry, but you see, we deliver anywhere, and when
Mrs. Farinholt ordered an anchovy pizza, we zipped right
over to the island. Here's my assistant. We'll be shoving
off. You ever come down with a case of the munchies,
give us a ring."

Buck waved me aboard, walked the Boston Whaler into
the Bay, and vaulted over the gunwale.

Syms Island was falling far off to our stern, its outline
a few faint pencil marks on the horizon, when I said, "Is
it possible Pierce or Elaine—"

"Listen to me for once in your goddamn life, Tommy.
Let go!"

7

I retreated to my parents' home, to the tall, lopsided house that looked like a larger structure that had been whittled down to half size. There, behind the facade of fake fieldstone, I regressed to childhood. No, I regressed further—to infancy, to a primitive stage of utter dependence and oral gratification. In the following days I may have eaten a bite or two, but I only remember drinking, then nodding off to troubled sleep and Technicolor dreams. I drank beer, wine, whiskey; it didn't matter. I liked the taste, and as Big Tom had said of his own craving for booze, I liked what it did to me. For hours at a stretch, it blotted out thought and kept me unconscious.

Sometimes I came to in the kitchen, my cheek glued to the tabletop. Other times, I woke in the TV room, having cratered on the BarcaLounger. Luke was always with me, the tube was tuned to the Olympics, and he was providing a nonstop commentary on the games in Seoul and events closer to home. "Got cops in the neighborhood asking questions, which I'm not surprise. Got reporters crawling around the front yard waiting for you, even wanting to know who I am. I tell them, 'I'm the baby-sitter. Unpaid,' I say so the VA won't cut my benefits on account of I'm supposed to be too disabled to work would be the stated reason."

During the basketball competition, Luke chattered more about his worries than mine. He didn't like the U.S. team's chances or its racial composition. "Normally I'm the last man in this world to bitch they got nothing but blacks on the squad, except one white boy that plays like he's black too. But this here's international ball, which you can argue back and forth, but one sure thing, you don't have to go airborne to win with these rules. You need white boys that grew up in the suburbs aiming at a hoop on a garage door, guys that don't never go near the paint. You need players that park out there in the ozone and stick those three-pointers.''

It's possible Buck had asked Luke not to leave me alone. Maybe they feared I'd do some irreparable damage to myself. But the damage had been done, and I had the sensation of sitting on a train, facing backward, watching scenes fade and disappear. My life, my career, was being unwritten before my eyes. Having set out to discover the identity of a victim as well as the murderer, I had failed on both counts. I was the only one exposed, the only culprit incriminated in this case.

When Gant and Quinn came to take my statement, I didn't claim journalistic privilege, didn't do as I had so often done in the past—save the juiciest tidbits for a book. I told them almost everything I knew or had reasonable cause to suspect. The one fact I held back was the identity of Clay's father. When they pressed that subject, I repeated Elaine's assurances that the child wasn't mine.

They didn't buy that or much of the rest of what I said. The only point I managed to persuade them of was that the cases had to be connected. Still, they kept pounding away with questions. What were my feelings toward my father? How would I characterize our relationship?

''Complicated,'' I told them. ''Complicated on both counts.''

When I produced my passport and proved I had been in Italy the night Big Tom was shot, they started in on Buck. Did he have reason to resent his father? Was I aware of my brother's financial problems? How much did he stand to inherit?

''For Chrissake,'' I said, ''you really think he killed his own father, then murdered two people he never met to throw suspicion on a person—Elaine's kid—he never knew about?"

"How we have it figured"—Quinn was sitting about six inches from my face—"you and Buck worked it out between yourselves. Buck caps the old man. Then you fly back and take care of your business."

"So why would I check in with the cops the first chance I got?" I appealed to Gant, who sat with his arms folded, his hands cupping the meaty curve of his biceps. "Tell him who brought you the bullet."

"There's different ways of explaining why you'd do that," Quinn cut in.

"Tell him who kept pushing the investigation, feeding you information."

"The thing of it is," Gant said, "they traced that trey-eight, the murder weapon. Last one in line is a bozo Buck represented."

"You should be questioning the bozo. Not me."

"We have," Quinn said. "He's slammed up, serving five to seven for armed robbery. That's some fabulous public defender, your brother."

"Maybe he had a guilty client. It happens, you know."

"Yeah, it also happens PDs get too close to their clients. Get ideas from them. Get guns from them."

"Is this guy claiming he gave Buck the .38?"

"He's not claiming anything just yet," Gant said. "He's waiting to climb on the car, see what's in it for him."

"I get it. You knock a few years off his sentence and he rolls over on Buck. Or anybody else you point to."

"It's not like that," Gant said.

"Yeah, well, it's like this. I've said all I'm going to say."

Once I got rid of Gant and Quinn, I called Buck. But he was way ahead of me. "They been here two or three times, and they keep schmoozing with this dildo up at the House of Corrections."

"Well?"

"Well what?" Buck said.

"Did he give you a gun?"

"You ask me a question like that, Tommy, you must have a hole in your head."

"Come on. I saw that cannon in your glove compartment. You told me how you got it."

"Number one, I don't appreciate what you're implying—like there's the slightest chance this is true."

"No, I just—"

"No, you just listen," he steamed on. "Number two, I'm not in love with the idea of talking on the telephone, not knowing how far a dickhead like Quinn would push things. Let's cut this short—which is what I should've done weeks ago when you brought it up."

"Before you go jumping down my throat, why don't you talk to your client? Find out what he did with that .38."

"*Former* client. You follow? I can't visit him without his permission or a court order."

"I assume you've tried."

"Good assumption, bro. Another assumption you should consider, they got him like in a luxury hospitality suite where he's not in any hurry to make up his mind what happened to his gun. Meanwhile, I was you, I'd stop everything—stop talking to cops, stop thinking, stop sticking your nose where it doesn't belong."

"Jesus, Buck, I'm sorry. I didn't mean—"

"Just let's stop right here, Tommy."

That sent me skidding back to the bottle, and I stayed there the next day when the news broke about Buck's link—they made it sound as if he were joined at the hip—to the convict who owned the Smith & Wesson. My brother and I were described as primary suspects. We were also described as unavailable for comment. When reporters phoned or rang the doorbell, I said nothing, wouldn't even acknowledge my name much less that I had had an affair with Elaine recently or in the remote past.

I didn't have much more to say when my agent, then my publisher, called to discuss six- and seven-figure deals, wraparound contracts and docudramas. "Nightline" wanted an interview, my agent said. So did the *Washington Post*. The *New York Times* invited me to write an op-ed piece. CBS asked to send a camera crew for a segment of "48 Hours" entitled "Celebrity Under Siege." My publisher warned that if I didn't make a preemptive strike, I couldn't expect to keep the story to myself. In New York, book proposals were circulating. On the West Coast, the concept was being pitched at script conferences.

I told them to deal me out.

Luke took to answering the door and the phone, and he dismissed everybody with his version of no comment. "In other words of verbalizing it, my man's got nothing to say."

We warmed up for the basketball semifinal between the United States and the Soviet Union with a bottle of Jim Beam. From the opening tip-off, the Russians outmuscled and outshot the U.S., and Luke gloomily predicted catastrophe. "What'd I tell you? You gotta have them suburban jump shooters."

In the second half, he began beating his crutches against the footrest of the BarcaLounger every time the Soviets scored. "How come, all the mean motherfuckers in this country, we couldn't find a few to block those Commies off the boards?"

While the U.S.A. whipped itself into a last-minute lather of futile energy, Luke went limp with resignation and bourbon, and by the time the Russians advanced to the gold-medal round, he was snoring softly and was in no condition to hear the phone. I wasn't in much better shape myself. I let it ring fifteen or twenty times before I realized it might be Buck or Marisa. Staggering to the kitchen dizzy and confused, I clung to the receiver as if to a life raft. Gradually, it registered who was yammering in my ear—Curtis Koontz.

"You and me got business to discuss," he said.

"No, what we've got to discuss"—my brain was shedding cobwebs filament by filament—"is why you told Whiting Pierce about my father."

"Oh, that," he said like a kid caught in some small mischief. "That's old news."

"Not for me. Murders don't get old."

"Look, you want to talk murder, mind if we do it in person? My rule of thumb, never discuss felonies on the telephone."

"How'd you even know he was dead?"

"Who?"

"My father."

"It's my business to know. Hell, it was in the paper, in the Metro section. They're my meat and potatoes, those inside pages. I read them every day, checking on old clients, scouting for new ones. Now are we going to do business or aren't we?"

"What are you pitching?"

"I know who did it—who offed all three of them."

My mind snapped into focus, but the rest of my swaying body went on working fuzzily and at half speed. "Why call me? Why not the police?"

Koontz guffawed. "That's rich. You're asking, you want to know, why I don't fork it over free when there's producers and directors drooling to buy this story?"

"I told you I—"

"Sure, you don't pay for interviews. What I'm asking, do you pay for info that'll get you and your brother off the hook? Or you two rather hang out to dry while I shop this around?"

"Where are you?"

"The Hitching Post Motel. Route One, right before you reach Laurel. I'm not waiting all night."

While water was heating in the microwave, I moved over to the sink, turned on the cold spigot, and stuck my wrists, then my head, under the faucet. Drenched and drunk, I fixed a mug of coffee and left without waking Luke, without bothering to dry my hands and head.

In front of the house, a few creeps with cameras shot

footage of me fumbling with the keys to the Toronado, glassy-eyed, mouth agape, wet hair wild. I could imagine how I'd look on the evening news—crazy and guilty. But that didn't slow me down. Neither did their shouted questions.

I switched on the Oldsmobile's AC and aimed the vents at my face. The cold air helped no more than the hot coffee. When I hit U.S. 1, it was all I could do to steer a straight line and remember to stop at red lights.

I considered calling Buck, asking him to meet me at the motel. But I could guess his response. No sense dragging him in deeper until I saw where this thing bottomed out.

The Hitching Post, a horseshoe-shaped loop of cinder-block cottages, used to cater to grooms and exercise boys from Laurel Race Track. Now its office windows were boarded up, the roadside sign was a Swiss cheese of bullet holes, and the parking lot was crowded with earth-moving equipment that bore the lion's-head logo of a local construction company. Outside unit eight, dwarfed by a tractor tire, Curtis Koontz was in one of his baggy, rumpled designer suits, looking as forlorn as I felt. No boyish grin, no spark in his cornflower-blue eyes. His sunburnt dome gleamed in the light of one of the summer's last days.

As I climbed out of the car, he reached toward me with trembling hands. For an instant I thought he meant to embrace me and cry on my shoulder. Instead, he frisked me, starting at the chest and patting down to my ankles.

"You think I'm carrying?" I asked.

"I'm less concerned you have a piece than you're wearing a wire. What we're doing this afternoon, it's strictly off the record till we agree on a price."

When Koontz stood up, he still seemed on the brink of tears or some terrible breakdown that might tumble him from sadness into rage. "Careerwise," he said, "my big problem has always been unreliable clients. Take Darryl Perry—" He shoved open the door and led me inside.

The room was hot and smelled of sweat and ammonia.

A fluorescent bulb in the bathroom provided the only light—barely enough to illuminate a box-spring mattress and the distorted shape of what I slowly came to see as a body, someone in a V-neck T-shirt with a bloodstained wad of towels between the legs.

Koontz jostled me closer to the mattress. I noticed the dark hair and high, round belly. I would never have recognized Doreen's face. Both eyes were black, her lips were swollen and split, and her nose was broken. If it hadn't been for the spasms in her belly, I'd have taken her for dead. Bourbon and coffee churned in my stomach.

"Darryl beat her like a punching bag." Koontz pulled a board of nicotine gum from his pocket, pressed out a piece, and popped it into his mouth. "Here she's carrying a baby worth a fortune, and that loony tune's too wired to care."

"We better get her to a hospital."

"You can't believe what a bitch of a day it's been." He groaned as though Doreen's problems were nothing compared to his. "She's hemorrhaging all over my car, and I'm searching for a place to stash her so Darryl won't find her while I'm off with Pierce."

"Pierce?"

"To get a settlement. I couldn't risk taking her to the emergency room, having the other side find out the shape she's in."

"Are you nuts? She'll die if we don't get her to a doctor."

"The baby's dead already. She's sure of that. Fucking Pierce, naturally he knows something's wrong. Any worthwhile lawyer, he gets a whiff of weakness, he's like a wolf. He won't offer a dime. Says we'll wait till the baby's born, see about the blood test." Koontz slicked a hand back over his scalp. "I'm so stressed out, I'm about to start smoking again. So much work, so much planning, and this is what we're down to."

"Look, goddammit." I grabbed his arm. "I'm not going to stand here and let her bleed to death."

He pried my fingers loose. "You're not interested in hearing who committed the murders?"

"Yes, but—"

"Listen to her and tell me what it's worth."

"I'll listen on the way to the hospital."

"No, listen first." Koontz knelt next to the bed like a distraught pilgrim at an altar. "Doreen, honey, the writer's here. Tell him. Who did this to you?"

I crouched beside Koontz. My belly, like Doreen's, had gone into spasms.

"Darryl did it," she gasped between contractions.

"Why? What did you find out?" Koontz cued her.

"He's insane."

"Yeah but—" He squeezed her hand. It was pale and limp as a dead lily. "But why'd he go insane?"

Her discolored eyelids were open, but I can't say whether she saw me or anything else. Her life had been reduced to one wretched ball of pain and this last stab at making money out of her misery.

"Because I know who killed them."

"Killed who?" I asked.

"Clay, his grandfather, and that other guy."

"Who was it?" Koontz asked.

"Darryl and—"

"Darryl was in jail," I said.

"Let her finish. Tell us, honey, who killed them."

"Darryl and Clay, they planned it. Darryl shot the first man, then gave Clay the gun and got himself arrested. Next night Clay was supposed to do his granddaddy, but he didn't know nothing about guns and he got killed too."

"How do you know?" I asked.

"Because she overheard Darryl talk about it," Koontz said. "That's why he beat her."

"Were you in on it?"

"Don't answer, honey. He's had a taste. He wants more, let's see his money."

Koontz urged me to my feet. "Outside," he said.

After the stale, stinking air of the room, it was some

relief to be on the parking lot, lost in the labyrinth of bulldozers and Caterpillars. Over the rolling thunder of traffic on Route 1, I heard the rush of blood through my inner ear.

Koontz wasn't having an easy time of it either. Yet even bent double by a disappointment very close to despair, he hadn't quit hustling. That was the truest sign of his capacity for self-delusion; he believed he had something to sell. "Where do we start?" he asked.

"We start by taking her to a doctor."

"No, first, lemme hear a number."

"You can't lock this up like an exclusive in the *National Enquirer*. The cops are going to know."

"Not until I have a deal."

"You're not getting one from me. You'll be lucky Doreen doesn't do time."

He spat his gum into the scoop of a steam shovel. "They can't blame her for what she overheard. How's she supposed to believe anything those goofballs said? The both of them beamed up on one kind of junk or another? She couldn't be sure till Darryl turned zootie on her."

"You're not that dumb, Koontz. What'll you tell the cops when they ask where your deadhead clients got the brains for their plan?"

He tried to grin, but couldn't bring it off. The merriment never quite reached his eyes. "Are you blaming me?" He had his hand in his baggy pants pocket. Maybe digging for another piece of gum. Maybe not.

"Let's stop bullshitting and get Doreen to a doctor."

"I'll handle that."

"I'll help." I stepped toward the room; he blocked the way.

"I said I'll handle it."

I looked Koontz up and down. He didn't weigh a hundred fifty pounds; his neck and wrists appeared no stronger than pipe stems. But there was no point in pushing it and finding out he had more than gum in his pocket.

"Suit yourself." I backed toward Big Tom's Toronado

and didn't take my eyes off him until I was in the car, accelerating around the earth movers.

At a truck stop, I hid the Oldsmobile between two huffing, chugging refrigerator rigs and hurried into the diner, dialed 911, and told the dispatcher to send an ambulance for Doreen. When he asked my name, I hung up and stayed in the phone booth, serenaded by Waylon Jennings on a jukebox. I was struggling to get things straight in my mind before I tried to make anyone else understand. Of all the combinations I had considered, I never pictured Darryl and Clay working together, and I still wasn't convinced. But I could see how it made sense—somebody ambushing Big Tom, then passing the .38 on to Clay, who was too fouled up to do his part without getting wasted. The question was who would believe me when I described this scenario? I had blown my credibility with Gant, I'd never had any with Quinn, and even Buck might not listen.

In the end I had no choice but to call my brother. Before Peggy put him on the line, she said, "You sound weird. Have you been drinking?"

"Not for half an hour or so."

"Great! You're on the road to recovery."

Buck was less encouraging. "This is more theories and guesswork, Tommy, I don't want to hear it."

"I'm not guessing now." I told him what Koontz and Doreen had said. "If there's nothing to it, why would she finger her brother and her boyfriend?"

"Money. You said they wanted money. Then again," he mused, "maybe they're scared somebody's about to snitch them out and they need to get there first. Koontz might have figured—his mistake—you carry weight with the cops, and when you accused Darryl, they'd believe you."

"What do we do?"

"Go back to the house. I'll meet you there."

"Why not contact Gant and Quinn and let them run Darryl down?"

"We weren't already in deep shit," Buck said, "that's

what I'd do. But when we talk to them this time, I want
to be damn sure we're right.''

"Hate to cause more trouble, drag you out on a week-
end evening.''

"Fuck you, Tommy, okay,'' said the brother I knew
best.

I ordered a large Coke to go, but it did little to settle my
stomach on the return trip to Hyattsville. Overcompensat-
ing, cautious about keeping to my side of the yellow line,
I reviewed the shrinking list of players. They were down
to a skeleton crew now, a clutch of puny figures, and my
narrative sense rebelled at the notion that the suspects were
so contemptible, the motive so blatant. My father's murder
and everything that followed from it seemed to require
more—some grand all-inclusive conspiracy. But this assumption, I suddenly saw, wasn't just a flaw in logic. It
was the fault line that ran through my writing, through my
character. In everything I did I had been out to settle a
score.

Our street was deserted, the neighborhood quiet, everyone indoors eating dinner, stoking up for tonight. The TV
and newspaper teams had abandoned their stakeout. Footage of me soused and soaking wet must have satisfied
them.

Unlocking the front door, I crossed the living room,
which was murky with evening light. I might have missed
Darryl if he hadn't spoken up. ''Suppose you know there's
a drunk nigger sleeping it off in your TV room.''

Caved in on the maroon velour couch, Darryl was
smoking a cigarette, tapping his ashes into a beer can. He
wore greasy blue jeans and a sweat-stained tank top that
hung from his shoulders as if from hooks. I couldn't see
to the bottom of his whirlpool eyes, but he didn't appear
to be speeding. His rope-muscled arms were limp, his
movements sluggish.

"Luke came over to watch the Olympics,'' I said in a
loud, jolly voice as if I welcomed having Darryl here too.

"The U.S. crashed and burned against Russia. We better hope they don't learn football."

"You got a point there." Easing over by the morris chairs, I kept them between him and me. Darryl's jeans were too tight to conceal anything in the pockets. But I wondered about under the tank top, stuck in his belt.

He dropped his cigarette butt into the can. It hissed in the dregs of beer. "Last bazooka of the day. It's nice you don't mind I let myself in the back door." He slouched lower, molding his spine to the rock-hard contours of the couch. "Don't guess I gotta tell you about Doreen."

Paralyzed between lying and telling the truth, I said, "Koontz called."

"So you know their side of it."

"What's yours?"

"She say I beat her up? She say why?" He sounded like my boys postponing bedtime with sleepy singsong questions. Maybe he had done a lude with the beer. "She tell you I shot your father?"

I concentrated on his hands. Oil-stained and blacknailed, they lay in his lap, as inert as disassembled auto parts. "I want to hear your side of it, Darryl."

"They're framing me. Her and Koontz. Heard them talk about it on the telephone. Doreen's saying no sweat. Things hot up, they can always blame me because I'm tied to the murder weapon."

"What about the shooting?"

"I never shot nobody. Just got the gun from a guy I know."

Tense as fused steel, I was poised to run at him or away from him. But Darryl stayed limp as a twist of licorice. "A guy in jail?" I asked.

"Wouldn't be surprised if that's where the asshole ended up."

"Why'd you need a gun?"

"Seems like they was always asking me favors there wasn't anybody else dumb enough to do."

"Who's 'they'? Doreen and Koontz?"

"Them and Clay. Clay's the one first asked could I get him a piece."

"Why?"

His filthy fingers pinched a crease in his jeans. "Type guy I am, I don't ask questions. I just, you know, assumed it had something to do with his grandfather."

"Something like taking the old man out?"

He sighed. "Like I say, he's a friend. Him and my sister's real tight. He needs a favor. What am I supposed to do—walk away?"

"Did you shoot my father?"

"I told you, I never shot nobody."

"What time were you arrested that night?"

"Early. Real early. Still light out, I remember."

"Doreen claims it was part of the plan—your getting collared."

"I never been part of no plan."

"When you heard what happened to Clay and his grandfather, what did you figure?"

"Just that's Clay for you. A great dude. Smoke dope, party, drive his cars—that's what he was into. Anything more complicated . . . well, you could bet money he'd be too cracked out to come through."

"What about my father? Clay was in Connecticut. You were in the slam. Who did it?"

"Hey, man, work it out."

"Doreen?"

"Eight months pregnant? How do you see it like that?"

"Koontz?"

"Who else? Him and Doreen's always yakking about their millions, how they're going to spend it. Nobody mentions me, and I don't ask for a dime. The thanks I get, they set me up."

"Why tell me? Why not the cops?"

"Who's going to believe my word against a lawyer?"

"They know when you were arrested."

"Hell, when they hear what I did to Doreen, they'll

change the booking record. I didn't mean to unload on her like that. How bad is she?''

I didn't see any percentage in telling him he might soon be up on a different murder charge. I'd wait for Buck. Then the three of us would drive down to the station and speak to Detective Gant. "Like another beer?"

His hands slithered off his lap to either side of his legs. "Whatever."

Tapped out and inattentive though he acted, I didn't turn my back. I watched him suck up the energy to ooze off the couch, and while I waited I caught sight of someone walking past the windows out front. A woman, a slim blond in tan slacks and a navy-blue pullover. Elaine, I thought.

My eyes still on Darryl, I eased over to the door and opened it for her. "There's something you should know."

"I'm all ears, sweetie." It was Curtis Koontz in a peroxide wig. He stuck a snub-nose .38 in my face and waved it for me to back away.

If Darryl had a gun, now was the time he'd use it. Weak-kneed and wobbly, I was ready to dive out of the cross fire. But Darryl was laid back so low he looked as if he were about to be embalmed.

"Been hunting for you," Koontz said to him, holding the .38 on me.

"Been around. When did you start cross dressing?"

"It's a fluid world we live in, Darryl. You're inflexible, you crack. I adapt."

"How about pointing that somewhere else," I said.

"Sure." He turned it on Darryl. "Anybody else in the house?"

I said no, and Darryl didn't contradict me.

"Darryl, Darryl." The boyish gleam was back in Koontz's eyes. "You had me worried half sick when I couldn't find you. Then it dawned on me where you'd be. There's always this predictability factor that you'll do something stupid. Like show up here and run your mouth."

"Sorry to fuck up your plan."

"Hey, no problem." Koontz stepped closer to Darryl, affable, disarming. "I'm a very inventive fellow. You fuck up Plan A, I fill in with Plan B." He jammed the gun barrel against Darryl's front teeth and pulled the trigger.

Darryl didn't have anywhere to fall. The shot flattened the back of his head against the velour and splashed his brains up the wall.

I took off toward the kitchen. I wasn't thinking, I was running, bumping into chairs, skidding on the linoleum, skittering back to my feet, and running again. Koontz's second shot caught me in the shoulder, spun me around, and flung me against the refrigerator. As I fell, blood streamed down my shirtsleeve and pooled in the palm of my hand. Then my right arm started twitching and the blood gushed over the floor.

"This is so silly, so pointless." Koontz closed in for a sure shot. He hadn't stopped grinning. That grin, his mocking, not-unfriendly manner, my own deepening shock—I couldn't believe he meant to kill me.

"Darryl didn't—"

"You like to talk Darryl?" he said. "Lemme say about Darryl, he's a rare example where to call him a dickhead isn't an insult, it's a clinical description. If I found him before he came here blabbing, I wouldn't give a flying fuck whether you went on living."

He was near enough now for me to smell his after-shave. It was like those times as a boy when I made the mistake of letting Big Tom get too close. "The dumb shit thought you could save him," Koontz said. "You're the one could have been saved. All you had to do was call the cops on Darryl. Instead you send an ambulance. Oh, well, they'll dump it on Darryl anyway. He killed Doreen, shot you, then himself. End of story."

I knew Luke had to be awake. I hoped Buck was on the way. I played for time. "Doreen's dead?"

He nodded. "Like I say, unreliable clients are my

downfall. We each did our part, we shoulda been home free.''

"And your part was killing my father?''

"Sorry. Another screwup.'' He almost sounded sincere. "Clay wormed the name out of his grandfather. Tells me his mother got knocked up by some yokel from Hyattsville. I look in the phone directory and bingo! Tom Heller! All the police have to do is draw a line from dot to dot and they'll pin the murders on the bastard that wrote the letters. But the father was the key. What if he comes forward, says his son's living in East Jesus, New Mexico, and there's no chance he shot Andrew? What if he knows his son's dead and someone else must have written the letters? So he had to go.''

"Then I showed up and you realized you murdered the wrong man?'' I lowered my gaze from the gun muzzle. There was a putrid stench in my nostrils, a compound of gunpowder, my own sweat, and the stink of the kitchen floor.

"I expected more from you,'' Koontz said. "Something creative. A famous true-crime writer—I thought you'd cop a terrific plea for your life. But you're flaking out on me.''

The next sound I heard was like a scythe humming in the air. It was followed by the *thwack* of a blade through meat. Koontz screamed and the gun went off. A bullet whammed into the refrigerator, and his wig floated to the floor.

I raised my head, and my eyes rolled back flooding with red. Koontz was bleeding from the scalp; strips of skin flapped around his eyebrows. Luke was teetering behind him, swinging his metal crutches, walloping Koontz on the skull, spraying blood.

The gun went off again, and a round ricocheted off the ceiling, raining plaster. I scissored my legs at Koontz, knocking him off balance. He fired wildly, chipping wood off the wall. Then Luke was stumbling backward into the TV room, pinwheeling his arms. His crutches clattered across the kitchen floor.

"Crazy fucking nigger," Koontz kept hollering. He smoothed a hand over his head, slicking the skin back like a toupee. With a sleeve of his pullover, he mopped the blood from his eyes and caught me crawling toward the table.

He appeared to be grinning, but it was a grimace. His eyebrows arched and his forehead laddered with wrinkles as he contorted his face to hold his flayed scalp in place. But the loose flesh came caterpillaring down his brow.

Standing over me, he stared down the gun barrel. I waited for the muzzle flash. I never saw it, but I heard an enormous explosion. Koontz slammed against the refrigerator, slithering down its side, fingers scrabbling for a grip. He landed on top of me. I kicked and shoved, rolling him over onto his back. Blood geysered out of a hole in his neck.

At the other end of the kitchen, Buck was crouched in a shooter's stance, holding the Colt Python in both hands, ready to fire again. He didn't have to.

8

"Alert and oriented." For the rest of the night, that's how I was described by paramedics and emergency-room doctors. Yet although I retain a crystalline image of isolated moments, some scenes are scrambled, like film footage unreeled out of sequence, and for minutes at a stretch, I must have fallen unconscious. After recoiling from Koontz's body, I wasn't aware of moving, but I came to on the far side of the kitchen, slumped against the cabinet under the sink, catching a child's-eye view of the room—clear sight-lines from the waist down.

Buck was crouched next to Koontz, feeling vainly for a pulse in his carotid artery. Then he plunked the four-pound pistol on the table and squatted beside me, ripped my shirtsleeve up the seam and wrapped a dish towel around my shoulder. "Doesn't look like it hit bone. The ambulance'll be here in a minute. I was at the front door when I heard the shots. Had to run back to the Isuzu for my gun. Believe me, bro, I considered calling the cops and waiting for reinforcements."

"If you'd done that, I'd be dead. Thanks for coming in."

"Can't say I'm crazy about your investigative technique. You keep dangling yourself like bait and getting clobbered. But it looks like you got the right guy."

"Where the hell's my crutches?" Luke hollered.

I was afraid he had been shot too, but it was the force of his wild swinging that had toppled him backward. Buck hauled him upright, and once Luke had a leg under him, he hopped into the kitchen, not bothering about his crutches. Puckered linoleum popped under his foot.

"What it is, I'm so pissed off at the Russians," he raved on in the same hyperventilating speed-rap as he had used to update me during the Olympics, "I decide to get me some sleep. I wake up listening how Mr. Skinhead here offed Big Tom and he's fixing to do Tommy next and I'm thinking, How am I going to make the cops believe this? Then I flash, How you make them believe is the easy part. First you gotta stop the sonuvabitch. I come out swinging like Hank Aaron."

When I thanked him, Luke leaned precariously forward for a look at the bloody towels on my shoulder. "Don't worry, Tommy. I seen worse. This one's a million-dollar wound, gets you sent back home."

What it got me more immediately was a howling sixty-mile-an-hour ambulance ride to the hospital, the same one where my father died. There the filmstrip really started to flicker. An anesthesiologist knocked me out, but my dreams were so vivid I imagined I stayed awake all during the operation. I thought I saw the scalpels and sutures, and I heard Gaillard and Buck accuse me of meddling. Quinn and Gant swore I was lying. Elaine, Marisa, and Doreen—their faces had merged—lamented that I had let them down. Big Tom, standing off to the side with Kevin and Matt, shook his head at my sad-assed efforts.

At some point, I was pushed on a gurney out of the operating room and deposited in a cool bed between starched sheets. A nurse or a nun—someone in white—arranged an IV over my head, and as the medication dripped into my veins, I continued a heated colloquy with the faces that swirled around me.

Eventually, the faces evolved into images of the deer on Syms Island streaking through my field of vision like eye floaters; of Doreen hemorrhaging away the last of her life; of Curtis Koontz splashing against the refrigerator. I tried, but couldn't recall the formula for reading high-velocity blood.

When Elaine glided into the room, I had no reason to assume she wasn't another in a nightlong succession of hallucinations. She wore a summer dress draped from the shoulders and cinched at the waist. Her hair was pinned up as her father preferred it, and she was twirling her sunglasses by the earpiece as she had on the plane to Texas.

"How are you feeling?" She moved around the foot of the bed to stand beside me.

"What time is it?" Somehow I thought if I pinned down this moment precisely, I'd realize whether it was an illusion.

"Eight-thirty, nine."

"Morning or evening?"

"Morning." She smiled as she might at a kid who had overslept. "I came as soon as I could."

I started to sit up, but coils of pain spiraled over my shoulders, down to my fingertips. Bristling with tubes and drains, my right arm was strapped to a pillow beside me.

"Don't move." She put a hand to my forehead, smoothing back my hair. "I only have a few minutes. They didn't want to let me in. I told them I'm your wife and I just flew over from Italy. Do I look like your wife?"

It didn't deserve an answer. Her breezy intimacy, her knack of getting her way, my fear that under medication I might mistake what she said, brought on a wariness I have never been able to separate from my other feelings for Elaine. "Why did you come?"

"Because I was worried. Because I wanted to say I'm sorry. If I hadn't asked for an affidavit, I'm sure you think none of this would have happened. Even if Curtis Koontz was the one that killed your father, I can understand why you'd hold me responsible."

"Koontz wasn't in it alone."

"The police told me about Clay and those other two." She glanced behind her, searching for a chair. Then she sat on the edge of the bed, holding my good hand. Her gestures struck me as a strange cross between the maternal and the manipulative.

"There's another reason I came. To set things straight between us."

"It's a little late for that."

"No, there's your book, your research," she said with what seemed to be a perfect absence of irony. "You need to know all the facts."

I smiled. However painful or appalling, there was always some pleasure in learning the truth. She had come to try again to convince me not to write about the case.

"You are still planning to do a book, aren't you?" she asked.

"What do you think?"

"I think you ought to know everything before you make up your mind."

"My problem is I already know too much about you."

"No. You don't know the worst. But if you want, I'll tell you."

I was tempted to say I could live without it, to say her version of events was bound to be self-serving and carry a secret price tag. For once I wanted to turn away from "the worst." But I waited silently and Elaine went ahead, staring down into my eyes the way Koontz had stared down the gun barrel, aiming for a kill shot. I had a deep foreboding she was about to tell me I was Clay's father.

Instead she said, "He didn't do it. Clay didn't kill Daddy."

"Doreen, Darryl, Koontz, they told me he did."

"No," she said. "I killed him."

She paused, and I expected her to add some anticlimactic qualification, to say, "I'm to blame because I didn't do a better job of raising Clay." Or, "If I'd been there, I could have stopped him." I was reminded of the time in Texas when she lay beside me in bed and told me her father had killed her mother, then quickly emended that to an admission that he had as good as caused her death with his indifference.

But now she repeated, "I did it. When I came into the library that night, Clay was on the floor dead, and Daddy was at the desk. He was drunk and he was crying. The gun was in front of him. He told me Clay had attacked him, tried to murder him, and he, Daddy, shot him in the struggle. He said he'd been sitting there for hours, waiting for me, wondering what to do.

"I didn't believe him," Elaine said. "You knew Daddy. Would you have believed him? All I could think was, He's wrecked everything. He drove mother to suicide, virtually put the pills in her mouth. He bullied me and everybody else with his money. He ruined any chance I had to be happy. Now I was sure he killed Clay because Clay threatened to turn those letters over to the newspapers. So I just—I didn't even think twice—I just grabbed the gun and shot Daddy. Then I called Whiting and made up a story to tell the police."

"Does Pierce know the truth?"

"No. But I had to tell you."

"When did you realize you were wrong about Andrew?"

"I wasn't wrong about him," she said. "He did everything he could to make me miserable. The only thing he didn't do was kill Clay. I started to suspect that when Koontz told us about your father. Like you, I sensed there had to be a connection, maybe some scheme that involved Clay."

"Why didn't you tell me?"

"I was afraid. I'm still afraid. But when you got shot, I decided this had gone far enough."

It wasn't in my nature to take things on trust. This woman and a host of others before and after her had taught me better, had taught me the guiding principle of my life— not to accept anything on faith. I demanded facts. Yet I believed her. I believed her as I never had when she swore she loved me. I believed she was more open and naked to me now than all those times when I had buried my fingers and face and seed in her. This was the ultimate act of intimacy, as close as I would ever come to her turbulent core—to hear her confess to murder, to feel that she was not only begging me to drop the book, she was seeking solace and forgiveness and a release from the prison of secrecy.

After a moment had passed, she asked, "What are you going to do?"

"I don't know. Go back to Rome, I guess." Her hand was still in mine. "I'm sorry, Elaine."

"So am I." It was she who let go first and stood up. "Well, I promised the nurse I wouldn't tire you."

There should have been something final to say, something as sweeping and incisive as what she had told me. I was searching for the words when Buck burst into the room, noisy and ebullient. He came at me as if to give me a bear hug, but then saw Elaine and stopped.

"Hello, Buck," she said. "I was just leaving." She leaned down and brushed her lips lightly against mine. "Hope you get better soon."

"What about you?" I asked.

She laughed. "Oh, I'm as good as I'm ever going to get." Then she was gone.

"What the hell was that?" Buck was stunned.

"A visit."

"A visit my ass! Are you out of your mind? Haven't you had enough trouble with her?"

"I didn't invite her. And I wasn't in any condition to chase her away."

"You and Koontz are a perfect pair, the two of you completely cracked." He was pacing the room. "Just talked to Gant. He leaked a few lines from the autopsy. Turns out Koontz had a hell of a coke habit. He needed a million-dollar settlement to keep his nose open. I knew the guy was a slimebucket, but I didn't think he was that dumb."

"He was any smarter, he'd have shot me before you and Luke could stop him."

"Old Luke, I don't believe I've ever seen anybody prouder of himself."

"He's got a right to be. He could have hung back in the TV room and Koontz would never have known he was there."

"Write him into the book. Promise him Eddie Murphy'll play his role in the movie."

"Now you remind me of Koontz." At once I regretted the remark. Buck's shoulders sagged. "What I mean is he was always hyping the case as a surefire best-seller."

"You said something like that yourself, Tommy, that night in Annapolis when we talked down on the dock."

"A lot's changed since then." I nodded to my arm, which lay cushioned like a relic displayed in a Roman church. "Luke called it a million-dollar wound, the kind that gets you sent home."

"Hey, you *are* home. What are you telling me? You're hightailing it back to Italy?"

"I'd better if I hope to stay married. I've been gone a long time. Too long. I miss Marisa and the boys, and I've got a lot to make up to them."

"Weren't you the one reminded me planes run in both directions?"

"Come on, Buck. I can't pull the kids out of school."

"Put them in school here. It won't hurt Kevin and Matt to spend time in the States while we're doing the book."

"That's the problem, Buck, what I'm trying to tell you. I can't do a book. I'm too close to the story. I'm part of it."

"You'll find a way to deal with that."

"No, even if Elaine was willing to cooperate—which I doubt—I couldn't cope with being around her."

"Why?" he demanded, hands on hips, corduroy jacket spread away from his huge chest and belly. "Because you were wrong about her?"

"That's part of it."

"You had damn good reason to suspect her. She's the

one suckered you back into her life, lying about the past, never letting on about Clay. She used you.''

''Yeah, well, I used her too. More than once.''

''Okay, it was an honest error. And you apologized. Has she?''

''Matter of fact, she has. Look, Buck, accusing her of triple murder isn't the only mistake I made. Those pictures of us at the motel, I can't promise it wouldn't happen again. I can't pretend to have a professional relationship with Elaine.''

He raked at his beard with both hands. ''Jesus, the woman's like a fishhook in your ass. Aren't you ever going to shake loose?''

What he said struck me as mordantly funny. I laughed, and a shock of pain sizzled down my arm.

''It's not a joke,'' he said. ''I was counting on this.''

''If it's a matter of money—''

''It's not the goddamn money.'' He yanked off his coat as if to challenge me to a fistfight. ''This was our chance— probably the last one—to be with each other, to work together on something. For a guy that bitches about feeling like the family outsider, the one dumped on by Big Tom, you do an awful lot of that yourself—kissing people off, keeping them at arm's length. We didn't chase you away. We didn't leave you. You left us. Now you've turned it around and—aw, shit, Tommy, don't make me whine about it. I'll miss you. You'll go back to Rome and when the hell will I see you again?''

I held out my left hand. After some hesitation, he took it. ''I'll miss you too,'' I said. ''I'm sorry, I really am, for dragging you into this mess. If I'd listened to you, I'd have saved myself a lot of lumps. Under the circumstances, it sounds crazy, but I've enjoyed being here with you.''

''Then stay.''

''And do what?''

''Whatever you'd do in Rome.''

I thought of my study, the ''porno den,'' as Marisa

called it. I thought of the autopsy reports, the crime-scene photos, and file cards filled with forensic information. There was nothing there I was eager to return to.

"You don't want to do a book, forget it," Buck said. "You and I got lots of other things to talk about. Bring your family down to the beach and spend some time with us. Take your boys to a ball game."

"I don't know. It'd be a big change for Kevin and Matt."

"I'm sure they'd handle it."

"I'm tired, Buck." Actually I was more depressed than tired, and it was the thought of my study in Rome, of all the hours I had holed up there, that brought me down. "Mind if we talk about this later?"

"Anytime. Like me to phone Marisa, tell her you're all right?"

"No, I'd better do that. I need to talk to her—if I can ever decide what to say."

A nurse came and chased Buck out, then needled in another ampule of antibiotics that sent me whirling back into a woozy state where any explanation to Marisa seemed impossible. To make her understand the past month—the murders, my mistakes and self-deceptions—I'd have to recreate a world that would be as unfathomable to her as Italy often was to me, and she'd need to learn more about my childhood than I'd ever told her before.

In my haze of hallucinatory reasoning I thought she'd even have to know about the Washington Senators, now no more than a memory, and the Redskins as they used to be—hapless and all white and quarterbacked by a midget. She'd need to able to picture Buck and me playing basketball in the distant reaches of the metro area—in Anacostia where black guys like Luke were nicknamed King Kangaroo or the Elevator Man, and in Chevy Chase where the stars were always called Chad or Porter, and those girls with faultless skin and supercilious smiles sat up in the bleachers, coolly taking our measure, their presence both a reproach and a provocation. I'd have to persuade her that that had somehow led to my falling in love with Elaine and following her to Texas, hitchhiking through states that Kevin and Matt would mispronounce with inflections that probably echoed the original Indian names.

Of course, it was also crucial for her to come to grips with Big Tom and the enormous force-field he exerted even after his death. But since I was in the process of revising my picture of this man whose portrait I had previously believed was cast in bronze, I knew we'd have to depend on Buck and Luke if we hoped to see my father as he actually was.

What I desperately wanted to avoid was the one subject that would most deeply interest Marisa. No matter how I told my tale, regardless of my digressions and smoke screens, she was bound to ask, as she had on the phone, why I had never mentioned Elaine, why I had shut her and the boys out of so much of my life.

The answer seemed self-evident; I had sealed off the past the way you'd close the compartments of a sinking ship. Fearful that the smallest leak had the potential to turn into a flood that would drown us, I had felt it was safer to keep away from the people and places I came from.

Yet for all my efforts at evasion, the past had crashed in on us anyway, and I couldn't hold it back any longer. If we were to have any chance of going on from here, I had to do what Elaine had done today—confide in Marisa, break through the bars of secrecy I had built up between us.

Postponing the call, I weighed where I should recount this story. Our apartment in Rome struck me as wrong—too crowded with Kevin and Matt's benign presence, too suffused with our personal history to allow scope for the chaotic narrative and sprawling cast I had to deal with.

I imagined leading Marisa out to the terrace where we'd sit on the wire-harp chairs surrounded by pastel oleanders and purple scrolls of bougainvillea. But this, too, seemed the wrong spot—too sunny, too dense with golden light, for some of the dark scenes I had to describe. Faced with the familiar horizon of the Alban Hills and the city's famous slabs of marble, the monuments of dead emperors and domes of celebrated cathedrals, how could Marisa envision Hyattsville?

No, she'd have to be here, have to explore my parents' house and the neighborhood as though sifting the rubble at an archaeological site. To get any inkling of what had happened this summer, she'd have to live in the States awhile.

In the end I never placed the call. Marisa phoned me—she'd heard the news from friends—and said she and the boys were flying to the States. I told her to take her time, close the apartment, and pack for a long stay. When she asked why, I said, "It'd take a book to explain."

AFTERWORD

On the trip to Baltimore-Washington Airport, Peggy drove ahead with the kids in the Isuzu while Buck followed at the wheel of the Toronado. Luke sat up front with him, alternately discoursing on the Olympics and on Curtis Koontz. My arm in a sling, I rode in back, riddled with last-minute doubts.

As we waited beside the sculpture of the crab, Buck, sweating in a tweed jacket, watched a lively crowd disembark from an Air Jamaica flight. "The Coke and Ganja Express," he called it. "Half the passengers'll be arrested for smuggling," he said, "and I'll wind up representing them. I should arrange for the stewardesses to pass around my card right after takeoff."

While Luke was describing to the younger kids, Brendan and Beth, how he had cracked Curtis Koontz on the noggin, Peggy huddled with Megan and Marty, handing them what appeared to be a folded bed sheet from her canvas tote bag. "Goochy" was scrawled in black letters on the bag. When she noticed I was watching, Peggy gave me a sharp look and said, "I trust you brought a terrific present for Marisa."

"Just myself."

"God, are you in trouble." She brushed at the lapels of my suit. "You don't look too bad—sort of gaunt and soulful. Getting shot was a smart play for sympathy. Even if she hasn't forgiven you, I doubt Marisa would slug an invalid."

"Would you forgive me?"

Her small, brown face was upturned to mine. She seemed to be giving the question serious consideration. "Not at first. Not till you said you were sorry."

"I am, Peggy. I know this has been a bitch for you and Buck. I'll make it up to you."

She gave me a peck on both cheeks. "It's enough seeing how happy Buck is that you're staying."

I suppose their arrival lacked the heartrending emotion and dramatic resonance of those film clips we've all seen of grubby emigrants catching their first glimpse of America, breaking into tears at sight of the Statue of Liberty lifting her torch high above New York harbor, holding out the promise of a new life. Still, Marisa, Kevin, and Matt were visibly touched that so many people had gathered to greet them and that their cousins had unfurled a banner from the Goochy bag and hung it from the giant crab's claws. *Benvenuti!* it said.

Kevin had filled out, and after a few weeks in the sun, his hair was as blond as mine. Matt had grown too, but was still light enough for me to lift with my left arm, still small enough to want to be hugged. When I set him down, Marisa filled the space he had left. She kissed me and said, "You're so skinny, so pale."

"I've been worried what I'd tell you."

"Che scemo," she said. What a fool. "I don't want to hear that now. Just let me be with you."

After kissing Uncle Buck and Aunt Peggy and ceremoniously shaking hands with their cousins, the boys came to Luke, and Matt asked with all the grave candor of a six-year-old, "Are you in our family?"

Luke shifted on his crutches and nibbled at his bebop tuft. "More like a friend," he said. "I live next door to your granddaddy's house."

"He's the one who helped Buck save my life," I said.

Matt glanced at my arm in the sling, then at Luke's empty pantleg, and asked, "Did you get shot too?"

"You better believe it. Five rounds from a fifty-caliber

machine gun,'' Luke said. Then seeing Matt's stricken expression, he added, ''but don't worry, it ain't slowed me down none.''